SUNDAY AFTER THE WAR

SUNDAY

AFTER THE WAR

*"I always carry over 40,000 gold
francs about with me in my belt.
They weigh about 40 pounds, and
I am beginning to get dysentery
from the load."*

HENRY MILLER

NEW DIRECTIONS

ACKNOWLEDGMENT

"Good News! God Is Love" was first published in *Horizon* (London); "The Gigantic Sunrise" in *Athene* (Chicago); "Today, Yesterday and Tomorrow" in *The National Herald* (New York); "The Most Lovely Inanimate Object in Existence" in *The Harvard Advocate*; and "Letter to Anais Nin Regarding One of her Books" in *Circle* (Berkeley, Cal.).

Manufactured in the United States of America.
New Directions Books are published by James Laughlin at Norfolk, Connecticut. New York Office: 333 Sixth Avenue, New York 14.

Dedicated

'To Melpo, last of the winter queens"

CONTENTS

	PAGE
'GOOD NEWS! GOD IS LOVE!'	9
ORIGINAL PREFACE TO "HOLLYWOOD'S HALLUCINATION"	39
THE GIGANTIC SUNRISE	57
REUNION IN BROOKLYN	63
TO-DAY, YESTERDAY AND TO-MORROW	107
A FRAGMENT FROM "THE ROSY CRUCIFIXION"	116
OF ART AND THE FUTURE	146
ANOTHER FRAGMENT FROM "THE ROSY CRUCIFIXION"	161
A DEATH LETTER TO EMIL	189
A THIRD FRAGMENT FROM "THE ROSY CRUCIFIXION"	212
SHADOWY MONOMANIA (D. H. LAWRENCE)	232
MORE ABOUT ANAIS NIN	276
THE MOST LOVELY INANIMATE OBJECT IN EXISTENCE	298

'GOOD NEWS! GOD IS LOVE!'

(Fragment from *The Air-conditioned Nightmare*)

It was in a hotel in Pittsburgh that I finished the *Life of Rama-krishna* by Romain Rolland. Pittsburgh and Ramakrishna—could any more violent contrast be possible? The one the symbol of brutal power and wealth, the other the very incarnation of love and wisdom.

We begin here, then, in the very quick of the nightmare, in the crucible where all values are reduced to slag.

I am in a small, supposedly comfortable room of a modern hotel equipped with all the latest conveniences. The bed is clean and soft, the shower functions perfectly, the toilet seat has been sterilized since the last occupancy, if I am to believe what is printed on the paper band which garlands it; soap, towels, lights, stationery, everything is provided in abundance.

I am depressed, depressed beyond words. If I were to occupy this room for any length of time I would go mad—or commit suicide. The spirit of the place, the spirit of the men who made it the hideous city it is, seeps through the walls. There is murder in the air. It suffocates me.

A few moments ago I went out to get a breath of air. I was back again in Czarist Russia. I saw Ivan the Terrible followed by a cavalcade of snouted brutes. There they were, the Cossacks, armed with clubs and revolvers. They had the look of men who obey with zest, who shoot to kill on the slightest provocation. The very sight of them inspires hatred and rebellion. One longs to pull them down off their prancing steeds and bash their thick skulls in. One wants to put an end to this sort of law and order.

Never has the *status quo* seemed more hideous to me. This is not the worst place, I know. But I am here and what I see hits me hard.

It was fortunate, perhaps, that I didn't begin my tour of America via Pittsburgh, Youngstown, Detroit; fortunate that I didn't start out by visiting Bayonne, Bethlehem, Scranton and such like. I might never have gotten as far as Chicago. I might have turned into a human bomb and exploded. By some canny instinct of self-preservation I turned south first, to explore the so-called 'backward' States of the Union. If I was bored for the most part I at least knew peace. Did I not see suffering and misery in the South too? Of course I did. There is suffering and misery everywhere throughout this broad land. But there are kinds and degrees of suffering; the worst, in my opinion, is the sort one encounters in the very heart of progress.

At this moment we are talking about the defense of our country, our institutions, our way of life. It is taken for granted that these must be defended, whether we are invaded or not. But there are things which ought not to be defended, which ought to be allowed to die; there are things which we should destroy voluntarily, with our own hands.

Let us try to make an imaginative recapitulation. Let us try to think back to the days when our forefathers first came to these shores. To begin with they were running away from something; like the exiles and expatriates whom we are in the habit of denigrating and reviling, they too had abandoned the homeland in search of something nearer to their heart's desire.

One of the curious things about these progenitors of ours is that though avowedly searching for peace and happiness, for political and religious freedom, they began by robbing, poisoning, murdering, almost exterminating the race to whom this vast continent belonged. Later, when the gold rush started, they did the same to the Mexicans as they had to the Indians. And when the Mormons sprang up they practised the same cruelties, the same intolerance and persecution upon their own white brothers.

I think of these ugly facts because as I was riding from Pittsburgh to Youngstown, through an Inferno which exceeds anything that Dante imagined, the idea suddenly came to me that I ought to have an American Indian by my side, that he ought to share this voyage with me, communicate to me silently or otherwise his emotions and reflections. By preference I would like to have had a descendant of one of the admittedly 'civilized' Indian tribes, a Seminole, let us say, who had passed his life in the tangled swamps of Florida.

Imagine the two of us then standing in contemplation before the hideous grandeur of one of those steel mills which dot the railway line. I can almost hear him thinking—'so it was for this that you deprived us of our birthright, took away our slaves, burned our homes, massacred our women and children, poisoned our souls, broke every treaty which you made with us and left us to die in the swamps and jungles of the Everglades!'

Do you think it would be easy to get him to change places with one of our steady workers? What sort of persuasion would you use? What now could you promise him that would be truly seductive? A used car that he could drive to work in? A slap-board shack that he could, if he were ignorant enough, call a home? An education for his children which would lift them out of vice, ignorance and superstition but still keep them in slavery? A clean, healthy life in the midst of poverty, crime, filth, disease and fear? Wages that barely keep your head above water and often not? Radio, telephone, cinema, newspaper, pulp magazine, fountain pen, wrist watch, vacuum cleaner or other gadgets *ad infinitum*? Are these the baubles that make life worth while? Are these what make us happy, care-free, generous-hearted, sympathetic, kindly, peaceful and godly? Are we now prosperous and secure, as so many stupidly dream of being? Are any of us, even the richest and most powerful, certain that an adverse wind will not sweep away our possessions, our authority, the fear or the respect in which we are held?

This frenzied activity which has us all, rich and poor, weak and powerful, in its grip—where is it leading us? There are two things in life which it seems to me all men want and very few ever get (because both of them belong to the domain of the spiritual) and they are health and freedom. The druggist, the doctor, the surgeon are all powerless to give health; money, power, security, authority do not give freedom. Education can never provide wisdom, nor churches religion, nor wealth happiness, nor security peace. What is the meaning of our activity then? To what end?

We are not only as ignorant, as superstitious, as vicious in our conduct as the 'ignorant, bloodthirsty savages' whom we dispossessed and annihilated upon arriving here—we are worse than they by far. We have degenerated; we have degraded the life which we sought to establish on this continent. The most productive nation in the world, yet unable to properly feed, clothe and shelter over a third of its population. Vast areas of valuable soil turning to waste land because of neglect, indifference, greed and vandalism. Torn some eighty years ago by the bloodiest civil war in the history of man and yet to this day unable to convince the defeated section of our country of the righteousness of our cause, nor able, as liberators and emancipators of the slaves, to give them true freedom and equality, but instead enslaving and degrading our own white brothers. Yes, the industrial North defeated the aristocratic South—the fruits of that victory are now apparent. Wherever there is industry there is ugliness, misery, oppression, gloom and despair. The banks which grew rich by piously teaching us to save, in order to swindle us with our own money, now beg us not to bring our savings to them, threatening to wipe out even that ridiculous interest rate they now offer should we disregard their advice. Three-quarters of the world's gold lies buried in Kentucky. Inventions which would throw millions more out of work, since by the queer irony of our system every potential boon to the human race is converted into an evil, lie idle on the shelves of the Patent Office or are bought up and destroyed by the powers that control our destiny. The land thinly populated and producing in a wasteful, haphazard way enormous surpluses of every kind, is deemed by its owners, a mere handful of men, unable to accommodate not only the starving millions of Europe but our own starving hordes. A country which makes itself ridiculous by sending out missionaries to the most remote parts of the globe, asking for pennies now of the poor in order to main-

13

tain the Christian work of these deluded devils who no more represent Christ than I do the Pope, and yet unable through its churches and missions at home to rescue the weak and defeated, the miserable and the oppressed. The hospitals, the insane asylums, the prisons filled to overflowing. Counties, some of them big as a European country, practically uninhabited, owned by an intangible corporation whose tentacles reach everywhere and whose responsibilities nobody can formulate or clarify. A man seated in a comfortable chair in New York, Chicago or San Francisco, a man surrounded by every luxury and yet paralysed with fear and anxiety, controls the lives and destinies of thousands of men and women whom he has never seen, whom he never wishes to see and whose fate he is thoroughly uninterested in.

This is what is called progress in the year 1941 in these United States of America. Since I am not of Indian, Negro or Mexican descent I do not derive any vengeful joy in delineating this picture of the white man's civilization. I am a descendant of two men who ran away from their native land because they did not wish to become soldiers. My descendants, ironically enough, will no longer be able to escape that duty; the whole white world has at last been turned into an armed camp.

Well, as I was saying, I was full of Ramakrishna on leaving Pittsburgh. Ramakrishna who never criticized, who never preached, who accepted all religions, who saw God everywhere in everything: the most ecstatic being, I imagine, that ever lived. Then came Coraopolis, Aliquippa, Wampum. Then Niles, the birth-place of President McKinley, and Warren, the birthplace of Kenneth Patchen. Then Youngstown, and two girls are descending the bluff beside the railroad tracks in the most fantastic setting I have laid eyes on since I left Crete. Instantly I am back on that ancient Greek island, standing at the edge of a crowd on the outskirts of Heraklion just a few miles from Knossus. There is no railroad on the island, the sanitation is bad, the dust is thick, the flies are everywhere, the food is lousy—but it is a wonderful place, one of the most wonderful places in the whole world. As at Youngstown by the railroad station there is a bluff here and a Greek peasant woman is slowly descending, a basket on her head, her feet bare, her body poised. *Here the resemblance ends. . . .*

As everybody knows, Ohio has given the country more Presidents than any other State in the Union. Presidents like McKinley, Hayes, Garfield, Grant, Harding—weak, characterless men. It has also given us writers like Sherwood Anderson * and Kenneth Patchen, the one looking for poetry everywhere and the other driven almost mad by the evil and ugliness everywhere. The one walks the streets at night in solitude and tells us of the imaginary life going on behind closed doors; the other is so stricken with pain and chagrin by what he sees that he re-creates the cosmos in terms of blood and tears, stands it upside down, and walks out on it in loathing and disgust. I am glad I had the chance to see these Ohio towns, this Mahoning River which looks as if the poisonous bile of all humanity had poured into it, though in truth it may contain nothing more evil than the chemicals and waste products of the mills and factories. I am glad I had the chance to see the colour of the earth here in winter, a colour not of age and death but of disease and sorrow. Glad I could take in the rhinoceros-skinned banks that rise from the river's edge and in the pale light of a wintry afternoon reflect the lunacy of a planet given over to rivalry and hatred. Glad I caught a glimpse of those slag heaps which look like the accumulated droppings of sickly prehistoric monsters which passed in the night. It helps me to understand the black and monstrous poetry which the younger man distils in order to preserve his sanity; helps

* Written before his death.

15

me to understand why the older writer had to pretend madness in order to escape the prison which he found himself in when he was working in the paint factory. It helps me to understand how prosperity built on this plane of life can make Ohio the mother of Presidents and the persecutor of men of genius.

The saddest sight of all are the automobiles parked outside the mills and factories. The automobile stands out in my mind as the very symbol of falsity and illusion. There they are, thousands upon thousands of them, in such profusion that it would seem as if no man were too poor to own one. In Europe, Asia, Africa the toiling masses of humanity look with watery eyes towards this Paradise where the worker rides to work in his own car. What a magnificent world of opportunity it must be, they think to themselves. (At least, we like to think that they think that way!) They never ask what one must do to have this great boon. They don't realize that when the American worker steps out of his shining tin chariot he delivers himself body and soul to the most stultifying labour a man can perform. They have no idea that it is possible, even when one works under the best possible conditions, to forfeit all rights as a human being. They don't know that the best possible conditions (in American lingo) mean the biggest profits for the boss, the utmost servitude for the worker, the greatest confusion and disillusionment for the public in general. They see a beautiful, shining car which purrs like a cat; they see endless concrete roads so smooth and flawless that the driver has difficulty in keeping awake; they see cinemas which look like palaces; they see department stores with mannikins dressed like princesses. They see the glitter and paint, the baubles, the gadgets, the luxuries; they don't see the bitterness in the heart, the scepticism, the cynicism, the emptiness, the sterility, the despair, the hopelessness which is eating up the American worker. They don't want to see this—they are full of misery themselves. They want a way out: they want the lethal comforts, conveniences, luxuries. And they follow in our footsteps—blindly, heedlessly, recklessly.

Of course not all American workers ride to work in automobiles. In Beaufort, S. C., only a few weeks ago I saw a man on a two-wheeled cart driving a bullock through the main street. He was a black man, to be sure, but from the look on his face I take it that he was far better off than the poor devil in the steel mill who drives his own car. In Tennessee I saw white men hitching their own bodies to the plough; I saw them struggling desperately to scratch a living from the thin soil on the side of a mountain. I saw the shacks they live in and wondered if it were possible to put together anything more primitive. But I can't say that I felt sorry for them. No; they are not the sort of people to inspire pity. On the contrary, one has to admire them. If they represent the 'backward' people of America, then we need more backward people. In the subway in New York you can see the other type, the bookworm who revels in social and political theories and lives the life of a drudge, foolishly flattering himself that because he is not working with his hands (nor with his brain either, for that matter) he is better off than the poor white trash in the South.

Those two girls in Youngstown coming down the slippery bluff —it was like a bad dream, I tell you. But we look at these bad dreams constantly with eyes open, and when someone remarks about it we say, 'Oh, yes, that's right, that's just how it is!' and we go on about our business or we take to dope, the dope which is worse by far than opium or hashish—I mean the newspapers, the radio, the movies. Real dope gives you the freedom to dream your own dreams; the American kind forces you to swallow the perverted dreams of men whose only ambition is to hold their job regardless of what they are bidden to do.

17

The most terrible thing about America is that there is no escape from the treadmill which we have created. There isn't one fearless champion of truth in the publishing world, not one film company devoted to art instead of profits. We have no theatre worth the name, and what we have of theatre is practically concentrated in one city; we have no music worth talking about except what the Negro has given us, and scarcely a handful of writers who might be called creative. We have murals decorating our public buildings which are about on a par with the aesthetic development of high school students, and sometimes below that level in conception and execution. We have art museums that are crammed with lifeless junk for the most part. We have war memorials in our public squares that must make the dead in whose name they were erected squirm in their graves. We have an architectural taste which is about as near the vanishing point as it is possible to achieve. In the ten thousand miles that I have travelled thus far I have come across two cities which have each of them a little section worth a second look—I mean Charleston and New Orleans. As for the other cities, towns and villages through which I passed, I hope never to see them again. Some of them have such marvellous names, too, which only makes the deception more cruel. Names like Chattanooga, Pensacola, Tallahassee, like Mantua, Phoebus, Bethlehem, Paoli, like Algiers, Mobile, Natchez, Savannah, like Baton Rouge, Saginaw, Poughkeepsie: names that revive glorious memories of the past or awaken dreams of the future. Visit them, I urge you. See for yourself. Try to think of Schubert or Shakespeare when you are in Phoebus, Virginia. Try to think of North Africa when you are in Algiers, Louisiana. Try to think of the life the Indians once led here when you are on a lake, a mountain or river bearing the names we borrowed from them. Try to think of the dreams of the Spaniards when you are motoring over the old Spanish Trail. Walk around in the old French quarter of New Orleans and try to reconstruct the life that once this city knew. Less than a hundred years have elapsed since this jewel of America faded out. It seems more like a thousand. Everything that was of beauty, significance or promise has been destroyed and buried in the avalanche of false progress. In the thousand years of almost incessant war Europe has not lost what we have lost in a hundred years of 'peace and progress'. No foreign enemy ruined the South. No barbaric vandals devastated the great tracts of land which are as barren and hideous as the dead surface of the moon. We can't attribute to the Indians the transformation of a peaceful, slumbering island like Manhattan into the most hideous city in the world. Nor can we blame the collapse of our economic system on the hordes of peaceful, industrious immigrants whom we no longer want. No, the European nations may blame one another for their miseries, but we have no such excuse—we have only ourselves to blame.

Less than two hundred years ago a great social experiment was begun on this virgin continent. The Indians whom we dispossessed, decimated and reduced to the status of outcasts, just as the Aryans did with the Dravidians of India, had a reverent attitude towards this land. The forests were intact, the soil rich and fertile. They lived in communion with Nature on what we choose to call a low level of life. Though they possessed no written language they were poetic to the core and deeply religious. Our forefathers came along and, seeking refuge from their oppressors, began by poisoning the Indians with alcohol and venereal disease, by raping their women and murdering their children. The wisdom of life which the Indians possessed they scorned and denigrated. When they had finally completed their work of conquest and extermination they herded the miserable remnants of a great race into concentration camps and proceeded to break what spirit was left in them.

19

Not long ago I happened to pass through a tiny Indian reservation belonging to the Cherokees in the mountains of North Carolina. The contrast between this world and ours is almost unbelievable. The little Cherokee reservation is a virtual Paradise. A great peace and silence pervades the land, giving one the impression of being at last in the happy hunting grounds to which the brave Indian goes upon his death. In my journey thus far I have struck only one other community which had anything like this atmosphere, and that was in Lancaster County, Pennsylvania, among the Amish people. Here a small religious group, clinging stubbornly to the ways of their ancestors in comportment, dress, beliefs and customs, have converted the land into a veritable garden of peace and plenty. It is said of them that ever since they settled here they have never known a crop failure. They live a life in direct opposition to that of the majority of the American people—and the result is strikingly apparent. Only a few miles away are the hell-holes of America where, as if to prove to the world that no alien ideas, theories or isms will ever get a foothold here, the American flag is brazenly and tauntingly flown from roofs and smokestacks. And what sorry-looking flags they are which the arrogant, bigoted owners of these plants display! We have two American flags always—one for the rich and one for the poor. When the rich fly it, it means that things are under control; when the poor fly it, it means danger, revolution, anarchy. In less than two hundred years the land of liberty, home of the free, refuge of the oppressed, has so altered the meaning of the Stars and Stripes that today when a man or woman succeeds in escaping from the horrors of Europe, when he finally stands before the bar under our glorious national emblem, the first question put to him is: 'How much money have you?' If you have no money but only a love of freedom, only a prayer for mercy on your lips, you are debarred, returned to the slaughter-house, shunned as a leper. This is the bitter caricature which the descendants of our liberty-loving forefathers have made of the national emblem.

Everything is caricatural here. I take a plane to see my father on his deathbed, and up there in the clouds, in a raging storm, I overhear two men behind me discussing how to put over a big deal, the big deal involving paper boxes, no less. The stewardess, who has been trained to behave like a mother, a nurse, a mistress, a cook, a drudge, never to look untidy, never to lose her Marcel wave, never to show a sign of fatigue or disappointment, or chagrin or loneliness, the stewardess puts her lily-white hand on the brow of one of the paper box salesmen and in the voice of a ministering angel says: 'Do you feel tired this evening? Have you a headache? Would you like a little aspirin?' We are up in the clouds and she is going through this performance like a trained seal. When the plane lurches suddenly she falls and reveals a tempting pair of thighs. The two salesmen are now talking about buttons, where to get them cheaply, how to sell them dearly. Another man, a weary banker, is reading the war news. There is a great strike going on somewhere—several of them, in fact. We are going to build a fleet of merchant vessels to help England—*next December!* The storm rages. The girl falls down again—she's full of black and blue marks. But she comes up smiling, dispensing coffee and chewing gum, putting her lily-white hand on someone else's forehead, inquiring if he is a little low, a little tired, perhaps. I ask her if she likes her job. For answer she says, 'It's better than being a trained nurse.' The salesmen are going over her points; they talk about her like a commodity. They buy and sell, buy and sell. For that they have to have the best rooms in the best hotels, the fastest, smoothest planes, the thickest, warmest overcoats, the biggest, fattest purses.

21

We need their paper boxes, their buttons, their synthetic furs, their rubber goods, their hosiery, their plastic this and that. We need the banker, his genius for taking our money and making himself rich. The insurance man, his policies, his talk of security, of dividends—we need him too. *Do we?* I don't see that we need any of these carnivora. I don't see that we need any of these cities, these hell-holes I've been in. I don't think we need a two-ocean fleet either. I was in Detroit a few nights ago. I saw the Mannerheim Line in the movies. I saw how the Russians pulverized it. I learned the lesson. *Did* you? Tell me what it is that man can build, to protect himself, which other men cannot destroy? What are we trying to defend? Only what is old, useless, dead, indefensible. Every defence is a provocation to assault. Why not surrender? Why not give —give all? It's so damned practical, so thoroughly effective and disarming. Here we are, we the people of the United States: the greatest people on earth, so we think. We have everything—everything it takes to make people happy. Or so we think. We have land, water, sky and all that goes with it. We could become the great shining example of the world; we could radiate peace, joy, power, benevolence. But there are ghosts all about, ghosts whom we can't seem to lay hands on. We are not happy, not contented, not radiant, not fearless.

We bring miracles about and we sit in the sky taking aspirin and talking paper boxes. On the other side of the ocean they sit in the sky and deal out death and destruction indiscriminately. We're not doing that yet, not yet, but we are committed to furnishing the instruments of destruction. Sometimes, in our greed, we furnish them to the wrong side. But that's nothing—everything will come out right in the end. Eventually we will have helped to wipe out or render prostrate a good part of the human race—not savages this time, but civilized 'barbarians'. Men like ourselves, in short, except that they have different views about the universe, different ideological principles, as we say. Of course, if we don't destroy them they will destroy us. That's logic—nobody can question it. That's political logic and that's what we live and die by. A flourishing state of affairs. Really exciting, don't you know. 'We live in such exciting times.' Aren't you happy about it? The world changing so rapidly and all that—isn't it marvellous! Think what it was a hundred years ago. Time marches on. Progress and Invention. What we dream we become. We'll get the knack of it soon. We'll learn how to annihilate the whole planet in the wink of an eye—just wait and see.

The capital of the new planet—the one, I mean, which will kill itself off—is, of course, Detroit. I realized that the moment I arrived. At first I thought I'd go and see Henry Ford, give him my congratulations. But then I thought—what's the use? He wouldn't know what I was talking about. Neither would Mr. Cameron most likely. That lovely Ford evening hour! Every time I hear it announced I think of Céline—Ferdinand, as he so affectionately calls himself. Yes, I think of Céline standing outside the factory gates (pp. 222-225, I think it is: *Journey to the End of the Night*). Will he get the job? Sure he will. He gets it. He goes through the baptism—the baptism of stultification through noise. He sings a wonderful song there for a few pages about the machine, the blessings that it showers upon mankind. Then he meets Molly. Molly is just a whore. You'll find another Molly in *Ulysses*, but Molly the whore of Detroit is much better. Molly has a soul. Molly is the milk of human kindness. Céline pays a tribute to her at the end of the chapter. It's remarkable because all the other characters are paid off in one way or another. Molly is whitewashed. Molly, believe it or not, looms up bigger and holier than Mr. Ford's huge enterprise. Yes, that's the beautiful and surprising thing about Céline's chapter on Detroit—that he makes the body of a whore triumph over the soul of the machine. You wouldn't suspect that there was such a thing as a soul if you went to Detroit. Everything is too new, too slick, too bright, too ruthless. Souls don't grow in factories. Souls are killed in factories—even the niggardly ones. Detroit can do in a week for the white man what the South couldn't do in a hundred years with the Negro. That's why I like the Ford evening hour—it's so soothing, so inspiring.

Of course Detroit isn't the worst place—not by a long shot. That's what I said about Pittsburgh. That's what I'll say about other places too. None of them is the worst. There is no worst or worstest. The worst is in process of becoming. It's inside us now, only we haven't brought it forth. Disney dreams about it—and he gets paid for it, that's the curious thing. People bring their children to look and scream with laughter. (Ten years later it happens now and then that they don't recognize the little monster who so joyfully clapped his hands and screamed with delight. It's always hard to believe that a Jack-the-Ripper could have sprung out of your own loins.) However . . . It's cold in Detroit. A gale is blowing. Happily I am not one of those without work, without food, without shelter. I am stopping at the gay Detroiter, the Mecca of the futilitarian salesmen. There is a swanky haberdashery shop in the lobby. Salesmen love silk shirts. Sometimes they buy cute little panties too—for the ministering angels in the aeroplanes. They buy any and everything—just to keep money in circulation. The men of Detroit who are left out in the cold freeze to death in woollen underwear. The temperature in winter is distinctly sub-tropical. The buildings are straight and cruel. The wind is like a double-bladed knife. If you're lucky you can go inside where it's warm and see the Mannerheim Line. A cheering spectacle. See how ideological principles can triumph in spite of sub-normal temperatures. See men in white cloaks crawling through the snow on their bellies; they have scissors in their hands, big ones, and when they reach the barbed wire they cut, cut, cut. Now and then they get shot doing it—but then they become heroes— and besides, there are always others to take their places, all armed with scissors. Very edifying, very instructive. Heartening, I should say. Outside, on the streets of Detroit, the wind is howling and people are running for shelter. But it's warm and cosy in the cinema. After the spectacle a nice warm cup of chocolate in the lobby of the hotel. Men talking buttons and chewing gum there. Not the same as in the aeroplane—different ones. Always find them where it's warm and comfortable. Always buying and selling. And of course a pocketful of cigars. Things are picking up in Detroit. Defence orders, you know. The taxi driver told me he expected to get his job back soon. In the factory, I mean. What would happen if the war stopped suddenly I can't imagine. There would be a lot of broken hearts. Maybe another crisis. People wouldn't know what to do for themselves if peace were suddenly declared. Every- body would be laid off. The bread lines would start up. Strange, how we can manage to feed the world and not learn how to feed ourselves.

I remember when the wireless came about how everybody thought —how wonderful! Now we will be in communication with the whole world! And television—how marvellous! Now we shall be able to see what's going on in China, in Africa, in the remotest parts of the world! I used to think that perhaps one day I'd own a little apparatus and that by just turning a dial I would see Chinamen walking through the streets of Pekin or Shanghai, or see savages in the heart of Africa performing the rites of initiation. What do we actually see and hear today? What the censors permit us to see and hear, nothing more. India is just as remote as it ever was—in fact, I think it is even more so now than it was fifty years ago. In

China a great war is going on—a revolution fraught with far greater significance for the human race than this little affair in Europe. Do you see anything of it in the news reels? Even the newspapers have very little to say about it. Five million Chinese can die of flood, famine or pestilence, or be driven from their homes by the invader, and the news (a headliner for one day usually) leaves us unruffled. In Paris I saw one news reel of the bombing of Shanghai and that was all. It was too horrible—the French couldn't stomach it. To this day we haven't been shown the real pictures of the First World War. You have to have influence to get a glimpse of those fairly recent horrors. There are the 'educational' pictures, to be sure. Have you seen them? Nice, dull, soporific, hygienic, statistical poems fully castrated and sprinkled with lysol. The sort of thing the Baptist or Methodist Church could endorse.

The news reels deal largely with diplomatic funerals, christenings of battleships, fires and explosions, aeroplane wrecks, athletic contests, beauty parades, fashions, cosmetics and political speeches. Educational pictures deal largely with machines, fabrics, commodities and crime. If there's a war on we get a glimpse of foreign scenery. We get about as much information about the other peoples of this globe, through the movies and the radio, as the Martians get about us. And this abysmal separation is reflected in the American physiognomy. In the towns and cities you find the typical American everywhere. His expression is mild, bland, pseudo-serious and definitely fatuous. He is usually neatly dressed in a cheap ready-made suit, his shoes shined, a fountain pen and pencil in his breast pocket, a brief-case under his arm—and of course he wears glasses, the model changing with the changing styles. He looks as though he were turned out by a university with the aid of a chain-store cloak and suit house. One looks like the other, just as the automobiles, the radios and the telephones do. This is the type between twenty-five and forty. After that age we get another type—the middle-aged man who is already fitted with a set of false teeth, who puffs and pants, who insists on wearing a belt though he should be wearing a truss. He is a man who eats and drinks too much, smokes too much, sits too much, talks too much and is always on the edge of a breakdown. Often he dies of heart failure in the next few years. In a city like Cleveland this type comes to apotheosis. So do the buildings, the restaurants, the parks, the war memorials. The most typical American city I have struck thus far. Thriving, prosperous, active, clean, spacious, sanitary, vitalized by a liberal infusion of foreign blood and by the ozone from the lake, it stands out in my mind as the composite of many American cities. Possessing all the virtues, all the prerequisites for life, growth, blossoming, it remains, nevertheless, a thoroughly dead place—a deadly, dull, dead place. (In Cleveland to see *The Doctor's Dilemma* is an exciting event.) I would rather die in Richmond somehow, though God knows Richmond has little enough to offer. But in Richmond, or in any Southern city for that matter, you do see types now and then which depart from the norm. The South is full of eccentric characters; it still fosters individuality. And the most individualistic are of course from the land, from the out-of-the-way places. When you go through a sparsely settled state like South Carolina you do meet men, interesting men—jovial, cantankerous, disputative, pleasure-loving, independent thinking creatures who disagree with everything, on principle, but who make life charming and gracious. There can hardly be any greater contrast between two regions, in these United States, in my mind, than between a State like Ohio and a State like South Carolina. Nor can there be a greater contrast in these States than between two cities like Cleveland and Charleston, for example. In the latter place you actually have to pin a man to the mat before you can talk business to him. And if

27

he happens to be a good business man, this chap from Charleston, the chances are that he is also a fanatic about something unheard of. His face registers changes of expression, his eyes light up, his hair stands on end, his voice swells with passion, his cravat slips out of place, his suspenders are apt to come undone, he spits and curses, he coos and prances, he pirouettes now and then. And there's one thing he never dangles in front of your nose—his time-piece. He has time, oodles of time. And he accomplishes everything he chooses to accomplish in due time, with the result that the air is not filled with dust and machine oil and cash-register clickings. The great time-wasters, I find, are in the North, among the busy-bodies. Their whole life, one might truly say, is just so much time wasted. The fat, puffy, wattle-faced man of forty-five who has turned asexual is the greatest monument to futility that America has created. He's a nymphomaniac of energy accomplishing noth-ing. He's a statistical bundle of fat and jangled nerves for the in-surance man to convert into a frightening thesis. He sows the land with prosperous, restless, empty-headed, idle-handed widows who gang together in ghoulish sororities where politics and diabetes go hand in hand.

About Detroit, before I forget it—yes, it was here that Swami Vivekenanda kicked over the traces. Some of you who read this may be old enough to remember the stir he created when he spoke before the Parliament of Religions in Chicago back in the early 'nineties. The story of the pilgrimage of this man who electrified the American people reads like a legend. At first unrecognized, re-jected, reduced to starvation and forced to beg in the streets, he was finally hailed as the greatest spiritual leader of our time. Offers of all kinds were showered upon him; the rich took him in and tried to make a monkey of him. In Detroit, after six weeks of it, he rebelled. All contracts were cancelled and from that time on he went alone from town to town at the invitation of such or such a society. Here are the words of Romain Rolland:

'His first feeling of attraction and admiration for the formidable power of the young Republic had faded. Vivekenanda almost at once fell foul of the brutality, the inhumanity, the littleness of spirit, the narrow fanaticism, the monumental ignorance, the crushing incomprehension, so frank and sure of itself with regard to all who thought, who believed, who regarded life differently from the paragon nation of the human race. . . . And so he had no patience. He hid nothing. He stigmatized the vices and crimes of the Western civilization with its characteristics of violence, pillage and destruction. Once when he was to speak at Boston on a beautiful religious subject particularly dear to him (Ramakrishna), he felt such repulsion at the sight of his audience, the artificial and cruel crowd of men of affairs and of the world, that he refused to yield them the key of his sanctuary, and brusquely changing the subject, he inveighed furiously against a civilization represented by such foxes and wolves. The scandal was terrific. Hundreds noisily left the hall and the Press was furious. He was especially bitter against false Christianity and religious hypocrisy: "With all your brag and boasting, where has your Christianity succeeded without the sword? Yours is a religion preached in the name of luxury. It is all hypocrisy that I have heard in this country. All this prosperity, all this from Christ! Those who call upon Christ care nothing but to amass riches! Christ would not find a stone on which to lay his head among you. . . . You are not Christians. Return to Christ!" '

Rolland goes on to contrast this reaction with that inspired by England. 'He came as an enemy and he was conquered.' Vivekenanda himself admitted that his ideas about the English had been revolutionized. 'No one,' he said, 'ever landed on English soil with more hatred in his heart for a race than I did for the English. . . .

29

There is none among you . . . who loves the English people more than I do now.'

A familiar theme—one hears it over and over again. I think of so many eminent men who visited these shores only to return to their native land saddened, disgusted and disillusioned. There is one thing America has to give, and that they are all in agreement about: MONEY. And as I write this there comes to my mind the case of an obscure individual whom I knew in Paris, a painter of Russian birth who, during the twenty years that he lived in Paris, knew scarcely a day that he was not hungry. He was quite a figure in Montparnasse—every one wondered how he managed to survive so long without money. Finally he met an American who made it possible for him to visit this country which he had always longed to see and which he hoped to make his adopted land. He stayed a year, travelling about, making portraits, received hospitably by rich and poor. For the first time in his whole life he knew what it was to have money in his pocket, to sleep in a clean, comfortable bed, to be warm, to be well nourished—and, what is more important, to have his talent recognized. One day, after he had been back a few weeks, I ran into him at a bar. I was extremely curious to hear what he might have to say about America. I had heard of his success and I wondered why he had returned.

He began to talk about the cities he had visited, the people he had met, the houses he had put up at, the meals he had been fed, the museums he had visited, the money he had made. 'At first it was wonderful,' he said. 'I thought I was in Paradise. But after six months of it I began to be bored. It was like living with children —but *vicious* children. What good does it do to have money in your pocket if you can't enjoy yourself? What good is fame if nobody understands what you're doing? You know what my life is like here. I'm a man without a country. If there's a war I'll either be put in a concentration camp or asked to fight for the French. I could have escaped that in America. I could have become a citizen and made a good living. But I'd rather take my chances here. Even if there's only a few years left those few years are worth more here than a lifetime in America. There's no real life for an artist in America—only a living death. By the way, have you got a few francs to lend me? I'm broke again. But I'm happy. I've got my old studio back again—I appreciate that lousy place now. Maybe it was good for me to go to America—if only to make me realize how wonderful is this life which I once thought unbearable.'

How many letters I received while in Paris from Americans who had returned home—all singing the same song. 'If I could only be back there again. I would give my right arm to be able to return. I didn't realize what I was giving up.' Et cetera, et cetera. I never received one letter from a repatriated American saying that he was happy to be home again. When this war is over there will be an exodus to Europe such as this country has never seen. We try to pretend now, because France has collapsed, that she was degenerate. There are artists and art critics in this country who, taking advantage of the situation, endeavour with utter shamelessness to convince the American public that we have nothing to learn from Europe, that Europe, France more particularly, is dead. What an abominable lie! France prostrate and defeated is more alive than we have ever been. Art does not die because of a military defeat, or an economic collapse, or a political débâcle. Moribund France produced more art than young and vigorous America, than fanatical Germany or proselytising Russia.

There are evidences of a very great art in Europe as long ago as twenty-five thousand years, and in Egypt as far back as sixty thousand years. Money had nothing to do with the production of these treasures. Money will have nothing to do with the art of the future. Money will pass away. Even now we are able to realize the futility of money. Had we not become the arsenal of the world, and thus staved off the gigantic collapse of our industrial system, we might have witnessed the spectacle of the richest nation on earth starving to death in the midst of the accumulated gold of the entire world. The war is only an interruption of the inevitable disaster which impends. We have a few years ahead of us and then the whole structure will come toppling down and engulf us. Putting a few millions back to work making engines of destruction is no solution of the problem. When the destruction brought about by war is complete, another sort of destruction will set in. And it will be far more drastic, far more terrible than the destruction which we are now witnessing. The whole planet will be in the throes of revolution. And the fires will rage until the very foundations of this present world crumble. Then we shall see who has life, the life more abundant. Then we shall see whether the ability to make money and the ability to survive are one and the same. Then we shall see the meaning of true wealth.

Meanwhile I have good news—I'm going to take you to Chicago, to the Mecca Apartments on the South Side. It's a Sunday morning and my cicerone has borrowed a car to take me around. We stop at a flea market on the way. My friend explains to me that he was raised here in the ghetto; he tries to find the spot where his home used to be. It's a vacant lot now. There are acres and acres of vacant lots here on the South Side. It looks like Belgium did after the World War. Worse, if anything. Reminds me of a diseased jawbone, some of it smashed and pulverized, some of it charred and ulcerated. The flea market is more reminiscent of Cracow than of Clignancourt, but the effect is the same. We are at the backdoor of civilization amidst the dregs and debris of the disinherited. Thousands, hundreds of thousands, maybe millions of Americans, are still poor enough to scrimmage through this offal in search of some needed object. Nothing is too dilapidated or rust-bitten or disease-laden to attract some hungry buyer. You would think the five and ten cent store would satisfy the humblest wants, but the five and ten cent store is really expensive in the long run, as one soon learns. The congestion is terrific—we have to elbow our way through the throng. It's like the banks of the Ganges except that there is no odour of sanctity about. As we push our way through the crowd my feet are arrested by a strange sight. There in the middle of the street, dressed in full regalia, is an American Indian. He's selling a snake oil. Instantly the thought of the other miserable derelicts stewing around in this filth and vermin is gone. *A World I Never Made*, wrote James Farrell. Well, there stands the real author of the book—an outcast, a freak, a hawker of snake oil. On that same spot the buffaloes once roamed; now it is covered with broken pots and pans, with worn-out watches, with dismantled chandeliers, with busted shoes which even an Igorote would spurn. Of course if you walk on a few blocks you can see the other side of the picture—the grand façade of Michigan Avenue, where it seems as if the whole world were composed of millionaires. At night you can see the great monument to chewing gum lit up by floodlights and marvel that such a monstrosity of architecture should be singled out for special attention. If you wander down the steps leading to the rear of the building and squint your eyes and sharpen your imagination a bit you can even imagine yourself back in Paris on the Rue Broca. No Bubu here, of course, but perhaps you will run into one of Al Capone's ex-comrades. It must be pleasant to be stuck up behind the glitter of the bright lights.

We dig further into the South Side, getting out now and then

33

to stretch our legs. Interesting evolution going on here. Rows of old mansions flanked by vacant lots. A dingy hotel sticking up like a Mayan ruin in the midst of yellow fangs and chalk teeth. Once respectable dwelling-places given up now to the dark-skinned people we 'liberated'. No heat, no gas, no plumbing, no water, no nothing —sometimes not even a window-pane. Who owns these houses? Better not inquire too deeply. What do they do with them when the darkies move out? Tear them down, of course. Federal housing projects. Model tenement houses. I'm thinking of old Genoa, one of the last ports I stopped at on my way back to America. Very old, this section. Nothing much to brag about in the way of conveniences. But what a difference between the slums of Genoa and the slums of Chicago! Even the Armenian section of Athens is preferable to this. For twenty years the Armenian refugees of Athens have lived like goats in the little quarter which they made their own. There were no old mansions to take over—not even an abandoned factory. There was just a plot of land on which they erected their homes out of whatever came to hand. Men like Henry Ford and Rockefeller contributed unwittingly to the creation of this paradise which was entirely built of remnants and discarded objects. I think of this Armenian quarter because as we were walking along my friend called my attention to a flower-pot on the windowsill of one of these gutted homes. 'You see,' he said, 'even the poorest among them have their flowers.' But in Athens I saw dovecotes, solariums, verandas floating without support, rabbits sunning themselves on the roofs, goats kneeling before ikons, turkeys tied to the door-knobs. Everybody had flowers—not just flowerpots. A door might be made of Ford fenders and look inviting. A chair might be made of gasoline tins and be pleasant to sit on. There were bookshops where you could read about Buffalo Bill and Jules Verne or Hermes Trismegistus. There was a spirit here which a thousand years of misery had not squelched. Chicago's South Side, on the other hand, is like a vast, unorganized lunatic asylum. Nothing can flourish here but vice and disease. I wonder what the great Emancipator would say if he could see the glorious freedom in which the black man moves now. He made them free, yes—free as rats in a dark cellar.

Well, here we are—the Mecca Apartments! A great quadrangular cluster of buildings, once in good taste, I suppose—architecturally. After the whites moved out the coloured people took over. Before it reached its present condition it went through a sort of Indian Summer. Every other apartment was a dive. The place glowed with prostitution. It must have been a Mecca indeed for the lonely darkie in search of work.

It's a queer building now. The locks are dismantled, the doors unhinged, the globes busted. You enter what seems like the corridor of some dismal Catholic institution, or a deaf and dumb asylum, or a Bronx sanatorium for the discreet practice of abortion. You come to a turn and you find yourself in a court surrounded by several tiers of balconies. In the centre of the court is an abandoned fountain covered with a huge wire mesh like the old-fashioned cheese covers. You can imagine what a charming spot this was in the days when the ladies of easy virtue held sway here. You can imagine the peals of laughter which once flooded the court. Now there is a strained silence, except for the sound of roller skates, a dry cough, an oath in the dark. A man and woman are leaning over the balcony rail above us. They look down at us without any expression in their faces. Just looking. Dreaming? Hardly. Their bodies are too worn, their souls too stunted, to permit even of that cheapest of all luxuries. They stand there like animals in the field. The man spits. It makes a queer, dull smack as it hits the pavement. Maybe that's his way of signing the Declaration of Independence.

35

Maybe he didn't know he spat. Maybe it was his ghost that spat. I look at the fountain again. It's been dry a long time. And maybe it's covered like a piece of old cheese so that people won't spit in it and bring it back to life. It would be a terrible thing for Chicago if this black fountain of life should suddenly erupt! My friend assures me there's no danger of that. I don't feel so sure about it. Maybe he's right. Maybe the Negro will always be our friend, no matter what we do to him. I remember a conversation with a coloured maid in the home of one of my friends. She said: 'I do think we have more love for you than you have for us.' 'You don't hate us ever?' I asked. 'Lord, no!' she answered, 'we just feel sorry for you. You has all the power and the wealth but you ain't happy.'

We got into the car, rode a few blocks and got out to visit another shell crater. The street was deserted except for some chickens grubbing for food between the slats of a crumbling piazza. More vacant lots, more gutted houses; fire escapes clinging to the walls with their iron teeth, like drunken acrobats. A Sunday atmosphere here. Everything serene and peaceful. Like Louvain or Rheims between bombardments. Then suddenly I saw it chalked up on the side of a house in letters ten feet high: 'GOOD NEWS! GOD IS LOVE!' When I saw these words I got down on my knees in the open sewer which had been conveniently placed there for the purpose and I offered up a short prayer, a silent one, which must have registered as far as Mound City, Illinois, where the coloured muskrats have built their igloos. It was time for a good stiff drink of cod-liver oil, but as the varnish factories were all closed we had to repair to the abattoir and quaff a bucket of blood. Never has blood tasted so wonderful! It was like taking Vitamins A, B, C, D, E in quick succession and then chewing a stick of cold dynamite. Good news! Aye, wonderful news—for Chicago. I ordered the chauffeur to take us immediately to Mundelein so that I could bless the cardinal and all the real estate operations, but we only got as far as the Bahai Temple. A workman who was shovelling sand opened the door of the temple and showed us around. He kept telling us that we all worshipped the same God, that all religions were alike in essence. In the little pamphlet which he handed us to read I learned that the Forerunner of the Faith, the Founder of the Faith, and the authorized Interpreter and Exemplar of Bahà'u'llàh's teachings, all suffered persecution and martyrdom for daring to make God's love all-inclusive. It's a queer world, even in this enlightened period of civilization. The Bahai temple has been twenty years building and is not finished yet. The architect was Mr. Bourgeois, believe it or not. The interior of the temple, in its unfinished state, makes you think of a stage setting for Joan of Arc. The circular meeting place on the ground floor resembles the hollow of a shell and inspires peace and meditation as few places of worship do. The movement has already spread over most of the globe, thanks to its persecutors and detractors. There is no colour line, as in Christian churches, and one can believe as he pleases. It is for this reason that the Bahai movement is destined to outlast all the other religious organizations on this continent. The Christian Church in all its freakish ramifications and efflorescences is as dead as a door-nail; it will pass away utterly when the political and social system in which it is now embedded collapses. The new religion will be based on deeds, not beliefs. 'Religion is not for empty bellies,' said Ramakrishna. Religion is always revolutionary, far more revolutionary than bread-and-butter philosophies. The priest is always in league with the devil, just as the political leader always leads to death. People are trying to get together, it seems to me. Their representatives, in every walk of life, keep them apart by breeding hatred and fear. The exceptions are so rare that when they occur the impulse is to set them apart, make supermen of them or gods,

37

anything but men and women like ourselves. And in removing them thus to the ethereal realms the revolution of love which they came to preach is nipped in the bud. But the good news is always there, just around the corner, chalked up on the wall of a deserted house: 'GOD IS LOVE!' I am sure that when the citizens of Chicago read these lines they will get up *en masse* and make a pilgrimage to that house. It is easy to find because it stands in the middle of a vacant lot on the South Side. You climb down a manhole in La Salle Street and just let yourself drift with the sewer water. You can't miss it because it's written in white chalk in letters ten feet high. All you need to do when you find it is to shake yourself like a sewer-rat and dust yourself off. God will do the rest. . . .

ORIGINAL PREFACE TO
"HOLLYWOOD'S HALLUCINATION"*

IT WAS always my intention to write a book about Hollywood. Since reading this book by Parker Tyler I know I shall never do it; the job has been done in a way beyond anything I could ever hope to accomplish.

Why do we go to the movies? Most every intelligent person puts this question to himself at one time or another, often repeatedly and disgustedly, and always out of a sense of shame. It's the modern version of the medieval query: Why does man sin? It has to be answered, even though the answer in no way affects one's

* Written at Parker Tyler's request but rejected by the publishers of his book.

behavior. We will all continue to go to the movies, just as our forefathers continued to wallow in sin.

Why do we go then? Well, it seems to me that the reason we go to the movies, or skip the movies and get drunk, the reason we read detective stories or switch now and then to Marcel Proust or Thomas Mann, the reason we have International Business Machines and the Bible Society, the reason we make poison gas and organize societies for the prevention of cruelty to animals, the reason we are at war, though there was never a period in history when people as a whole were less interested in making war, the reason for a thousand and one contradictory motives, thoughts and deeds, is one and the same. We have reached the point where black and white are interchangeable. To the man in the street it makes no difference whether you talk elephants or cuspidors—they are identical. The tragedy that has befallen the world, a tragedy inherent in our evolution, is that we can no longer give meaning and significance to events. The color has gone out of life and with it the drama. We are left with the sound and the fury of emptiness. In a world which boasts of progress there is the most amazing lack of intelligence, the most unprecedented absence of will. In obedience to our compulsive fears we show a remarkable ability to organize for self-destruction, but none whatever for creation.

There is no way to combat the pernicious influence of Hollywood unless we are ready and willing to combat all the other pernicious influences which make Hollywood what it is and which it represents with the deceptive faithfulness of a mirror. If Hollywood is America's hallucination, as Parker Tyler pretends, then the soul of America—or perhaps we'd better speak only of the psyche—is in a bad way. Do we want to change?—that is the question.

Recently I was reading a book by Claude Houghton, just off the press.* In it he has one of his characters declare: "We are all going to change—or perish. We are going to become regenerate—or disappear into the abyss. Surely that's clear! Either we're going to become persons with different desires, different thoughts, different emotions—or we are all going to become members of a vast suicide club. . . . There will be a new world directly enough people want a new world. Somebody once said that there are doors which will not open till millions stand before them. When enough people want a new world, it will arise. And not before. Ideals won't bring it—and neither will schemes for a utilitarian Utopia. Neither prayers will bring it, nor planning. It's what we all really want most that counts. What we really want when we're alone. Not the ideals we profess—that's just moral exhibitionism."

What aroused my admiration, when reading the first instalment of Tyler's book in the pages of "View," was the author's almost uncanny penetration of the matrix in which all Hollywood's progeny, good, bad, or indifferent, is conceived. In discussing "The Maltese Falcon" Parker Tyler threw a revolving beam of light on the world of crime and punishment which so fascinates the American audience. In the opening chapter of this book he makes a statement which sheds another kind of light on the Hollywood approach to life. He speaks of the watchful comet awaiting its chance to shine, illuminating more by its bad taste and illogicality than by its isolated triumphs. This phenomenal aspect of the cinema is of absorbing interest. It means for one thing that when a picture like "The Informer" appears on the horizon there is no telling whether we shall have to wait ten years or a hundred years for a production of equal splendor and magnitude. It means that

* All Change, Humanity!

when you see a picture such as "Night Must Fall" you are to conclude that it was a sheer accident and nothing more. You are never to permit your hopes to be roused, never to fall into the error of believing that at last the cinema is coming into its own; you must remain cynical, blasé, disillusioned, relying for your enjoyment and understanding of the films only upon the ever-increasing faculty of clairvoyance.

It goes without saying that, given an audience composed of Parker Tylers, there would be no cinema such as we know it today. There is a kind of criticism at work here which overleaps the subject and indicts not only the sponsors and producers of this form of entertainment, indicts not only the audience which suffers it to be, but levels an unanswerable condemnation at our whole way of life. Hallucinations are real and proceed from a guilty conscience or a diseased mind, really one and the same at bottom. Hollywood, as I see it, is just as guilty or innocent of crime as any or all of us. And that perhaps is what really infuriates us, when the subject comes up. Nothing can be done about it, just as nothing could be done to prevent Sacco and Vanzetti from going to the electric chair. The judge who imposed this monstrous sentence was not guilty; the American people were guilty—and they are still guilty. The judges who perpetrate these crimes are as helpless as the victims whom they condemn to death. As I write these lines the headlines are screaming the news of Earl Browder's release. He suffered enough, says our good, magnanimous president. What arrogant clap-trap! We want to know why he suffered at all. His timely release is just as much of a bad joke as his untimely incarceration. . . .

In one of Wassermann's books there is a prison-keeper named Klakusch who makes simple, homely declarations which I find extremely apropos. One goes like this: "Stop, world of humans, and attack the problem from a different angle!" Another goes this way:

"Then we must destroy the world and create people who think differently." *

Does all this seem far-fetched? I wonder. Either it's perfectly clear and indisputable what the situation is or one can go on being polite and admitting differences of opinion ad infinitum. Opinions don't matter a damn any more. The fact is that the situation is out of hand. Fate now holds the trump card.

How and why things are the way they are Hollywood shows us day in and day out at a price which is modest ("box office prices within reach of all," says Will Hays) when one takes into consideration the vast import hidden behind this seemingly innocuous form of entertainment. ("Motion pictures furnish entertainment, relaxation, information, and inspiration to millions every week"— Will Hays.) It is far more instructive, if you are interested in studying your own death warrant, to go to the cinema than to read books or listen to political speeches. It requires only the barest training to acquire the faculty of sight-reading. Once in possession of this faculty the entertainment is priceless. *How to interpret unreality*—that's what it amounts to. The highest metaphysical task ever offered to a limp and uncritical public. In terms of life the reward is nil. One has to enjoy it for its own sake, or forego it absolutely. Any truths perceived, any realization achieved, any urge precipitated, advances one nowhere. You step out of one shadow world into another, out of one dream into another—the other being always the same. It's like becoming conscious while still in the womb, and falling back into unconsciousness out of despair and futility. Christ himself, if he were to step out of the Normandie at Park Avenue and 53rd Street, N. Y., could not alter the configuration by a hair, even if he were to possess powers a hundred-fold more miraculous than his disciples credited him with. Somehow,

* *The Maurizius Case.*

when you step out of a place like the Normandie—and even more so when you step out of Grauman's Chinese Theatre, Hollywood —you know as you never knew before that Christ was indeed crucified, rose from the dead, and ascended on high. "A man of sorrows and acquainted with grief." (Courtesy of the International Bible Machine Corporation, Park Avenue, N. Y.) Yes, you know it deep in your guts. You know that his life was not only tragic and symbolic, but that it came to absolutely no fruition. (Otherwise you wouldn't be coming out of the movies with a forlorn, dejected air.) You know something more too. You know that every man-jack alive will be crucified, not once as Christ was, but a million times. You know that it makes no difference whether you throw a bomb or receive the Nobel Prize for aiding and abetting the most holy peace. You get a delirious feeling of being *foutu*. What makes you more delirious is that you paid good money (or bad) to see yourself being made *foutu*. Never, never will you have the chance to see yourself as the angel you long to be. You may become a hero, you may become a Guggenheim Prize winner, you may even become President, God forbid! but you will never discover a way out of the rat trap. The exits are closed, the hatches down. The best film of the year might just as well be the worst film of the year. Nothing is altered by any awards or condemnations. Nothing can be altered. Nobody, absolutely nobody, is to blame; neither is anybody to be praised, criticized or condemned. If it drives you mad you can smash the mirror, but that will not change the face of things, and you know it.

"Motion pictures are the democratic art of the 20th century," says Will Hays, in the name of the Motion Picture Producers and Distributors of America. To appreciate the significance of this statement one should read some of the accompanying facts compiled by this great Sanhedrin of the motion picture industry. In the year 1941, according to "Film Facts", motion pictures furnished regular employment to 282,000 persons; the annual payroll amounted to $400,000,000; 276 trades, crafts and professions were required for their production. These facts go hand in hand with the Production Code whose general principles are formulated thus:

1. No picture shall be produced which will lower the moral standards of those who see it. Hence the sympathy of the audience should never be thrown to the side of crime, wrong-doing, evil or sin.

2. Correct standards of life, subject only to the requirements of drama and entertainment, shall be presented.

3. Law, natural or human, shall not be ridiculed, nor shall sympathy be created for its violation.

The "particular applications" of these general principles, which are set forth in detail, are worthy of serious study—i.e., by some serious nincompoop such as Thorstein Veblen. I will cite just a few to indicate the benevolent tenor of these lofty, self-appointed guardians of public morals. . . .

"The technique of murder must be presented in a way that will not inspire imitation."

"Revenge in modern times shall not be justified."

"The use of liquor in American life, when not required by the plot or for proper characterization, will not be shown."

"The sanctity of the institution of marriage and the home shall be upheld. Pictures shall not infer that low forms of sex relationship are the accepted or common thing."

"Scenes of passion should not be introduced when not essential to the plot."

"In general, passion should so be treated that these scenes do not stimulate the lower and baser element."

"Seduction and rape are never the proper subject for comedy."

"Sex perversion or any inference of it is forbidden."

"Miscegenation (sex relationships between the white and black races) is forbidden."

"Sex hygiene and venereal diseases are not subjects for motion pictures."

"Scenes of actual childbirth, in fact or in silhouette, are never to be presented."

"Children's sex organs are never to be exposed."

"The treatment of low, disgusting, unpleasant, though not necessarily evil, subjects should be subject always to the dictate of good taste and a regard for the sensibilities of the audience."

"Ministers of religion in their character as ministers of religion should not be used as comic characters or as villains."

"The treatment of bedrooms must be governed by good taste and delicacy."

Under the heading "Repellent Subjects" there is this: "The following subjects must be treated within the careful limits of good taste:

1. Actual hangings or electrocutions as legal punishment for crime.

2. Third Degree methods.

3. Brutality and possible gruesomeness.

4. Branding of people or animals.

5. Apparent cruelty to children or animals.

6. The sale of women, or a woman selling her virtue.

7. Surgical operations."

Then follows a code dealing with "Special Regulations re Crime in Motion Pictures", which is a sinister masterpiece, apparently by the same genius who devised the foregoing, in which whitewash and revelation proceed in a contrapuntal fugue.

When we wonder, in our weak and senile moments, why so few

good films are produced, let us remember that the good fathers who of their own free will drew up this neo-Hammurabic Code had as their guiding principle the elevation of good taste, which is the apotheosis of negation. Let us be indulgent and forgiving, since their supreme concern is the augmentation of box office receipts. They represent the spiritual elect of our time. They work for truth, justice and decency—on a cold cash basis. They provide entertainment, relaxation, information and inspiration to all at a price which is so modest, so reasonable, that rather than commit suicide we go to their luxurious exhibition halls and masturbate in our sleep. God bless you, dear provident angels of mercy! We thank you for your abundant gifts. . . .

Before giving the "all clear" signal let's strum a few lethal dichotomies on the dialectical guitar. There is the robot and the labor leader, the gangster and the politically fixed judge, the prostitute and the vice crusader. Carry it out in the key of *Ut mineur* through every realm and layer of life and you have an *enchainement* which is as nearly perfect as divine justice can be. As Klakusch says: "The initiated simply laugh at the idea of either protection or improvement."

All clear? *Bon!* And now about zombies. . . .

The proletariat are the zombies of the earth. Over them are the cruel masters of the earth, also zombies, but unlike the proletariat, doomed to perpetuate their breed without benefit of a Lincoln or a Lenin. Since the dawn of history only a handful of men have been concerned with breaking the spell. They had the originality to conceive of a world without zombies. What is more, they had the courage to act as *if* that distant fact were already truth. The most surprising thing about the advent of these forerunners is this: the zombies, both master and slave, continued to remain zombies, only they developed a spiritual cast, or taint, as you wish.

None of them thought of emulating the emancipated ones. They became worshipful, that's all, and incidentally, more vicious.

A super-zombie, even if he were powerless to free the world, would at least have the intelligence to know that intelligence is nothing if we have only the illusion that we are free. Under a thrall freedom and slavery are easily interchangeable. A super-zombie would not want to be a millionaire any more than he would want to be a highly paid mechanic at the Ford Motor Works. He would not want to be a dictator any more than he would want to be an Untouchable. His sole plan of action would be to smash the pattern—i.e., break the trance. It would not be a solution, because there are no solutions. It would be liberation, a chance to jump clear of the clock-work. Snap out of it and see what happens!—that would be the pass-word. He would simply break the dam and turn the still lake into a torrent of foaming energy. "Still lake" is a euphemism. Stagnant pool is better.

In the stagnant pool of life the zombies breed like bacteria. There is nothing wrong with bacteria per se. Nothing wrong with zombies either, when all the world's a zombie. But we know in our frozen zombie hearts that this trance-like condition in which we have been breeding like lice for thousands of years is only a partial aspect of life. Part of us is zombie and another part is undefinable, but by comparison infinitely free. It is this vast area of our being which Hollywood not just ignores, which would mean that it knows and rejects, but is oblivious to. Now and then an artist reveals that he has an inkling of it, but to preoccupy himself with this greater, unexplored domain would be tantamount to courting suicide, as artist. The whole vast cultural world floats above our heads like incense rising from the sweat of slaves. Art is the balsam which we apply to our bruises. It is the aesthetic mouthwash of constipated ninnies who have not only lost their appetite for life but the teeth with which to chew their devitalized food products.

So long as we are all hitched to the chain-gang, so long as we are all shackled and manacled, so long as we answer yes to a number and wear the same striped uniform, the cultural arts will always make a soothing cough syrup. At least, that's what the cultured souls try to make us believe. Yet somehow we're not thoroughly convinced. Somehow we've always been expecting of the creative spirits something more, something "liberating", shall I say? There seems to be a vast misunderstanding all along the line as to the nature of the creative gift. We have never decided whether it's a narcotic or a missing vitamin. In our confusion and restlessness—because zombies thrash around too, just like victims of the nightmare—we crucify our geniuses first and then vainly try to resurrect them. If the "genius" had a secret clue to the mystery of life we would never know, because whenever he opens his mouth we crack down on him. We prefer to listen to the dead ones—because whatever is dead awakens a response in us.

The art of the cinema may indeed be a very ancient one, but in its present guise it reaches its apogee. There was never a more perfect synchronization of supply and demand than in this realm of the "democratic art". Movies, quickies, quackies—it's all one consistent, deleterious ectoplasm. If we were capable of protest, capable of distinction and evaluation, Donald Duck would have been murdered just as quickly as Hitler. (By the way, is it strange or isn't it that Hitler hasn't been murdered yet?)

There is mention in Tyler's book of foreign films, foreign actors, foreign directors. Subtle differences are touched upon, differences which every sensitive being perceived and felt before the crack-up. Undoubtedly in the work of foreign artists there was a larger element of art as well as a more human touch. Today these differences seem negligible. When the ice caps begin to slide towards the Equator the qualitative as well as the quantitative differences between one form of life and another become even less than an academic question. The European artist cannot pump new life into us, and even if he could, it would be of no avail. The form of life which permitted us to sit back in a comfortable seat and analyze these subtle differences is on the toboggan. The whole shebang is doomed, and that includes the projection room. As we approach the fatal day Hollywood becomes the one and only maw, the ineluctable hopper in which all the arts, foreign and domestic, are made grist for the mill. The hallucination becomes the autoscope. . . . When you get this slant on things you realize that even such an inspiring figure as Mahatma Gandhi is nothing but a spiritual zombie. And that makes you not sad so much as sick to the stomach.

Somewhere I read once that every language begins as poetry and ends as algebra. So too all art might be thought of as beginning out of soul stuff and ending in celluloid and cellophane. When recently I felt myself being carried away by those moving passages on the Cathedral of Chartres, in André Malraux's latest book, I had the strange repercussion afterwards that this all-too-human language was something of an anachronism. My thoughts reverted to the words of a lesser known Frenchman who, on the eve of the débâcle, wrote: "It is time to abandon the world of civilized men and its light. It is too late to try to be reasonable and cultivated—this has led to a life that is without interest. Secretly or not, we must needs become quite different, or cease being." *

We rail about the censorship, about the nefarious powers of the church, about the humiliating tyranny of the matriarchal system,

* *The Sacred Conspiracy*, by Georges Bataille—from "Vertical", edited by Eugene Jolas.

about the glittering eye that is forever fastened upon the cash register. We credit the Hollywood nabobs with being Machiavellian, because they pander so successfully to the low taste of the mob. We pretend that there is an unholy partnership between Church, State, Factory and Cinema, and the pretension is just. But get a close-up of these cruel, cunning arbiters of our destiny and you get a picture of Everyman when he has emerged from his larval state. They are all walking the treadmill, all harried and ridden, all responding with automatic inflexibility. You have to feel just as sorry for the Pope or a toothless Rockefeller, as you do for the Georgia convict or Bertha the poor sewing machine girl. The Hollywood stars and the men who promote them toss in their sleep with the same unremitting anguish as the street-walker and her pimp. And while Hitler is at large we all do the goose-step with good grace— all except Mahatma Gandhi who, according to the zombie logic, must obviously be out of his mind.

From Gandhi to Disney, or from heliotropes to knucklebones: an interesting glissando. If there is mystery surrounding Hitler's powers of self-preservation, if there is ambiguity attached to Gandhi's logic, there is nothing but clarity, wisdom and justice connected with Walt Disney's astronomical rise to fame. The animated cartoon, brought to box-office perfection by the mastermind of the American Unconcious, is the dramatic and puissant epilogue to the *Ding an Sich*. It's the picturization of the little man's epicene drive towards the spiritual bonanzas of the universe. How much longer, I ask myself, are we going to bother to preserve the convention, or the fiction, of living actors and actresses—"even in silhouette"? Why not simplify? Why not get down to bed-rock? From poetry to algebra, and from algebra to the astral concentration camps. Why stop to invent non-Euclidian geometries? We've already crossed the line: we're in the world of the abstracts. Nonrepresentational art galvanized by the squirt gun. A world of utter purity in which the censor, tongue-tied and web-footed, has sunk for another Manwantara below the subliminal threshold. Sometimes, when I contemplate this world, I miss the homely idiocies of the zombies I used to play with. I feel as though I were surrounded by nothing but Lennie Frankensteins, all very animated, don't you know, and often quite articulate in a disgusting sort of way, but all so hungry for a bit of—well, what the game-keeper might have suggested to Lady Chatterley. As Parker Tyler so aptly says, in the chapter called "The Daylight Dream"—"all the monsters of Hollywood cannot compare with the luminous and authentic monstrosity of a little child's drawing or the painting of the insane."

There's one feature of the Hollywood art factory which I notice the author has ignored—that's the news reel. Particularly the Voice which accompanies the march of events. It's the same Voice, of course, which speaks to us over the radio: the anonymous Voice of the anonymous herd. It's the phony voice that should have been given to Frankenstein. If the latter were allowed to talk naturally —in character, so to speak—he would probably talk like Raymond Swing, or like that other mellifluous warbler whom I've been listening to for thousands of years but whose name escapes me for the moment. The peculiar feature of this news Voice is that no matter what it narrates it never loses its toneless lustre. If it's Quaker Oats that's being featured it warbles about Quaker Oats with the dulcet tones of a violoncello; if it's Elgin watches ditto; if it's a football match ditto; if it's a hurricane ditto; if it's the fall of Singapore ditto; if it's a new bathing suit ditto; if it's birth control ditto; if it's higher education ditto; if it's the second coming of Christ ditto; if it's a bull market ditto; if it's Carter's Little Liver Pills ditto. If the end of the world were at hand it would report the event in the same dramatically undramatic tone of voice. . . .

This voice is an achievement which no other age has given us. It says, in effect, X always equals Y. *And it gets paid for doing it!* Z is never mentioned, because Z stands for Zebra and other unmentionable things. To glide from the fall of Paris to the latest metal clip garter not the slightest modulation is demanded. The fall of Berlin, or the fall of Moscow—it doesn't matter which to the Voice—can always be neatly sandwiched in between the latest lynching bee and the newest brand of pop.

Everybody has seen and heard Mussolini talk. Quite a treat, too. People laugh or hiss, according to their glandular pattern. With Hitler it's different, I've noticed. Why, it's hard to say, because he's every bit as ridiculous as Benito. But people take him more seriously—which is a bad sign, incidentally. However, let's skip Hitler: for a bad joke a hell of a lot of words have been wasted on him, to say nothing of ammunition. Let's take Stalin—or the Chinese impresarios. I notice that only Park Avenue idiots laugh at Stalin, rather hysterically, too. Stalin seems to be talking a brand new language, a language he learned all by himself. He talks like a man who means what he says, which is quite frightening to people who have been accustomed all their lives to adjusting themselves to lies and chicanery. By comparison Roosevelt and Churchill seem utterly unconvincing, as though they were reading it out of a book—a hymn book. The *pièce de résistance* is that dynastic queen of the yellow world, Madame Chiang Kai-shek. Of course nobody knows what she's saying—probably not even the Chinese —but it's impressive, thoroughly impressive. (How impressive you can appreciate better by listening to Eleanor Roosevelt.) This little woman, as precious almost as the beautiful Nefertiti, seems to be saying, very politely, very graciously, of course, that all white

53

people are impotent, and not only impotent but cowardly, and not only cowardly but dastard, and not only dastard but boorish. "I've only got coolies behind me," is the way I translate her words, "but I can perform miracles with them. Thank you ever so much for the three aeroplanes you sent last winter." And then she seems to blow a kiss whilst gathering up her hobble skirt and rolling up her sleeves to comb the lice out of some poor orphan's poll. The Generalissimo is waiting for her in the wings. If they're waiting for a bombardment you may see them sit down to a game of chess—it's a good news reel technique for saving face. . . .

And so, as we follow the races, or follow the retreating British armies, the Voice pursues us. As it explains to us what happened six weeks ago—forgetful of the fact that we also read the newspapers—none of the dread events which are rocking the world disturb us any longer. The Voice eliminates anything which will mar the main event—which is the feature film of course. It gets us set for the trance.

(I often wonder what the Voice does during the interim between reels. Does It play pool and visit Turkish baths? Or does It sit home all day and read the newspapers? And on what sort of toothpaste does It feed?)

Anyway, it gets paid for it! It's important to remember that. That inner voice which Socrates distrusted! Maybe now you get the idea. . . . Nietzsche, in his cruel way, loved to fling gibes at Socrates about this weakness. Nietzsche thought the inner man had something. Socrates knew better. Now everybody knows . . . it's an open secret.

Can it be that this Voice, which is as smooth and consistent as the most refreshing toothpaste, is the voice of the monster? Is this the Voice which even the Czar of Hollywood is powerless to prevail against? Think of Clifton Fadiman, that beautiful, impersonal dialectic of his, rising like the ghost of Oscar Hammerstein above the spray of facts and figures which bring us sorely needed information in such an entertaining way. Or Raymond Gram Swing when he opens his trap to call to his mate—the box office, that is. A hundred million Lennie Frankenstein Juniors listen breathlessly. Such delicious, thrilling information—and free! free as the air! Don't these entertaining warblers make Roosevelt and Willkie look like droopy Harz canaries? Well, anyway, it's all gravy that they hand out—every word of it. But then suddenly, quite mysteriously too, sometimes you hear Elizabeth Bergner calling—*long distance*. She sounds like an interplanetary voice. Is she hysterializing, or what? Some say she's being cast for Seraphita soon—or was it Bixby's stove polish? Anyway, god-damn it! *she suffers*—and that's something. That's why they're so unearthly, her performances. She weeps over a little thing like a broken heart, imagine that! *And gets paid for it!* Though, to be frank, not quite as handsomely as Donald Duck or Mickey Mouse. . . .

. One thing you have to give Hollywood credit for: it puts money into circulation. It demonstrates that the most horrible, as well as the most vacuous, things can be made to pay. How pleasant now to sit back and watch the bloody Civil War as it affected those charming creatures—Leslie Howard and Vivian Leigh.

Something more up to date, you say? Why certainly. How about the destruction of Warsaw or Shanghai or Rotterdam? Maybe you'd like Chungking better. Wonderful photography! Especially during that moment of silence after the Japanese bombers moved on. And that lovely scenic railway trip up the Burma Road . . . those strange Tibetan monks outside the lamasery. You remember? Remember the pilgrim who walked a few steps and prostrated himself? Over and over again—perhaps for a thousand miles. Curious, wasn't it? Like something on Mars. Edifying, though. If we didn't have wars we might never know how these strange people live. Of course, in peace times we do have educational features . . . can't deny that. But nothing like these documentary pictures, what! All very expert, even down to the musical accompaniments. I wonder who'll arrange the score when they show the bombing of New York? Anyway, you see now how it is in other parts of the world. Aren't you glad you live in the United States of North America? No need to move from the spot: Hollywood brings it to you on a silver platter. We should be grateful to Hollywood—and to Mr. and Mrs. Roosevelt also—for making everything so ducky-wucky here in North America while the rest of the world is in flames. . . .

And don't think for a minute, because I seem to accuse them of complacency, that they don't want new ideas in Hollywood! Yes indeedy, they do! It may be hard to believe it, when the whole world is in such a dither and ferment, but honestly, they're always short of material in Hollywood. As though life didn't move fast enough. And yet, Christ knows, we're all doing our bit to speed up the destruction. But there it is. Hollywood always has its scouts out for new material—human or otherwise. Sometimes it smells a bit strong, a bit like the stock-yards, if you get what I mean. But if anybody has an idea, something original . . . you know, some clever little idea . . . something in good taste and of correct standards . . . say, for instance, a woman falling in love with her ironing board . . . something original and entertaining, like that . . . they'll take it. And what's more—*you'll get paid for it!* Don't give them the story of your life! They can invent that much better than you can live it. No, something "original".

THE GIGANTIC SUNRISE

For me Anghelos Sikelianos is one of those rare spirits whom one understands immediately or not at all. One does not approach his work through the intellect. To follow him in all his manifestations, and they are myriad, demands a collaboration of the whole being, which in turn implies a faith in the inscrutable continuity of life.

Coming at a time when the peoples of the earth seem more disunited than ever Sikelianos appears on the horizon like a reborn sun. We of this epoch have felt only the first slanting rays of this luminous orb. The thick, dark folds of the past still envelop us; we are not yet aware that the herald of a new dawn is appealing to us, warming us with his oracular breath.

The failure of the Delphic Idea is only a seeming one. A seed was dropped which no power on earth can prevent unfolding. With the last oracle a curtain fell which obscured the true source of light and power. Since the days of ancient Greece man has known only a Purgatorial existence. The body, once radiant and part of a holy trinity, has wandered blindly through the labyrinth of the senses. Only when summoned to murder en masse has it recaptured any of its ancient splendor. It has not responded to love and worship; it has not been animated by the one and only source of life which is faith.

In every work of Sikelianos, whether prose or poetry,* there recur certain words and phrases which distinguish him as an emissary of light. Even though only fragments of his writings were to remain, even though these were to come to us through some unfamiliar tongue such as Bantu, we could not fail to grasp the meaning and the portent of his vision. As poet, prophet, visionary, he illumines for us not only the splendor and significance of the past but the splendor and significance contained in every passing moment. He stresses what is active, "overseeingly active". He revives the sense of drama which is rooted in pain, joy, mystery. He sees the earth as a vast experimental stage on which problems of super-cosmic dimension are foreshadowed.

Only in the sense that he is concerned with the destiny of all mankind can he be said to be a true Hellene. Greece alone cannot claim him. He begins where his ancient forbears left off. For the ancient Greeks were the true evangels of the Western world;

* As yet there are no books of Sikelianos available here in English translation, though New Directions hopes soon to publish one; meanwhile readers are referred to the December, 1943 number of the magazine *Athene* (919 Wellington Avenue, Chicago 14, Illinois).

it was only when they had turned their faces away from the light that they perished. To no other people on earth was there given such a glorious opportunity of illuminating the earth as to the ancient Greeks. Emerging at this darkest hour Sikelianos appears like a reincarnation not of any one particular illustrious spirit of the past but of the very effulgent substance of that luminous past. Of and by himself, like that mystic sword-blade he speaks of in "The Sibyl", he opens Memory like a double wound deep within us.

As poet Sikelianos ventures far beyond the poets of our time. To say that all his poems are poems of initiation is not enough; they are also poems of ordination. Whoever follows him in his empyrean flights must realize with a conviction never before vouchsafed that the true leaders of the world are the men of imagination, the seers. To unite man with man and peoples with peoples is not the work of politicians or of social reformers; men are united only through illumination. The true poet is an awakener; he does not promise bread and jobs. He knows that struggle and conflict are at the very core of life; he does not offer himself as a balm. All ideas of government fail insofar as they exclude the poet and the seer who are one. The democratic idea is operative only at the base of the pyramid; the pivotal, dynamic element is the aristocratic. They are not oppositional; unless translated crudely. On the contrary they are complementary to one another. In his every day social life man is essentially a democrat, or else a clod or a buffoon; in his relation to the eternal man is an aristocrat, or else a renegade. The same gap, the same barriers, which exist between peoples or between classes exist within the soul of every man. We cannot advance with eyes shut and hearts closed; we cannot act without obedience to the law of spontaneity. To act without regard for the whole of life is to destroy all spontaneous impulse, all rhythm, all polarity. The egotist spreads chaos throughout the whole universe. It is not enough that men act in concert on the principle of the lowest common denominator: the quest of mass comfort, or of mass satisfaction, is just as capable of producing rivers of blood as are the mad dreams of the Caesars. Unison has the divine beat of the blood but the source of inspiration is above. In every land there are a chosen few who speak a universal language. Together throughout eternity they may be said to form "a river of luminous saintliness." Keep them apart and the earth itself will dry up. And that is what the temporizing men of action endeavor to do. Under the spell of false prophets, false leaders, whole nations curl up and die—after orgiastic displays of pomp and power. To-day all the great nations of the earth are locked in combat. No man can say which one of them will be great or greatest to-morrow. But this much one can say—those which worshipped power, whether secretly or acknowledged, will perish. "Intelligence," says Sikelianos, "must enlarge and deepen the power of Love." The intelligence which spends itself in constructing engines of destruction, or in seeking to protect itself, is doomed. Intelligence has to transcend itself; it has to blossom forth with a solar radiance which will transfuse the activities of man with joyous significance. The supreme intelligence of the poet, who situates himself at the heart of the universe, has that beneficent, luminous quality. If he is mad then madness is the sine qua non. If he utters nonsense, then nonsense must be the order of all our days. If he is to be rejected from the councils of men then let us reject all hope, all wisdom.

In urging "a return to our deepest historic self" Sikelianos sought to shift the attention of the Greek people from the pettifogging rivalries and ambitions of the other European peoples. Everything of value that is European stems from Greece. Why look to Europe where all had become confused? Look within yourselves, he pleaded. You have lost nothing; you have simply forgotten, you have been asleep. Indeed, where else dare the people of Greece look to-day? To Russia? To America? To England? In her hour of greatest need Greece was betrayed by the great powers of the earth. What in fact can they supply her with, assuming that they regain ascendancy over the common enemy? Food, machinery, money perhaps. And distorted codes of justice, of education, of economy. And in return for these dubious gifts? In return they will ask, as all great powers have always asked, that Greece obediently play the role of cat's paw. Perhaps they will renew their archaeological burrowings, turn up new ruins, new evidences of ancient splendor. And they will weep copious crocodile tears over the things of the past while rearming themselves to befoul the present beauties of the earth. They will encourage their heroic little ally to fight again with ancient ardor in the name of all that is un-Greek, un-Mediterranean. At the utmost they will only be able to teach the people of Greece how to become efficient, soulless work dogs. Where in the Western world is there a program which has any altitude? Where in the Western world is there a nation which has any enthusiasm for life beyond the mere goal of preservation? Where is that superabundance of vitality, that excess of joy, that wisdom which exalts, such as was common to the men of ancient Greece? What faith was it that inspired the shambles of a Christian Europe? Who are the leaders in this hour of crisis? Do they resemble even remotely the lesser geniuses of the Hellenic world? Never was there such confusion, such disillusionment, such pitiful cringing and caterwauling. It is a disembodied world screaming in agony. It is the ghost fighting the ghost.

I believe that only those ideas which strike the prosaic rulers of the world as chimerical have validity. I believe that nothing works as easily, as smoothly, as perfectly as the miraculous. Ask men to surpass themselves and you liberate them. Ask them to be reasonable and you kill the springs of action. The sensible thing, for a small nation like Greece, would be to feather her nest. The sublime thing, and perhaps the only thing which will save Europe, would be for her to send forth her eagles. The nest which was plundered has become a rock whither in their restless flight the eagles come to alight. To right and left, to north and south, only quicksands are visible. A new species of bird seeks to dominate the airs. It is a soulless bird and its life will be of short duration. It seeks not to reach the sun but to spread desolation. It bears no message from gods or men; under its wings it carries only the promise of pain, terror, devastation.

Somewhere to-day on Greek soil there is an eagle who has shown himself capable of soaring above the highest flights of the new mechanical birds of the air. Time and again he has flown straight towards the sun, and his wings have not been melted nor his spirit quenched. Neither has he been proved insane. Nor accused of immunity to pain or suffering. He waits, he bides his time, like the great world actor which he is. When the smoke clears away, when the air ceases to be rent with the screams of bursting bombs, we shall be able perhaps to follow him with reverence and understanding.

REUNION IN BROOKLYN

I ARRIVED at the dock in practically the same condition in which I had left, that is, penniless. I had been away exactly ten years. It seemed much longer, more like twenty or thirty. What sustained me more than anything else during my residence abroad was the belief that I would never be obliged to return to America.

I had of course kept up a correspondence with the family during this period; it was not a very fulsome correspondence and I am sure it gave them very little idea of what my life really was like. Towards the end of my stay in Paris I received a letter informing me of my father's illness; the nature of it was such that I entertained little hope of finding him alive on my return.

What plagued me all the time I was away, and with renewed force as I was crossing the ocean, was the realization that I could give them no help. In the fifteen years which had elapsed since I began my career I had not only proved incapable of supporting myself by my efforts but I had substantially increased my debts. I was not only penniless, as when I left, but I was further in the hole, so that actually my position was far worse than on leaving the country. All I had to my credit were a few books which more than likely will never be published in this country, at least not as they were written. The few gifts which I had brought with me I was obliged to leave at the Customs because I lacked the money to pay the necessary duty.

As we were going through the immigration formalities the officer asked me jokingly if I were *the* Henry Miller to which I replied in the same vein that the one he meant was dead. He knew that, of course. Asked as to what I had been doing in Europe all that time I said—"enjoying myself"—an answer which had the double merit of being true and of forestalling further questions.

Almost the first words out of my mother's mouth, after we had greeted each other, were: "Can't you write something like *Gone With the Wind* and make a little money?" I had to confess I couldn't. I seem to be congenitally incapable of writing a best-seller. At Boston, where we first put in, I remember my astonishment on wandering through the railway station when I saw the staggering heaps of books and magazines for sale. (It was my first glimpse of America and I was rather dazzled and bewildered.) *Gone With the Wind* was all over the place, apparently, in a cheap movie edition which looked more interesting to me, accustomed to the paper-covered books of France, than the original format. I wondered vaguely how many millions of dollars had been put in circulation by this book. I noticed that there were other women writers whose works were displayed among the best-sellers. They all seemed to be huge tomes capable of satisfying the most voracious reader. It seemed perfectly natural to me that the women writers of America should occupy such a prominent place. America is essentially a woman's country—why shouldn't the leading novelists be women?

How I had dreaded this moment of returning to the bosom of the family! The thought of walking down this street again had always been a nightmare to me. If any one had told me when in Greece that two months hence I would be doing this I would have told him he was crazy. And yet, when I was informed at the American Consulate in Athens that I would be obliged to return to America I made no effort to resist. I accepted their unwarranted interference as if I were obeying the voice of Fate. Deep down, I suppose, was the realization that I had left something unfinished in America. Moreover, when the summons came I must confess that I was morally and spiritually stronger than I had ever been in my life. "If needs be," I said to myself, "I can go back to America," much as one would say, "I feel strong enough to face anything now!"

Nevertheless, once back in New York it took me several weeks to prepare myself for the ordeal. I had, of course, written my folks that I was on my way. They very naturally expected me to telephone them immediately on my arrival. It was cruel not to do so but I was so intent on easing my own pain that I postponed communicating with them for a week or more. Finally I wrote them from Virginia, where I had fled almost at once, unable to bear the sight of my native city. What I was hoping for above all, in trying to gain a little time, was a sudden turn of fortune, the advent of a few hundred dollars from a publisher or editor, some little sum with which to save my face. Well, nothing turned up. The one person whom I had vaguely counted on failed me. I mean my American publisher. He hadn't even been willing to assist me in getting back to America, so I learned. He feared that if he sent me the passage money I would squander it on drink or in some other foolish way. He probably means well and he certainly writes well about honoring the artist in our midst, giving him food and drink and that sort of thing. "*Welcome home, Henry Miller. . . .*" I often thought of that phrase of his which he inserted in the preface of my book as I turned about in the rat trap. It's easy to write such things, but to substantiate words with deeds is quite another matter.

It was towards evening when I set out to visit the folks. I came up out of the new Eighth Avenue subway and, though I knew the neighborhood well, immediately proceeded to lose my bearings. Not that the neighborhood had changed much; if anything it was I who had changed. I had changed so completely that I couldn't find my way any more in the old surroundings. I suppose too that getting lost was a last unconscious effort to avoid the ordeal.

As I came down the block where the house stands it seemed to me as if nothing had changed. I was infuriated, in fact, to think that this street which I loathe so much had been so impervious to the march of time. I forget. . . . There was one important change. On the corner where the German grocery store had been, and where I had been horsewhipped as a boy, there now stood a funeral parlor. A rather significant transformation! But what was even more striking is the fact that the undertaker had originally been a neighbor of ours—in the old 14th Ward which we had left years ago. I recognized the name at once. It gave me a creepy feeling, passing his place. Had he divined that we would shortly be in need of his services?

As I approached the gate I saw my father sitting in the arm-chair by the window. The sight of him sitting there, waiting for me, gave me a terrible pang. It was as though he had been sitting there waiting all these years. I felt at once like a criminal, like a murderer.

It was my sister who opened the iron gate. She had altered considerably, had shrunk and withered like a Chinese nut. My mother and father were standing at the threshold to greet me. They had aged terribly. For the space of a moment I had the uncomfortable sensation of gazing at two mummies who had been removed from the vault and galvanized into a semblance of life. We embraced one another and then we stood apart in silence for another fleeting moment during which I comprehended in a flash the appalling tragedy of their life and of my own life and of every animate creature's on earth. In that moment all the strength which I had accumulated to fortify myself was undone; I was emptied of everything but an overwhelming compassion. When suddenly my mother said, "Well, Henry, how do we look to you?" I let out a groan followed by the most heart-rending sobs. I wept as I had never wept before. My father, to conceal his own feelings, withdrew to the kitchen. I hadn't removed my coat and my hat was still in my hand. In the blinding flood of tears everything was swimming before my eyes. "God Almighty!" I thought to myself, "what have I done? Nothing I thought to accomplish justifies this. I should have remained, I should have sacrificed myself for them. Perhaps there is still time. Perhaps I can do *something* to prove that I am not utterly selfish. . . ." My mother meanwhile said nothing. Nobody uttered a word. I stood there in the middle of the room with my overcoat on and my hat in my hand and I wept until there were no more tears left. When I had collected myself a bit I dried my eyes and looked about the room. It was the same immaculate place, showing not the least sign of wear or tear, glowing a little brighter, if anything, than before. Or did I imagine it because of my guilt? At any rate, I thanked God, it did not seem poverty-stricken as I had feared it might look. It was the same modest, humble place it had always been. It was like a polished mausoleum in which their misery and suffering had been kept brightly burning.

The table was set; we were to eat in a few moments. It seemed natural that it should be thus, though I hadn't the slightest desire to eat. In the past the great emotional scenes which I had witnessed in the bosom of the family were nearly always associated with the table. We pass easily from sorrow to gluttony.

We sat down in our accustomed places, looking somewhat more cheerful, if not actually merry, than we had a few moments ago. The storm had passed; there would only be slight and distant reverberations henceforth. I had hardly taken the spoon in my hand when they all began to talk at once. They had been waiting for this moment a long time; they wanted to pour out in a few minutes all that had been accumulating for ten years. Never have I felt so willing to listen. Had they poured it out for twenty-four hours on end I would have sat patiently, without a murmur, without a sign of restlessness, until the last word had been uttered. Now at last they had me and could tell me everything. They were so eager to begin, so beside themselves with joy, that it all came out in a babble. It was almost as if they feared that I would run off again and stay away another ten years.

It was about time for the war news and so they turned the radio on, thinking that I would be interested. In the midst of the babble and confusion, boats going down, ammunition works blasted, and the same smooth dentifricial voice switching from calamities to razor blades without a change of intonation or inflection, my mother interrupted the hubbub to tell me that they had been thinking about my homecoming and had planned that I should share a bed with my father. She said she would sleep with my sister in the little room where I had slept as a boy. That brought on another choking fit. I told them there was no need to worry about such things, that I had already found a place to stay and that everything was jake. I tried to tell them jokingly that I was now a celebrity, but it didn't sound very convincing either to them or to myself.

"Of course," said my mother, ignoring what I had just said, "it may be a little inconvenient for you; father has to get up now and then during the night—but you'll get used to it. I don't hear him any more."

I looked at my father. "Yes," he said, "since the operation, the last one, I'm lucky if I get three or four hours' sleep." He drew aside his chair and pulled up the leg of his trousers to show me the bag which was strapped to his leg. "That's what I have to wear now," he said. "I can't urinate any more the natural way. It's a nuisance, but what can you do? They did the best they could for me." And he went on hurriedly to tell me of how good the doctor had been to him, though he was a perfect stranger and a Jew to boot. "Yes," he added, "they took me to the Jewish hospital. And I must say I couldn't have had better treatment anywhere."

I wondered how that had come about—the Jewish hospital—because my mother had always been scared to death of anything remotely connected with the Jews. The explanation was quite simple. They had outlived the family doctor and all the other doctors in the neighborhood whom they once knew. At the last moment some one had recommended the Jewish doctor, and since he was not only a specialist but a surgeon they had acquiesced. To their astonishment he had proved to be not only a good doctor but an extremely kind and sympathetic person. "He treated me as if he were my own son," said my father. Even my mother had to admit that they couldn't have found a better man. What seemed to impress them most about the hospital, I was amazed to learn, was the wonderful grub which they served there. One could eat à la carte apparently—and as much as one cared to. But the nurses were not Jewish, they wanted me to know. They were Scandinavian for the most part. The Jews don't like such jobs, they explained. "You know, they never like to do the dirty work," said my mother.

In the midst of the narrative, hardly able to wait for my mother to finish, my father suddenly recalled that he had made a note of some questions he wished to put to me. He asked my sister to get the slip of paper for him. Whereupon, to my surprise, my sister calmly told him to wait, that she hadn't finished her meal yet. With that he gave me a look, as much as to say—"you see what I have to put up with here!" I got up and found the piece of paper on which he had listed the questions. My father put on his spectacles and began to read.

"Oh, first of all," he exclaimed, "what pier did you dock at?"

I told him.

"That's what I thought," he said. "Now, what was the grub like on board the boat? Was it American cooking or Greek?"

The other questions were in a similar vein. Had we received the wireless news every day? Did I have to share my cabin with others? Did we sight any wrecks? And then this—which took me completely by surprise: "What is the Parthenon?"

I explained briefly what the Parthenon was.

"Well, that's all right," he said, as though to say—"no need to go into that any further." "I only asked," he added, looking up over the top of his spectacles, "because mother said she thought it was a park. I knew it wasn't a park. How old did you say it was again?" He paused a moment to hmmn. "The place must be full of old relics," he added. Well, anyway, it must have been very interesting in Greece, that's what he thought. As for himself he had always wanted to see Italy—and London. He asked about Saville Row where the merchant tailors have their shops. "You say the tailors (meaning the workmen on the bench) are all English? No Jews or Italians, eh?" "No," I said, "they all seemed to be English, from their looks anyway." "That's queer," he reflected. "Must be a strange place, London."

He moved over to the arm-chair near the window. "I can't sit here very long," he said, "it sinks down too low. In a moment I'll change to the hard chair. You see, with all this harness on it gets pretty uncomfortable at times, especially when it's warm." As he talked he kept pressing the long tube which ran down his leg. "You see, it's getting gritty again. Just like sand inside. You'd never think that you pass off all that solid matter in your urine, would you? It's the damndest thing. I take all the medicines he prescribes religiously, but the damned stuff *will* accumulate. That's my condition, I suppose. When it gets too thick I have to go to the doctor and let him irrigate me. About once a month, that is. *And does that hurt!* Well, we won't talk about that now. Some times it's worse than other times. There was one time I thought I couldn't stand it any more—they must have heard me for blocks around. If everything goes well I can stretch the visits to five or six weeks. It's five dollars a crack, you know."

I ventured to suggest that it might be better if he went oftener instead of trying to stretch it out.

"That's just what I say," he responded promptly. "But mother says we have to economize—there's nothing coming in any more, you know. Of course she doesn't have to stand the pain."

I looked at my mother inquiringly. She was irritated that my father should have put it thus. "You can't run to the doctor every time you have a little pain," she said scoldingly, as if to rebuke him for having brought up the subject. "I've told him time and again that's his condition."

By condition she meant that he would have to endure his suffering until . . . well, if she had to put it baldly she would say—*until the end*. He was lucky to be alive, after all he had gone through. "If it weren't for that old bag, for that awful leakage," she ruminated aloud, "father would be all right. You see what an appetite he has—and what a color!"

"Yes," my sister put in, "he eats more than any of us. We do all the work; he has it easy."

My father gave me another look. My mother, catching his mute appeal, tried to pass it over lightly with a little joke, one of those crude jokes which the family were fond of. "Look at him," she said with a slightly hysterical laugh, "hasn't he a good color? Why, he's as tough as an old rooster. You couldn't kill him off with an axe!"

It was impossible for me to laugh at this. But my sister, who had learned to take her cue from my mother, suddenly grew apoplectic with indignation. "Look at us," she exclaimed, rolling her head from side to side. "Look how thin we got! Seventy times a day I climbed the stairs when father was in bed! Everybody tells me how bad I look, that I must take care of myself. We don't even have a chance to go to the movies. I haven't been to New York for over a year."

"And I have a cinch of it, is that it?" my father put in pepperily. "Well, I wish I could change places with you, that's all I want to say."

"Come now," said my mother, addressing my father as if he were a petulant child, "you know you shouldn't talk like that. We're doing our best, you know that."

"Yes," said my father, his tone getting more caustic, "and what about that cranberry juice I'm supposed to drink every day?"

With this my mother and sister turned on him savagely. How could he talk that way, they wanted to know, when they had been working themselves to the bone nursing and tending him? They turned to me. I must try to understand, they explained, that it was difficult sometimes to get out of the house, even to go as far as the corner.

"Couldn't you use the phone?" I asked.

The phone had been disconnected long ago, they told me. Another of my mother's economies, it seemed.

"But supposing something happened during the night?" I ventured to say.

"That's just what I tell them," my father put in. "That was mother's idea, shutting off the phone. I never approved of it."

"The things you say!" said my mother, trying to silence him with a frowning grimace. She turned to me, as if I were the very seat of reason. "All the neighbors have phones," she said. "Why, they won't even let me pay for a call—but of course I do in some other way. And then there's Teves up at the corner. . . ."

"You mean the undertaker?" I said.

"Yes," said my father. "You see, when the weather permits I often take a stroll as far as the corner. If Teves is there he brings a camp chair out for me—and if I want to make a call why I use his phone. He never charges me for it. He's been very decent, I must say that." And then he went on to explain to me how nice it was to be able to sit up there at the corner and watch the promenade. There was more life there, he reflected almost wistfully. "You know, one gets sick of seeing the same faces all the time, isn't that so?"

"I hope you're not sick of us!" said my mother reproachfully.

"You know that's not what I mean," replied my father, obviously a little weary of this sort of exchange.

As I got up to change my seat I noticed a pile of old newspapers on the rocker. "What are you doing with those?" I asked.

"Don't touch them!" screamed my sister. "Those are for me!"

My father quickly explained that my sister had taken to reading the papers since my absence. "It's good for her," he said, "it takes her mind off things. She's a little slow, though . . . always about a month behind."

"I am not," said my sister tartly. "I'm only two weeks behind. If we didn't have so much work to do I'd be up to date. The minister says. . . ."

"All right, you win," said my father, trying to shut her up. "You can't say a word in this house without stepping on some one's toes."

There was a Vox-Pox program due over the radio any minute. They wanted to know if I had ever heard it, but before I could say yes or no my sister put in her oar—she wanted to listen to the choir singing carols. "Perhaps he'd like to hear some more war news," said my mother. She said it as though, having just come from Europe, I had a special proprietary interest in the grand carnage.

"Have you ever heard Raymond Gram Swing?" asked my father.

I was about to tell him I hadn't when my sister informed us that he wasn't on this evening.

"How about Gabriel Heatter then?" said my father.

"He's no good," said my sister, "he's a Jew."

"What's that got to do with it?" said my father.

"I like Kaltenborn," said my sister. "He has such a beautiful voice."

"Personally," said my father, "I prefer Raymond Swing. He's very impartial. He always begins—'Good Evening!' Never 'Ladies and gentlemen' or 'My friends,' as President Roosevelt says. You'll see. . . ."

This conversation was like a victrola record out of the past. Suddenly the whole American scene, as it is portrayed over the radio, came flooding back—chewing gum, furniture polish, can openers, mineral waters, laxatives, ointments, corn cures, liver pills, insurance policies; the crooners with their eunuch-like voices; the comedians with their stale jokes; the puzzlers with their inane questions (how many matches in a cord of wood?); the Ford Sunday evening hour, the Bulova watch business, the xylophones, the quartets, the bugle calls, the roosters crowing, the canaries warbling, the chimes bringing tears, the songs of yesterday, the news fresh from the griddle, the facts, the facts, the facts. . . . Here it was again, the same old stuff, and as I was soon to discover, more stupefying and stultifying than ever. A man named Fadiman, whom I was later to see in the movies with a quartet of well-informed nit-wits, had organized some kind of puzzle committee—*Information Please*, I think it was called. This apparently was the *coup de grâce* of the evening's entertainment and befuddlement. This was real education, so they informed me. I squirmed in my seat and tried to assume an air of genuine interest.

It was a relief when they shut the bloody thing off and settled down to telling me about their friends and neighbors, about the accidents and illnesses of which seemingly there was no end. Surely I remembered Mrs. Froehlich? Well, all of a sudden—she was the picture of health, mind you!—she was taken to the hospital to be operated on. Cancer of the bladder it was. Lasted only two months. And just before she died—"she doesn't know it," said my father, absent-mindedly using the present tense—her husband met with an accident. Ran into a tree and had his head taken off—just as clean

75

as a razor. The undertakers had sewn it back on, of course—wonderful job they made of it too. Nobody would have been able to tell it, seeing him lying there in the coffin. Marvellous what they can do nowadays, the old man reflected aloud. Anyway, that's how it was with Mrs. Froehlich. Nobody would have thought that those two would pass on so quickly. They were only in their fifties. . . .

Listening to their recital I got the impression that the whole neighborhood was crippled and riddled with malignant diseases. Everybody with whom they had any dealings, friend, relative, neighbor, butcher, letter-carrier, gas inspector, every one without exception carried about with him perpetually a little flower which grew out of his own body and which was named after one or the other of the familiar maladies, such as rheumatism, arthritis, pneumonia, cancer, dropsy, anemia, dysentery, meningitis, epilepsy, hernia, encephalitis, megalomania, chilblains, dyspepsia and so on and so forth. Those who weren't crippled, diseased or insane were out of work and living on relief. Those who could use their legs were on line at the movies waiting for the doors to be thrown open. I was reminded in a mild way of *Voyage au Bout de la Nuit*. The difference between these two worlds otherwise so similar lay in the standard of living; even those on relief were living under conditions which would have seemed luxurious to that suburban working class whom Céline writes about. In Brooklyn, so it seemed to me, they were dying of malnutrition of the soul. They lived on as vegetable tissue, flabby, sleep-drugged, disease-ridden carcasses with just enough intelligence to enable them to buy oil-burners, radios, automobiles, newspapers, tickets for the cinema. One whom I had known as a ball-player when I was a boy was now a retired policeman who spent his evenings writing in old Gothic. He had composed the Lord's Prayer in this script on a small piece of cardboard, so they were telling me, and when it was finished he discovered that he had omitted a word. So he was doing it over again, had been at it over a month already. He lived with his sister, an old maid, in a lugubrious big house which they had inherited from their parents. They didn't want any tenants—it was too much bother. They never went anywhere, never visited anybody, never had any company. The sister was a gossip who sometimes took three hours to get from the house to the corner drug store. It was said that they would leave their money to the Old Folks' Home when they died.

My father seemed to know every one for blocks around. He also knew who came home late at night because, sitting in the parlor at the front window all hours of the night waiting for the water to flow, he got a slant on things such as he'd never had before. What amazed him apparently was the number of young women who came home alone at all hours of the night, some of them tight as a pig-skin. People no longer had to get up early to go to work, at least not in this neighborhood. When he was a boy, he remarked, work began at daylight and lasted till ten in the evening. At eight-thirty, while these good for nothings were still turning over in bed, he was already having a second breakfast, meaning some pumper-nickel sandwiches and a pitcher of beer.

The recital was interrupted because the bag was beginning to fill up. In the kitchen my father emptied the contents of the bag into an old beer pitcher, examined it to see if the urine looked cloudy or sandy, and then emptied it in the toilet. His whole atten-tion, since the advent of the bag, was concentrated on the qual-ity and flow of his urine. "People say hello, how are you getting on, and then biffo! they forget about you," he said, as he came back and resumed his place by the window. It was a random remark, apropos of nothing as far as I can remember, but what he meant evidently was that others *could* forget whereas he couldn't. At night, on going to bed, he had always the comforting thought that in an hour or two he would be obliged to get up and catch the urine before it began to leak out of the hole which the doctor had drilled in his stomach. There were rags lying about everywhere, ready to catch the overflow, and newspapers, in order to prevent the bedding and furniture from being ruined by the endless flow. Sometimes it would take hours for the urine to begin flowing and at other times the bag would have to be emptied two or three times in quick succession; now and then it would come out in the natural way also, as well as from the tube and the wound itself. It was a humiliating sort of malady as well as a painful one.

Out of a clear sky my mother, in an obviously false natural voice, suddenly requested me to accompany her upstairs, saying that she wanted to show me some of the improvements which had been made during my absence. We no sooner got to the landing than she began explaining to me in muffled tones that my father's condition was incurable. "He'll never get well," she said, "it's . . . ," and she mentioned that word which has come to be synonymous with modern civilization, the word which holds the same terror for the man of to-day as did leprosy for the men of old. It was no surprise to me, I must say. If anything, I was amazed that it was only that and nothing more. What bothered me more than anything was the loud voice in which she was whispering to me, for the doors were all open and my father could easily have heard what she was saying had he tried. I made her walk me through the rooms and tell me in a natural voice about the various renovations, about the thermostat, for instance, which was hanging on the wall under my grandfather's portrait. That fortunately brought up the subject of the new oil burner, thus precipitating a hurried visit of inspection to the cellar.

The appearance of the cellar was a complete surprise. It had been denuded, the coal bins removed, the shelves taken out, the walls whitewashed. Like some mediaeval object used by alchemists, there stood the oil burner neat, immaculate, silent except for a spasmodic ticking whose rhythm was unpredictable. From the reverence with which my mother spoke of it I gathered that the oil burner was quite the most important object in the house. I gazed at it in fascination and astonishment. No more coal or wood, no ashes to haul, no coal gas, no watching, no fussing, no fuming, no dirt, no smoke; temperature always the same, one for day and one for night; the little instrument on the parlor wall regulated its functioning automatically. It was as though a magician had secreted himself in the walls of the house, a new electro-dynamic, super-heterodyne god of the hearth. The cellar, which had once been a frightening place filled with unknown treasures, had now become bright and habitable; one could serve lunch down there on the concrete floor. With the installation of the oil burner a good part of my boyhood was wiped out. Above all I missed the shelves where the wine bottles covered with cobwebs had been kept. There was no more wine, no more champagne, not even a case of beer. Nothing but the oil burner—and that peculiar, unnaturally rhythmed ticking which however muffled always gave me a start.

As we climbed the stairs I observed another sacred object also ticking in a mechanically epileptic way—the refrigerator. I hadn't seen a refrigerator since I left America and of course those I had known then were long since outmoded. In France I hadn't even used an ice-box, such as we had been accustomed to at home. I bought only as much as was required for the current meal; what was perishable perished, whatever turned sour turned sour, that was all. Nobody I knew in Paris owned a refrigerator; nobody I knew ever thought of refrigerators. As for Greece, where coal was at a premium, the cooking was done on charcoal stoves. And, if one had any culinary instincts, the meals could be just as palatable, just as delicious and nourishing as anywhere else. I was reminded of Greece and the charcoal stoves because I had suddenly become aware that the old coal stove in the kitchen was missing, its place taken now by a shining white enamelled gas range, another indispensable, just-as-cheap and equally sacred object as the oil burner and the refrigerator. I began to wonder if my mother had become a little daffy during my absence. Was everybody installing these new conveniences? I inquired casually. Most everybody, was the answer, including some who couldn't afford to do so. The Gothic maniac and his sister hadn't, to be sure, but then they were eccentric—they never bought anything unless they had to. My mother, I couldn't deny, had the good excuse that they were getting old and that these little innovations meant a great saving of labor. I was glad, in fact, that they had been able to provide for themselves so well. At the same time, however, I couldn't help but think of the old ones in Europe; they had not only managed to do without these comforts but, so it seemed to me, they remained far healthier, saner and more joyous than the old ones in America. America has comforts; Europe has other things which make all these comforts seem quite unimportant.

During the conversation which ensued my father brought up the subject of the tailor shop which he hadn't set foot in for over three years. He complained that he never heard a word from his former partner. "He's too miserly to spend a nickel on a telephone call," he said. "I know there was an order from So-and-So for a couple of suits; that was about six months ago. I haven't heard a word about it since." I naturally volunteered to pay a visit to the shop one day and inquire about things. "Of course," he said, "he doesn't have to worry any more whether things go or not. His daughter is a movie star now, you know." It was possible too, he went on to say, that the client had gone off on a cruise; he was always knocking about somewhere in his yacht. "By the time he comes in again he'll have either gained a few pounds or lost a few, and then everything will have to be altered. It may be a year or two before he's ready to take the clothes."

I learned that there were now about a dozen customers left on the books. No new ones forthcoming, of course. It was like the passing of the buffaloes. The man with the yacht who had ordered two precious suits of clothes, for which he was in no apparent hurry, used formerly to order a dozen at a time, to say nothing of cutaways, overcoats, dinner jackets, and so on. Nearly all the great merchant tailors of the past were either out of business, in bankruptcy, or about to give up. The great English woollen houses which had once served them were now shrunk to insignificant size. Though we have more millionaires than ever, fewer men seem inclined to pay $200.00 for an ordinary sack suit. Curious, what!

It was not only pathetic, it was ludicrous, to hear him talking about those two suits which, by the way, I was to remember to ask his partner not to leave hanging on the rack by the front window because they would be faded by the time the man called for a fitting. They had become mythical, legendary—the two suits ordered by a millionaire in the year '37 or '38 just prior to a short cruise in the Mediterranean. If all went well why possibly two years hence there would be ten or fifteen dollars accruing to the old man as his share of the transaction. Wonderful state of affairs! Somehow the two legendary suits belonged with the oil-burner and the frigidaire —part and parcel of the same system of luxurious necessity and generous waste. Meantime, just to take a random shot, the fumes from the copper smelting plant at Ducktown, Tennessee, had rendered absolutely death-like and desolate the whole region for fifty miles around. (To see this region is to have a premonition of the fate of still another planet—our Earth—should the human experiment fail. Here Nature resembles the raw backside of a sick chimpanzee.) The president of the plant, undisturbed by the devastation, to say nothing of the premature deaths in the mines, may possibly be getting ready to order a hunting jacket on his coming trip to New York. Or he may have a son who is preparing to enter the army as a brigadier-general for whom he will put in an order for the appropriate outfit when the time comes. That disease which boss tailors acquire, just like other people, won't be such a terrifying thing to the president of Copper Hill, should it strike him down, because with trained nurses to irrigate him every few hours and a specialist to summon by taxi when he has a little pain, he can have quite a tolerable time of it—perhaps not as much rich food as he is used to having, but plenty of good things just the same, including a game of cards every night or a visit to the cinema in his wheel chair.

As for my father, he has his little pleasure too every month or so, when he is given a joy ride to the doctor's office. I was a little annoyed that my father should be so grateful to his friend for acting as a chauffeur once a month. And when my mother began to lay it on about the kindness of the neighbors—letting her telephone free of charge and that sort of thing—I was about ready to explode. "What the devil," I remarked, "it's no great favor they're doing. A nigger would do as much for you—more maybe. That's the least one can do for a friend."

My mother looked aggrieved. She begged me not to talk that way. And in the next breath she went on to say how good the people next door were to her, how they left the morning paper for them at the window every evening. And another neighbor down the block was thoughtful enough to save the old rags which accumulated. Real Christians, I must say. Generous souls, what!

"And the Helsingers?" I said, referring to their old friends who were now millionaires. "Don't they do anything for you?"

"Well," my father began, "you know what a stinker he always was. . . ."

"How can you talk that way!" exclaimed my mother.

"I'm only telling the truth," said the old man innocently.

They had been very kind and thoughtful too, my mother tried to say. The proof of it was that they had remembered on their last visit—eight months ago—to bring a jar of preserves from their country estate.

"So that's it!" I broke out, always enraged by the very mention of their name. "So that's the best they can do, is it?"

"They have their own troubles," said my mother reprovingly. "You know Mr. Helsinger is going blind."

"Good," I said bitterly. "I hope he grows deaf and dumb too—and paralyzed to boot."

Even my father thought this a bit too vehement. "Still," he said, "I can't say that I ever knew him to do a generous deed. He was always close, even from the beginning. But he's losing it all now—the boy is going through it fast."

"That's fine," I said. "I hope he loses every penny of it before he croaks. I hope he dies in want—and in pain and agony."

Here my sister suddenly popped up. "You shouldn't talk that way," she said, "you'll be punished for it. Pastor Liederkranz says we must only speak good of one another." And with the mention of the pastor's name she began to ramble on about Greece which his holiness, the Episcopal cheese of the diocese, had visited last year during his vacation.

"And what have they done for you all?" (meaning the church) I asked, turning to my father and mother.

"We never belonged to any church, you know," said my mother softly.

"Well, *she* belongs, doesn't she?" I said, nodding in my sister's direction. "Isn't that enough for them?"

"They have their own to take care of."

"*Their own!*" I said sneeringly. "That's a good excuse."

"He's right," said my father. "They could have done *something*. You take the Lutheran Church—we're not members of that either, but they send us things just the same, don't they. And they come and visit us, too. How do you explain that?" and he turned on my mother rather savagely, as if to show that he was a bit fed up with her continuous whitewashing of this one and that.

At this juncture my sister, who always became alert when the church was involved, reminded us that a new parish house was being built—there would be new pews installed too, we shouldn't forget that either. "That costs something!" she snarled.

"All right, you win!" yelled my father. I had to laugh. I had never realized before what an obstinate, tenacious creature my sister could be. Half-witted though she was, she seemed to realize that she needn't let my father bulldoze her any longer. She could even be cruel, in her witless way. "No, I won't get any cigarettes for you," she would say to the old man. "You smoke too much. We don't smoke and we're not sick."

The great problem, the old man confided to me when we were alone for a few minutes, was to be able to have a quarter in his pocket at all times—"in case anything should happen," as he put it. "They mean well," he said, "but they don't understand. They think I ought to cut out the cigarettes, for instance. By God, I have to do something to while away the time, don't I? Of course it means fifteen cents a day, but. . . ."

I begged him not to say any more about it. "I'll see that you have cigarettes at least," I said, and with that I fished out a couple of dollars and blushingly thrust the money in his hand.

"Are you sure you can spare it?" said my father, quickly hiding it away. He leaned forward and whispered: "Better not let them know you gave me anything—they'll take it away from me. They say I don't need any money."

I felt wretched and exasperated.

"Understand," he went on, "I don't mean to complain. But it's like the doctor business. Mother wants me to delay the visits as long as possible. It's not right, you know. If I wait too long the pains get unbearable. When I tell her that she says—*"it's your condition."* Half the time I don't dare tell her I'm in pain; I don't want to annoy her. But I do think if I went a little oftener it would ease things up a bit, don't you?"

I was so choked with rage and mortification I could scarcely answer him. It seemed to me that he was being slowly tortured and humiliated; they behaved as if he had committed a crime by becoming ill. Worse, it was as if my mother, knowing that he would never get well, looked upon each day that he remained alive as so much unnecessary expense. She delighted in depriving herself of things, in order to impress my father with the need of economizing. Actually the only economy he could practise would be to die. That's how it looked to me, though I dare say if I had put it to my mother that way she would have been horrified. She was working herself to the bone, no doubt about that. And she had my sister working the treadmill too. But it was all stupid—unnecessary labor for the most part. They *created* work for themselves. When any one remarked how pale and haggard they looked they would reply with alacrity—"Well, some one has to keep going. We can't all afford to be ill." As though to imply that being ill was a sinful luxury.

As I say, there was a blend of stupidity, criminality and hypocrisy in the atmosphere. By the time I was ready to take leave my throat was sore from repressing my emotions. The climax came when, just as I was about to slip into my overcoat, my mother in a tearful voice came rushing up to me and, holding me by the arm, said: "Oh Henry, there's a thread on your coat!" A thread, by Jesus! That was the sort of thing she would give attention to! The way she uttered the word thread was as if she had spied a leprous hand sticking out of my coat pocket. All her tenderness came out in removing that little white thread from my sleeve. Incredible— and disgusting! I embraced them in turn rapidly and fled out of the house. In the street I allowed the tears to flow freely. I sobbed and wept unrestrainedly all the way to the elevated station. As I entered the train, as we passed the names of familiar stations, all of them recalling some old wound or humiliation, I began enacting in my mind the scene I had just been through, began describing it as if I were seated before the typewriter with a fresh piece of paper in the roller. "Jesus, don't forget that about the head that was sewn on," I would say to myself, the tears streaming down my face and blinding me. *"Don't forget this . . . don't forget that."* I was conscious that everybody's eyes were focussed on me, but still I continued to weep and to write. When I got to bed the sobbing broke out again. I must have gone on sobbing in my sleep for in the early morning I heard some one rapping on the wall and awoke to find my face wet with tears. The outburst continued intermittently for about thirty-six hours; any little thing served to make me break out afresh. It was a complete purge which left me exhausted and refreshed at the same time.

On going for my mail the next day, as if in answer to my prayers, I found a letter from a man whom I thought was my enemy. It was a brief note saying that he had heard I was back and would I stop in to see him some time. I went at once and to my astonishment was greeted like an old friend. We had hardly exchanged greetings when he said to me: "I want to help you—what can I do for you?" These words, which were wholly unexpected, brought on another weeping fit. Here was a Jew whom I had met only once before, with whom I had exchanged barely a half dozen letters while in Paris, whom I had offended mortally by what he considered my anti-Semitic writings, and now suddenly, without a word of explanation for his *volte face*, he puts himself completely at my service. *I want to help you!* These words which one so seldom hears, especially when one is in distress, were not new to me. Time and again it has been my fortune to be rescued either by an enemy or by an utter stranger. It has happened so often, in fact, that I have almost come to believe that Providence is watching over me.

To be brief, I now had a sufficient sum in my pocket for my needs and the assurance that more was forthcoming should I need it. I passed from the anguish of utter doubt and despair to radiant, boundless optimism. I could return to the house of sorrow and bring a ray of cheer.

I telephoned immediately to communicate the good news. I told them I had found an editor for my work and had been given a substantial advance. I hinted that I would be shortly given a contract for a new book, a lie which was soon to become a fact. They were amazed and a bit sceptical, as they had always been. My mother, in fact, as though failing to grasp what I had said, informed me over the telephone that they could give me a little work to do, if I wanted it, such as painting the kitchen and repairing the roof. It would give me a little pocket money anyway, she added.

As I hung up the receiver it came back to me in a flash how long ago, when I had just begun to write, I used to sit at the window by the sewing table, and batter my brains trying to write the stories and essays which the editors never found acceptable. I remember the period well because it was one of the bitterest I have ever gone through. Because of our abject poverty my wife and I had decided to separate for a while. She had returned to her parents (so I thought!) and I was returning to mine. I had to swallow my pride and beg to be taken back to the fold. Of course there had never been any thought in their mind of refusing my request, but when they discovered that I had no intention of looking for a job, that I was still dreaming of earning a living by writing, their disappointment was soon converted into a deep chagrin. Having nothing else to do but eat, sleep and write I was up early every morning, seated at the sewing table which my aunt had left behind when she was taken to the insane asylum. I worked until a neighbor called. The moment the bell rang my mother would come running to me and beg me frantically to put my things away and hide myself in the clothes closet. She was ashamed to let any one know that I was wasting my time at such a foolish pursuit. More, she was even concerned for fear that I might be slightly touched. Consequently, as soon as I saw some one entering the gate I gathered up my paraphernalia, rushed with it to the bathroom, where I hid it in the tub, and then secreted myself in the clothes closet where I would stand in the dark choking with the stink of camphor balls until the neighbor took leave. Small wonder that I always associated my activity with that of the criminal! Often in my dreams I am taken to the penitentiary where I immediately proceed to install myself as comfortably as possible with typewriter and paper. Even when awake I sometimes fall into a reverie wherein, accommodating myself to the thought of a year or two behind the bars, I begin planning the book I will write during my incarceration. Usually I am provided with the sewing table by the window, the one on which the telephone stood; it is a beautiful inlaid table whose pattern is engraved in my memory. In the center of it is a minute spot to which my eyes were riveted when, during the period I speak of, I received one evening a telephone call from my wife saying that she was about to jump in the river. In the midst of a despair which had become so tremendous as to freeze all emotion I suddenly heard her tearful voice announcing that she could stand it no longer. She was calling to say goodbye—a brief, hysterical speech and then click! and she had vanished and her address was the river. Terrible as I felt I nevertheless had to conceal my feelings. To their query as to who had called I replied—"Oh, just a friend!" and I sat there for a moment or two gazing at the minute spot which had become the infinitesimal speck in the river where the body of my wife was slowly disappearing. Finally I roused myself, put on my hat and coat, and announced that I was going for a walk.

When I got outdoors I could scarcely drag my feet along. I thought my heart had stopped beating. The emotion I had experienced on hearing her voice had disappeared; I had become a piece of slag, a tiny hunk of cosmic debris void of hope, desire, or even fear. Knowing not what to do or where to turn I walked about aimlessly in that frozen blight which has made Brooklyn the place of horror which it is. The houses were still, motionless, breathing gently as people breathe when they sleep the sleep of the just. I walked blindly onward until I found myself on the border of the old neighborhood which I love so well. Here suddenly the significance of the message which my wife had transmitted over the telephone struck me with a new impact. Suddenly I grew quite frantic and, as if that would help matters, I instinctively quickened my pace. As I did so the whole of my life, from earliest boyhood on, began to unroll itself in swift and kaleidoscopic fashion. The myriad events which had combined to shape my life became so fascinating to me that, without realizing why or what, I found myself growing enthusiastic. To my astonishment I caught myself laughing and weeping, shaking my head from side to side, gesticulating, mumbling, lurching like a drunkard. I was alive again, that's what it was. I was a living entity, a human being capable of registering joy and sorrow, hope and despair. It was marvellous to be alive—just that and nothing more. Marvellous to have lived, to remember so much. If she had really jumped in the river then there was nothing to be done about it. Just the same I began to wonder if I oughtn't to go to the police and inform them about it. Even as the thought came to mind I espied a cop standing on the corner, and impulsively I started towards him. But when I came close and saw the expression on his face the impulse died as quickly as it had come. I went up to him nevertheless and in a calm, matter of fact tone I asked him if he could direct me to a certain street, a street I knew well since it was the one I was living on. I listened to his directions as would a penitent prisoner were he to ask the way back to the penitentiary from which he had escaped.

When I got back to the house I was informed that my wife had just telephoned. "What did she say?" I exclaimed, almost beside myself with joy.

"She said she would call you again in the morning," said my mother, surprised that I should seem so agitated.

When I got to bed I began to laugh; I laughed so hard the bed shook. I heard my father coming upstairs. I tried to suppress my laughter but couldn't.

"What's the matter with you?" he asked, standing outside the bedroom door.

"I'm laughing," I said. "I just thought of something funny."

"Are you sure you're all right?" he said, his voice betraying his perplexity. "We thought you were crying. . . ."

I am on my way to the house with a pocketful of money. Unusual event for me, to say the least. I begin to think of the holidays and birthdays in the past when I arrived empty-handed, sullen, dejected, humiliated and defeated. It was embarrassing, after having ignored their circumstances all these years, to come trotting in with a handful of dough and say, "Take it, I know you need it!" It was theatrical, for one thing, and it was creating an illusion which might have to be sadly punctured. I was of course prepared for the ceremony my mother would go through. I dreaded that. It would have been easier to hand it to my father, but he would only be obliged to turn it over to my mother and that would create more confusion and embarrassment.

"You shouldn't have done it!" said my mother, just as I had anticipated. She stood there holding the money in her hand and making a gesture as if to return it, as if she couldn't accept it. For a moment I had the uncomfortable feeling that she might possibly have thought I stole the money. It was not beyond me to do a thing like that, especially in such a desperate situation. However, it was not that, it was just that my mother had the habit, whenever she was offered a gift, be it a bunch of flowers, a crystal bowl or a discarded wrapper, of pretending that it was too much, that she wasn't worthy of such a kindness. "You oughtn't to have done it!" she would always say, a remark that always drove me crazy. "Why shouldn't people do things for one another?" I used to ask. "Don't you enjoy giving gifts yourself? Why do you talk that way?" Now she was saying to me, in that same disgusting fashion, "We know you can't afford it—why did you do it?"

"But didn't I tell you I *earned* it—and that I'll get lots more? What are you worrying about?"

"Yes," she said, blushing with confusion and looking as if I were trying to injure her rather than aid her, "but are you sure? Maybe they won't take your work after all. Maybe you'll have to return the money. . . ."

"For God's sake, stop it!" said my father. "Take it and be done with it! We can use it, you know that. You bellyache when we have no money and you bellyache when you get it." He turned to me. "Good for you, son," he said. "I'm glad to see you're getting on. It's certainly coming to you."

I always liked my father's attitude about money. It was clean and honest. When he had he gave, until the last cent, and when he didn't have he borrowed, if he could. Like myself he had no compunctions about asking for help when he needed it. He took it for granted that people should help, because he himself was always the first to help when any one was in need. It's true he was a bad financier; it's true he made a mess of things. But I'm glad he was that way; it wouldn't seem natural to think of him as a millionaire. Of course, by not managing his affairs well he forced my mother to become the financier. Had she not contrived to salt a little away during the good years no doubt the three of them would have been in the poor house long ago. How much she had salvaged from the wreckage none of us knew, not even my father. Certainly, to observe the way she economized, one would imagine it to be a very insignificant sum. Not a scrap of food ever went into the garbage can; no piece of string, no wrapping paper was ever thrown out; even the newspapers were preserved and sold at so much the pound. The sweater which she wore when it got chilly was in rags. Not that she had no other, oh no! She was saving the others carefully—they were put away in camphor balls—until the day that the old one literally fell apart. The drawers, as I accidentally discovered when searching for something, were crammed full of things which would come in handy some time, some time when things would be much worse than now. In France I was accustomed to seeing this stupid conservation of clothes, furniture and other objects, but to see it happening in America, in our own home, was something of a shock. None of my friends had ever shown a sense of economy, nor any sentiment for old things. It wasn't the American way of looking at life. The American way has always been to plunder and exploit and then move on.

Now that the ice had been broken my visits to the house became quite frequent. It's curious how simple things are when they're faced. To think that for years I had dreaded the very thought of walking into that house, had hoped to die first and so on. Why, it was actually pleasant, I began to realize, to run back and forth, particularly when I could come with hands full as I usually did. It was so easy to make them happy—I almost began to wish for more difficult circumstances, in order to prove to them that I was equal to any emergency. The mere fact of my presence seemed to fortify them against all the hazards and dangers which the future might hold in store. Instead of being burdened by their problems I began to feel lightened. What they asked of me was nothing compared to what I had stupidly imagined. I wanted to do more, much more, than anything they could think of asking me to do. When I proposed to them one day that I would come over early each morning and irrigate my father's bladder—a job which I felt my mother was doing incompetently—they were almost frightened. And when I followed that up, since they wouldn't hear of such a thing, by proposing to hire a nurse I could see from the expression on their faces that they thought I was losing my head. Of course they had no idea how guilty I felt, or if they had they were tactful enough to conceal it. I was bursting to make some sacrifice for them, but they didn't want sacrifices; all that they ever wanted of me, I slowly began to comprehend, was myself.

Sometimes in the afternoons, while the sun was still warm, I would sit in the backyard with my father and chat about old times. They were always proud of the little garden which they kept there. As I walked about examining the shrubs and plants, the cherry tree and the peach tree which they had grown since I left, I recalled how as a boy I had planted each little bush. The lilac bushes in particular impressed me. I remembered the day they were given me, when I was on a visit to the country, and how the old woman had said to me—"They will probably outlast you, my young bucko." Nothing was dying here in the garden. It would be beautiful, I thought to myself, if we were all buried in the garden among the things we had planted and watched over so lovingly. There was a big elm tree a few yards away. I was always fond of that tree, fond of it because of the noise it made when the wind soughed through the thick foliage. The more I gazed at it now the more its personality grew on me. I almost felt as if I would be able to talk to that tree if I sat there long enough.

Other times we would sit in the front, in the little areaway where once the grass plot had been. This little realm was also full of memories, memories of the street, of summer nights, of mooning and pining and planning to break away. Memories of fights with the children next door who used to delight in tantalizing my sister by calling her crazy. Memories of girls passing and longing to put my arms around them. And now another generation was passing the door and they were regarding me as if I were an elderly gentleman. "Is that your brother I see sitting with you sometimes?" some one asked my father. Now and then an old playmate would pass and my father would nudge me and say—"There goes Dick So-and-So" or "Harry this or that". And I would look up and see a middle-aged man passing, a man I would never have recognized as the boy I once used to play with. One day it happened that as I was going to the corner a man came towards me, blocking my path, and as I tried to edge away he planked himself square in front of me and stood there gazing at me fixedly, staring right through me. I thought he was a detective and was not altogether sure whether he had made a mistake or not. "What do you want?" I said coldly, making as if to move on. "What do I want?" he echoed. "What the hell, don't you recognize an old friend any more?" "I'm damned if I know who you are," I said. He stood there grinning and leering at me. "Well, I know who you are," he said. With that my memory came back. "Why of course," I said, "it's Bob Whalen. Of course I know you; I was just trying to kid you." But I would never have known him had he not forced me to remember. The incident gave me such a start that when I got back to the house I went immediately to the mirror and scrutinized my countenance, trying in vain to detect the changes which time had made in it. Not satisfied, and still inwardly disturbed, I asked to see an early photograph of myself. I looked at the photograph and then at the image in the mirror. There was no getting round it— it was not the same person. Then suddenly I felt apologetic for the casual way in which I had dismissed my old boyhood friend. Why, come to think of it, we had been just as close as brothers once. I had a strong desire to go out and telephone him, tell him I would be over to see him and have a good chat. But then I remembered that the reason why we had ceased relations, upon growing to manhood, was because he had become an awful bore. At twenty-one he had already become just like his father whom he used to hate as a boy. I couldn't understand such a thing then; I attributed it to sheer laziness. So what would be the good of suddenly renewing our friendship? I knew what his father was like; what good would it do to study the son? We had only one thing in common—our youth, which was gone. And so I dismissed him from my mind then and there. I buried him, as I had all the others from whom I had parted.

Sitting out front with my father the whole miniature world of the neighborhood passed in review. Through my father's comments I was privileged to get a picture of the life of these people such as would have been difficult to obtain otherwise. At first it seemed incredible to me that he should know so many people. Some of those whom he greeted lived blocks away. From the usual neighborly salutations relations had developed until they became genuine friendships. I looked upon my father as a lucky man. He was never lonely, never lacking visitors. A steady stream passed in and out of the house bringing thoughtful little gifts or words of encouragement. Clothes, foodstuffs, medicines, toilet articles, magazines, cigarettes, candy, flowers—everything but money poured in liberally. "What do you need money for?" I said one day. "Why, you're a rich man." "Yes," he said meekly, "I certainly can't complain."

"Would you like me to bring you some books to read?" I asked another time. "Aren't you tired of looking at the magazines?" I knew he never read books but I was curious to see what he would answer.

"I used to read," he said, "but I can't concentrate any more."

I was surprised to hear him admit that he had ever read a book. "What sort of books did you read?" I asked.

"I don't remember the titles any more," he said. "There was one fellow—Ruskin, I think it was."

"You read *Ruskin?*" I exclaimed, positively astounded.

"Yes, but he's pretty dry. That was a long time ago, too."

The conversation drifted to the subject of painting. He remembered with genuine pleasure the paintings with which his boss, an English tailor, had once decorated the walls of the shop. All the tailors had paintings on their walls then, so he said. That was back in the '80's and '90's. There must have been a great many painters in New York at that time, to judge from the stories he told me. I tried to find out what sort of paintings the tailors went in for at that period. The paintings were traded for clothes, of course.

He began to reminisce. There was So-and-so, he was saying. He did nothing but sheep. But they were wonderful sheep, so life-like, so real. Another man did cows, another dogs. He asked me parenthetically if I knew Rosa Bonheur's work—those wonderful horses! And George Inness! There was a great painter, he said enthusiastically. "Yes," he added meditatively, "I never got tired of looking at them. It's nice to have paintings around." He didn't think much of the modern painters—too much color and confusion, he thought. "Now Daubigny," he said, "there was a great painter. Fine sombre colors—something to think about." There was one large canvas, it seems, which he was particularly fond of. He couldn't remember any more who had painted it. Anyway, the thing which impressed him was that nobody would buy this painting, though it was acknowledged to be a masterpiece. "You see," he said, "it was too sad. People don't like sad things." I wondered what the subject could have been. "Well," he said, "it was a picture of an old sailor returning home. His clothes were falling off his back; he looked glum and melancholy. But it was wonderfully done—I mean the expression on his face. But nobody would have it; they said it was depressing."

As we were talking he paused to greet some one. I waited a few minutes until he beckoned me to approach and be introduced.

"This is Mr. O'Rourke," he said, "he's an astrologer." I pricked up my ears. "An astrologer?" I echoed. Mr. O'Rourke modestly replied that he was just a student. "I don't know so very much about it," he said, "but I did tell your father that you would return and that things would change for the better with your coming. I knew that you must be an intelligent man—I studied your horoscope carefully. Your weakness is that you're too generous; you give right and left."

"Is that a weakness?" I said laughingly.

"You have a wonderful heart," he said, "and a great intelligence. You were born lucky. There are great things in store for you. I told your father that you will be a great man. You'll be very famous before you die."

My father had to run inside a moment to empty the bag. I stood chatting with Mr. O'Rourke a few minutes. "Of course," he said, "I must also tell you that I say a prayer every night for your father. That helps a great deal, you know. I try to help everybody—that is, if they will listen to me. Some people, of course, you can't help —they won't let you. I'm not very fortunate myself but I have the power to aid others. You see, I have a bad Saturn. But I try to overcome it with prayer—and with right living, of course. I was telling your mother the other day that she has five good years ahead of her. She was born under the special protection of St Anthony—June the 13th is her birthday, isn't it? St Anthony never turns a deaf ear to those who beseech his favor."

"What does he do for a living?" I asked my father when Mr. O'Rourke had gone.

"He doesn't do anything, as far as I can make out," said my father. "I think he's on relief. He's a queer one, isn't he? I was wondering if I shouldn't give him that old overcoat that mother put away in the trunk. I've got enough with this one. You notice he looks a bit seedy."

There were lots of queer ones walking about the street. Some had become religious through misfortune and sorrow. There was one old woman who sent my father Christian Science tracts. Her husband had become a drunkard and deserted her. Now and then she would drop in to see my father and explain the writings of the Master. "It's not all nonsense," said my father. "Everything has its points, I suppose. Anyway, they don't mean any harm. I listen to them all. Mother thinks it's silly, but when you have nothing to do it takes your mind off things."

It was strange to me to see how the church had finally gotten its grip on every one. It seemed to lie in wait for the opportune moment, like some beast of prey. The whole family seemed to be touched with one form of religiosity or another. At one of the family reunions I was shocked to see an old uncle suddenly rise and pronounce grace. Thirty years ago any one who had dared to make a gesture like that would have been ridiculed and made the butt of endless jokes. Now everybody solemnly bowed his head and listened piously. I couldn't get over it. One of my aunts was now a deaconess. She loved church work, especially during festivities, when there were sandwiches to be made. They spoke of her proudly as being capable of waiting on fifty people at once. She was clever, too, at wrapping up gifts. On one occasion she had astounded everybody by presenting some one with a huge umbrella box. And what do you suppose was in the umbrella box when they undid it? Five ten-dollar bills! Quite original! And that was the sort of thing she had learned at the church, through all the fairs and bazaars and what not. So you see. . . .

During one of these reunions a strange thing happened to me. We were celebrating somebody's anniversary in the old house which my grandfather had bought when he came to America. It was an occasion to meet all the relatives at once—some thirty to forty aunts, cousins, nephews, nieces. Once again, as in olden times, we would all sit down to table together, a huge creaking board laden with everything imaginable that was edible and potable. The prospect pleased me, particularly because of the opportunity it would give me to have another look at the old neighborhood.

While the gifts were being distributed—a ceremony which usually lasted several hours—I decided to sneak outdoors and make a rapid exploration of the precincts. Immediately I set foot outdoors I started instinctively in search of the little street about which I used to dream so frequently while in Paris. I had been on this particular street only two or three times in my life, as a boy of five or six. The dream, I soon discovered, was far more vivid than the actual scene. There were elements which were missing now, not so much because the neighborhood had changed but because these elements had never existed, except in my dreams. There were two realities which in walking through the street now began to fuse and form a composite living truth which, if I were to record faithfully, would live forever. But the most curious thing about this incident lies not in the fitting together of the dream street and the actual street but the discovery of a street I had never known, a street only a hand's throw away, which for some reason had escaped my attention as a child. This street, when I came upon it in the evening mist, had me gasping with joy and astonishment. Here was the street which corresponded exactly with that ideal street which, in my dream wanderings, I had vainly tried to find.

In the recurrent dream of the little street which I first mentioned the scene always faded at the moment when I came upon the bridge that crossed the little canal, neither the bridge nor the canal having any existence actually. This evening, after passing beyond the frontier of my childhood explorations, I suddenly came upon the very street I had been longing to find for so many years. There was in the atmosphere here something of another world, another planet. I remember distinctly the premonition I had of approaching this other world when, passing a certain house, I caught sight of a young girl, obviously of foreign descent, poring over a book at the dining room table. There is nothing unique, to be sure, in such a sight. Yet, the moment my eyes fell upon the girl I had a thrill beyond description, a premonition, to be more accurate, that important revelations were to follow. It was as if the girl, her pose, the glow of the room falling upon the book she was reading, the impressive silence in which the whole neighborhood was enveloped, combined to produce a moment of such acuity that for an incalculably brief, almost meteoric flash I had the deep and quiet conviction that everything had been ordained, that there was justice in the world, and that the image which I had caught and vainly tried to hold was the expression of the splendor and the holiness of life as it would always reveal itself to be in moments of utter stillness. I realized as I pushed ecstatically forward that the joy and bliss which we experience in the profound depths of the dream—a joy and bliss which surpasses anything known in waking life—comes indubitably from the miraculous accord between desire and reality. When we come to the surface again this fusion, this harmony, which is the whole goal of life, either falls apart or else is only fitfully and feebly realized. In our waking state we toss about in a troubled sleep, the sleep which is terrifying and death-dealing because our eyes are open, permitting us to see the trap into which we are walking and which we are nevertheless unable to avoid.

The interval between the moment of passing the girl and the first glimpse of the long-awaited ideal street, which I had searched for in all my dreams and never found, was of the same flavor and substance as those anticipatory moments in the deep dream when it seems as if no power on earth can hinder the fulfillment of desire. The whole character of such dreams lies in the fact that once the road has been taken the end is always certain. As I walked past the row of tiny houses sunk deep in the earth I saw what man is seldom given to see—the reality of his vision. To me it was the most beautiful street in the world. Just one block long, dimly lit, shunned by respectable citizens, ignored by the whole United States—a tiny community of foreign souls living apart from the great world, pursuing their own humble ways and asking nothing more of their neighbors than tolerance. As I passed slowly from door to door I saw that they were breaking bread. On each table there was a bottle of wine, a loaf of bread, some cheese and olives and a bowl of fruit. In each house it was the same: the shades were up, the lamp was lit, the table spread for a humble repast. And always the occupants were gathered in a circle, smiling good-naturedly as they conversed with one another, their bodies relaxed, their spirit open and expansive. Truly, I thought to myself, this is the only life I have ever desired. For the briefest intervals only have I known it and then it has been rudely shattered. And the cause? Myself undoubtedly, my inability to realize the true nature of Paradise. As a boy, knowing nothing of the great life outside, this ambiance of the little world, the holy, cellular life of the microcosm, must have penetrated deep. What else can explain the tenacity with which I have clung for forty years to the remembrance of a certain neighborhood, a certain wholly inconspicuous spot on this great earth? When my feet began to itch, when I became restless in my own soul, I thought it was the larger world, the world outside, calling to me, beseeching me to find a bigger and greater place for myself. I expanded in all directions. I tried to embrace not only this world but the worlds beyond. Suddenly, just when I thought myself emancipated, I found myself thrust back into the little circle from which I had fled. I say "the little circle", meaning not only the old neighborhood, not only the city of my birth, but the whole United States. As I have explained elsewhere, Greece, tiny though it appears on the map, was the biggest world I have ever entered. Greece for me was the home which we all long to find. As a country it offered me everything I craved. And yet, at the behest of the American consul in Athens, I consented to return. I accepted the American consul's intervention as the bidding of fate. In doing so I perhaps converted what is called blind fate into something destined. Only the future will tell if this be so. At any rate, I came back to the narrow, circumscribed world from which I had escaped. And in coming back I not only found everything the same, but even more so. How often since my return have I thought of Nijinsky who was so thoughtlessly awakened from his trance! What must he think of this world on which he had deliberately turned his back in order to avoid becoming insane like the rest of us! Do you suppose he feels thankful to his specious benefactors? Will he stay awake and toss fitfully in his sleep, as do we, or will he choose to close his eyes again and feast only upon that which he knows to be true and beautiful?

The other day, in the office of a newspaper, I saw in big letters over the door: "Write the things which thou hast seen and the things which are." I was startled to see this exhortation, which I have religiously and unwittingly followed all my life, blazing from the walls of a great daily. I had forgotten that there were such words recorded in *Revelations. The things which are!* One could ponder over that phrase forever. One thing is certain, however, and that is that the things which are are eternal. I come back to that little community, that dream world, in which I was raised. In microcosm it is a picture of that macrocosm which we call the world. To me it is a world asleep, a world in which the dream is imprisoned. If for a moment there is an awakening the dream, vaguely recalled, is speedily forgotten. This trance, which continues twenty-four hours of the day, is only slightly disturbed by wars and revolutions. Life goes on, as we say, but smothered, damped down, hidden away in the vegetative fibres of our being. Real awareness comes intermittently, in brief flashes of a second's duration. The man who can hold it for a minute, relatively speaking, inevitably changes the whole trend of the world. In the span of ten or twenty thousand years a few widely isolated individuals have striven to break the deadlock, shatter the trance, as it were. Their efforts, if we look at the present state of the world superficially, seem to have been ineffectual. And yet the example which their lives afford us points conclusively to one thing, that the real drama of man on earth is concerned with Reality and not with the creation of civilizations which permit the great mass of men to snore more or less blissfully. A man who had the slightest awareness of what he was doing could not possibly put his finger to the trigger of a gun, much less cooperate in the making of such an instrument. A man who wanted to live would not waste even a fraction of a moment in the invention, creation and perpetuation of instruments of death. Men are more or less reconciled to the thought of death, but they also know that it is not necessary to kill one another. They know it intermittently, just as they know other things which they conveniently proceed to forget when there is danger of having their sleep disturbed. To live without killing is a thought which could electrify the world, if men were only capable of staying awake long enough to let the idea soak in. But man refuses to stay awake because if he did he would be obliged to become something other than he now is, and the thought of that is apparently too painful for him to endure. If man were to come to grips with his real nature, if he were to discover his real heritage, he would become so exalted, or else so frightened, that he would find it impossible to go to sleep again. To live would be a perpetual challenge to create. But the very thought of a possible swift and endless metamorphosis terrifies him. He sleeps now, not comfortably to be sure, but certainly more and more obstinately, in the womb of a creation whose only need of verification is his own awakening. In this state of sublime suspense time and space have become meaningless concepts. Already they have merged to form another concept which, in his stupor, he is as yet unable to formulate or elucidate. But whatever the role that man is to play in it, the universe, of that we may be certain, is not asleep. Should man refuse to accept his role there are other planets, other stars, other suns waiting to go forward with the experiment. No matter how vast, how total, the failure of man here on earth, the work of man will be resumed elsewhere. War leaders talk of resuming operations on this front and that, but man's front embraces the whole universe.

In our sleep we have discovered how to exterminate one another. To abandon this pleasant pursuit merely to sleep more soundly, more peacefully, would be of no value. We must awaken —or pass out of the picture. There is no alarm clock which man can invent to do the trick. To set the alarm is a joke. The clock itself is an evidence of wrong thinking. What does it matter what time you get up if it is only to walk in your sleep?

Now extinction seems like true bliss. The long trance has dulled us to everything which is alive and awake. Forward! cry the defenders of the great sleep. *Forward to death!* But on the last day the dead will be summoned from their graves: they will be made to take up the life eternal. To postpone the eternal is impossible. Everything else we may do or fail to do, but eternity has nothing to do with time, nor sleep, nor failure, nor death. Murder is postponement. And war is murder, whether it be glorified by the righteous or not. I speak of the things which are, not because they are of the moment but because they always have been and always will be. The life which every one dreams of, and which no one has the courage to lead, can have no existence in the present. The present is only a gateway between past and future. When we awaken we will dispense with the fiction of the bridge which never existed. We will pass from dream to reality with eyes wide open. We will get our bearings instantly, without the aid of instruments. We will not need to fly around the earth in order to find the paradise which is at our feet. When we stop killing—not only actually, but in our hearts—we will begin to live, and not until then.

I believe that it is now possible for me to have my being anywhere on earth. I regard the entire world as my home. I inhabit the earth, not a particular portion of it labelled America, France, Germany or Russia. I owe allegiance to mankind, not to a particular country, race or people. I answer to God and not to the Chief Executive, whoever he may happen to be. I am here on earth to work out my own private destiny. My destiny is linked with that of every other living creature inhabiting this planet—perhaps with those on other planets too, who knows? I refuse to jeopardize my destiny by regarding life within the narrow rules which are now laid down to circumscribe it. I dissent from the current view of things as regards murder, as regards religion, as regards society, as regards our well-being. I will try to live my life in accordance with the vision I have of things eternal. I say "Peace to you all!" and if you don't find it, it's because you haven't looked for it.

TO-DAY, YESTERDAY AND
TO-MORROW

THE QUESTION most often put to me by my American compatriots
on my return from Greece was this: are the Greeks of to-day anything like the Greeks of old? To answer in the affirmative was invariably to cause astonishment. Of course it never occurred to these
good souls to ask themselves if the Americans of to-day are anything like the Americans of Washington and Jefferson's time.

To me it's always been a curious and lamentable thing that,
when one speaks of the Greeks, it is the fifth century Greek that
is referred to. It is typical of the Western mind to want to convert
an apogee into a stasis. Contrary to the rhythm of the universe,

contrary to all organic law, such a desire can only be construed as expressive of childish longing. In the religious sphere it manifests itself by the creation of a beyond which, though represented as bliss, can only be regarded as an exquisite form of perpetual torture.

Fortunately for the living Greek, whom we so blithely seek to ignore, the evidence of a continuous tradition of greatness leads deep into the past and bespeaks a future just as glorious. The idea voiced by Spengler, that with the death of a culture the peoples who created the great civilizations of the past live on merely as biological phenomena, seems disproved by the logic of current events.

Perhaps the greatest example of the rebirth of a nation is that given us by the Chinese. Like India, also going through the throes of rebirth, though less spectacularly (hampered as she is by a jealous and tyrannical foster-parent), China after this war will undoubtedly rise to a position of supreme eminence among the great powers. Indeed, I think it is not too rash to predict that the picture of the world to come will be given its form and content by the three countries hitherto regarded as dead or backward: I mean China, India and Russia.

This most unexpected awakening by what, up until a few years ago, were regarded as dormant peoples is a phenomenon worthy of the deepest study. As every one knows, what is happening is that the conglomerate, dispersed elements which composed the above-mentioned peoples are unifying, cohering into wholes again. They are becoming nationalized. At the moment when the hope of the world seems to lie in de-nationalization this tendency would appear to be counter-clockwise. But, just as with the individual, it is first necessary to become integrated before taking part in the world's activities, so with peoples. The centrifugal movement makes way for the centripetal one. Systole and diastole. The hitherto dispersed "elements" are now being coordinated into functional wholes in order that eventually, and perhaps in the not too distant future, the whole globe will function as a planetary being. It is important that in the process the infinite parts which go to make up the total entity retain their individuality. The brotherhood of man, when it comes about, will be a brotherhood of true individuals. It will be an aristocracy, based on the recognition of the common divinity of all.

The failure of the democratic principle is due, in my opinion, to the fact that even the most democratic peoples have never gone the whole hog: i.e., neither low enough nor high enough. In a democracy such as ours, for example, one half the country rules the other half, depending on which gets the whip hand. In Periclean Greece, the so-called Golden Age, the free men decided the fate of the more numerous helots. A people can be just as tyrannical as a dictator or an absolute monarch. The people are their own worst enemy. And yet, just as no man can look to any one but himself, in the last analysis, so neither can the people as a whole look to any but themselves. Leaders—yes. But the real leaders are seldom those who are in the limelight—perhaps never.

It is curious, in this connection, that the very word individuality has come to have a pejorative sense. It is an accusation often levelled against the ancient Greeks, that they were too individualistic. It has also been levelled against the men of the Renaissance, and latterly against the democratic Americans. In reading Edith Hamilton's book, *The Great Age of Greek Literature*, the chapters which impressed me most were those devoted to the man who wrote "The Retreat of the Ten Thousand" and to the man who wrote about war (Thucydides) as no other historian ever has. In the space of a few generations, as Miss Hamilton emphasizes, the Greek who was so magnificent in defeat became the Greek who became so ugly and merciless in triumph and power. It is not power, of course, that was at fault, but the love of power. Since that fatal period in Greek history other nations have learned the same bitter lesson, and some are learning it even now.

Psychoanalysis has revived a term—individuation--which points to the limitations, as well as the cure, of individualism. A robber baron, for example, and the type is still with us, may have great individuality, but he certainly has not attained individuation. What distinguishes him, makes him a conspicuous individual, is the lesser side of him, his predatory nature. Lincoln understood perfectly the goal to be attained when he said: "As I would not want to be a slave so I would not want to be a master." Eugene V. Debs, when brought to trial for his refusal to bear arms, expressed it better still: "While there is a lower class I am in it; while there is a criminal element I am of it; while there is a soul in prison, I am not free." These words broaden and deepen the meaning of the Emancipation Proclamation; they lead us out into the open world of the future, constitute the platform of the democrats to come. No one is free, in short, no one can enjoy the powers which are rightfully his—and which only then are truly unlimited—until each and every man is free and equal absolutely. In this sense the task of every man is unending, and the goal never attainable, except on the level of spiritual understanding. The process, or the way, is all. The way and the means are the end.

Nothing is truer than that we become what we are. Now if any people on earth reflect what they are, and not merely what they have become, it is the Greeks. I had no false worship of the Greeks when I set out in 1939 on my "pilgrimage", for that is what it became as I journeyed on. I was not in search of the past, or the future. I wanted to see what was. But, looking squarely at what Greece was then, I saw into the past and the future. I looked into the soul of the Greek people. And the particularity of the Greek soul, let me add rapidly, is the phenomenal, which, thank God, is still a good Greek word. Everything about the Greek is phenomenal, using the word in the sense of extraordinary, as we now vulgarly do, and thereby testifying unconsciously that we do regard all which comes to pass as miraculous. Only a super-endowed people could have chosen as motto and inspiration the words inscribed on the temple of Apollo at Delphi—"Nothing to the extreme". The sense of measure and proportion was born of the heroic. It had nothing to do with timidity and caution, as is implied by our word "moderation". In Paris a blind professor of music, one of the greatest teachers I have ever met, said to me: "Genius is the norm." I believe it utterly. I think it was the realization of this truth which led to the birth of such a profusion of geniuses as Greece gave to the world, and is still giving.

Beside the inquisitive, restless, vivacious Greek the Englishman, for example, seems ill at ease. He looks upon the Greek as a freak or an eccentric. Eccentric! What connotations the French have given to that word! So revelatory of their own smug and petty self-centeredness. Indeed, when one finally comes upon the Greek, sees him in his own habitat, one instinctively feels that the yardstick with which he has been accustomed to measuring his neighbors has to be lengthened. Suddenly the word "human" acquires a new dignity and significance. Suddenly one realizes that what we have taken for granted as normal is really abnormal, or more properly speaking, sub-normal. The Greek is oversize in every respect. Because he is nearer to the node. Because he of all peoples still carries within him the notion of cosmos. He is a pan-human soul, so to speak. He is not locked up in himself, not chauvinistic, not limited by his fears or ambitions. It is the tragedy of the Greeks, I truly believe, that they so heroically persist in remaining human, in carrying the cosmos about with them, each and every one, as though they were personal emissaries of the gods. It makes them seem archaic to the degenerate souls who have questioned away the very nature of the universe and who seek nothing but power, power, power.

Nothing could be more typical of this supreme quality of the Greeks than their recent unlooked-for resistance to the Italian and German invaders. What did they hope to attain by venturing such an impossible stand? They must have known from the start that they were doomed. It couldn't be possible, could it, that they, "the wily Greeks", were duped? Reason, with which they are so heavily endowed, would have counselled them to surrender without a fight. Shrewd, practical wisdom, for the exercise of which they are so often reproached, might have dictated still another course. But the heroic instinct demanded action, no matter what the outcome . . . It was an object lesson to the world. To all the little peoples of the earth Greece, by her immeasurable self-sacrifice, gave hope. It was the darkest hour of the war, and, in my opinion, the true turning point of the war. Once again Greece had performed her mission— to lead and inspire the world. Looking back upon this miraculous exploit of an impoverished, ill-equipped nation, one is obliged to admit that it was "phenomenal". There was no precedent for it, save at Marathon, Thermopylae, Salamis.

At the present moment Greece seems in danger of being snuffed out. Her reward appears to take the form of total starvation. Even before the war her condition was one which the ordinary American would find it difficult to comprehend. Wherein then does her hope lie? What can save her from complete annihilation?

I shall have to utter now a most horrible truth. If, when this war is over, only a thousand out of her former population of seven million are left Greece will not perish. Reduced to the final inexpugnable nucleus, it is even possible that the Greeks will achieve the apotheosis towards which they were verging in the glorious period of their cultural flowering. As in the game of chess it is often necessary, if the pawns are to reveal their true power, that the board first be cleared. The transition from pawn to queen, when it comes about, is not gradual but sudden, as swift and miraculous as a conversion. The art of war, which is poetized in the game of chess, has this at least to teach us—that the mighty are often laid low by the humble. The grand strategy is so to marshal one's forces that the pawns become eventually strong as queens. Great deeds require not time so much as space, freedom of operation. I have remarked elsewhere how huge a country, though it occupies but the tip of Europe, Greece seems. This is not an illusion, but a reality. It has to do with the fact that, as I stated previously, there is still something "cosmic" about the Greeks. It is not numbers with the Greek, but number: the world of idea, not the world of things. This is the phenomenal quality of the Greek, to-day as of yesterday, and to-morrow as of to-day: he sees the act which is hidden in the word. The Greeks make verbs, and verbs are symbols. Symbols are indestructible.

Alexander the Great, upon reaching India, was smitten, it is said, by the wisdom of a holy man. Finding it impossible to persuade the holy man to join his retinue, and return to Greece with him, he threatened to kill him. Whereupon the holy man gave out a great horse laugh. "Kill me?" he roared mockingly—"how can you kill me? I'm indestructible!"

When reduced to desperation people no longer rely on a leader. "Every one of you is the leader," said Xenophon to his men once. This utterance is characteristically Greek. The undeniability of it colors all Greek history, even down to the present day.

Terrible as it is, this is not the darkest moment in Greek history. The domination by the Axis powers will be of brief duration. The invasion of the continent is imminent. Greece will be liberated and the Balkans set aflame once again. I tremble to think what will happen to the present invaders of Greece when that moment arrives.

"Swift! Bring me an axe that can slay. I will know now if I am to win or lose. I stand here on the height of misery."

These words which Aeschylus put in the mouth of Clytemnestra apply now with frightful eloquence. Aye, bring an axe that can slay! And bring tanks and bombers and heavy artillery! *Bring food!* No need to bring men. One Greek is worth a hundred trained foot-soldiers. Greece needs food and weapons.

The danger which menaces Greece to-day is the horrible fate which overtook the remnants of the International Brigades at Le Vernet. "They had done nothing," says Arthur Koestler, "but put into practice what we had preached and believed; they had been admired and worshipped, and thrown on the rubbish-heap like a sackful of potatoes, to putrefy." (*Scum of the Earth*, by Arthur Koestler, Macmillan, 1941). To read what happened to the hundred and fifty men who formed the Leper Barrack at Le Vernet is something to make one's blood run cold. But in Greece at this very moment there are several *million* individuals who are suffering this same shameful neglect, humiliation and torture. We ask them to be patient and wait for deliverance—but are we in the meantime racking our brains to devise ways and means of succoring them? I doubt it.

As with individuals so with nations—each seems to have his role to play. The role of the Greeks is the hardest of all: it is to remain human when the very meaning of cosmos is lost. In the midst of opposing trends—individualism versus collectivism—the Greeks alone have the true sense of proportion. A tiny microcosm among the peoples of the earth, they nevertheless retain the image and the significance of the macrocosm. Theirs is the middle way—between heaven and earth.

This means virtually that the Greeks have a different polarity from that of their neighbors. They take their stance in the very heart of the world; their axis is a vertical one; they live and die in the center of a whirlwind. But just this fact of being situated at the core, where the very breath of life is danger, is what guarantees them immunity from destruction. The more fiercely the fires rage the more they become imbued with courage and wisdom. They are forever being tested in the fiery crucible. It is this extraordinary destiny which lends to the Greeks their phenomenal aspect or quality. They suffer more and enjoy more, they see further and act quicker than other peoples. Their metabolism is, so to speak, electrified. They live according to a rhythm which will one day be the norm. Meanwhile, just because they are in advance of the rest of the world, they suffer the tortures of the damned.

For over two thousand years now this Promethean drama has been going on. The true liberation of Greece depends on the world's liberation. Until that day is ushered in Greece can not and will not relinquish her role. It is a phenomenal situation, a phenomenal impasse. And only a phenomenal people can solve it.

A FRAGMENT FROM
"THE ROSY CRUCIFIXION"

INSTEAD of rushing out of the house immediately after dinner that evening, as I usually did, I lay on the couch in the dark and fell into a deep reverie. "Why don't you try to *write?*" That was the phrase which had stuck in my crop all day, which repeated itself insistently even as I was saying thank you to my friend MacGregor for the ten-spot which I had wrung from him after the most humiliating wheedling and cajoling.

In the darkness I began to work my way back to the hub. I began to think of those most happy days of childhood, the long Summer days when my mother took me by the hand and led me over the fields to see my little friends, Joey and Tony. As a child it was impossible to penetrate the secret of that joy which comes from a sense of superiority. That extra sense, which enables one to participate and at the same time to observe one's participation, appeared to me to be the normal endowment of everyone. That I enjoyed everything more than the other boys I was unaware of. The discrepancy between myself and others only dawned on me as I grew older. I was made to feel that it was a defect resulting from my flagrant irresponsibility. From this ensued alternate moods of dejection in which I sank far below the normal level of despondency.

To write, I meditated, must be an act devoid of will. The word, like the deep ocean current, has to float to the surface of its own impulse. A child has no need to write, he is innocent. A man writes to throw off the poison which he has accumulated because of his false way of life. He is trying to recapture his innocence but all he succeeds in doing, by writing, is to inoculate the world with the virus of his disillusionment. No man would set a word down on paper if he had the courage to live out what he believed in. His inspiration is deflected at the source. If it is a world of truth, beauty and magic that he desires to create, why does he put millions of words between himself and the reality of that world? Why does he defer action—unless it be that like other men what he really desires is power, fame, success. "Books are human actions in death," said Balzac, and yet, having perceived the truth he deliberately surrendered the angel to the demon which possessed him.

A writer woos his public just as ignominiously as a politician or any other mountebank; he loves to finger the great pulse, to prescribe like a physician, to win a place for himself, to be recognized as a force, to receive the full cup of adulation, even if it be deferred a thousand years. He doesn't want a new world which might be established immediately, because he knows it would never suit him. He wants an impossible world in which he is the uncrowned puppet ruler dominated by forces utterly beyond his control. He is content to rule insidiously—in the fictive world of symbols—because the very thought of contact with rude and brutal realities frightens him. It is true he has a greater grasp of reality than other men, but he makes no effort to impose that higher reality on the world by force of example. He is satisfied just to preach, to drag along in the wake of disasters and catastrophes, a death-croaking prophet always without honor, always stoned, always shunned by those who, however unfitted for their task, are ready and willing to assume responsibility for the affairs of the world. The truly great writer does not want to write: he wants the world to be a place in which he can live the life of the imagination. The first quivering word he puts to paper is the word of the wounded angel: pain. The process of putting down words is equivalent to giving oneself a narcotic. Observing the growth of a book under his hands, he swells with delusions of grandeur. "I too am a conqueror—perhaps the greatest conqueror of all! My day is coming. I will enslave the world—by the magic of words. . . ." Et cetera ad nauseam.

The little phrase—*Why don't you try to write?*—involved me, as it had from the very beginning, in a hopeless bog of confusion. I wanted to enchant but not to enslave; I wanted a greater, richer life, but not at the expense of others; I wanted to free the imagination of all men at once, because without the support of the whole world, without a world imaginatively unified, the freedom of the imagination becomes a vice. I had no respect for writing *per se*, anymore than I had for God *per se*. Nobody, no principle, no idea has validity in itself. What is valid is only that much of anything, God included, which is realized by all men in common. People are always worried about the fate of the genius. I never worried about the genius—genius takes care of the genius in a man. My concern was always for the nobody, the man who is lost in the shuffle, the man who is so common, so ordinary, that his presence is not even noticed. One genius does not inspire another. All geniuses are leeches, so to speak. They feed from the same source—the blood of life. The most important thing for the genius is to make himself useless, to be absorbed in the common stream, to become a fish again and not a freak of nature. The only benefit, I reflected, which the act of writing could offer me was to remove the differences which separated me from my fellow-man. I definitely did not want to become an artist, in the sense of becoming something strange, something apart and out of the current of life.

The best part about writing is not the actual labor of putting word against word, brick upon brick, but the preliminaries, the spade work which is done in silence under any circumstances, in dream as well as in the waking state. In short, the period of gestation. No man ever puts down what he intended to say: the original creation, which is taking place all the time, whether one writes or doesn't write, belongs to the primal flux: it has no dimensions, no form, no time element. In this preliminary state, which is creation and not birth, what disappears suffers no destruction; something which was already there, something imperishable, like memory or matter or God, is summoned and in it one flings himself like a twig into a torrent. Words, sentences, ideas no matter how subtle or ingenious, the maddest flights of poetry, the most profound dreams, the most hallucinating visions, are but crude hieroglyphs chiselled in pain and sorrow to commemorate an event which is untransmissible. In an intelligently ordered world there would be no need to make the unreasonable attempt of putting such miraculous happenings down. Indeed, it would make no sense, for if men only stopped to realize it, who would be content with the counterfeit when the real is at every one's beck and call? Who would want to switch in and listen to Beethoven, for example, when he might himself experience the ecstatic harmonies which Beethoven so desperately strove to register? A great work of art, if it accomplishes anything, serves to remind us, or let us say to set us dreaming, of all that is fluid and intangible—which is to say, the universe. It cannot be understood—it can only be accepted or rejected; if accepted we are revitalized, if rejected we are diminished. Whatever it purports to be it is not: it is always something more for which the last word will never be said. It is all that we put into it out of hunger for that which we deny every day of our lives. If we accepted *ourselves* as completely as the work of art the whole world of art would die of malnutrition. Every man Jack of us moves without feet at least a few hours a day, when his eyes are closed and his body prone. The art of dreaming when wide awake will be in the power of every man one day. Long before that books will cease to exist, for when most men are wide awake and dreaming their powers of communication (with one another and with the spirit that moves all men) will be so enhanced as to make writing seem like the harsh and raucous squawks of an idiot.

I think and know all this, lying in the dark memory of a Summer's day, without having mastered, or even half-heartedly attempted to master, the art of the crude hieroglyph. Before ever I begin I am disgusted with the efforts of the acknowledged masters. Without the ability or the knowledge to make so much as a portal in the façade of the grand edifice I criticize and lament the architecture itself. If I were only a tiny brick in the vast cathedral of this antiquated style I would be infinitely happier, I would have life, the life of the whole structure, even as an infinitesimal part of it. But I am outside, a barbarian who cannot make even a crude sketch, let alone a plan, of the edifice he dreams of inhabiting. I dream a new blazingly magnificent world which collapses as soon as the light is turned on. A world that vanishes but does not die, for I have only to become still again and stare wide-eyed into the darkness and it reappears. There is then a world in me which is utterly unlike any world I know of. I do not think it is my exclusive property—it is only the angle of my vision which is exclusive in that it is unique. If I talk the language of my unique vision nobody will understand; the most colossal edifice may be reared and yet remain invisible. The thought of that haunts me. What good will it do to make an invisible temple?

Drifting with the flux—because of that little phrase. This is the sort of thinking that went on whenever the word writing came up. In ten years of sporadic efforts I had managed to write a million words or so. You might as well say—a million blades of grass. To call attention to this ragged lawn was humiliating. All my friends knew that I had the itch to write—that's what made me good company now and then: *the itch. . . .*

I had more in common with Ulric than with any of my other friends. For me he represented Europe, its softening, civilizing influence. We would talk by the hour of this other world where art had some relation to life, where you could sit quietly in public watching the passing show and think your own thoughts. Would I ever get there? Would it be too late? How would I live? What would I do for money? What language would I speak? When I thought about it realistically it seemed hopeless. Only hardy, adventurous spirits could realize such dreams. Ulric had done it—for a year—by dint of hard sacrifice. For ten years he had done the things he hated to do—in order to make a dream come true. Now the dream was over and he was back where he had started. Farther back than ever, really, because he could never again adapt himself to the treadmill. For him it had been a Sabbatical leave, a dream which turns to gall and wormwood as the years roll by and one feels himself being dragged down into the morass of the daily grind. I could never do as Ulric had done. I could never make a sacrifice of that sort, nor could I be content with a mere vacation however long or short it might be. My policy has always been to burn my bridges behind me. My face is always set towards the future. If I make a mistake it is fatal. When I am flung back I fall all the way back—to the very bottom. My one safeguard is my resiliency. So far I have always bounced back. Sometimes the re-bound has resembled a slow motion performance, but in the eyes of God speed has no particular significance.

It was in Ulric's studio not so many months ago that I finished my first book—the book about the twelve messengers. I used to work in his brother's room where some short time previously a magazine editor, after reading a few pages of an unfinished story, informed me cold-bloodedly that I hadn't an ounce of talent, that I didn't know the first thing about writing—in short that I was a complete flop and the best thing to do, my lad, is to forget it, try to make an honest living. Another nincompoop who had written a highly successful book about Jesus the carpenter had told me the same thing. And if rejection slips mean anything there was ample corroboration to support the criticism of these discerning minds. "Who are these shits?" I used to say to Ulric. Where do they get off to tell me these things? What have they done, except to prove that they know how to make money?"

Well, I was talking about Joey and Tony, my little friends. I was lying in the dark, a little twig floating in the Japanese current. I was getting back to simple abracadabra, the straw that makes bricks, the crude sketch, the temple which must take on flesh and blood and make itself manifest to all the world. I got up and put on a soft light. I felt calm and lucid, like a lotus opening up. No violent pacing back and forth, no tearing the hair out by the roots. I sank slowly into a chair by the table and with a pencil I began to write. I described in simple words how it felt to take my mother's hand and walk across the sun-lit fields, how it felt to see Joey and Tony rushing towards me with arms open, their faces beaming with joy. I put one brick upon another like an honest brick-layer. Something of a vertical nature was happening—not blades of grass shooting up but something structural, something planned. I didn't strain myself to finish it; I stopped when I had said all I could. I read it over quietly, what I had written. I was so moved that the tears came to my eyes. It wasn't something to show an editor: it was something to put away in a drawer, to keep as a reminder of natural processes, as a promise of fulfillment.

Every day we slaughter our finest impulses. That is why we get a heart-ache when we read those lines written by the hand of a master and recognize them as our own, as the tender shoots which we stifled because we lacked the faith to believe in our own powers, our own criterion of truth and beauty. Every man, when he gets quiet, when he becomes desperately honest with himself, is capable of uttering profound truths. We all derive from the same source. There is no mystery about the origin of things. We are all part of creation, all kings, all poets, all musicians: we have only to open up, only to discover what is already there.

What happened to me in writing about Joey and Tony was tantamount to revelation. It was revealed to me that I could say what I wanted to say—if I thought of nothing else, if I concentrated upon that exclusively—and if I were willing to bear the consequences which a pure act always involves.

Two or three days later I met Mara for the first time in broad daylight. I was waiting for her in the Long Island depot over in Brooklyn. It was about six in the afternoon, daylight saving time, which is a strange sun-lit rush hour that enlivens even such a gloomy crypt as the waiting room of the Long Island Railroad. I was standing near the door when I spotted her crossing the car tracks under the elevated line; the sunlight filtered through the hideous structure in shafts of powdered gold. She had on a dotted Swiss dress which made her full figure seem even more opulent; the breeze blew lightly through her glossy black hair, teasing the heavy chalk-white face like spray dashing against a cliff. In that quick lithe stride, so sure, so alert, I felt again a renewed sense of life; it was the animal breaking through the flesh with flowery grace and fragile beauty. This was her day-time self, a fresh, healthy creature who dressed with utter simplicity and talked almost like a child.

We had decided to spend the evening at the beach. I was afraid it would be too cool for her in that light dress but she said she never felt the cold. We were so frightfully happy that the words just babbled out of our mouths. We had crowded together in the motorman's compartment, our faces almost touching and glowing with the fiery rays of the setting sun. How different this ride over the roof-tops from the lonely anxious one that Sunday morning when I set out for her home! Was it possible that in such a short span of time the world could take on such a different hue? The world! What is the world if it is not something which we carry in our hearts? That fiery sun going down in the West—what a symbol of joy and warmth! It fired our hearts, illuminated our faces, magnetized our souls. It's warmth would last far into the night, would flow back from below the curved horizon in defiance of the night. In this fiery blaze I handed her the manuscript to read. I couldn't have chosen a more favorable moment or a more favorable critic. It had been conceived in darkness and it was being baptized in light. As I watched her expression I had such a strong feeling of exaltation that I felt as if I had handed her a message from the Creator Himself. I didn't need to know her opinion—I could read it on her face. For years I cherished this souvenir, reviving it in those dark moments when I had broken with every one, walking back and forth in a lonely attic in a foreign city, reading the freshly written pages and struggling to visualize on the faces of all my coming readers this expression of unreserved love and admiration. When people ask me if I have a definite audience in mind when I sit down to write I tell them no, I have no one in mind, but the truth is that I have before me the image of a great crowd, an anonymous crowd in which perhaps I recognize here and there a friendly face: in that crowd I see accumulating the slow, burning warmth which was once a single image: I see it spread, take fire, rise into a great conflagration. The only time a writer receives his due reward is when someone comes to him burning with this flame which he fanned in a moment of solitude. Honest criticism means nothing: what one wants is unrestrained passion, fire for fire.

When one is trying to do something beyond his known powers it is useless to seek the approval of friends. Friends are at their best in moments of defeat—at least that is my experience. Then they either fail you bitterly or they surpass themselves. Sorrow is the great link—sorrow and misfortune. But when you are testing your powers, when you are trying to do something new, the best friend is apt to prove a traitor. The very way he wishes you luck, when you broach your chimerical ideas, is enough to dishearten you. He believes in you only as far as he knows you; the possibility that you are greater than you seem is disturbing, for friendship is founded on mutuality. It is almost a law that when a man embarks on a great adventure he must cut all ties. He must take himself off to the wilderness, and when he has wrestled it out with himself, he must return and choose a disciple. It doesn't matter how poor in quality the disciple may be: it matters only that he believes implicitly. For a germ to sprout some other person, some one individual out of the crowd, has to show faith. Artists, like great religious leaders, show amazing perspicacity in this respect. They never pick the likely one for their purpose, but always some obscure, frequently ridiculous person.

What aborted me in my beginnings, what almost proved to be a tragedy, was that I could find no one who believed in me implicitly, either as a person or as a writer. There was Mara, it is true, but Mara was not a friend, hardly even another person, so closely did we unite. I needed some one outside the vicious circle of false admirers and envious denigrators. I needed a man from the blue.

Ulric did his best to understand what had come over me, but he hadn't it in him then to perceive what I was destined to become. How can I forget the way he received the news about Mara? It was the day after we had gone to the beach. I had gone to the office as usual in the morning, but by noon I was so feverishly inspired that I took a trolley and rode out into the country. Ideas were pouring into my head. As fast as I jotted them down others came crowding in. At last I reached that point where you abandon all hope of remembering your brilliant ideas and you simply surrender to the luxury of writing a book in your head. You know that you'll never be able to recapture these ideas, not a single line of all the tumultuous and marvellously dove-tailed sentences which sift through your mind like sawdust spilling through a hole. On such days you have for company the best companion you will ever have—the modest, defeated, plodding workaday self which has a name and which can be identified in public registers in case of accident or death. But the real self, the one who has taken over the reins, is almost a stranger. He is the one who is filled with ideas; he is the one who is writing it in the air; he is the one who, if you become too fascinated with his exploits, will finally expropriate the old, worn-out self, taking over your name, your address, your wife, your past and your future. Naturally, he doesn't wish to concede immediately that you have another life, a life apart in which he has no share. He says quite naïvely—"Feeling rather high today, eh?" And you say yes almost shamefacedly.

"Look, Ulric," I said, bursting in on him in the midst of a Campbell's Soup design, "I've got to tell you something. I'm bursting with it."

"Sure, fire away," he said, dipping his water color brush in the big pot on the floor beside him. "You don't mind if I go on with this bloody thing, do you? I've got to finish it by tonight."

I pretended I didn't mind but I was disconcerted. I pitched my voice lower in order not to disturb him too much. "You remember the girl I was telling you about—the girl I met at the dance hall? Well, I met her again. We went to the beach together last night...."

"How was it . . . good going?"

I could see from the way he slid his tongue over his lips that he was priming himself for a good juicy yarn.

"Listen, Ulric, do you know what it is to be in love?"

He didn't even deign to look up in answer to this. As he deftly mixed his colors in the tin tray he mumbled something about having normal instincts.

I went on unabashed. "Do you think you might meet a woman someday who would change your whole life?"

"I've met one or two who've tried—not with entire success, as you can see," he responded.

"Shit! Drop that stuff a moment, will you? I want to tell you something . . . I want to tell you that I'm in love, madly in love. I know it sounds silly, but this is different—I've never been like this before. You want to know if she's a good piece of tail. Yes, she's magnificent. But I don't give a shit about that . . ."

"Oh, you don't? Well, that's something new."

"Do you know what I did today?"

"You went to the Houston Street Burlesk maybe."

"I went to the country. I was walking around like a madman. . . ."

"What do you mean—did she give you the gate already?"

"No. She told me she loved me. . . . I know, it sounds childish, doesn't it?"

"I wouldn't say that exactly. You might be temporarily deranged that's all. Everybody acts a bit queer when he falls in love. In your case it's apt to last longer. I wish I didn't have this damned job on my hands—I might listen more feelingly. You couldn't come back a little later, could you? Perhaps we could eat together, yes?"

"All right, I'll come back in an hour or so. Don't run out on me, you bastard, because I haven't a cent on me."

I blew down the stairs and headed for the park. I was all riled up. It was silly to get all steamed up before Ulric. Always cool as a cucumber, that guy. How can you make another person understand what is really happening inside you? If I were to break a leg he would drop everything. But if your heart is breaking with joy— well, it's a bit boring, don't you know. Tears are easier to put up with than joy. Joy is destructive: It makes others uncomfortable. Weep and you weep alone—what a lie that is! Weep and you will find a million crocodiles to weep with you. The world is forever weeping. The world is drenched in tears. Laughter, that's another thing. Laughter is momentary—it passes. But joy, joy is a kind of ecstatic bleeding, a disgraceful sort of super-contentment which overflows from every pore of your being. You can't make people joyous just by being joyous yourself. Joy has to be generated by oneself: it is or it isn't. Joy is founded on reasons too profound to be understood and communicated. To be joyous is to be a madman in a world of sad ghosts. . . .

Reflections of this order always excited me to the breaking point. Ten minutes of introspective reverie and I was bursting to write a book. I thought of Mona. If only for her sake I ought to begin. And where would I begin? In this room which was like the lobby of an insane asylum? Begin with Kronski looking over my shoulder?

Somewhere I had read recently about an abandoned city of Burma, the ancient capital of a region where in the compass of a hundred miles there once flourished eight thousand thriving temples. The whole area was now empty of inhabitants, had been so for a thousand years or more. Only a few lone priests, probably half-crazed, were now to be found among the empty temples. Serpents and bats and owls infested the sacred edifices; at night the jackals howled amidst the ruins.

Why should this picture of desolation cause me such painful depression? Why should eight thousand empty, ruined temples awaken such anguish? People die, races disappear, religions fade away: it is in the order of things and one accepts. But that something of beauty should remain and be powerless to affect, powerless to attract us, was an enigma which weighed me down. *For I had not even begun to build!* In my mind I saw my own temples in ruins, before even one brick had been laid upon another. In some freakish way I and the goofy messengers who were to aid me were prowling about the abandoned places of the spirit like the jackals which howled at night. We wandered amidst the halls of an ethereal edifice, a dream stupa, which would be abandoned before it could take earthly shape. In Burma the invader had been responsible for driving the spirit of man into the ground. It had happened over and over in the history of man and it was an explicable, if also a sad, happening. But what prevented us, the dreamers of this continent, from giving form and substance to our fabulous edifices? The race of visionary architects was as good as extinct. The genius of man had been canalized and directed into other channels. So it was said. I could not accept it. I have looked at the separate stones, the girders, the portals, the windows which even in buildings are like the eyes of the soul; I have looked at them as I have looked at separate pages of books and the lines which formed the pages of these books, and I have seen one architecture informing the lives of our people, be it in book, in law, in stone, in custom; I saw that it was created, seen first in the mind, then objectified, given light, air and space, given purpose and significance, given a rhythm which would rise and fall, a growth from seed to flourishing tree, a decline from shrivelled leaf and branch to seed again, and a compost to nourish the seed. I saw this continent as other continents before and after: creations in every sense of the word, including the very catastrophes which would make their existence forgotten.

After Kronski and Ghompal had retired I felt so wide awake, so stimulated by the thoughts which were racing through my head that I felt impelled to go for a long walk. As I was putting on my things I looked at myself in the mirror. I made that whistling grimace of Sheldon's and felicitated myself on my powers of mimicry. Once upon a time I had thought I might make a good clown. There was a chap in school who passed as my twin brother; we were very close to one another and later, when we had graduated, we formed a club of twelve which we called the Xerxes Society. We two possessed all the initiative—the others were just so much slag and driftwood. In desperation sometimes George Marshall and I would perform for the others, an impromptu clowning which kept them in stitches. Later I used to think of these moments as having quite a tragic quality; the dependency of the others was really pathetic. It was a foretaste of the general inertia and apathy which I was to encounter all through life. Thinking of George Marshall, I began to make more faces; I did it so well that I began to get a little frightened of myself. For suddenly I remembered the day when for the first time in my life I looked into the mirror and realized that I was gazing at a stranger. It was after I had been to the theatre with George Marshall and MacGregor. George Marshall had said something that night which disturbed me profoundly. I was angry with him for his stupidity, but I couldn't deny that he had put his finger on a sore spot. He had said something which made me realize that our twinship was over, that in fact we would become enemies henceforth. And he was right, though the reasons he had given were false. From that day forth I began to ridicule my bosom friend, George Marshall. I wanted to be the opposite of him in every way. It was like the splitting of a chromosome. George Marshall remained in the world, with it, of it, for it; he took root and grew like a tree, and there was no doubt but that he had found his place and with it a relatively full measure of happiness. But as I looked in the mirror that night, disowning my own image, I knew that what George Marshall had predicted about my future was only superficially correct. George Marshall had never really understood me; the moment he suspected I was *different* he had renounced me.

I was still looking at myself as these memories flitted through my head. My face had grown sad and thoughtful. I was no longer looking at my image but at the image of a memory of myself at another moment—when sitting on a stoop one night listening to a Hindu "boy" named Tawde. Tawde too had said something that night which had provoked in me a profound disturbance. But Tawde had said it as a friend. He was holding my hand, the way

Hindus do. A passer-by looking at us might have thought we were making love. Tawde was trying to make me see things in a different light. What baffled him was that I was "good at heart" and yet . . . I was creating sorrow all about me. Tawde wanted me to be true to myself, that self which he recognized and accepted as my "true" self. He seemed to have no awareness of the complexity of my nature, or if he did, he attached no importance to it. He couldn't understand why I should be dissatisfied with my position in life, particularly when I was doing so much good. That one could be thoroughly disgusted with being a mere instrument of good was unthinkable to him. He didn't realize that I was only a blind instrument, that I was merely obeying the law of inertia, and that I hated inertia even if it meant doing good.

I left Tawde that night in a state of despair. I loathed the thought of being surrounded by dumb clucks who would hold my hand and comfort me in order to keep me in chains. A sinister gayety came over me as I drew farther away from him; instead of going home I went instinctively to the furnished room where the waitress lived with whom I was carrying on a romantic affair. She came to the door in her night shift, begging me not to go upstairs with her because of the hour. We went inside, in the hallway, and leaned against the radiator to keep warm. In a few minutes I had it out and was giving it to her as best I could in that strained position. She was trembling with fear and pleasure. When it was over she reproached me for being inconsiderate. "Why do you do these things?" she whispered, snuggled close against me. I ran off, leaving her standing at the foot of the stairs with a bewildered expression. As I raced through the streets a phrase repeated itself over and over: "Which is the true self?"

It was this phrase which accompanied me now, racing through the morbid streets of the Bronx. Why was I racing? What was driving me on at this pace? I slowed down, as if to let the demon overtake me. . . .

If you persist in throttling your impulses you end by becoming a clot of phlegm. You finally spit out a gob which completely drains you and which you only realize years later was not a gob of spit but your inmost self. If you lose that you will always race through dark streets like a madman pursued by phantoms. You will always be able to say with perfect sincerity: "I don't know what I want to do in life." You can push yourself clean through the filament of life and come out at the wrong end of the telescope, seeing everything beyond you, out of grasp, and diabolically twisted. From then on the game's up. Whichever direction you take you will find yourself in a hall of mirrors; you will race like a madman, searching for an exit, to find that you are surrounded only by distorted images of your own sweet self.

What I disliked most in George Marshall, in Kronski, in Tawde and the incalculable hosts which they represented, was their surface seriousness. The truly serious person is gay, almost nonchalant. I despised people who, because they lacked their own proper ballast, took on the problems of the world. The man who is forever disturbed about the condition of humanity either has no problems of his own or has refused to face them. I am speaking of the great majority, not of the emancipated few who, having thought things through, are privileged to identify themselves with all humanity and thus enjoy that greatest of all luxuries: service.

There was another thing I heartily disbelieved in—work. Work, it seemed to me even at the threshold of life, is an activity reserved for the dullard. It is the very opposite of creation, which is play, and which just because it has no raison d'être other than itself is the supreme motivating power in life. Has any one ever said that God created the universe in order to provide work for Himself? By a chain of circumstances having nothing to do with reason or intelligence I had become like the others—a drudge. I had the comfortless excuse that by my labors I was supporting a wife and child. That it was a flimsy excuse I knew, because if I were to drop dead on the morrow they would go on living somehow or other. To stop everything, and play at being myself, why not? The part of me which was given up to work, which enabled my wife and child to live in the manner they unthinkingly demanded, this part of me which kept the wheel turning—a completely fatuous, ego-centric notion!—was the least part of me. I gave nothing to the world in fulfilling the function of bread-winner; the world exacted its tribute of me, that was all.

The world would only begin to get something of value from me the moment I stopped being a serious member of society and be-came—myself. The State, the nation, the united nations of the world, were nothing but one great aggregation of individuals who repeated the mistakes of their forefathers. They were caught in the wheel from birth and they kept at it till death—and this treadmill they tried to dignify by calling it "life." If you asked any one to explain or define life, what was the be all and the end all, you got a blank look for answer. Life was something which philosophers dealt with in books that no one read. Those in the thick of life, the plugs in harness, had no time for such idle questions. "You've got to eat, haven't you?" This query, which was supposed to be a stop-gap, and which had already been answered if not in the abso-lute negative at least in a disturbingly relative negative by those who knew, was a clue to all the other questions which followed in a veritable Euclidian suite. From the little reading I had done I had observed that the men who were most *in* life, who were moulding life, who were life itself, ate little, slept little, owned little or noth-ing. They had no illusions about duty, or the perpetuation of their kith and kin, or the preservation of the State. They were interested in truth and truth alone. They recognized only one kind of activity —*creation*. Nobody could command their services because they had of their own accord pledged themselves to give all. They gave gratuitously, because that is the only way to give. This was the way of life which appealed to me: it made sound sense. It *was* life—not the simulacrum which those about me worshipped.

I had understood all this—with my mind—at the very brink of manhood. But there was a great comedy of life to be gone through before this vision of reality could become anything like a dire necessity. The tremendous hunger for life which others sensed in me acted like a magnet; it attracted those who needed my particular kind of hunger. The hunger was magnified a thousand times. It was as if those who clung to me like iron filings, becoming themselves sensitized, attracted others in turn. Sensation ripened into experience and experience engendered experience.

What I secretly longed for was to disentangle myself of all those lives which had woven themselves into the pattern of my own life and were making my destiny a part of theirs. To shake myself free of these accumulating experiences which were mine only by force of inertia required a violent effort. Now and then I lunged and tore at the net, but only to become more enmeshed. My liberation seemed to involve pain and suffering, perhaps destruction, for those whom my powers of attraction had caused to identify their lives with my own. Every move I made for my own private good brought about reproach and condemnation. I was a traitor a thousand times over. I had lost even the right to become ill—because "they" needed me. I wasn't *allowed* to remain inactive. Had I died I think they would have galvanized my corpse into a semblance of life. *The dance of life!* Quite a ghoulish affair, looking at it from a wholly selfish, personal standpoint.

"I stood before a mirror and said fearfully: 'I want to see how I look in the mirror with my eyes closed.' "

These words of Richter's, when I first came upon them, made an indescribable commotion in me. As did the following, which seems almost like a corollary of the above—from Novalis:

"The seat of the soul is where inner world and outer world touch each other. For nobody knows himself, if he is only himself and not also another one at the same time."

"To take possession of one's transcendental I, to be the I of one's I, at the same time," as Novalis expressed it again.

There is a time when ideas tyrannize over one, when one is just a hapless victim of another's thoughts. This "possession" by another seems to occur in periods of depersonalization, when the warring selves come unglued, as it were. Normally one is impervious to ideas; they come and go, are accepted or rejected, put on like shirts, taken off like dirty socks. But in those periods which we call crises, when the mind sunders and splinters like a diamond under the blows of a sledge-hammer, those innocent ideas of a dreamer take hold, lodge in the crevices of the brain, and by some subtle process of infiltration bring about a definite, irrevocable alteration of the personality. Outwardly no great change takes place; the individual affected does not suddenly behave differently; on the contrary, he may behave in more "normal" fashion than before. This seeming normality assumes more and more the quality of a protective device. From surface deception he passes to inner deception. With each new crisis, however, he becomes more strongly aware of a change which is no change, but rather an intensification of something hidden deep within. Now when he closes his eyes he can really look at himself. He no longer sees a mask. He sees without seeing, to be exact. Vision without sight, a fluid grasp of intangibles: the merging of sight and sound: the heart of the web.

Here stream the distant personalities which evade the crude contact of the senses; here the overtones of recognition discreetly lap against one another in bright, vibrant harmonies. There is no language employed, no outlines delineated.

When the ship founders it settles slowly; the spars, the masts, the rigging float away. On the ocean floor of death the bleeding hull bedecks itself with jewels; remorselessly the atomic life begins. What was ship becomes the nameless indestructible.

Like ships, men founder time and again. Only memory saves them from complete dispersion. Poets drop their stitches in the loom, straws for drowning men to grasp as they sink into extinction. Ghosts climb back on watery stairs, make imaginary ascents, vertiginous drops, memorize numbers, dates, events in passing from gas to liquid and back again. There is no brain capable of registering the changing changes. Nothing happens in the brain, except the gradual rust and detrition of the cells. But in the mind worlds unclassified, undenominated, unassimilated, form, break, unite, dissolve and harmonize ceaselessly. In the mind-world ideas are the indestructible elements which form the jewelled constellations of the interior life. We move within their orbits, freely if we follow their intricate patterns, enslaved or possessed if we try to subjugate them. Everything external is but a reflection projected by the mind machine.

Creation is the eternal play which takes place at the border-line; it is spontaneous and compulsive, obedient to law. One remove from the mirror and the curtain rises. *Séance permanente.* Only madmen are excluded. Only those who "have lost their mind", as we say. For these never cease to dream that they are dreaming. They stood before the mirror with eyes open and fell sound asleep; they sealed their shadow in the tomb of memory. In them the stars collapse to form what Hugo called "a blinding menagerie of suns which, through love, make themselves the poodles and the New-foundlands of immensity".

The creative life! Ascension. Passing beyond oneself. Rocketing out into the blue, grasping at flying ladders, mounting, soaring, lifting the world up by the scalp, rousing the angels from their ethereal lairs, drowning in stellar depths, clinging to the tails of comets. Nietzsche had written of it ecstatically—and then swooned forward into the mirror to die in root and flower. "Stairs and contradictory stairs", he wrote, and then suddenly there was no longer any bottom; the mind, like a splintered diamond, was pulverized by the hammer-blows of truth.

There was a time when I acted as my father's keeper. I was left alone for long hours, cooped up in the little booth which was used as an office. While he was drinking with his cronies I was feeding from the bottle of creative life. My companions were the free spirits, the overlords of the soul. The young man sitting there in the dingy yellow light was completely unhinged; he lived in the crevices of great thoughts, crouched like a hermit in the barren folds of a lofty mountain range. From truth he passed to imagination and from imagination to invention. At this last portal, through which there is no return, fear beset him. To venture farther was to wander alone, to rely wholly upon oneself. The purpose of discipline is to promote freedom. But freedom leads to infinity and infinity is terrifying. Then arose the comforting thought of stopping at the brink, of setting down in words the mysteries of impulsion, compulsion, propulsion, of bathing the senses in human odors. To become utterly human, the compassionate fiend incarnate, the locksmith of the great door leading beyond and away and forever isolate.

Men founder like ships. Children also. There are children who settle to the bottom at the age of nine, carrying with them the secret of their betrayal. There are perfidious monsters who look at you with the bland, innocent eyes of youth; their crimes are unregistered, because we have no names for them. Why do lovely faces haunt us so? Do extraordinary flowers have evil roots?

Studying her morsel by morsel, feet, hands, hair, lips, ears, breasts, travelling from navel to mouth and from mouth to eyes, the woman I fell upon, clawed, bit, suffocated with kisses, the woman who had been Mara and was now Mona, who had been and would be other names, other persons, other assemblages of appendages, was no more accessible, penetrable, than a cool statue in a forgotten garden of a lost continent. At nine or earlier, with a revolver that was never intended to go off, she might have pressed a swooning trigger and fallen like a dead swan from the heights of her dream. It might well have been that way, for in the flesh she was dispersed, in the mind she was as dust blown hither and thither. In her heart a bell tolled, but what it signified no one knew. Her image corresponded to nothing that I had formed in my heart. She had intruded it, slipped it like thinnest gauze between the crevices of the brain in a moment of lesion. And when the wound closed the imprint had remained, like a frail leaf traced upon a stone.

Haunting nights when filled with creation I saw nothing but her eyes and in those eyes, rising like bubbling pools of lava, phantoms came to the surface, faded, vanished, reappeared, bringing dread, apprehension, fear, mystery. A being constantly pursued, a hidden flower whose scent the blood-hounds never picked up. Behind the phantoms, peering through the jungle brush, stood a shrinking child who seemed to offer herself lasciviously. Then the swan dive, slow, as in motion pictures, and snow-flakes falling with the falling body, and then phantoms and more phantoms, the eyes becoming eyes again, burning like lignite, then glowing like embers, then soft like flowers, and then the nose, mouth, cheeks, ears looming out of chaos, heavy as the moon, a mask unrolling and flesh taking form, face, feature.

Night after night, from words to dreams to flesh to phantoms. Possession and depossession. The flowers of the moon, the broad-backed palms of jungle growth, the baying of blood-hounds, the frail white body of a child, the lava bubbles, the rallitando of the snow-flakes, the floorless bottom where smoke blooms into flesh. And what is flesh but moon? And what is moon but night? Night is longing, longing beyond all endurance.

"Think of us!" she said that night when she turned and flew up the steps rapidly. And it was as if I could think of nothing else. We two and the stairs ascending infinitely. Then "contradictory stairs": the stairs in my father's office, the stairs leading to crime, to madness, to the portals of invention. How *could* I think of anything else?

Creation. To create the legend in which I could fit the key which would open her soul.

A woman trying to deliver her secret. A desperate woman, seeking through love to unite herself with herself. Before the immensity of mystery one stands like a centipede that feels the ground slipping beneath its feet. Every door that opens leads to a greater void. One must swim like a star in the trackless ocean of time. One must have the patience of radium buried beneath a Himalayan peak.

It is about twenty years now since I began the study of the photogenic soul; in that time I have conducted hundreds of experiments. The result is that I know a little more—about myself. I think it must be very much the same with the political leader or the military genius. One discovers nothing about the secrets of the universe; at the best one learns something about the nature of destiny.

In the beginning one wants to approach every problem directly. The more direct and insistent the approach, the more quickly and surely one succeeds in getting caught in the web. No one is more helpless than the heroic individual. And no one can produce more tragedy and confusion than such a type. Flashing his sword above the Gordian knot, he promises speedy deliverance. A delusion which ends in an ocean of blood.

The creative artist has something in common with the hero. Though functioning on another plane, he too believes that he has solutions to offer. He gives his life to accomplish imaginary triumphs. At the conclusion of every grand experiment, whether by the statesman, the warrior, the poet or the philosopher, the problems of life present the same enigmatic complexion. The happiest peoples, it is said, are those which have no history. Those which have a history, those which have made history, seem only to have emphasized through their accomplishments the eternality of struggle. These disappear too, eventually, just as those who made no effort, who were content merely to live and to enjoy.

The creative individual, in wrestling with his medium, is supposed to experience a joy which balances, if it does not outweigh, the pain and anguish which accompany the struggle to express himself. He lives in his work, we say. But this unique kind of life varies extremely with the individual. It is only in the measure that he is aware of more life, the life abundant, that he may be said to live in his work. If there is no realization there is no purpose or advantage in substituting the imaginative life for the purely adventurous one of reality. Everyone who lifts himself above the activities of the daily round does so not only in the hope of enlarging his field of experience, or even of enriching it, but of quickening it. Only in this sense does struggle have any meaning. Accept this view, and the distinction between failure and success is nil. And this is what every great artist comes to learn en route—that the process in which he is involved has to do with another dimension of life, that by identifying himself with this process he *augments* life. In this view of things he is permanently removed—and protected—from that insidious death which seems to triumph all about him. He divines that the great secret will never be apprehended but incorporated in his very substance. He has to make himself a part of the mystery, live *in* it as well as with it. Acceptance is the solution: it is an art, not an egotistical performance on the part of the intellect. Through art then one finally establishes contact with reality: that is the great discovery. Here all is play and invention; there is no solid foothold from which to launch the projectiles which will pierce the miasma of folly, ignorance and greed. The world has *not* to be put in order: the world *is* order incarnate. It is for us to put ourselves in unison with this order, to know what is the world order in contradistinction to the wishful-thinking orders which we seek to impose on one another. The power which we long to possess, in order to establish the good, the true and the beautiful, would prove to be, if we could have it, but the means of destroying one another. It is fortunate that we are powerless. We have first to acquire vision, then discipline and forbearance. Until we have the humility to acknowledge the existence of a vision beyond our own, until we have faith and trust in superior powers, the blind must lead the blind. The men who believe that work and brains will accomplish everything must ever be deceived by the quixotic and unforeseen turn of events. They are the ones who are perpetually disappointed; no longer able to blame the gods, or God, they turn on their fellowmen and vent their impotent rage by crying "Treason! Stupidity!" and other hollow terms.

The great joy of the artist is to become aware of a higher order of things, to recognize by the compulsive and spontaneous manipulation of his own impulses the resemblance between human creations and what is called "divine" creations. In works of fantasy the existence of law manifesting itself through order is even more apparent than in other works of art. Nothing is less mad, less chaotic, than a work of fantasy. Such a creation, which is nothing less than pure invention, pervades all levels, creating, like water, its own level. The endless interpretations which are offered up contribute nothing, except to heighten the significance of what is seemingly unintelligible. This unintelligibility somehow makes profound sense. Everyone is affected, including those who pretend not to be affected. Something is present, in works of fantasy, which can only be likened to an elixir. This mysterious element, often referred to as "pure nonsense", brings with it the flavor and the aroma of that larger and utterly impenetrable world in which we and all the heavenly bodies of which our earth is but a microcosmic speck have their being. The term nonsense is one of the most baffling words in our vocabulary. It has a negative quality only, like death. Nobody can explain nonsense: it can only be demonstrated. To add, moreover, that sense and nonsense are interchangeable is only to labor the point. Nonsense belongs to other worlds, other dimensions, and the gesture with which we put it from us at times, the finality with which we dismiss it, testifies to its disturbing nature. Whatever we cannot include within our narrow framework of comprehension we reject. Thus profundity and nonsense may be seen to have certain unsuspected affinities.

Why did I not launch into sheer nonsense immediately? Because, like others, I was afraid of it. And deeper than that was the fact that, far from situating myself in a beyond, I was caught in the very heart of the web. I had survived my own destructive school of Dadaism: I had progressed, if that is the word, from scholar to critic to pole-axer. My literary experiments lay in ruins, like the cities of old which were sacked by the vandals. I wanted to build, but the materials were unreliable and the plans had not even become blue-prints. If the substance of art is the human soul, then I must confess that with dead souls I could visualize nothing germinating under my hand.

To be caught in a glut of dramatic episodes, to be ceaselessly participating, means among other things that one is unaware of the outlines of that bigger drama of which human activity is but a small part. The act of writing puts a stop to one kind of activity in order to release another. When a monk, prayerfully meditating, walks slowly and silently down the hall of a temple, and thus walking sets in motion one prayer-wheel after another, he gives a living illustration of the act of sitting down to write. The mind of the writer, no longer preoccupied with observing and knowing, wanders meditatively amidst a world of forms which are set spinning by a mere brush of his wings. No tyrant, this, wreaking his will upon the subjugated minions of his ill-gotten kingdom. An explorer, rather, calling to life the slumbering entities of his dream. The act of dreaming, like a draught of fresh air in an abandoned house, situates the furniture of the mind in a new ambiance. The chairs and tables collaborate; an effluvia is given off, a game is begun.

To ask the purpose of this game, how it is related to life, is idle. As well ask the Creator, why volcanoes? why hurricanes? since obviously they contribute nothing but disaster. But, since disasters are disastrous only for those who are engulfed in them, whereas they can be illuminating for those who survive and study them, so it is in the creative world. The dreamer who returns from his voyage, if he is not shipwrecked en route, may and usually does convert the collapse of his tenuous fabric into other stuff. For a child the pricking of a bubble may offer nothing but astonishment and delight. The student of illusions and mirages may react differently. A scientist may bring to a bubble the emotional wealth of a world of experience. The same phenomenon which causes the child to scream with delight may give birth, in the mind of an earnest experimenter, to a dazzling vision of truth. In the artist these contrasting reactions seem to combine or merge, producing that ultimate one, the great catalyzer called *realization*. Seeing, knowing, discovering, enjoying—these faculties or powers are pale and lifeless without realization. The artist's game is to move over into reality. It is to see beyond the mere "disaster" which the picture of a lost battlefield renders to the naked eye. For, since the beginning of time the picture which the world has presented to the naked human eye can hardly seem anything but a hideous battle-ground of lost causes. It has been so and will be so until man ceases to regard himself as the mere seat of conflict. Until he takes up the task of becoming the "I of his I".

OF ART AND THE FUTURE*

To MOST men the past is never yesterday, or five minutes ago, but distant, misty epochs some of which are glorious and others abominable. Each one reconstructs the past according to his temperament and experience. We read history to corroborate our own views, not to learn what scholars think to be true. About the future there is as little agreement as about the past, I've noticed. We stand in relation to the past very much like the cow in the meadow —endlessly chewing the cud. It is not something finished and done with, as we sometimes fondly imagine, but something alive, con-

* Written expressly for Cyril Connolly.

stantly changing, and perpetually with us. But the future too is with us perpetually, and alive and constantly changing. The difference between the two, a thoroughly fictive one, incidentally, is that the future we create whereas the past can only be recreated. As for that constantly vanishing point called the present, that fulcrum which melts simultaneously into past and future, only those who deal with the eternal know and live in it, acknowledging it to be all.

At this moment, when almost the entire world is engaged in war, the plight of a few artists—for we never have more than a handful, it seems—appears to be a matter of the utmost unimportance. At the outbreak of the war art was by universal agreement at a perilously low ebb. So was life, one might say. The artist, always in advance of his time, could register nothing but death and destruction. The normal ones, i.e., the unfeeling, unthinking ones, regarded the art products of their time as morbid, perverse and meaningless. Just because the political picture was so black they demanded of their hirelings that they paint something bright and pleasing. Now all are bogged down, those who saw and those who did not, and what the future contains is dependent on that very creative quality which unfortunately seems vital only in times of destruction. Now every one is exhorted to be creative—with gun in hand.

To every man fighting to bring the war to a victorious end the result of the conflict calls up a different picture. To resume life where one left off is undoubtedly the deepest wish of those now participating in the holocaust. It is here that the greatest disillusionment will occur. To think of it descriptively we have to think of a man jumping off a precipice, escaping miraculously from certain death and then, as he starts to climb back, suddenly discovering that the whole mountain side has collapsed. The world we knew before September 1939 is collapsing hour by hour. It had

147

been collapsing long before that, but we were not so aware of it, most of us. Paris, Berlin, Prague, Amsterdam, Rome, London, New York—they may still be standing when peace is declared, but it will be as though they did not exist. The cultural world in which we swam, not very gracefully, to be sure, is fast disappearing. The cultural era of Europe, and that includes America, is finished. The next era belongs to the technician; the day of the mind machine is dawning. God pity us!

Taking a rough, uncritical view of history we realize at a glance that in every stage of civilization the condition of the common man has been anything but a civilized one. He has lived like a rat —through good epochs and bad ones. History was never written for the common man but for those in power. The history of the world is the history of a privileged few. Even in its grandeur it stinks.

We are not suddenly going to turn a new page with the cessation of this fratricidal war. Another wretched peace will be made, never fear, and there will be another breathing spell of ten or twenty years and then we shall go to war again. And the next war will also be regarded as a just and holy war, as is this one now. But whatever the reason for or nature of the coming war, it will no more resemble this one than this one resembles the previous one which, significantly enough, we speak of as "World War No. 1." In the future we shall have only "world wars"—that much is already clear.

With total wars a new element creeps into the picture. From now on every one is involved, without exception. What Napoleon began with the sword, and Balzac boasted he would finish with the pen, is actually going to be carried through by the collaboration of the whole wide world, including the primitive races whom we study and exploit shamelessly and ruthlessly. As war spreads wider and wider so will peace sink deeper and deeper into the hearts of men. If we must fight more whole-heartedly we shall also be obliged to live more whole-heartedly. If the new kind of warfare demands that everybody and everything under the sun be taken cognizance of, so will the new kind of peace. Not to be able to be of service will be unthinkable. It will constitute the highest treason, probably punishable by death. Or perhaps a more ignominious end awaits the unfit and unserviceable: in lieu of becoming cannon fodder they may become just fodder.

The first world war ushered in the idea of a league of nations, an international court of arbitration. It failed because there was no real solidarity among the so-called nations, most of them being only cats' paws. This war will bring about the realization that the nations of the earth are made up of individuals, not masses. The common man will be the new factor in the world-wide collective mania which will sweep the earth.

The date most commonly agreed upon (by professional prophets) for the end of this war is the Fall of 1947. But by 1944 it is quite possible that the war will assume its true aspect, that of world-wide revolution. It will get out of the control of those now leading "the masses" to slaughter. The masses will slaughter in their own fashion for a while. The collapse of Germany and Italy will precipitate the débâcle, thereby creating a rift between the British and American peoples, for England (her men of power) is still more fearful of a Russian victory than of a German defeat. France has still to play her true role. Fired by the success of the Soviets, she will overleap all bounds, and, just as in the French Revolution, amaze the world by her spirit and vitality. There will be more blood shed in France than in any other part of Europe, before a quietus is established.

An era of chaos and confusion, beginning in 1944, will continue until almost 1960. All boundaries will be broken down, class lines obliterated, and money become worthless. It will be a caricature of the Marxian Utopia. The world will be enthralled by the ever-unfolding prospects seeming to offer nothing but good. Then suddenly it will be like the end of a debauch. A protracted state of *Katzenjammer* will set in. Then commences the real work of consolidation, when Europe gets set to meet the Asiatic invasion, due about the turn of the century. For, with the culmination of this war, China and India will play a most prominent and important part in world affairs. We have roused them from their lethargy and we shall pay for having awakened them. The East and the West *will* meet one day—in a series of death-like embraces.* After that the barriers between peoples and races will break down and the melting-pot (which America only pretends to be) will become an actuality. Then, and only then, will the embryonic man of the new order appear, the man who has no feeling of class, caste, color or country, the man who has no need of possessions, no use for money, no archaic prejudices about the sanctity of the home or of marriage with its accompanying tread-mill of divorce. A totally new conception of individuality will be born, one in which the collective life is the dominant note. In short, for the first time since the dawn of history, men will serve one another, first out of an enlightened self-interest, and finally out of a greater conception of love.

The distinctive feature of this "epoch of the threshold", so to speak, will be its visionary-realistic quality. It will be an era of realization, accomplishment and vision. It will create deeper, more insoluble problems than ever existed before. Immense horizons will open up, dazzling and frightening ones. The ensuing conflicts

* The present strife with Japan is more a clash of rivals than of genuine antagonists. But it serves to damage irreparably our unwarranted prestige in the East.

will assume more and more the character of clashes between wizards, making our wars appear puny and trifling by comparison. The white and the black forces will come out in the open. Antagonisms will be conscious and deliberate, engaged in joyously and triumphantly, and to the bitter end. The schisms will occur not between blocs of nations or peoples but between two divergent elements, both clear-cut and highly aware of their goals, and the line between them will be as wavering as the flow of the zodiacal signs about the ecliptic. The problem for the next few thousand years will be one of power, power in the abstract and ultimate. Men will be drunk with power, having unlocked the forces of the earth in ways now only dimly apprehended. The consolidation of the new individuality, rooted in the collective (man no longer worshipping the Father but acknowledging sources of power greater than the Sun) will dissolve the haunting problem of power. A dynamic equilibrium, based upon the recognition of a new creative center, will establish itself, permitting the free play of all the fluid, potent forces locked within the human corpus. Then it may be possible to look forward to the dawn of what has already been described as "The Age of Plentitude".*

Before the present conflict is terminated it is altogether likely that we shall see unleashed the deadly secret weapon so often hinted at on all sides. At the very beginning of the war I described (in an unpublished book on America) the ironic possibilities which the discovery and use of a deadly "human flit" would entail. The ambivalent attitude of dread and ridicule which this idea generally elicits is significant. It means that the inconceivable and unconscionable has already become a dire possibility. That the men of science will be coerced into yielding up the secret now in their possession I have no doubt. If the Japanese can unblushingly carry

* Title of Dane Rudhyar's new and as yet unpublished book.

on their program of systematically doping their victims it is not at all unthinkable that we on our side will come forth with an even more effective, certainly a more drastic and immediate, weapon of destruction. All the rules of warfare which have hitherto obtained are destined to be smashed and relegated to the scrap-heap. This is merely a corollary to the dissolution of the Hague Tribunal, the Maginot Line and all our fond conceptions of peace, justice and security. It is not that we have become more brutal and cynical, more ruthless and immoral—it is that ever since the last war we are consciously or unconsciously (probably both) making war upon war. The present methods of making war are too ineffectual, too protracted, too costly in every sense. All that impedes us thus far is the lack of imaginative leaders. The common people are far more logical, ruthless and totalitarian in spirit than the military and political cliques. Hitler, for all that has been said against him, is hardly the brilliant imaginative demon we credit him with being. He merely served to unleash the dark forces which we tried to pretend did not exist. With Hitler Pluto came out into the open. In England and America we have far more realistic, far more ruthless, types. All that deters them is fear of consequences: they are obsessed by the image of the boomerang. It is their habit to act obliquely, shamefacedly, with guilty consciences. But this conscience is now being broken down, giving way to something vastly different, to what it was originally, what the Greeks called *syneidesis*. Once a deep vision of the future opens up these types will proceed with the directness and remorselessness of monomaniacs.

The problem of power, what to do with it, how to use it, who shall wield it or not wield it, will assume proportions heretofore unthinkable. We are moving into the realm of incalculables and imponderables in our every-day life just as for the last few generations we have been accustoming ourselves to this realm through the play of thought. Everything is coming to fruition, and the harvest will be brilliant and terrifying. To those who look upon such predictions as fantastic I have merely to point out, ask them to imagine, what would happen should we ever unlock the secret patents now hidden in the vaults of our unscrupulous exploiters. Once the present crazy system of exploitation crumbles, and it is crumbling hourly, the powers of the imagination, heretofore stifled and fettered, will run riot. The face of the earth can be changed utterly overnight once we have the courage to concretize the dreams of our inventive geniuses. Never was there such a plenitude of inventors as in this age of destruction. And there is one thing to bear in mind about the man of genius—even the inventor—usually he is on the side of humanity, not the devil. It has been the crowning shame of this age to have exploited the man of genius for sinister ends. But such a procedure always acts as a boomerang: ultimately the man of genius always has his revenge.

Within the next fifteen years, when the grand clean-up goes into effect, the man of genius will do more to liberate the fettered sleeping giants than was ever done in the whole history of man. There will be strange new offices, strange new powers, strange new rules. It will seem for a while as though everything were topsy-turvy, and so it will be, regarded from to-day's vantage point. What is now at the bottom will come to the top, and vice versa. The world has literally been standing on its head for thousands of years. So great has been the pressure from above that a hole has been bored through the very stuff of consciousness. Into the empty vessel of life the waters are now pouring. The predatory few, who sought to arrange life in their own vulpine terms, will be the first to be drowned. "The few", I say, but in all truth they are legion. The floods of destruction sweep high and low; we are all part and parcel of the same mould; we have all been abetting the crime of man against man. The type of man we represent will be drowned out utterly. A new type will arise, out of the dregs of the old. That is why the stirring of sleepy Asia is fraught with such fateful consequences for the man of Europe, or shall I say, the man of the Western world. All this muck, these lees and dregs of humanity, the coolies and Untouchables, will have to be absorbed in our blood-stream. The clash of East and West will be like a marriage of the waters; when the new dry land eventually appears the old and the new will be indistinguishable.

The human fundament is in the East. We have talked breathlessly about equality and democracy without ever facing the reality of it. We shall have to take these despised and neglected ones to our bosom, melt into them, absorb their anguish and misery. We cannot have a real brotherhood so long as we cherish the illusion of racial superiority, so long as we fear the touch of yellow, brown, black or red skins. We in America will have to begin by embracing the Negro, the Indian, the Mexican, the Filipino, all those Untouchables whom we so blithely dismiss from our consciousness by pointing to our Bills of Rights. We have not even begun to put the Emancipation Proclamation into effect. The same is true of course for England, for imperialist Holland, and colonial France. Russia took the first genuine steps in this direction, and Russia, nobody will dispute, has certainly not been weakened by carrying out her resolution to the letter.

And now, what about Art? What is the place and the future of art in all this turmoil? Well, in the first place, it seems to me that what we have hitherto known as art will be non-existent. Oh yes, we will continue to have novels and paintings and symphonies and statues, we will even have verse, no doubt about it. But all this will be as a hangover from other days, a continuation of a bad dream which ends only with a full awakening. The cultural era is past.

The new civilization, which may take centuries or a few thousand years to usher in, will not be *another* civilization—it will be the open stretch of realization which all the past civilizations have pointed to. The city, which was the birth-place of civilization, such as we know it to be, will exist no more. There will be nuclei of course, but they will be mobile and fluid. The peoples of the earth will no longer be shut off from one another within states but will flow freely over the surface of the earth and intermingle. There will be no fixed constellations of human aggregates. Governments will give way to management, using the word in a broad sense. The politician will become as superannuated as the dodo bird. The machine will never be dominated, as some imagine; it will be scrapped, eventually, but not before men have understood the nature of the mystery which binds them to their creation. The worship, investigation and subjugation of the machine will give way to the lure of all that is truly occult. This problem is bound up with the larger one of power—and of possession. Man will be forced to realize that power must be kept open, fluid and free. His aim will be not to possess power but to radiate it.

At the root of the art instinct is this desire for power—vicarious power. The artist is situated hierarchically between the hero and the saint. These three types rule the world, and it is difficult to say which wields the greatest power. But none of them are what might be called adepts. The adept is the power behind the powers, so to speak. He remains anonymous, the secret force from which the suns derive their power and glory.

To put it quite simply, art is only a stepping-stone to reality; it is the vestibule in which we undergo the rites of initiation. Man's task is to make of himself a work of art. The creations which man makes manifest have no validity in themselves; they serve to awaken, that is all. And that, of course, is a great deal. But it is not the all. Once awakened, everything will reveal itself to man as creation. Once the blinders have been removed and the fetters unshackled, man will have no need to recreate through the elect cult of genius. Genius will be the norm.

Throughout history the artist has been the martyr, immolating himself in his work. The very phrase, "a work of art", gives off a perfume of sweat and agony. Divine creation, on the other hand, bears no such connotation. We do not think of sweat and tears in connection with the creation of the universe; we think of joy and light, and above all of play. The agony of a Christ on Calvary, on the other hand, illustrates superbly the ordeal which even a Master must undergo in the creation of a perfect life.

In a few hundred years or less books will be a thing of the past. There was a time when poets communicated with the world without the medium of print; the time will come when they will communicate silently, not as poets merely, but as seers. What we have overlooked, in our frenzy to invent more dazzling ways and means of communication, is to communicate. The artist lumbers along with crude implements. He is only a notch above his predecessor, the cave man. Even the film art, requiring the services of veritable armies of technicians, is only giving us shadow plays, old almost as man himself.

No, the advance will not come through the aid of subtler mechanical devices, nor will it come through the spread of education. The advance will come in the form of a break through. New forms of communication will be established. New forms presuppose new desires. The great desire of the world to-day is to break the bonds which lock us in. It is not yet a conscious desire. Men do not yet realize what they are fighting for. This is the beginning of a long fight, a fight from within outwards. It may be that the present war will be fought entirely in the dark. It may be that the revolution ensuing will envelop us in even greater darkness. But even in the blackest night it will be a joy and a boon to know that we are touching hands around the world. That has never happened before. We can touch and speak and pray in utter darkness. And we can wait for the dawn—no matter how long—provided we all wait together.

The years immediately ahead of us will be a false dawn, that is my belief. We cannot demolish our educational, legal and economic pediments overnight, nor even our phony religious superstructures. Until these are completely overthrown there is not much hope of a new order. From birth we live in a web of chaos in which all is illusion and delusion. The leaders who now and then arise, by what miracle no one knows, these leaders who come forward expressly to lead us out of the wilderness, are nearly always crucified. This happens on both sides of the fence, not just in the domain of Axis tyrants. It can happen in Soviet Russia too, as we know. And it happens in a less spectacular but all the more poisonous, insidious way in the United States, "home of the brave and land of the free." It is idle to blame individuals, or even classes of society. Given the educational, legal, economic and religious background of the cultural nations of this day, the results are inevitable. The savagery of a Céline is like the prattle of a child to those who can look into the heart of things with naked eye. Often, when I listen to the radio, to a speech by one of our politicians, to a sermon by one of our religious maniacs, to a discourse by one of our eminent scholars, to an appeal by one of our men of good will, to the propaganda dinned into us night and day by the advertising fiends, I wonder what the men of the coming century would think could they listen in for just one evening.

I do not believe that this repetitious cycle of insanity which is called history will continue forever. I believe there will be a great break through—within the next few centuries. I think that what we are heralding as the Age of Technic will be nothing more than a transition period, as was the Renaissance. We will need, to be sure, all our technical knowledge and skill to settle once and for all the problem of securing to every man, woman and child the fundamental necessities. We will make a drastic revision, it also goes without saying, of our notion of necessities, which is an altogether crude and primitive one. With the concomitant emancipation of woman, entailed by this great change, the awakening of the love instinct will transform every domain of life. The era of neuters is drawing to a close. With the establishment of a new and vital polarity we shall witness the birth of male-and-female in every individual. What then portends in the realm of art is truly unthinkable. Our art has been masculine through and through, that is to say, lop-sided. It has been vitiated by the unacknowledged feminine principle. This is as true of ancient as of modern art. The tyrannical, subterranean power of the female must come to an end. Men have paid a heavy tribute for their seeming subjugation of the female.

If we dare to imagine a solution of these seemingly fixed problems, dare to imagine an end of perhaps ten thousand years of pseudo-civilization, dare to imagine a change as radical as from the Stone Age to the Age of Electricity, let us say, for in the future we will not advance slowly step by step as in the past but with the rush of the whirlwind, then who can say what forms of expression art will assume? Myself I cannot see the persistence of the artist type. I see no need for the individual man of genius in such an order. I see no need for martyrs. I see no need for vicarious atonement. I see no need for the fierce preservation of beauty on the part of a few. Beauty and Truth do not need defenders, nor even expounders. No one will ever have a lien on Beauty or Truth; they are creations in which all participate. They need only to be apprehended; they exist eternally. Certainly, when we think of the conflicts and schisms which occur in the realm of art, we know that they do not proceed out of love of Beauty or Truth. Ego worship is the one and only cause of dissension, in art as in other realms. The artist is never defending art, but simply his own petty conception of art. Art is as deep and high and wide as the universe. There is nothing but art, if you look at it properly. It is almost banal to say so yet it needs to be stressed continually: all is creation, all is change, all is flux, all is metamorphosis. But how many deeply and sincerely believe that? Are we not devotees of the static? Are we not always on the defensive? Are we not always trying to circumscribe, erect barriers, set up tabus? Are we not always preparing for war? Are we not always in the grip of "fear and trembling"? Are we not always sanctifying, idolizing, martyrizing, proselytizing? What a pitiful, ignominious spiritual shambles, these last ten thousand years! *Civilized*, we say. What a horrible word! What bedeviled idiocy skulks behind that arrogant mark! Oh, I am not thinking of this war, nor of the last one, nor of any or all the wars men have waged in the name of *Civilization*. I am thinking of the periods in between, the rotten, stagnant eras of peace, the lapses and relapses, the lizard-like sloth, the creepy mole-like burrowing in, the fungus growths, the barnacles, the stink-weeds; I am thinking of the constant fanatical dervish dance that goes on in the name of all that is unreal, unholy and unattainable, thinking of the sadistic-masochistic tug of war, now one getting the upper hand, now the other. In the name of humanity when will we cry *Enough!*

There are limits to everything, and so I believe there is a limit to human stupidity and cruelty. But we are not yet there. We have not yet drained the bitter cup. Perhaps only when we have become full-fledged monsters will we recognize the angel in man. Then, when the ambivalence is clear, may we look forward with confidence to the emergence of a new type of man, a man as different from the man of to-day as we are from the *pithecanthropus erectus*. Nor is this too much to hope for, even at this remote distance. There have been precursors. Men have walked this earth who, for all they resemble us, may well have come from another planet. They have appeared singly and far apart. But to-morrow they may come in clusters, and the day after in hordes. The birth of Man follows closely the birth of the heavens. A new star never makes its appearance alone. With the birth of a new type of man a current is set in motion which later enables us to perceive that he was merely the foam on the crest of a mighty wave.

I have a strange feeling that the next great impersonation of the future will be a woman. If it is a greater reality we are veering towards then it must be woman who points the way. The masculine hegemony is over. Men have lost touch with the earth; they are clinging to the window-panes of their unreal superstructures like blind bats lashed by the storms of oceanic depths. Their world of abstractions spells babble.

When men are at last united in darkness woman will once again illumine the way—by revealing the beauties and mysteries which enfold us. We have tried to hide from our sight the womb of night, and now we are engulfed in it. We have pretended to be single when we were dual, and now we are frustrate and impotent. We shall come forth from the womb united, or not at all. Come forth not in brotherhood, but in brotherhood and sisterhood, as man and wife, as male and female. Failing, we shall perish and rot in the bowels of the earth, and time pass us by ceaselessly and remorselessly.

ANOTHER FRAGMENT FROM
"THE ROSY CRUCIFIXION"

WHY IS IT that all is so quiet? The black floral pieces are dripping with condensed milk. A man named Silverberg is chewing the lips of a mare. Another called Vittorio is mounting a ewe. A woman without name is shelling peanuts and stuffing them between her legs.

And at this same hour, almost to the minute, a dark, sleek chap nattily attired in a tropical worsted with a bright yellow tie and a white carnation in his button-hole takes his stand in front of the Hotel Astor on the third step, leaning his weight lightly on the bamboo cane which he sports at this hour of the day.

His name is Osmanli, obviously an invented one. He has a roll of ten, twenty and fifty dollar bills in his pocket. The fragrance of an expensive toilet water emanates from the silk kerchief which cautiously protrudes from his breast pocket. He is as fresh as a daisy, dapper, cool, insolent—a real Jim Dandy. To look at him one would never suspect that he is in the pay of an ecclesiastical organization, that his sole mission in life is to spread poison, malice, slander, that he enjoys his work, sleeps well and blossoms like the rose.

Tomorrow noon he will be at his accustomed place in Union Square, mounted on a soap box, the American flag protecting him; the foam will be drooling from his lips, his nostrils will quiver with rage, his voice will be hoarse and cracked. Every argument that man has trumped up to destroy the appeal of Communism he has at his disposal, can shake them out of his hat like a cheap magician. He is there not only to give argument, not only to spread poison and slander, but to foment trouble: he is there to create a riot, to bring on the cops, to go to court and accuse innocent people of attacking the Stars and Stripes.

When it gets too hot for him in Union Square he goes to Boston or Providence or some other American city, always wrapped in the American flag, always surrounded by his trained fomenters of discord, always protected by the shadow of the Church. A man whose origin is completely obscured, who has changed his name dozens of times, who has served all the Parties, red, white and blue, at one time or another. A man without country, without principle, without faith, without scruples. A servant of Beelzebub, a stooge, a stool pigeon, a traitor, a turn-coat. A master at confusing men's minds, an adept of the Black Lodge.

He has no close friends, no mistress, no ties of any kind. When he disappears he leaves no traces. An invisible thread links him to those whom he serves. On the soap box he seems like a man possessed, like a raving fanatic. On the steps of the Hotel Astor, where he stands every night for a few minutes, as though surveying the crowd, as though slightly abstracted, he is the picture of self-possession, of suave, cool nonchalance. He has had a bath and a rub-down, his nails manicured, his shoes shined; he has had a sound nap, too, and following that a most excellent meal in one of those quiet, exclusive restaurants which cater only to the gourmet. Often he takes a short stroll in the Park to digest the repast. He looks about with an intelligent, appreciative eye, aware of the beauties of earth and sky. Well read, travelled, with a taste for music and a passion for flowers, he often muses as he walks on the follies of man. He loves the flavor and savour of words; he rolls them over on his tongue, as he would a delicious morsel of food. He knows that he has the power to sway men, to stir their passions, to goad them and confound them at will. But this very ability has made him contemptuous, scornful and derisive of his fellow-man.

Now on the steps of the Astor, disguised as a boulevardier, a flaneur, a Beau Brummel, he gazes meditatively over the heads of the crowd, unperturbed by the chewing gum lights, the flesh for hire, the jingle of ghostly harnesses, the look of absentia-dementia in passing eyes. He has detached himself from all parties, cults, isms, ideologies. He is a free-wheeling ego, immune to all faiths, beliefs, principles. He can buy whatever he needs to sustain the illusion that he needs nothing, no one. He seems this evening to be more than ever free, more than ever detached. He admits to himself that he feels like a character in a Russian novel and he wonders vaguely why he should be indulging in such sentiments. He recognizes that he had just dismissed the idea of suicide; he is a little startled to find that he had been entertaining such ideas.

He had been arguing with himself; it had been quite a prolonged affair, now that he retraces his thoughts. The most disturbing thought is that he does not recognize the self with which he had discussed the question of suicide. This hidden being had never made its wants known before. There had always been a vacuum around which he had built a veritable cathedral of changing personalities. When he retreated behind the façade he had always found himself alone. And now he had made the discovery that he was not alone, that despite all the change of masks, all the architectural camouflage, some one was living with him, some one who knew him intimately, and who was now urging him to make an end of it.

The most fantastic part of it was that he was being urged to do it at once, to waste no time. It was preposterous because, admitting that the idea was seductive and appealing, he nevertheless felt the very human desire to enjoy the privilege of living out his own death in his imagination, at least for an hour or so. He seemed to be begging for time, which was strange, because never in his life had he entertained the notion of doing away with himself. He should have dismissed the thought instead of pleading like a convicted criminal for a few moments of grace. But this emptiness, this solitude into which he usually retreated, now began to assume the pressure and the explosiveness of a vacuum. The bubble was about to burst. He knew it. He knew he could do nothing to stay it. He walked rapidly down the steps of the Astor and plunged into the crowd. He thought for a moment that he would perhaps lose himself in the midst of all these bodies but no, he became more and more lucid, more and more self-conscious, more and more determined to obey the imperious voice which goaded him on. He was like a lover on his way to a rendezvous. He had only one thought—his own destruction. It burned like a fire, it illumined the way.

As he turned down a side street in order to hasten to his appointment he understood very clearly that he had already been taken over, as it were, and that he had only to follow his nose. He had no problems, no conflicts. Certain automatic gestures he made without even slackening his pace. For instance, passing a garbage can he tossed his bank roll into it as though he were getting rid of a banana peel; at a corner he emptied the contents of his inside coat pocket down a sewer; his watch and chain, his ring, his pocket knife went in similar fashion. He patted himself all over, as he walked, to make sure that he had divested himself of all personal possessions. Even his handkerchief, after he had blown his nose for the last time, he threw in the gutter. He felt as light as a feather and moved with increasing celerity through the sombre streets. At a given moment the signal would be given and he would give himself up. Instead of a tumultuous stream of thoughts, of last minute fears, wishes, hopes, regrets, such as we imagine to assail the doomed, he knew only a singular and ever more expansive void. His heart was like a clear blue sky in which not even the faintest trace of a cloud is perceptible. One might think that he had already crossed the frontier of the other world, that he was now before his actual bodily death already in the coma, and that emerging and finding himself on the other side he would be surprised to find himself walking so rapidly. Only then perhaps would he be able to collect his thoughts; only then would he be able to ask himself why he had done it.

Overhead the El is rattling and thundering. A man passes him running at top speed. Behind him is an officer of the law with a drawn revolver. He has begun to run too. Now all three of them are running. He doesn't know why, he doesn't even know that some one is behind him. But when the bullet pierces the back of his skull and he falls flat on his face a gleam of blinding clarity reverberates through his whole being.

Caught face downward in death there on the sidewalk, the grass already sprouting in his ears, Osmanli redescends the steps of the Hotel Astor, but instead of rejoining the crowd he slips through the back door of a modest little house in a village where he spoke a different language. He sits down at the kitchen table and sips a glass of buttermilk. It seems as though it were only yesterday that, seated at this same table, his wife had told him she was leaving him. The news had stunned him so that he had been unable to say a word; he had watched her go without making the slightest protest. He had been sitting there quietly drinking his buttermilk and she had told him with brutal, direct frankness that she never loved him. A few more words equally unsparing and she was gone. In those few minutes he had become a completely different man. Recovering from the shock he experienced the most amazing exhilaration. It was as if she had said to him: "You are now free to act!" He felt so mysteriously free that he wondered if his life up to that moment had not been a dream. To act! It was so simple. He remembered going out into the yard and seeing an axe he had picked it up without thinking; and then, with the same spontaneity, he had walked to the dog kennel, whistled to the animal, and when it stuck its head out he had chopped it off clean. That's what it meant—to act! So extremely simple, it made him laugh. He knew now that he could do anything he wished. He went inside and called the maid. He wanted to take a look at her with these new eyes. There was nothing more in his mind than that. An hour later, having raped her, he went directly to the bank and from there to the railway station where he took the first train that came in.

166

From then on his life had assumed a kaleidoscopic pattern. The few murders he had committed were carried out almost absent-mindedly, and without malice, hatred or greed. He made love almost in the same way. He knew neither fear, timidity, nor caution.

In this manner ten years had passed in the space of a few minutes. The chains which bind the ordinary man had been taken from him; he had roamed the world at will, had tasted freedom and immunity, and then in a moment of utter relaxation, surrendering himself to the imagination, he had concluded with pitiless logic that death was the one luxury he had denied himself. And so he had descended the steps of the Hotel Astor and a few minutes later, falling face downward in death, he realized that he was not mistaken when he understood her to say that she had never loved him. It was the first time he had ever thought of it again, and though it would be the last time he would ever think of it he could not make any more of it than when he first heard it ten years ago. It had not made sense then and it did not make sense now. He was still sipping his buttermilk. He was already a dead man. He was powerless, that's why he had felt so free. But he had never actually been free, as he had imagined himself to be. That had been simply an hallucination. To begin with, he had never chopped the dog's head off, otherwise it would not now be barking with joy. If he could only get to his feet and look with his own eyes he would know for certain whether everything had been real or hallucinatory. But the power to move had been taken from him. From the moment she had uttered those few telling words he knew he would never be able to move from the spot. Why she had chosen that particular moment when he was drinking the buttermilk, why she had waited so long to tell him, he could not understand and never would. He would not even try to understand. He had heard her very distinctly, quite as if she had put her lips to his ear and shouted the words into it. It had travelled with such speed to all parts of his body that it was as though a bullet had exploded in his brain. Then, could it have been just a few moments later or an eternity, he had emerged from the prison of his old self much as a butterfly emerges from its chrysalis. Then the dog, then the maid, then this, then that—innumerable incidents repeating themselves as if in accordance with a pre-established plan. Everything of a pattern, even down to the three or four casual murders.

As in the legends where it is told that he who forsakes his vision tumbles into a labyrinth from which there is no issue save death, where through symbol and allegory it is made clear that the coils of the brain, the coils of the labyrinth, the coils of the serpents which entwine the backbone are one and the same strangling process, the process of shutting doors behind one, of walling in the flesh, of moving relentlessly towards petrification, so it was with Osmanli, an obscure Turk, caught by the imagination on the steps of the Hotel Astor in the moment of his most illusory freedom and detachment. Looking over the heads of the crowd he had perceived with shuddering remembrance the image of his beloved wife, her dog-like head turned to stone. The pathetic desire to overreach his sorrow had ended in the confrontation with the mask. The monstrous embryo of unfulfillment blocked every egress. With face pressed against the pavement he seemed to kiss the stony features of the lost woman. His flight, pursued with skillful indirection, had brought him face to face with the bright image of horror reflected in the shield of self-protection. Himself slain, he had slain the world. He had reached his own identity in death.

(Cleo was terminating her dance. The last convulsive movements had coincided with the fantastic retrospection on Osmanli's death. . . .)

The incredible thing about such hallucinations is that they have their substance in reality. When Osmanli fell face forward on the sidewalk he was merely enacting a scene out of my life in advance. Let us jump a few years into the pot of horror.

The damned have always a table to sit at, whereon they rest their elbows and support the leaden weight of their brains. The damned are always sightless, gazing out at the world with blank orbs. The damned are always petrified and in the center of their petrifaction is the essence of emptiness. The damned have always the same excuse—the loss of the beloved.

It is night and I am sitting in a cellar. This is our home. I wait for her night after night, like a prisoner chained to the floor of his cell. There is a woman with her whom she calls her friend. They leave me without food, without heat, without light, without water. They tell me to amuse myself until they return.

Through months of shame and humiliation I have come to hug my solitude. I no longer seek help from the outside world. I no longer answer the door-bell. I live by myself, in the turmoil of my fears. Trapped in my own phantasms I wait for the flood to rise and drown me out.

When they return to torture me I behave like the animal which I have become. I pounce on the food with ravenous hunger. I eat with my fingers. And as I devour the food I grill them mercilessly, as though I were a mad, jealous Czar. I pretend that I am angry; I hurl vile insults at them, I threaten them with my fists, I growl and spit and rage.

I do this night after night in order to stimulate my almost extinct emotions. I have lost the power to feel. To conceal this defect I simulate every passion. There are nights when I amuse them no end by roaring like a wounded lion. At times I knock them down with a velvet-thudded paw. I have even peed on them when they rolled about on the floor convulsed with hysterical laughter.

They say that I have the makings of a clown. They say they will bring some friends down one night and have me perform for them. I grind my teeth and move my scalp back and forth to signify approval. I am learning all the tricks of the zoo.

My greatest stunt is to pretend jealousy. Jealousy over little things, particularly. Never to inquire whether she slept with this one or that, but only to know if he kissed her hand. I can become furious over a little gesture like that. I can pick up the knife and threaten to slit her throat. On occasion I go so far as to give her inseparable friend a tender jab in the buttocks. I bring iodine and court plaster and I kiss her inseparable friend's ass first.

Let us say that they come home of an evening and find the fire out. Let us say that this evening I am in an excellent mood, having conquered the pangs of hunger with an iron will, having defied the onslaught of insanity alone in the dark, having almost convinced myself that only egotism can produce sorrow and misery. Let us say further that, entering the prison cell, they seem insensitive to the victory which I have won. They sense nothing more than the dangerous chill of the room. They do not inquire if I am cold, they simply say it is cold here.

Cold, my little queens? Then you shall have a roaring fire. I take the chair and smash it against the stone wall. I jump on it and break it into tiny pieces. I kindle a little flame at the hearth with paper and splinters. I roast the chair piece by piece.

A charming gesture, they think. So far so good. A little food now, a bottle of cold beer. So you have had a good evening this evening? It was cold outdoors, was it? You collected a little money? Fine, deposit it in the Dime Savings Bank tomorrow! You, Hego-

roboru, run out and buy a flask of rum! I am leaving tomorrow.
. . . I am setting out on a journey.

The fire is getting low. I take the vacant chair and beat its brains
out against the wall. The flames leap up. Hegoroboru returns with
a grin and holds the bottle out. The work of a minute to uncork
it, guzzle a deep draught. Flames leap up in my gizzard. Stand up!
I yell. Give me that other chair! Protests, howls, screams. This is
pushing things too far. But it's cold outdoors, you say? Then we
need more heat. Get away! I shove the dishes on to the floor with
one swipe and tackle the table. They try to pull me away. I go
outside to the dust-bin and I find the axe. I begin hacking away.
I break the table into tiny pieces, then the commode, spilling
everything on to the floor. I will break everything to pieces, I warn
them, even the crockery. We will warm ourselves as we have never
warmed ourselves before.

A night on the floor, the three of us tossing like burning corks.
Taunts and gibes passing back and forth.

"He'll never go away . . . he's just acting."

A voice whispering in my ear: "Are you really going away?"

"Yes, I promise you I am."

"But I don't want you to go."

"I don't care what you want any longer."

"But I love you."

"I don't believe it."

"But you *must* believe me."

"I believe nobody, nothing."

"You're ill. You don't know what you're doing. I won't let you
go."

"How will you stop me?"

"Please, please, Val, don't talk that way . . . you worry me."
Silence.

A timid whisper: "How are you going to live without me?"

"I don't know, I don't care. As I lived before probably."

"But you need me. You don't know how to take care of yourself."

"I need nobody."

"I'm afraid, Val. I'm afraid something will happen to you."

In the morning I leave stealthily while they slumber. By stealing a few pennies from a blind newspaperman I get to the Jersey shore and set out for the highway. I feel fantastically light and free. In Philadelphia I stroll about as if I were a tourist. I get hungry. I ask for a dime from a passerby and I get it. I try another and another—just for the fun of it. I go into a saloon, eat a free lunch with a schooner of beer, and set out for the highway again.

I get a lift in the direction of Pittsburgh. The driver is uncommunicative. So am I. It's as though I had a private chauffeur. After a while I wonder where I'm going. Do I want a job? No. Do I want to begin life all over again? No. Do I want a vacation? No. I want nothing.

Then what *do* you want? I say to myself. The answer is always the same: Nothing.

Well, that's exactly what you have: Nothing.

The dialogue dies down. I become interested in the cigarette lighter which is plugged into the dashboard. The word cleat enters my mind. I play with it for a long time, then dismiss it peremptorily, as one would dismiss a child who wants to play ball with you all day.

Roads and arteries branching out in every direction. What would the earth be without roads? A trackless ocean. A jungle. The first road through the wilderness must have seemed like a grand accomplishment. Direction, orientation, communication. Then two roads, three roads. . . . Then millions of roads. A spider web and in the center of it man, the creator, caught like a fly.

We are travelling seventy miles an hour, or perhaps I imagine it. Not a word exchanged between us. He may be afraid to hear me say that I am hungry or that I have no place to sleep. He may be thinking where to dump me out if I begin to act suspiciously. Now and then he lights a cigarette on the electric grill. The gadget fascinates me. It's like a little electric chair. It burns you to a crisp.

"I'm turning off here," he says suddenly. "Where are you going?"

"You can leave me out here . . . thanks."

I step out into a fine drizzle. It's darkling. Roads leading to everywhere. I must decide where I want to go. I must have an objective.

I stand so deep in trance that I let a hundred cars go by without looking up. I haven't even an extra handkerchief, I discover. I was going to wipe my glasses but then, what's the use? I don't have to see too well or feel too well or think too well. I'm not going anywhere. When I get tired I can drop down and go to sleep. Animals sleep in the rain, why not man? If I could become an animal I would be getting somewhere.

A truck pulls up beside me; the driver is looking for a match.

"Can I give you a lift?" he asks.

I hop in without asking where to. The rain comes down harder, it has become pitch black suddenly. I have no idea where we're bound and I don't want to know. I feel content to be out of the rain sitting next to a warm body.

This guy is more convivial. He talks a lot about matches, how important they are when you need them, how easy it is to lose them, and so on. He makes conversation out of anything. It seems strange to talk so earnestly about nothing at all when really there are the most tremendous problems to be solved. Except for the fact that we are talking about material trifles this is the sort of conversation that might be carried on in a French salon. The roads have connected everything up so marvellously that even emptiness can be transported with ease.

As we pull into the outskirts of a big town I ask him where we are.

"Why, this is Philly," he says. "Where did you think you were?"

He grunted. Then he added: "You don't seem to care very much one way or another. You act like you were just riding around in the dark."

"You said it. That's just what I'm doing . . . riding around in the dark."

I sank back and listened to him tell about guys walking around in the dark looking for a place to flop. He talked about them very much as a horticulturist would talk about certain species of shrubs. He was a "space-binder," as Korbsyzki puts it, a guy riding all the highways and byways all by his lonesome. What lay to either side of the traffic lanes was the veldt, and the creatures inhabiting that void were vagrants hungrily bumming a ride.

The more he talked the more wistfully I thought of the meaning of shelter. After all, the cellar hadn't been too bad. Out in the world people were just as poorly off. The only difference between them and me was that they went out and got what they needed; they sweated for it, they tricked one another, they fought one another tooth and nail. I had none of those problems. My only problem was how to live with myself day in and day out.

I was thinking how ridiculous and pathetic it would be to sneak back into the cellar and find a little corner all to myself where I could curl up and pull the roof down over my ears. I would crawl in like a dog with his tail between his legs. I wouldn't bother them

174

any more with jealous scenes. I would be grateful for any crumbs that were handed me. If she wanted to bring her lovers in and make love to them in my presence it would be all right too. One doesn't bite the hand that feeds one. Now that I had seen the world I wouldn't ever complain again. Anything was better than to be left standing in the rain and not know where you want to go. After all, I still had a mind. I could lie in the dark and think, think as much as I chose, or as little. The people outside would be running to and fro, moving things about, buying, selling, putting money in the bank and taking it out again. That was horrible. I wouldn't ever want to do that. I would much prefer to pretend that I was an animal, say a dog, and have a bone thrown to me now and then. If I behaved decently I would be petted and stroked. I might find a good master who would take me out on a leash and let me make pipi everywhere. I might meet another dog, one of the opposite sex, and pull off a quick one now and then. Oh, I knew how to be quiet now and obedient. I had learned my little lesson. I would curl up in a corner near the hearth, just as quiet and gentle as you please. They would have to be terribly mean to kick me out. Besides, if I showed that I didn't need any-thing, didn't ask any favors, if I let them carry on just as if they were by themselves, what harm could come by giving me a little place in the corner?

The thing was to sneak in while they were out, so that they couldn't shut the gate in my face.

At this point in my reverie the most disquieting thought took hold of me. What if they had fled? What if the house were de-serted?

Somewhere near Elizabeth we came to a halt. There was some-thing wrong with the engine. It seemed wiser to get out and hail another car than to wait around all night. I walked to the nearest gas station and hung around for a car to take me into New York. I waited over an hour and then got impatient and lit off down the gloomy lane on my own two legs. The rain had abated; it was just coming down fine. Now and then, thinking how lovely it would be to crawl into the dog kennel, I broke into a trot. Elizabeth was about fifteen miles off.

Once I got so overjoyed that I broke into song. Louder and louder I sang, as if to let them know I was coming. Of course I wouldn't enter the house singing—that would frighten them to death.

The singing made me hungry. I bought a Hershey Almond Bar at a little stand beside the road. It was delicious. See, you're not so badly off, I said to myself. You're not eating bones or refuse yet. You may get some good dishes before you die. What are you thinking of—lamb stew? You mustn't think about palatable things . . . think only of bones and refuse. From now on it's a dog's life.

I was sitting on a big rock some seven or eight miles this side of Elizabeth when I saw a big truck approaching. It was the fellow I had left farther back. I hopped in. He started talking about engines, what ails them, what makes them go, and so on. "We'll soon be there," he said suddenly, apropos of nothing.

"Where?" I asked.

"New York of course . . . where do you think?"

"Oh, New York . . . yeah. I forgot."

"Say, what the hell are you going to do in New York, if I ain't getting too personal?"

"I'm going to rejoin my family."

"You been away long?"

"About ten years," I said, drawing the words out meditatively.

"Ten years! That's a hell of a long time. What were you doing, just bumming around?"

"Yeah, just bumming around."

"I guess they'll be glad to see you . . . your folks."

"I guess they will."

"You don't seem to be sure of it," he said, giving me a quizzical look.

"That's true. Well, you know how it is."

"I guess so," he answered. "I meet lots of guys like you. Always come back to the roost some time or other."

He said roost, I said kennel—under my breath, to be sure. I liked kennel better. Roost was for roosters, pigeons, birds of feather that lay eggs. I wasn't going to lay no eggs. Bones and refuse, bones and refuse. I repeated it over and over, to give myself the moral strength to crawl back like a beaten dog.

I borrowed a nickel from him on leaving and ducked into the subway. I felt tired, hungry, weather-beaten. The passengers looked sick to me. As though some one had just let them out of the hoosegow or the alms house. I had been out in the world, far, far away. For ten years I had been knocking about and now I was coming home. Welcome home, prodigal son! Welcome home! My goodness, what stories I had heard, what cities I had seen! What marvellous adventures! Ten years of life, just from morn to midnight. Would the folks still be there?

I tiptoed into the areaway and looked for a gleam of light. Not a sign of life. Well, they never came home very early. I would go in upstairs by way of the stoop. Perhaps they were in the back of the house. Sometimes they sat in Hegoroboru's little bedroom off the hall where the toilet box trickled night and day.

I opened the door softly, walked to the head of the stairs which were enclosed, and quietly, very quietly, lowered myself step by step. There was a door at the bottom of the steps. I was in total darkness.

Near the bottom I heard muffled sounds of speech. They were home! I felt terrifically happy, exultant. I wanted to dash in wagging my little tail and throw myself at their feet. But that wasn't the program I had planned to adhere to.

After I had stood with my ear to the panel for some minutes I put my hand on the door knob and very very slowly and noiselessly I turned it. The voices came much more distinctly now that I had opened the door an inch or so. The big one, Hegoroboru, was talking. She sounded maudlin, hysterical, as though she had been drinking. The other voice was low-pitched, more soothing and caressing than I had ever heard it. She seemed to be pleading with the big one. There were strange pauses, too, as if they were embracing. Now and then I could swear the big one gave a grunt, as though she were rubbing the skin off the other one. Then suddenly she let out a howl of delight, but a vengeful one. Suddenly she shrieked.

"Then you do love him still? You were lying to me!"

"No, no! I swear I don't. You *must* believe me, *please*. I never loved him."

"That's a lie!"

"I swear to you . . . I swear I never loved him. He was just a child to me."

This was followed by a shrieking gale of laughter. Then a slight commotion, as if they were scuffling. Then a dead silence, as if their lips were glued together. Then it seemed as if they were undressing one another, licking one another all over, like two calves in the meadow. The bed squeaked. The big one had probably thrown herself on top of the other. Fouling the nest, that was it. They had gotten rid of me as if I were a leper and now they were trying to do the man and wife act. It was good I hadn't been lying in the corner watching this with my head between my paws. I would have barked angrily, perhaps bitten them. And then they would have kicked me around like a dirty cur.

I didn't want to hear any more. I closed the door gently and sat on the steps in the total dark. The fatigue and hunger had passed. I was extraordinarily awake. I could have walked to San Francisco in three hours.

Now I must go somewhere! I must get very definite—or I will go mad. I know I am not just a child. I don't know if I want to be a man—I feel too bruised and battered—but I certainly am not a child!

Then a curious physiological comedy took place. *I began to menstruate.* I menstruated from every hole in my body. When a man menstruates it's all over in a few minutes. He doesn't leave any mess behind either.

I crept upstairs on all fours and left the house as silently as I had entered it. The rain was over, the stars were out in full splendor. A light wind was blowing. The Lutheran Church across the way which in the daylight was the color of baby shit had now taken on a soft ochrous hue which blended serenely with the black of the asphalt. I was still not very definite in my mind about the future. At the corner I stood a few minutes, looking up and down the street as if I were taking it in for the first time. When you have suffered a great deal in a certain place you have the impression that the record is imprinted in the street. But if you notice, streets seem peculiarly unaffected by the sufferings of private individuals. If you step out of a house at night, after losing a dear friend, the street seems really quite discreet. If the outside became like the inside it would be unbearable. Streets are breathing places. . . .

I move along, trying to get definite without developing a fixed idea. I pass garbage cans loaded with bones and refuse. Some have put old shoes, busted slippers, hats, suspenders, and other worn out articles in front of their dwellings. There is no doubt but that if I took to prowling around at night I could live quite handsomely off the discarded crumbs.

The life in the kennel is out. That's one thing very definite. I don't feel like a dog any more anyway. . . . I feel more like a tomcat. The cat is independent, anarchistic, a free-wheeler. It's the cat that rules the roost at night.

Getting hungry again. I wander down to the bright lights of Borough Hall where the cafeterias blaze. I look through the big windows to see if I can detect a friendly face. Pass on, from shop window to shop window, examining shoes, haberdashery, pipe tobaccos and so forth. Then I stand awhile at the subway entrance, hoping forlornly that some one will drop a nickel and not miss it. I look the newsstands over to see if there are any blind men about whom I can steal a few pennies from.

After a time I am walking on the bluff at Columbia Heights. I pass a sedate brown-stone house which I remember entering years and years ago to deliver a package of clothes to one of my father's customers. I remember standing in the big back room with the bay windows giving out on the river. It was a day of brilliant sunshine, a late afternoon, and the room seemed to me to be like a Vermeer, all brown and golden, and invested with a holy light. I had to help the old man on with his clothes. He was ruptured and when he stood in the middle of the room in his light underwear he seemed positively obscene.

Below the bluff ran a street full of warehouses. The terraces of the wealthy homes were like overhanging gardens ending abruptly some twenty or thirty feet above this dismal street with the dead windows and the grim archways leading to the wharves. I went to the end of a blind street and stood against a wall to take a leak. A drunk comes along and stands beside me. He pees all over himself and then suddenly he doubles up and begins to vomit. As I walk away I can hear it splashing over his shoes.

I run down a long flight of stairs leading to the docks and find myself face to face with a man in uniform swinging a big stick. He wants to know what I'm about, but before I can answer he begins to shove me and brandish the stick. I climb back up the long flight of stairs and sit on a bench. Facing me is an old-fashioned hotel where a school-teacher who used to be sweet on me lives. The last time I saw her I had taken her out to dinner and then as I was saying good-bye I had to ask her for a nickel. She gave it to me—just a nickel—with a look which I shall never forget. She had placed high hopes in me when I was a student. But that look told me all too plainly that she had since revised her opinion of me. I had become hopeless, I would never be able to cope with the world.

The stars were very bright. I stretched out on the bench and gazed at them intently. All my failures were now tightly bound up inside me like the embryo of unfulfillment. All that had happened to me now seemed extremely remote. I had nothing to do now but revel in my detachment. I began to voyage from star to star . . .

An hour or so later, chilled to the bone, I got to my feet and began walking briskly. An insane desire to repass the house I had been driven from took possession of me. I was dying to know if they were still up and about.

The shades were only partially drawn and the light from a candle near the bed gave the front room a quiet glow. I stole close to the window and put my ear to it. They were singing a Russian song which the big one was fond of. Apparently all was bliss in there.

I tiptoed out of the areaway and turned down Love Lane which was at the corner. It had been named Love Lane during the Revolution most likely; now it was simply a back alley dotted with garages and repair shops. More garbage cans, too.

I retraced my steps to the river, to that grim, dismal street which ran like a dried-up canal beneath the overhanging terraces of the rich. Nobody ever walked through this street late at night—it was considered too dangerous.

However, there was not a soul about. The passageways tunneled through the warehouses gave fascinating glimpses of the river life —barges lying lifeless, tugs gliding by like smoking ghosts, the sky-scrapers silhouetted against the New York shore, huge iron stan-chions with cabled hawsers slung around them, piles of bricks and lumber, sacks of coffee. The most poignant sight was the sky itself swept clear of clouds and studded with fistsful of stars which gleamed like the breast-plates of the high priests of old.

Finally I made to go through an archway. About half-way through I felt a huge rat race across my feet. I stopped with a shudder and another one slid over my feet. Then a panic seized me and I ran back to the street. On the other side of the street was a man standing close to the wall. I stood stock still, undecided which way to turn, and hoping that this silent figure would move first. But he remained immobile, watching me like a hawk. Again I felt panicky, but this time I steeled myself to walk away, fearing that if I ran he would also run. I walked as noiselessly as possible, my ear cocked to catch the sound of his steps. I didn't dare to turn my head back. I walked slowly, deliberately, hardly putting my heel down.

I had only walked a few yards when I had the certain sensation that he was following me, not on the other side of the street, but directly behind me, perhaps only a few yards away. I hastened my steps, still however making no sound. It seemed to me that he was moving faster than I, gaining on me. I could almost feel his breath on my neck. Suddenly I took a quick look around. He was there, almost within grasp. I knew I couldn't elude him now. I had a feeling that he was armed and that he would use his weapon, knife or gun, the moment I tried to make a dash for it.

Instinctively I turned and dove for his legs. He tumbled over my back and struck his head against the pavement. I knew I hadn't the strength to grapple with him. Again I had to move fast. He was just rolling over, slightly stunned, it seemed, as I sprang to my feet. His hand was reaching for his pocket. I kicked out and caught him square in the stomach. He groaned and rolled over. I bolted. I ran with all the strength I had in me. But the street was steep and long before I had come to the end of it I had to break into a walk. I turned again and listened. It was too dark to tell whether he had risen to his feet or was still lying on the sidewalk. Not a sound except the wild beating of my heart, the hammering of my temples. I leaned against the wall to catch my breath. I felt terribly weak, ready to faint. I wondered if I would have the strength to climb to the top of the hill.

Just as I was congratulating myself on my narrow escape I saw a shadow creeping along the wall down where I had left him. This time my fear turned my legs to lead. I was absolutely paralyzed. I watched him creeping closer and closer, unable to stir a muscle. He seemed to divine what had happened; his pace never quickened.

When he got within a few feet of me he flashed the gun. With that I instinctively put up my hands. He came up to me and frisked me. Then he put his gun back in his hip pocket. Never a word out of him. He went through my pockets, found nothing, cuffed me in the jaw with the back of his hand and then stepped back towards the gutter.

"Put your hands down," he said, low and tense.

I dropped them like two flails. I was petrified with fright.

He pulled the gun out again, levelled it, and said in the same even, low, tense voice: "I'm givin' it to you in the guts, you dirty dog." With that I collapsed and as I fell I heard the bullet spatter against the wall. It was the end. I expected a fusillade. I remember trying to curl up like a foetus, crooking my elbow over my eyes to protect them. Then came the fusillade, then I heard him running. I knew I must be dying, but I felt no pain.

Suddenly I realized that I hadn't even been scratched. I sat up and I saw a man running towards the fleeing assailant with a gun in his hand. He fired a few shots as he ran but they must have gone wide of the mark.

I rose to my feet unsteadily, felt myself all over again to make certain that I was really unhurt, and waited for the guard to return.

"Will you help me a bit," I said, "I'm pretty rocky."

He looked at me suspiciously, the gun still in his hand.

"What the hell are you doing around here at this hour of the night?" he said.

"I'm awfully weak," I said. "I'll tell you later. Help me home, will you?"

I told him where I lived, that I was a writer, that I had been out for a breath of fresh air. "He cleaned me out," I added. "Lucky you came along . . . he was going to do me in."

A little more of this lingo and he softened up enough to say—"Here, take this and get yourself a cab. You're all right I guess." He thrust a dollar bill in my hand.

I found a cab in front of a hotel and ordered the driver to take me to Love Lane. On the way I stopped a moment to get a package of cigarettes.

The lights were out this time. I went up by the stoop and slid lightly down to the hallway. Not a sound. I put my ear to the door of the front room and listened intently. Then I stole softly back to the little cell at the end of the hall where the big one usually slept. I had the feeling that the room was deserted. Slowly I turned the knob. When I had opened the door sufficiently I sank to all fours and crept in on my hands and knees, feeling my way carefully to the bed. There I raised my hand and felt the bed. It was empty. I undressed quickly and crawled in. There were some cigarette butts at the foot of the bed—they felt like dead bugs.

In a moment I was sound asleep. I dreamed that I was lying in the corner by the hearth; I had a coat of fur, padded paws and long ears. Between my paws was a bone which had been licked clean. I was guarding it jealously, even in my sleep. A man entered and gave me a kick in the ribs. I pretended not to feel it. He kicked me again, as though to make me growl—or perhaps it was to make me let go of the bone.

"Stand up!" he said, exposing a whip which he had hidden behind his back.

I was too weak to move. I looked up at him with piteous, bleary eyes, imploring him mutely to leave me in peace.

"Come on, get out of here!" he muttered, raising the butt end of the whip as if to strike.

I staggered to all fours and tried to hobble away. My spine seemed to be broken. I caved in, collapsed like a punctured bag.

Then the man coldly raised the whip again and with the butt end cracked me over the skull. I let out a howl of pain. Enraged at this he grasped the whip by the butt end and began lashing me unmercifully. I tried to raise myself but it was no use—my spine was broken. I wriggled over the floor like an octopus, receiving lash after lash. The fury of the blows had taken my breath away. It was only after he had gone, thinking that I was done for, that I began to give vent to my agony. At first I began to whimper, then as my strength returned I began to scream and howl. The blood was oozing from me as if I were a sponge. It flowed out in all directions, making a big dark spot, as in the animated cartoons. My voice got weaker and weaker. Now and then I let out a yelp.

When I opened my eyes the two women were bending over me, shaking me.

"Stop it, for God's sake, stop it!" the big one was saying.

The other was saying: "My God, Val, what's happened? Wake up, wake up!"

I sat up and looked at them with a dazed expression. I was naked and my body was full of blood and bruises.

"Where have you been? What happened?" their voices now chimed together.

"I was dreaming, I guess." I tried to smile but the smile faded into a distorted grin. "Look at my back," I said. "Is it broken?"

They laid me back on the bed and turned me over, as if I had been marked "fragile."

"You're full of bruises. You must have been beaten up."

I closed my eyes and tried to remember what had happened to me. All I could think of was the dream, the man standing above me with the whip and lashing me. He had kicked me in the ribs, as if I were a mangy cur. I'll give it to you in the guts, you dirty dog! My back was broken, I remembered distinctly. I had caved in and sprawled out on the floor like an octopus. And in that help-less position he had lashed away with a fury that was inhuman.

"Let him sleep," I heard the big one say.

"I'm going to call an ambulance," said the other.

They began to argue.

"Go away, leave me alone," I muttered.

It was quiet again. I fell asleep. I dreamed that I was in the dog show, that I was a chow and that I had a blue ribbon around my neck. In the next booth was another chow with a pink ribbon around his neck. It was a toss-up who would win the prize.

Two women whom I seemed to recognize were bickering about our respective merits and demerits. Finally the judge came over and placed his hand on my neck. The big woman strode away angrily, spitting in disgust. But the woman whose pet I was bent over and holding me by the ears raised my head and kissed me on the snout. "I knew you would win the prize for me," she whispered. "You're such a lovely, lovely creature," and she began stroking my fur. "Wait a moment now, my darling, and I'll bring you something nice. Just a moment. . . ."

When she returned she had a little package in her hand, wrapped in tissue paper and tied with a beautiful ribbon. She held it up before me and I stood on my hind legs and barked. "Woof woof! Woof woof!"

"Take it easy, dear," she said, undoing the package slowly. "Mother's brought you a beautiful little present."

"Woof woof! Woof woof!"

"That's a darling . . . that's it . . . easy now . . . easy."

I was furiously impatient to receive my gift. I couldn't understand why she was taking so long. It must be something terribly precious, I thought to myself.

The package was almost unwrapped now. She was holding the little gift behind her back.

"Up, up! That's it . . . up!"

I got up on my hind legs and began prancing and pirouetting before her.

"Now beg! Beg for it!"

"Woof woof! Woof woof!" I was ready to jump out of my skin with joy.

Suddenly she dangled it before my eyes. It was a magnificent knuckle bone full of marrow encircled in a gold wedding ring. I was furiously eager to seize it but she held it high above her head, tantalizing me mercilessly. Finally, to my astonishment, she stuck her tongue out and began to suck the marrow into her mouth. She turned it around and sucked from the other end. When she had made a clean hole in the center of the bone she caught hold of me and began to stroke me. She did it so masterfully that in a few seconds I stood out like a raw turnip. Then she took the bone with the wedding ring still around it and she slipped it over me. "Now you little darlin', I'm going to take you home and put you to bed," she whispered. And with that she picked me up and walked off, everybody laughing and clapping his hands. Just as we got to the door the bone slid off and fell to the ground. I tried to scramble out of her arms, but she held me tight to her bosom. I began to whimper like a little child. "Hush, hush!" she said, and sticking out her tongue she licked my face. "You dear, lovely, little creature!"

"Woof woof! Woof woof!" I barked. "Woof! woof! Woof, woof, woof!"

A DEATH LETTER TO EMIL

(From *Letters To Emil*)

Dear Emil:

Your letter came just as I am about to mail a bundle of letters to you. I had held them up owing to lack of postage money. (Verlaine: "please send me six sous for stamps and other little things.") To-day I have the dough and all goes out at once, with a vengeance. Your letter rouses my ire—a good-natured ire, slightly paranoiac, healthily so . . . healthy neurosis.

Emil, you are quite all cock-eyed. I must tell you so frankly. You don't know yet what it is all about. I am wondering if you have received all the pages I wrote on Lawrence, which L. was to forward to you (?) Otherwise I can't understand your writing thus about Lawrence and Spengler. Do you read these excerpts I send you? Ask me about them—not your Ernest Boyds and William Hales. . . . I am going to enlighten you a bit. I'm going to waste time and effort on you because, damn it all, if you don't get what I'm driving at who will?

You say: "I think that it is not the end. I think there is much more death in Europe than here. Perhaps more death in Paris than in Burgundy." You seem to think that there exists in Paris a school of death philosophers, of which F. L. A. and myself are amusing exponents. If F. rubs his eyes and asks if he's being kidded, when he receives L.'s death letters (?), it is probably because under the stars and stripes he doesn't recognize his own language any more. Perhaps! Perhaps L., who has a genius for putting things upside down and hindside front, has bewildered his brother acrobat in death logic. I don't know what passes between L. and F. There is a bit of mystic secrecy between them which it is not my business to pry into. I leave it alone, respectfully, admiringly. I know that when recently I renewed my acquaintance with L. it gave me great pleasure to hear him say—"I've come at length to believe that you and F. are geniuses." I had pleasure in hearing it, not for my part —because I don't need to be reassured as to that point—but for F.'s sake, for the sake of the F. L. friendship which was so near to disaster when F. departed these shores.

F.! If he were here now I would put my arms around him and hug him. Where is that little man with the bright glancing eye, the flame in his guts, the fire in his brain, the fierce, inquiring mind, the shameless arrogance and the humility that makes one weep, so deep it is and so genuine. F.! Why, little F., so despised, so misunderstood, so tortured and bound up with his inner conflicts—F. is a man, very much alive, a man with the Holy Ghost in his bowels, where it belongs. And if he is a philosopher of death, he breathes more life than all that crew combined . . . that vile, healthy, rosy-cheeked, piratical crew you describe. Smoking, steaming shits, these are! When it comes to life and death, you are all of you over there a lot of smoking, steaming shits. (I borrow the vituperative language from Lawrence.) There's no use hedging about it, Emil . . . I must say it.

You say that Europe is more death-like. You say, how can these rosy-cheeked, lusty young college men have insides full of ashes? Well, you know that that phrase was hurled against Gerald Crich, in *Women in Love*. Gerald Crich stands as a symbolic type of our Western Civilization. And by Western Civilization Spengler meant to include America too, no mistake about that. America is not a special, separate civilization. For heaven's sake, man, don't you know where America stands in the scheme of things? Do you think Spengler was talking about Germany, France, England alone? Spengler was talking about a very real condition manifesting itself as Culture, now dying off as Civilization, in a large part of the world. He speaks of a Western Culture because at present there is no other Culture. It is the sole, significant phenomenon on the historical horizon. What exists in remote parts, in India, China, Japan, Africa—these are all fag ends, the static perpetuity of something that once lived and had meaning, but no more. The Cultures rise and fall, they bob up as new species and races bob up in the biological world. They are historical, spiritual organisms which flourish and decay. Do you imagine that what is going on in China and Japan to-day is part of Japanese and Chinese culture? The Chinese and Japanese, qua Chinese and Japanese, are dead. The physical specimens labelled thus come out of a tradition of Chinese culture which is now receiving the impress of our Western culture. (God help them!) India the same . . . all living on as vermiform appendices in the great historical organism, the makan-thropos of man's spiritual world.

You say you don't understand the warfare over Lawrence, why he should have been attacked as a man of ideas and not just accepted as a poet. Fine. I am glad that you recognize the poet in him: that is his distinction, that marks him out separate and meaningful to us. A poet. That is to say, a prophet, a voice, a creator.

Lawrence was a man of ideas, was dominated, ridden by ideas. You cannot take the poetry and discard the ideas. He saw to it that that would be impossible. That's why the warfare goes on over his dead body. He embodied his ideas in his poetry. Or better, he gave body and spirit to his ideas through his poetic feeling and vision. As a man he was divided. As a poet he was single. He could not have got inside the horse and unicorn, the tortoise, the cobra and the dandelion, and all the other living manifestations of the Holy Spirit, unless he had been imbued with an Idea. One does not write poetry decoratively, as some excrescence . . . as excreta. One does not see the beauty and tragic mystery of life with two eyes alone—in fact, the eyes blind one to it all. Lawrence saw with the inner eye, with the flaming core of him. He saw beyond the visible death about him into the eternal livingness of things. He was a life-bringer. But he was anchored in death. He is an apostle of death, I repeat. But it is necessary to understand what this means. For his death is not the death you are talking about any more than his life is the life you glorify in those sexual numskulls over there. These athletes whom you mention are dead inside, tombs draped in flesh. Verily, their insides are full of ashes. You can make them lusty and vigorous in the sexual parts, you can put waves in their hair and give them sound teeth and clean breaths, you can put an elastic gait in their stride, *but you can't blow life into them.* What you are looking at is the biological organism, the immortal body which persists through race and species for ever and ever. But you have got to accustom yourself to looking at that body, that purely biological phenomenon, as a vessel of life, of ideas, of spirit. You have got to put an X-ray to that body and see through the mask of flesh into the spiritual interior, see the spiritual ossature and musculature. Then you will see, as Lawrence points out, that a great part of the organism is given over to the mere function of *devouring* . . . that it is intestinal. The rosy-cheeked young men you talk about may fuck beautifully, in the way we know at the stud farm. But there must be something more to it. There must be some hope and purpose behind all this beautiful fucking if we are to get something better than the yahoos who now make up the fag end of our glorious Western Civilization.

Lawrence accepts in toto, so far as I can see, the Spenglerian doctrine, the organic view of man's spiritual quest. As a prophet, he is full of doom. It fills his mouth perpetually. He states it and restates it in multifarious fashion. He begs us to die, to get it over with quickly. He hails America because America is more corrupt, more moribund—and therefore nearer to salvation, rebirth. You spoke of F. being a bit flustered, hesitant, stuttering, when employing his "death lingo" in your American midst. He had to admit, I think you said, that you were all going around in rompers. But what is that if not the evidence of senility? It is a second childhood you are celebrating. It is not virility, not springtime, not young manhood and womanhood. It is old age, diddering, gibbering old age playing the child again. America is senile, foolish, idiotic. "Pourrie avant d'être mûre," said a Frenchman.

Lawrence devotes his most magnificent acumen to explaining the appearance of a Herman Melville. In *Moby Dick* he sees a prophecy. The sinking of the Pequod was the previsioned sinking of the great white civilization, now represented by that Western Culture which Spengler describes. Doom! Lawrence goes to Melville like a blood-hound. Because Melville is the spokesman, the apocalyptic voice of doom. 1851 was the date of writing. And what has happened since? Post mortem effects, says Lawrence. The great Walt Whitman, pioneer of the soul, the man who brought the message of the Open Road, Whitman was for Lawrence a post mortem effect. (You will have to read the essay to grasp the full significance of this—why Whitman was tainted, why he failed in his earnest purpose. "He said *sympathy*, not love.")

That is the prophetic side of Lawrence, apostle of doom, apostle of death. He had enough vision and integrity to stick to that, despite all the gush of life in his veins. He went on producing, as few men of his generation have produced, whetted by the prospect of coming doom. *The End?* He could not have so rejoiced in the prospect of doom and death and destruction had he thought in terms of an end. The very idea of cyclical, organic life and death, of birth and growth and decay, forbids that. How people fall on Spengler and gnash their teeth—because he predicts what is so palpably inevitable. . . . All these spirits are in the grip of the Absolute. But this Absolute is utterly different from those of the past, from Plato, Pythagoras, Jesus, et alia. This is an Absolute of Life, not Death. I walk all around this subject for you, without ever getting to the dead centre. In a way, it is deliberate. I would like you to struggle a bit yourself, to realize the full purport of these words. I would like you to get that essay called "The Crown" and read there for yourself, in the most exalted, profound language Lawrence ever employed, the full significance of Life and Death. What is Absolute, what is Static, what is Corruption. . . .

Lawrence has brought salvation into the here and now, the eternal ever present. He lodges himself in the life-stream. He worships power, aristocracy, distinction, values. He does not promise a hereafter, a spiritual salvation when we are dead and selfless. He talks about consummation *now*, in the living moment. He runs against the whole trend of historical destiny. He stands out as anti-fate. He takes up his position in MAN, not in history, nor religion, nor culture, nor movements. He accepts death, biological, spiritual, ultimate. Death in all its phases. And, by refusing to avoid the issue (all man's spiritual progress has been a steady, persistent evasion of this death!) he finds life. The one great paralyzing influence to-day is the fear of life. That is the meaning of neuroticism. F. can make it clear to you, if it is not already so. F. is a neurotic. A productive one.

It is not a definite thing, fear of this or fear of that, but fear, large, terrible, irrational. That is why F. reaches out so eagerly for death. If he can take hold of that he knows he will have life again. But F. is trying to take hold of it as Idea, with his intellect, with his terrible logic. F. simply cannot, will not die. He is ashamed of himself, and he has a right to be. It is a disgrace to go on living that living death of his. F. has been dead a long time; it is only the ghost, the animated corpse of a man, who calls on you and fills you with his attenuated ideas. Listen, I adore F. I am not saying harsh, unjust things against him. I wish you would show him all I have written herein. If he were here I would put my arms around him and hug him. I prefer the corpse of F. to all the so-called live bodies around me here. I prefer that stench which he gives off to all the rosy-cheeked fragrance of the dead-alive athletes who can fuck so beautifully.

You say Europe is nearer to death than America. I say it is not so. Lawrence also had to admit it was not so. He said that Europe was more alive because people had lived and suffered and fought and struggled there, shed blood for their ideas, etc. People are freest, he said, when they are living in a homeland—meaning when

195

they remained and fought out the problems that beset them. Well, Europe is my homeland—not America. I am with Europe always. I have found my homeland. I think some day the tide of emigration will turn and all those hordes who poured over to America to work the soil and the mills, to erect that ghastly, empty edifice of Work and Progress over there, I think that bloody crew of ghosts and cadavers will return to Europe again and die here and refecundate the soil of Europe. Already we who have come over are prophets of the new phase of things. We are the advance sentinels, the little corps of reconnoiterers who must go forward and be shot down for the sake of informing the rest. . . . Europe is my homeland, though I speak none of her languages. But what language do I require to make myself understood? Not English certainly. Nor French, nor German. I have only to walk into the street here and I am understood, and I understand those around me. I understand perhaps a little better because I cannot speak the actual tongue. I speak symbolically. I hear symbolically. When I roll into the Gare St. Lazare from my excursions to Louveciennes, it is as though I heard with a thousand ears, saw with a thousand eyes. Already, in the train, as I approach the confines of Paris, my heart begins to leap. I go forward to meet Paris as a man goes forward to meet his mistress. I go from one woman to another. All that the actual one gives me fills me with lust for this other intangible, this vast, deep, spiritual woman which is Paris. And Paris is France, not Burgundy, not Anjou, not Savoy. Paris is the heart of France. When Paris speaks it is France speaking. The same goes for New York. It is one of those fatuous, delightfully naïve and idle remarks that seem to have currency now, when men feel themselves inwardly empty, to say that New York is not America, that Paris is not France. New York, Paris, Rome, Berlin, Madrid, London, these are the hearts of their countries; they beat with the keenest life blood, with the cultural, spiritual blood of their countries. The rest is intestinal, biological, racial, specious in the worst sense. . . . The peasant is the same everywhere. The peasant is the peasant: the dumb voice of nature, the clod rooted to the soil. A geographical phenomenon, not a spiritual one. The peasant is plant-like. The city man, the man who rises to his apogee and death and transfiguration in the great metropolises of the world, that man is the eternal spirit of man, the nomad, the poet, the artist, the creator.

I go to the peasant with no reverence. I am not a nature worshipper. I go to the peasant as I go to food and wine, to tree and beast, to air and sunshine. I go to plunder him, to rob him of his vitality, his fat, vegetable wealth, his inexhaustible vitality. But I convert that mass of blood and sunshine into spirit. I revitalize him too—don't forget that. I give him his spiritual background against which he too must move or perish. The peasant does not exist alone. He seems to . . . comes nearer to it than most men. The poet is the one who lives most truly alone . . . on the mountain tops. The peasant lives in the soil, rooted, perpetually rooted. He is like the grass which covers the earth. We tear it up continually to make way for fields, for patches of cultivation. And the moment we turn our backs, the moment we cease digging and planting and sowing, the grass returns, covers up all our efforts. That is the peasant. And the poet needs the peasant, more than he needs the dry, intellectual fodder of cities and provinces. The poet lives as a unity, a thing unto himself. He touches the peasant in order to keep alive his sense of reality. Because the reality of the athlete, of the book-worm, of the pedant and scholar, is insufficient to him. He must give all of them a new reality; he cannot take their feeble, false, sterile, make believe reality and hand back a synthetic or imaginative product. When Lawrence creates war about him, when any man creates war about him, know that it is because of his *ideas*. Know that he is giving back a new reality, a poetic and ineluctable reality—not a mirror of things as they are or seem to be. He gives back with his blood a passionate, living, experienced reality. And before man can accept that reality, move in it, breathe it, he must die. He must always die first and be reborn. He cannot breathe the new reality with his old dry lungs. The lungs collapse under the new pressure. . . .

Fuck it! It's a crime to stay in and write letters on a beautiful day like this. Fuck America! Fuck your death and corruption! *Allons!* The open road—Bougival, Charenton, Marly-le-roi, Garches la Coquette, Maison Lafitte, etc. . . .

24 hours later

I say Europe is not dead. It is America that is dead. . . . We had the ride, Bald, Fred and I. We went to Charenton and Alfort, on the Marne. We had a swim in the icy May waters of the Marne, red with mud and garbage. We picked up a French boy on the road, in the Bois de Vincennes, and we gave him a treat . . . swam with him, boxed with him, drank beer with him, ate fried fish with him. His father is champion feather-weight of France, has just come back from America. His father *adores* America, brought back ten suits of clothes, because the French tailors don't know how to make clothes. O. K. Chalk that up against the French . . . a little proof of their death, if you like. *They don't know how to make clothes!* And maybe, in your opinion over there, neither do they know how to make films. (I am writing to-day, in my Cinema folder, about two absurd masterpieces I saw last night: *Le Harpon Rouge* and *The Wax Museum*. Masterpieces of death and corruption, of sadism and virginity.)

I spoke a while back of what happens to me as I roll into the

Gare St. Lazare. It is an emotional triumph—*always*. I think the Gare St. Lazare is the greatest railway station man ever built—wild, romantic, unsupportable statement—but true, nevertheless. The Gare St. Lazare is the chief gateway to Paris. You have only to experience a ride into London or Vienna, or New York, to feel the difference. To enter New York by way of Park Avenue . . . can you picture anything more ghastly, more sordid, more foul and degrading? How it feels to ride into London Lawrence has described once and for all in *Women in Love*. Machen has given an earlier picture of it, equally vile and repulsive. But Park Avenue . . . from the elevated structure, looking down into those dark bedrooms, those filthy, crawling streets of the upper ghetto, that dreary, monotonous row of tenements, all brown and gray and sooty, all bedeviled by the lifeless lustre of our wonderful mechanical age. I know of no worse sight on earth. That I call death. Worse than death. I call it cancer, leprosy, gangrene.

Alors, St. Lazare! Twilight. The engines lined up neatly in the round-houses. The switch towers burnished by the setting sun. The walls gleaming like mocha and taffeta, like scalded milk. *Suze, Cinzano, Pernod fils*. The walls blazing with hideous advertisements in raw dyes . . . so hideous that they are lovely. *Savon Cadum*—probably the worst trade mark ever invented by man. And yet, I love that rosy-cheeked baby which was painted before the end of the century perhaps and which lives on as long as this advertising age will live.

Twilight. The Gare is humming with suburbanites. People dressed in ill-fitting clothes, mufflers around their necks, pull-overs over their dirty underwear, caps such as only a Polak or a Dago would wear in America. Black sack coats and striped trousers for the *rond-cuirs* (the swivelchair functionaries), who read in their leisure the best literature in the world. Shiny, greasy, green-black derbies to lend an air of respectability. Burnt out butts (*mégots*) hanging from the corner of their lips, more ash than butt. This masculine world, ill-garbed, garlic-breath'd, run down at the heel, semi-respectable, semi-ludicrous, earnest but not sombre, runs forward to meet the other half, the female side—not quite so ill-garbed, not quite so ludicrous. They meet in the Gare, or they meet on a terrasse, over an apéritif. The great confluence of traffic arteries that meet around the Gare St. Lazare is the most humming, the most alive, the most colorful (despite the drabness) of any crowd I have ever seen. *Between five and seven.* The streets are choked. To battle against the current in the rue du Havre is like going against a Spring torrent. No order. No one direction. Each one pushing on in his individual way. Each one going forward to meet some other one. Over an apéritif. And I who have just stepped out of the train, still in the dream of transit, I who am saturated with all the sun-splashed walls, the shiny locomotives, the curtainless windows, the substantial ineradicable fields, I who have swallowed en route the Eiffel Tower, the Bois de Boulogne, the Trocadero, the flower-beds and the cemeteries, I plunge now into the froth and bubble of the rush hour. The sky overhead is motionless, the winds are stilled; there is a chaste, delicate stilliness in the heavens which the chimney pots pierce and the sirens and klaxons rend and the brakes tear to ribbons. And, like the enamelled delicacy of the sky is the contented, peaceful expression of the passers-by. It is almost Oriental in its deep passivity. It is not bred of rank, sterile optimism, of senile idealism. It is the smile of an old people who have learned how to live, and, in order to live, have fortified themselves with the most impregnable weapons, military and spiritual. Perhaps the only great realistic people left in the world to-day, the French. Armed to the teeth, and yet peaceable. Fanatically jealous of their rights, and yet tolerant. Paralyzingly ironic, yet filled with a lust for life. Old, gnarled trees, with roots so deep that they touch the oldest layers of civilization. Frugal people, not miserly. Knowing the value of everything. Even of a good time. When a French workman invites a whore to sup with him there is a regal flavor to the scene such as no millionaire, no pork-packer, no steel magnate, could conjure up. The bucket of chilled wine, the slabs of cold roast veal and mayonnaise, the mellow cheese, the fresh fruit—these things live before the eyes of a French workman and a little trot-about of the boulevards just as a *nature morte* of Cézanne lives. Lives on perpetually. If it ceases at the Café Graf, it goes on at the Café Dupont. It is going on all the time . . . as soon as the lights go on and the asphalt gets its dose of embalming fluid.

And what gives the *nature morte* its eternal life is the electric juice in the male and female bodies participating. The little whore is not worn out with fucking. She lives by it. She has no germ of white idealism in her blood, no cancerous sin and conscience in her veins. And the worker is not going to hang his head in the morning because he deceived his wife or his sweetheart.

I am living on amongst them with a thousand eyes and ears. Speaking not their language but a deeper, fundamental, symbolical language. Thanking my stars that I do not know French too well, so that I may move among them. Walking up the rue Amsterdam, toward the Café Wepler, I think invariably of Paul Morand. I think of what a curse it is for a man to trot about the globe and know every language so well, be so adaptable that he can live anywhere, rootless, nomadic, the eternal wandering Jew who acquires everything and possesses nothing. I think of the great pity it is that the world will listen to this effete cosmopolitan who is at home in New York, Rome, London, Helsingfors, Bagdad, Tokio, Timbuctoo and so on, and who turns a deaf ear to Duhamel, the intense, fanatical, patriotic, righteous, moral, indignant, prejudiced stay-at-home Frenchman. Every word that Paul Morand writes about his spiritual excursions is a nail in the coffin of a great, civilized people. It is blasphemy and anathema, the more so in that it is tepid, palatable, suave, ingratiating. A man cannot admire the Automat and a restaurant for chauffeurs at the same time. He cannot admire a Ziegfeld beauty trimmed in monkey furs and a middle-aged Frenchwoman whose beauty is certainly not on the surface. The spiritual nomad who knows no frontiers, no antagonisms, no hatreds, no prejudices, is one with the scum that emigrates to America in search of food and clothes and sanitary toilets. A man must be for and against, even if it is only *for* the world and *against* the devil. He may embrace all peoples, all customs, all ideas, but he must be *against* something too. And Paul Morand is neither for nor against. He is an opportunist. He refuses to be assimilated. That is to say, refuses to be passionately convinced, spiritually corruptible. He lives on in the flesh, eternally, obeying an international peace and good-will—and prosperity of the intestines. He creates nothing, because he admits no conflict. He recognizes no evil save famine. He has no pride because he has no humility. He is a virtuoso instead of a composer, an impresario instead of a genius. He speaks all languages fluently and penetrates none. He adapts himself everywhere to everything without losing his identity, because, as Lawrence rightly points out, instead of a living, flaming core this type carries in his guts a tiny, hard pebble. He has a mineralogical immortality.

To be specific, that is the trouble with F. too. He has this polished stone immortality, this eternal gall-stone in his gizzard. He will not yield up his soul, either to America, to France, or to Jerusalem. The world is like a magnetic field for the compass in his belly. The needle will not stay pointed north. It is errant, erratic, fugitive. It obeys every galvanized current, every tremor of the earth, every subterranean quiver and impulse. The needle is paralyzed; it has no axis of its own.

In New York F. will deride this death nonsense. The skyscrapers attract him too powerfully. In France he will decry the virginal American woman, because the realism of the French is too powerful for him. In Burgundy he will write his death book—because the soil of the peasant has choked his jewel-like philosophy with rank marsh grass. He will rave to me about Lawrence—who opened my eyes to Lawrence if not F.?—and then go to America like a disillusioned Rimbaud. He will outdo Rimbaud in his dream phantasies, then rub his hands and count his money, groan over his mythical losses.

Is there a real F.? Is that F. over there who makes a caricature of his ghost? F. the heavy tragedian. F. the Shakepearean. F. the cunt chaser. F. the dubious one. Bah! It is saddening to me. If you would do him a good turn flagellate him, drive him out of America with the whip, burn the pants off him. This man is a burlesque star. He belongs in Miner's theatre—if it is not burned down.

I saw a man that was *not* these things. I believe in that man. He can deny his death wisdom, his dream language, his lapidary exegeses, his beyond good and evil—he can deny it over there, perhaps out of delicacy—who knows what F. is capable of?—but he can't deny it to me. I won't have it. F. can't come to me with his deflated stock stubs and his mythical bank figures and his dubious imagery. I walked with F. along the Seine and I listened to a very wise man. I listened to a poet. I acted very humbly as his amanuensis in composing a certain paper—and I saw how two minutes afterwards he could play the buffoon with a race-track man, an Armenian. Sad. Sad. F. would have me believe that he really believes this Armenian understood what he was talking about. F.

preferred to believe that only because he was disappointed in me, chagrined that I could not then understand him as I ought to have understood him. My mind was not as fluid and subtle as the race-track tout's. F. was seeking for men who could respond to his new Catechism. I was slow at learning my Catechism. I knew the 23rd Psalm once by heart, without understanding a word of it. They gave me a gilt-edged Bible for my parrot-wisdom and put the letters of my name in gold on the cover of the New Testament. The 23rd Psalm only made its appeal to me because of an anguished day with J. I had to run out of the house and buy a Bible. Suddenly the words which I had memorized 25 or 30 years ago flooded up in me with meaning. A door opened up on them and I burst out with a great light. . . .

The Lord is my shepherd; I shall not want.

He maketh me to lie down in green pastures; he leadeth me beside the still waters.

He restoreth my soul: he leadeth me in the paths of righteousness for his name's sake.

Yea, though I walk through the valley of the shadow of death, I will fear no evil: for thou art with me; thy rod and thy staff they comfort me.

Thou preparest a table before me in the presence of mine enemies: thou anointest my head with oil; my cup runneth over.

Surely goodness and mercy shall follow me all the days of my life: and I will dwell in the house of the Lord for ever. . . .

If I were to try to explain what that meant to me I should get a zero—from F. But once the Catechism is learned, once you possess it, there are no more zeros or hundred percents. I have been dwelling in the House of the Lord a long while now. I want nothing. Goodness and mercy have followed me everywhere.

God giveth and God taketh away. That is what the Jewish bride wails over the body of her beloved. I always said—what could be fairer? I said it like a zany, because I have no fear of the Lord, no fear of his hand, his hereafter, his now even. I can mock the Lord and I can revere him. The Lord is all things. The Lord is the Morning Star too. And the Lord is Quetzalcoatl. The Lord is what manifests himself in man through the office of the Holy Ghost. I will not deny Him.

And the Holy Ghost in F. is with me. I know it must sound very strange in a studio on East 9th Street, when the gin bottle is opened and a new cunt hangs on the wall and the newspapers are full of riots and famine, to hear about the Holy Ghost manifesting himself in Clichy. But it is a fact. The Holy Ghost is here, dwells in this room, accompanies me when my feet march lovingly over the worn cobblestones. The Holy Ghost is in the dirty water too that the red twigs are pushing towards the Seine. All that muck and vomit in the gutter, all those newspapers in the sewers with which nameless people wiped their ass, the Holy Ghost is laving all that filth too with his eternal spirit.

The Holy Ghost made F. a philosopher and a Surrealist. When the man F. went to sleep the poet in him created new words, words that "make love" (*faire l'amour*). In his poems F. stood in the "post-mechanical" street and surrendered his intestinal self. He put no antimacassars over his images, no condoms over his ideas. The words rushed forth from the dream of sleep and they fornicated. An apocalyptic fornication, Revelation of the 21st Century, a John knowing his circumcision. In his death book a bright green bile poured itself over the world. It seemed to me, when I read that biography, that the earth had grown a little younger. I read it as a Psalm, as I read the 23rd Psalm on a day of great anguish. I wrote a letter to F., as only a Gentile can write a Jew, the words hastening on their leaden feet to catch the fleeting spirit of a man who had risen from his tomb. Afterwards I sat with F. in cafés, and the spirit which had departed left the body of the man like heavy slag seated before me. It is strange that the day I came to F. I came in quest of food. I remember how eagerly he jumped up, at the end of our first, grotesque interview—I a reporter for a Jewish paper!—and ran to the kitchen to prepare me some nourishment. It was all very symbolical. He fed me. And his nourishment is with me yet. His nourishment was in the eye, the great restless orb in his bowels that shot round over all corners of the earth and came to light on me with a strange flame. His nourishment was in the wild hysterical laugh that ended our talk at night when we lay side by side in the Villa Seurat. His nourishment was in the stubborn refusal to feed my body, a gesture I appreciated even more than F. and for which I admire him always.

He gave me so many things, and by their gifts shall ye know them. It is how I know F. By his gifts. He gave me the icy snow above the monasteries, the violet light before dawn; he gave me little god T. and M. D., he gave me the fierce glow of that *bistrot* behind the Ursulines, some vulcan glow that never was seen there before and never will be again. He gave me the frozen spirit of Goethe and the hearty guts of Rabelais. He gave me the live, burning core of Lawrence and a music of transfiguration which I had only heard before in the concert hall. He gave me his sardonic smile which comforted me more than all the empty stomachic laughter of H. I put my hand in his bowels and I felt there the live embers. I saw that the body was asbestos.

I say to you, send that man home. Send him back to his twin, L., so that they may reign over the kingdom of life and death as the Gemini did of old. These men have visions, live by visions. Their words are terribly warped and askew, they enter the plasm of the living soul like gimlets, and they bore and bore like the piercing auguries of the Mysteries.

Send him back, I say, to his twin brother. I am of another world, another time. I am less anachronistic. I am only of the last century and the one to come. F. and L., they are of no century: they are apocalyptic. They dwell in the spirit, in the Africa of the soul. I, alas, am a man of flesh and blood. I go to all things with a heavy hand, a hand saturated with blood. I want to put my hands on everything and leave a stain. The spirit is too humble for me, too evanescent. I am anchored in the body, and I want to die in this body. I am a man of the old world, a seed that was transplanted by the wind and could not blossom in the Africa of America. I belong on the heavy tree of the past, ripe with its intimate fruit. . . . My soul is not an economic soul, as is the fashion in souls to-day. My soul is my own, and it is tremendously organic, tremendously physical. The climate for my soul is here where there is quickness and corruption. My soul is given up to this passing world which is going down before the intestinal soul of America. I am proud not to belong to this century. But my pride does not run toward immortality. I want to go down before this maggot war. I could not exist among the sanitary, sterile instruments of the economic soul. Your boasted Renaissance is a false alarm. America can have no Renaissance until it has tasted death. I have had my Renaissance.

Four hours later

Europe is not dead, I tell you. . . . We are eating dinner. A sumptuous banquet made entirely of delectables. Nothing but radishes, green salad, tomatoes, sardines, black olives, Jewish bread, cheese, bananas, apple sauce. A banquet, I tell you. It costs only a few francs. But the real banquet is outside the window, the stilly

Paris sky which allows the smouldering red of the roofs to burn into your consciousness. No elevator passes to erase the scene momentarily; no wind stirs to blow things into your eyes; no storm clouds roll up to overcast your mood. The sky, the roofs, the motionless panorama, fades out like an opium dream. . . . We are talking about opium, Fred and I. About the opium that Claude Farrère writes about in *La Bataille*. It is literary opium, says Fred. It is not literary opium, say I. "All that conversation with the American woman is false," says Fred. "It is not false, it is deeply true," I assert. We go on like that, arguing, as we always argue over the evening meal.

Here is what Claude Farrère did do with opium. He gave us an opium feast. He made us drunk, not drugged, with opium. He painted a Chinese mandarin who is of the very essence of old China. Such men never existed, save in literature. Even China did not know them. But such men are real; they made Chinese history. And the important thing about this Farrère Chinaman is the way he handled his opium. He got drunk on it. He was discoursing with the Frenchman on fundamental questions. The opium was there symbolically. The opium was the dream and the void between the races. Impassable void. As he talked he made himself drunk—with his opium philosophy. But he did it deliberately, sensually, with his eyes wide open, observing the world reel and float about him.

As the bout progresses we observe a curious reversal of the laws of drunkenness. Instead of becoming indifferent to the means he becomes more sensitive. He changes the pipe bowls frequently, and with each change the demand is more exacting, more precise, more refined. He reserves his most precious, most artistic, pipe for the last. In his grand and profound stupor, when his wisdom has been thoroughly saturated with the fumes, he calls for the rare bowl. As his consciousness recedes his sensuous nature expands. As the thinker falls away the artist emerges. Drunkenness. It is unconscious on Farrère's part, of course, but it is almost as if, to apprehend this forever inscrutable soul of the Chinese, the Frenchman had to fall back on the great drunken symbology of Rabelais. The Holy Bottle is transformed into the aesthetic bowl. The mysteries are touched on in a drunken orgy of drugs. When the room spins with the heaviness of the fumes and the drunken mandarin relapses into the primitive spirit of his race, the barrier is broken down. The opium beats in the blood like a heavy tocsin. The two old races, the French and the Chinese, speak across the void. They meet in the fumes of intoxication. Drunkenness assumes a dignity of race, a profound wisdom that pierces the very marrow of the geometric soul of Jew and Christian. What Cézanne tried vainly to realize, these two old world souls achieve in the confraternity of opium. The frontiers of the intellect are franchised. The blood speaks. And the blood pronounces doom, doom for the Japanese who have sold out to false gods. The battle later is only the manifest fulfillment of the prophecy. In that victory of the Japanese over the Russian forces there is projected a defeat that is becoming more and more realized as time goes on. The battle is symbolical. It is between the Oriental Rome and the hybrid Slav. The hybrid which has not yet evolved all the way, not yet emancipated itself from the animal world. The Russo-Japanese war was the death struggle—not between Russians and Japanese (they were merely the chess pieces) but between man-the-hybrid and man-the-god. Both sides succumbed. It was a stalemate. The conclusion was indicated before the pieces were manipulated. It was all useless, a game to pass away an idle night, a night saturated with lost lives and broken ideas. In 1907 a *revolution* was still possible—but there were no men to envisage it. The war was fought instead. When the revolution came it brought no new thing. The whole latter half of the 19th century had been given up to a theoretic working out of this silly revolution. Long before the city of St. Petersburg capitulated the revolution had been accomplished in theory. The world had become socialistic without knowing it.

In China, while the Russo-Japanese conflict went on, a truly profound race looked upon the conflict for what it might reveal in the game of Chinese chess. The battle of Port Arthur was written about by a learned mandarin—in a manual for chess-players. The Chinese attached only an aesthetic importance to the war. That is, the real Chinese . . . the ones you find in literature. So-called Young China altered its physiognomy. But that too was aesthetic merely. For the Chinese have from time immemorial played with the mask. Played in a very real, tragic sense. They have altered their physiognomy radically, cruelly, in twenty centuries. Now they are putting on a dramatic Occidental mask. They will discard it maybe five or six centuries hence. They have developed the art of the theatre to its furthest limit. There is nothing beyond the Chinese theatre, as art. Because every Chinaman has become a consummate actor. He does not need to study his lines, to rehearse his piece, to stand in front of the mirror. The whole drama is burned into his soul, and the world has become his stage and his mirror. He looks through the eye-slits of his changing masks and he beholds the changes that time works upon the spirit of man. Everything has become an art to him—even his philosophy, his wisdom. The terror of life intrigues him no more. He has passed beyond terror. China has immortalized her soul in the stone images that run over her hills: the long line of monsters which signal the approach to a city are the monsters which the Chinese soul has come to know and accept, and accepting, conquer.

The Chinaman has the cold feel of stone. He hides his eternal, inhuman face behind the masks of other races. His glance is un-fathomable, the eye inscrutable. He has ceased to have visions. He does not writhe in torture any more. He knows no ideals. Every-thing is ritualized in stone. China is free of *Weltschmerz* and neu-roticism and insanity. Free of moronism. China would not under-stand a word of Freud's doctrine, or rather, having grappled with it centuries ago, she has relegated it to the dust-bin. China has transmogrified all her problems into the art of the theatre. There are no new dramas, only the perpetual drama, written in blood.

All this on China because at dinner table, while Fred is attack-ing the "literature" of Claude Farrère, I have an image which I wish to retain and put in this portrait. . . .

HENRY

A THIRD FRAGMENT FROM
"THE ROSY CRUCIFIXION"

FREUD, Freud . . . A lot of things might be laid at his door. There is Dr. Kronski now, some ten years after our semantic life at Riverside Drive. Big as a porpoise, puffing like a walrus, emitting talk like a locomotive emits steam. An injury to the head has disregulated his entire system. He has become a glandular anomaly, a study in cross-purposes.

We had not seen each other for some years. We meet again in New York. Hectic confabulations. He learns that I have had more than a speaking acquaintance with psychoanalysis during my absence abroad. I mention certain figures in that world who are well-known to him—from their writings. He's amazed that I should know them, have been accepted by them—as a friend. He begins to wonder if he hadn't made a mistake about his old friend Henry Miller. He wants to talk about it, talk and talk and talk. I refuse. That impresses him. He knows that talking is his weakness, his vice.

After a few meetings I realize that he is hatching an idea. He can't just take it for granted that I know something about psycho-analysis—he wants proofs. "What are you doing now . . . in New York?" he says. I answer that I am doing nothing, really.

"Aren't you writing?"

"No."

A long pause. Then it comes out. An experiment . . . a grand experiment. I'm the man to do it. He will explain.

The long and short of it is that he would like me to experiment with some of his patients—his ex-patients, I should say, because he has given up his practise. He's certain I can do as good as the next fellow—maybe better. "I won't tell them you're a writer," he says. "You've been a writer, but during your stay in Europe you became an analyst. How's that?"

I smiled. It didn't seem bad at all, at first blush. As a matter of fact, I had long toyed with the very idea. I jumped at it. Settled then. To-morrow, at four o'clock, he would introduce me to one of his patients.

That's how it began. Before very long I had about seven or eight patients. They seemed to be pleased with my efforts. They told Dr. Kronski so. He of course had expected it to turn out thus. He thought he might become an analyst himself. Why not? I had to confess I could see no reason against it. Any one with charm, intelligence and sensitivity might become an analyst. There were healers long before Mary Baker Eddy or Sigmund Freud were heard of. Common sense played its role too.

"To be an analyst, however," I said, not intending it as a serious remark, "one should first be analyzed himself, you know that."

"How about you?" he said.

I pretended I had been analyzed. I told him Otto Rank had done the job.

"You never told me that," he said, again visibly impressed. He had an unholy respect for Otto Rank.

"How long did it last?" he asked.

"About three months. Rank doesn't believe in prolonged analyses, I suppose you know."

"That's true," he said, growing very thoughtful. A moment later he popped it. "What about analyzing me? No, seriously. I know it's not considered a good risk when you know one another as intimately as we do, but just the same . . ."

"Yes," I said slowly, feeling my way along, "perhaps we might even explode that stupid prejudice. After all, Freud had to analyze Rank, didn't he?" (This was a lie, because Rank had never been analyzed, even by Father Freud.)

"To-morrow then, at ten o'clock!"

"Good," I said, "and be on the dot. I'm going to charge you by the hour. Sixty minutes and no more. If you're not on time it's your loss . . ."

"You're going to charge me?" he echoed, looking at me as if I had lost my mind.

"Of course I am! You know very well how important it is for the patient to pay for his analysis."

"But I'm not a patient!" he yelled. "Jesus, I'm doing you a favor."

"It's up to you," I said, affecting an air of sang-froid. "If you can get some one else to do it for nothing, well and good. I'm going to charge you the regular fee, the fee you yourself suggested for your own patients."

"Now listen," he said, "you're getting fantastic. After all, I was the one who launched you in this business, don't forget that."

"I must forget that," I insisted. "This is not a matter of sentiment. In the first place I must remind you that you not only need analysis to become an analyst, you need it because you're a neurotic. You couldn't possibly become an analyst if you weren't neurotic. Before you can heal others you have to heal yourself. And if you're not a neurotic I'll make you one before I'm through with you, how do you like that?"

He thought it was a huge joke. But the next morning he came, and he was prompt too. He looked as though he had stayed up all night to be there on time.

"The money," I said, before he had even removed his coat.

He tried to laugh it off. He settled himself on the couch, as eager to have his bottle as any infant in swaddling clothes.

"You've got to give it to me now," I insisted, "or I refuse to deal with you." I enjoyed being firm with him—it was a new role for me also.

"But how do you know that we can go through with it?" he said, trying to stall. "I'll tell you . . . if I like the way you handle me I'll pay you whatever you ask . . . within reason, of course. But don't make a fuss about it now. Come on, let's get down to brass tacks."

"Nothing doing," I said. "No tickee, no shirtee. If I'm no good you can bring suit against me, but if you want my help then you've got to pay—and pay in advance. By the way, you're wasting time, you know. Every minute you sit there haggling about the money you're wasting time that might have been spent more profitably.

It's now"—and here I consulted my watch—"it's now twelve minutes after ten. As soon as you're ready we'll begin . . ."

He was sore as a pup about it but I had him in a corner and there was nothing to do but to shell out.

As he was dishing it out—I charged him ten dollars a séance—he looked up, but this time with the air of one who has already confided himself to the doctor's hands. "You mean to say that if I should come here one day without the money, if I should happen to forget or be short a few dollars, you wouldn't take me on?"

"Precisely," I said. "We understand one another perfectly. Shall we begin . . . *now?*"

He fell back on the couch like a sheep ready for the axe. "Compose yourself," I said soothingly, sitting behind him and out of his range of vision. "Just get quiet and relax. You're going to tell me everything about yourself . . . from the very beginning. Don't imagine that you can tell it all in one sitting. We're going to have many sessions like this. It's up to you how long or how short this relationship will be. Remember that it's costing you ten dollars every time. But don't let that get under your skin, because if you think of nothing but how much it's costing you you'll forget what you intended to tell me. This is a painful procedure, but it's in your own interest. If you learn how to adapt yourself to the role of a patient you will also learn how to adapt yourself to the role of analyst. Be critical with yourself, not with me. I am only an instrument. I am here to help you. . . . Now collect yourself and relax. I'll be listening whenever you're ready to deliver yourself. . . ."

He had stretched himself out full length, his hands folded over the mountain of flesh which was his stomach. His face was very pasty; it had the blenched look, his skin, of a man who has just returned from the water closet after straining himself to death. The body had the amorphous appearance of the helpless fat man who finds the effort to raise himself to a sitting posture almost as difficult as it would be for a tortoise to right itself when it has been capsized. Whatever powers he possessed seemed to have deserted him. He flipped about restlessly for a few minutes, a human flounder weighing itself.

My exhortation to talk had paralyzed that faculty of speech which was his prime endowment. To begin with there was no longer any adversary before him to demolish. He was being asked to employ his wits against himself. He was to deliver and reveal—in a word, to *create*—and that was something he had never in his life attempted. He was to discover the meaning of meaning in a new way, and it was obvious that the thought of it terrified him.

After wriggling about, scratching himself, flopping from one side of the couch to the other, rubbing his eyes, coughing, sputtering, yawning, he opened his mouth as if to talk—but nothing came out. After a few grunts he raised himself on his elbow and turned his head in my direction. There was something piteous in the expression of his eyes.

"Can't you ask me a few questions?" he said. "I don't know where to begin."

"It would be better if I didn't ask you any questions," I said. "You will find your way if you take your time. Once you begin you'll go on like a cataract. Don't force it."

He flopped back to a prone position and sighed heavily. It would be wonderful to change places with him, I thought to myself. During the silences my will was in abeyance; I was enjoying the pleasure of making silent confession to some invisible super-analyst. I didn't feel the least bit timid or awkward, or inexperienced. Indeed, once having decided to play the role I was thoroughly in it and ready for any eventuality. I realized at once that by the mere act of assuming the role of healer one becomes a healer in fact.

I had a pad in my hand ready for use should he drop anything of importance. As the silence prolonged itself I jotted down a few notes of an extra-therapeutic nature. I remember putting down the names of Chesterton and Herriot, two Gargantuan figures who, like Kronski, were gifted with an extraordinary verbal facility. It occurred to me that I had often remarked this phenomenon *chez les gros hommes*. They were like the Medusas of the marine world —floating organs who swam in the sound of their own voice. Polyps outwardly, there was an acute, brilliant concentration noticeable in their mental faculties. Fat men were often most dynamic, most engaging, most charming and seductive. Their laziness and sloven-liness were deceptive. In the brain they often carried a diamond. And, unlike the thin man, when they washed down troughs of food their thoughts sparkled and scintillated. They were often at their best when the gustatory appetites were invoked. The thin man, on the other hand, also a great eater frequently, tends to become sluggish and sleepy when his digestive apparatus is called into play. He is usually at his best on an empty stomach.

"It doesn't matter where you begin," I said finally, fearing that he would go to sleep on me. "No matter what you lead off with you will always come back to the sore spot." I paused a moment. Then in a soothing voice I said very deliberately: "You can take a nap too, if you like. Perhaps that would be good for you."

In a flash he was wide awake and talking. The idea of paying me to take a nap electrified him. He was spilling over in all directions at once. That wasn't a bad stratagem, I thought to myself.

He began, as I say, with a rush, impelled by the frantic fear that he was wasting time. Then suddenly he appeared to have become so impressed by his own revelations that he wanted to draw me into a discussion of their import. Once again I firmly and gently refused the challenge. "Later," I said, "when we have something to go on. You've only begun . . . you've only scratched the surface."

"Are you making notes?" he asked, elated with himself.

"Don't worry about me," I replied, "think about yourself, about your problems. You're to have implicit confidence in me, remember that. Every minute you spend thinking about the effect you're producing is wasted. You're not to try to impress me . . . your task is to get sincere with yourself. There is no audience here. . . . I am just a receptacle, a big ear. You can fill it with slush and nonsense, or you can drop pearls into it. Your vice is self-consciousness. Here we want only what is real and true and *felt*. . . ."

He became silent again, fidgeted about for a few moments, then grew quite still. His hands were now folded back of his head. He had propped the pillow up so as not to relapse into sleep.

"I've just been thinking," he said, in a more quiet, contemplative mood, "of a dream I had last night. I think I'll tell it to you. It may give us a clue. . . ."

This little preamble meant only one thing—that he was still worrying about *my* end of the collaboration. He knew that in analysis one is expected to reveal one's dreams. That much of the technique he was sure of—it was orthodox. It was curious, I reflected, that no matter how much one knows *about* a subject, to act is another matter. He understood perfectly what went on, in analysis, between patient and analyst, but he had never once confronted himself with the realization of what it meant. Even now, though he hated to waste his money, he would have been tremendously relieved if, instead of going on with his dream, I had suggested that we discuss the therapeutic nature of these revelations. He would actually have preferred to invent a dream and then hash it to bits with me rather than unload himself quietly and sincerely. I felt that he was cursing himself—and me too, of course—for having suggested a situation wherein he could only, as he imagined, allow himself to be tortured.

However, with much laboring and sweating, he did manage to unfold a coherent account of the dream. He paused, when he had finished, as if expecting me to make some comment, some sign of approval or disapproval. Since I said nothing he began to play with the idea of the significance of the dream. In the midst of these intellectual excursions he suddenly halted himself and, turning his head slightly, he murmured dejectedly: "I suppose I oughtn't to do that . . . that's your job, isn't it?"

"You can do anything you please," I said quietly. "If you prefer to analyze yourself—and pay me for it—I have no objection. You realize, I suppose, that one of the things you've come to me for is to acquire confidence and trust in others. Your failure to recognize this is part of your illness."

Immediately he started to bluster. He just had to defend himself against such imputations. It wasn't true that he lacked confidence and trust. I had said that only to pique him.

"It's also quite useless," I interrupted, "to draw me into argument. If your only concern is to prove that you know more than I do then you will get nowhere. I credit you with knowing much more than I do—but that too is part of your illness—that you know too much. You will never know everything. If knowledge could save you you wouldn't be lying there."

"You're right," he said meekly, accepting my statement as a chastisement which he merited. "Now let's see . . . where was I? I'm going to get to the bottom of things . . ."

At this point I casually glanced at my watch and discovered that the hour was up.

"Time's up," I said, rising to my feet and going over to him.

"Wait a minute, won't you?" he said, looking up at me irritably and as if I had abused him. "It's just coming to me now what I wanted to tell you. Sit down a minute."

"No," I said, "we can't do that. You've had your chance . . . I've given you a full hour. Next time you'll probably do better. It's the only way to learn." And with that I yanked him to his feet.

He laughed in spite of himself. He held out his hand and shook hands with me warmly. "By God," he said, "you're all right! You've got the technique down pat. I'd have done exactly the same had I been in your boots."

I handed him his coat and hat, and started for the door to let him out.

"You're not rushing me off, are you?" he said. "I'd like to have a little chat before I go."

"You'd like to discuss the situation, is that it?" I said, marching him to the door against his will. "That's out, Dr. Kronski. No discussions. I'll look for you to-morrow at the same hour."

"But aren't you coming over to the house to-night?"

"No, that's out too. Until you finish your analysis we will have no relation but that of doctor and patient. It's much better, you'll see." I took his hand, which was hanging limp, raised it and shook him a vigorous good-bye. He backed out of the door as if dazed.

He came every other day for the first few weeks, then he begged for a stagger schedule, complaining that his money was giving out. I knew of course that it was a drain on him, because since he had given up his practise his only income was from the insurance company. He had probably salted a tidy sum away, before the accident. The problem, however, was to rout him out of his state of dependency, drain him of every penny he owned, and restore the desire to earn a living again. One would hardly have believed it possible that a man of his energies, powers, could deliberately castrate himself in order to get the better of an insurance company. Undoubtedly the injuries he had sustained in the automobile accident had impaired his health. For one thing he had become quite a monster. Deep down I was convinced that the accident had merely accelerated the weird metamorphosis. When he popped the idea of becoming an analyst I realized that there was still a spark of hope in him. I accepted the proposition at face value, knowing that his pride would never permit him to confess that he had become "a case." I used the word "illness" deliberately always—to give him a jolt, to make him admit that he needed help. I also knew that, if he gave himself half a chance, he would eventually break down and put himself in my hands completely.

It was taking a big gamble, however, to presume that I could break down his pride. There were layers of pride in him, just as there were layers of fat around his girdle. He was one vast defense system, and his energies were constantly being consumed in repairing the leaks which sprang up everywhere. With pride went suspicion. Above all, the suspicion that he may have misjudged my ability to handle the "case." He had always flattered himself that he knew his friends' weak spots. Undoubtedly he did—it's not such a difficult thing to do. He kept alive the weaknesses of his friends in order to bolster the sense of his own superiority. Any improvement, any development, on the part of a friend he looked upon as a betrayal. It brought out the envious side of his nature. . . . In short, it was a vicious treadmill, his whole attitude toward others.

The accident had not essentially changed him. It had merely altered his appearance, exaggerated what was already there latent in his being. The monster which he had always been potentially was now a flesh and blood fact. He could look at himself every day in the mirror and see with his own eyes what he had made of himself. He could see in his wife's eyes the revulsion he created in

others. Soon his children would begin to look at him strangely—
that would be the last straw.

By attributing everything to the accident he of course succeeded
in gathering a few crumbs of comfort from the unwary. He also
succeeded in concentrating attention upon his physique and not
his psyche. But alone with himself he knew that it was a game
which would soon peter out. He couldn't go on forever making a
smoke screen of his enormous bundle of flesh.

When he lay on the couch unburdening himself it was curious
that no matter from what point in the past he started out he always saw himself as strange and monstrous. *Doomed* was more
precisely the way he felt about himself. Doomed from the very beginning. A complete lack of confidence as to his private destiny.
Naturally and inevitably he had imparted this feeling to others; in
some way or other he would manage to so manoeuvre that his
friend or sweetheart would fail him or betray him. He picked them
with the same foreknowledge that Christ displayed in choosing
Judas.

What kind of drama do you want to stage?

Kronski wanted a brilliant failure, a failure so brilliant that it
would outshine success. He seemed to want to prove to the world
that he could know as much and be as much as anybody, and at
the same time prove that it was pointless—to be anything or to
know anything. He seemed congenitally incapable of realizing that
there is an *inherent* significance in everything. He wasted himself
in an effort to prove that there never could be any final proofs,
never for a moment conscious of the absurdity of defeating logic
with logic. It reminded me, his attitude, of the youthful Céline
saying with furious disgust: "She could go right ahead and be even
lovelier, a hundred thousand times more luscious, she wouldn't get
any change out of me—not a sigh, not a sausage. She could try

223

every trick and wile imaginable, she could strip-tease for all she was worth to please me, rupture herself, or cut off three fingers of her hand, she could sprinkle her short hairs with stars—but never would I talk, never! Not the smallest whisper. I should say not! That's all there was about it . . ."

The variety of defense works with which the human being hedges himself in is just as astounding as the visible mechanisms in the animal and insect worlds. There is a texture and substance even to the psychic fortifications, as you discover when you begin to penetrate the forbidden precincts of the ego. The most difficult ones are not necessarily those who hide behind a plate of armor, be it of iron, steel, tin or zinc. Neither are they so difficult, though they offer greater resistance, who encase themselves in rubber, and who, *mirabile dictu*, appear to have acquired the art of vulcanizing the perforated barriers of the soul. The most difficult ones are what I would call the "Piscean malingerers". These are the fluid, solvent egos who lie still as a foetus in the uterine marshes of the stagnant self. When you puncture the sac, when you think Ah! I've got you at last!—you find nothing but clots of mucus in your hand. These are the baffling ones, in my opinion. They are like the "soluble fish" of the Dadaist metempsychology. They grow without a backbone; they dissolve at will. All you can ever lay hold of are the indissoluble, indestructible nuclei—the disease germs, so to say. About such individuals one feels that in body, mind and soul they are nothing but disease. They were born to illustrate the pages of text-books. In the realm of the psyche they are the gynae-cological monsters whose only life is that of the pickled specimen which adorns the laboratory shelf.

Their most successful disguise is compassion. How tender they can become! How considerate! How touchingly sympathetic! But if you could ever get a look at them—just one fluorescent glance!—

what a pretty egomaniac you would see. They bleed with every bleeding soul in the universe—but they never fall apart. At the crucifixion they hold your hand and slake your thirst, weep like drunken cows. They are the professional mourners from time immemorial, even in the Golden Age when there was nothing to weep about. Misery and suffering is their habitat, and at the equinox they bring the whole kaleidoscopic pattern of life to a glaucous glue.

There are psychical specimens of this order who walk out of the analyst's office to take their place in the ranks of dehumanized labor. They have been pared down to an efficient little bundle of mutilated reflexes. They not only earn their own living, they support their aged relatives. They refuse the niche of fame in the hall of horrors to which they are entitled; they elect to compete with other souls in a quasi-soulful way. They die hard, like knots of wood in a giant oak. They resist the axe, even when it is all up.

I wouldn't go so far as to say that Kronski was of this order, but I must confess that many a time he gave me such an impression. There was many a time when I felt like swinging the axe and finishing him off. Nobody would have missed him; nobody would have mourned his loss. He had got himself born a cripple and a cripple he would die, that's how it struck me. As an analyst I couldn't see of what benefit he would be to others. As analyst he would only see cripples everywhere, even among the god-like. Other analysts, and I had known some personally who were most successful, had recuperated from their crippledom, so to speak, and were of use to other cripples like themselves, because they had at least learned to use their artificial limbs with ease and perfection. They were good demonstrators.

There was one thought, however, which bored into me like a gimlet during these sessions with Kronski. It was the notion that every one, no matter how far gone he was, could be saved. Yes, if one had infinite time and infinite patience, it could be done. It began to dawn on me that the healing art was not at all what people imagined it to be, that it was something very simple, too simple, in fact, for the ordinary mind to grasp. To put it in the simple way it came to my mind I would say that it was like this: *everybody becomes a healer the moment he forgets about himself.* The sickness which we see everywhere, the bitterness and disgust which life inspires in so many of us, is only the reflection of the sickness which we carry within us. Prophylactics will never secure us against the world disease, because we bear the world within. No matter how marvellous human beings become the sum total will yield an external world which is painful and imperfect. As long as we live self-consciously we must always fail to cope with the world. It is not necessary to die in order to come at last face to face with reality. Reality is here and now, everywhere, gleaming through every reflection that meets the eye. Prisons and even lunatic asylums are emptied of their inmates when a more vital danger menaces the community. When the enemy approaches the political exile is recalled to share in the defense of his country. At the last ditch it gets dinned into our thick skulls that we are all part and parcel of the same flesh. When our very lives are threatened we begin to live. Even the psychic invalid throws away his crutches in such moments. For him the greatest joy is to realize that there is something more important than himself. All his life he has turned on the spit of his own roasted ego. He made the fire with his own hands. He drips in his own juices. He makes himself a tender morsel for the demons he liberated with his own hands. That is the picture of human life on this planet called the Earth. Everybody is a neurotic, down to the last man and woman. The healer, or the analyst, if you like, is only a super-neurotic. He has put the

Indian sign on us. To be cured we must rise from our graves and throw off the cerements of the dead. Nobody can do it for another—it is a private affair which is best done collectively. We must die as egos and be born again in the swarm, not separate and self-hypnotized, but individual and related.

As to salvation and all that . . . The greatest teachers, the true healers, I would say, have always insisted that they can only point the way. The Buddha went so far as to say: "Believe nothing, no matter where you read it or who has said it, *not even if I have said it*, unless it agrees with your own reason and your own common sense."

The great ones do not set up offices, charge fees, give lectures, or write books. Wisdom is silent, and the most effective propaganda for truth is the force of personal example. The great ones attract disciples, lesser figures whose mission it is to preach and to teach. These are the gospellers who, unequal to the highest task, spend their lives in converting others. The great ones are indifferent, in the profoundest sense. They don't ask you to believe: they electrify you by their behavior. They are the awakeners. What you do with your petty life is of no concern to them. What you do with your life is only of concern to you, they seem to say. In short, their only purpose here on earth is to inspire. And what more can one ask of a human being than that?

To be sick, to be neurotic, if you like, is to ask for guarantees. The neurotic is the flounder that lies on the bed of the river, securely settled in the mud, waiting to be speared. For him death is the only certainty, and the dread of that grim certainty immobilizes him in a living death far more horrible than the one he imagines but knows nothing about.

The way of life is toward fulfillment, however, wherever it may lead. To restore a human being to the current of life means not only to impart self-confidence but an abiding faith in the processes of life. A man who has confidence in himself *must* have confidence in others, confidence in the fitness and rightness of the universe. When a man is thus anchored he ceases to worry about the fitness of things, about the behavior of his fellowmen, about right and wrong, and justice and injustice. If his roots are in the current of life he will float on the surface like a lotus and he will blossom and give forth fruit. He will draw his nourishment from above and below; he will send his roots down deeper and deeper, fearing neither the depths nor the heights. The life that is in him will manifest itself in growth, and growth is an endless, eternal process. He will not be afraid of withering, because decay and death are part of growth. As a seed he began and as a seed he will return. Beginnings and endings are only partial steps in the eternal process. The process is everything . . . the way . . . the Tao.

The way of life! A grand expression. Like saying *Truth.* There is nothing beyond it. It is all.

And so the analyst says, "Adapt yourself!" He does not mean, as some wish to think—adapt yourself to this rotten state of affairs! He means—adapt yourself to life! *Become an adept!* That is the highest adjustment—to make oneself an adept.

The delicate flowers are the first to perish in a storm; the giant is laid low by a sling-shot. For every height that is gained new and more baffling dangers menace us. The coward is often buried beneath the very wall against which he huddled in fear and anguish. The finest coat of mail can be penetrated by a skillful thrust. The greatest armadas are eventually sunk; Maginot lines are always circumvented. The Trojan horse is always waiting to be trotted out. Where then does security lie? What protection can you invent that has not already been thought of? It is useless to think of security: there is none. The man who looks for security, even in the mind, is like a man who would chop off his limbs in order to have artificial ones which will give him no pain or trouble.

In the insect world is where we see the defense system par excellence. In the gregarious life of the animal world we see another kind of defense system. By comparison the human being seems a helpless creature. In the sense that he lives a more exposed life he is. But this ability to expose himself to every risk is precisely his strength. A god would have no recognizable defense whatever. He would be one with life, moving in all dimensions freely.

Fear, hydra-headed fear, which is rampant in all of us, is a hangover from lower forms of life. We are straddling two worlds, the one from which we have just emerged and the one toward which we are heading. That is the deepest meaning of the word human, that we are a link, a bridge, a promise. It is in us that the life process is being carried to fulfillment. We have a tremendous responsibility, and it is the gravity of that which awakens our fears. We know that if we do not move forward, if we do not realize our potential being, we shall relapse, sputter out, and drag the world down with us. We carry Heaven and Hell within us: we are the cosmogonic builders. We have choice—and all creation is our range. For some it is a terrifying prospect. It would be better, think they, if Heaven were above and Hell below—anywhere outside, but not within. But that comfort has been knocked from under us. There are no places to go to, either for reward or punishment. The place is always here and now, in your own person and according to your own fancy. The world is exactly what you picture it to be, always, every instant. It is impossible to shift the scenery about and pretend that you will enjoy another, a different act. The setting is permanent, changing with the mind and heart, not according to the dictates of an invisible stage director. You are the author, director and actor all in one: the drama is always going to be your own life, not someone else's. A beautiful, terrible, ineluctable drama, like a suit made of your own skin. Would you want it otherwise? Could you invent a better drama?

Lie down, then, on the soft couch which the analyst provides, and try to think up something different. The analyst has endless time and patience; every minute you detain him means money in his pocket. He is like God, in a sense—the God of your own creation. Whether you whine, howl, beg, weep, implore, cajole, pray or curse he listens. He is just a big ear minus a sympathetic nervous system. He is impervious to everything but truth. If you think it pays to fool him then fool him. Who will be the loser? If you think he can help you, and not yourself, then stick to him until you rot. He has nothing to lose. But if you realize that he is not a god but a human being like yourself, with worries, defects, ambitions, frailties, that he is not the repository of an all-encompassing wisdom but a wanderer, like yourself, along the path, perhaps you will cease pouring it out like a sewer, however melodious it may sound to your ears, and rise up on your own two legs and sing with your own God-given voice. To confess, to whine, to complain, to commiserate, always demands a toll. To sing it doesn't cost you a penny. Not only does it cost nothing—you actually enrich others. *Sing the praises of the Lord*, it is enjoined. Aye, sing out! Sing out, O Master-builder! Sing out, glad warrior! *But*, you quibble, how can I sing when the world is crumbling, when all about me is bathed in blood and tears? Do you realize that the martyrs sang when they were being burned at the stake? They saw nothing crumbling, they heard no shrieks of pain. They sang because they were full of faith. Who can demolish faith? Who can wipe out joy? Men have tried, in every age. But they have not succeeded. Joy and faith are inherent in the universe. In growth there is pain and struggle; in accomplishment there is joy and exuberance; in

230

fulfillment there is peace and serenity. Between the planes and spheres of existence, terrestrial and super-terrestrial, there are ladders and lattices. The one who mounts sings. He is made drunk and exalted by unfolding vistas. He ascends sure-footedly, thinking not of what lies below, should he slip and lose his grasp, but of what lies ahead. *Everything lies ahead.* The way is endless, and the farther one reaches the more the road opens up. The bogs and quagmires, the marshes and sink-holes, the pits and snares, are all in the mind. They lurk in waiting, ready to swallow one up the moment one ceases to advance. The phantasmal world is the world which has not been fully conquered over. It is the world of the past, never of the future. To move forward clinging to the past is like dragging a ball and chain. The prisoner is not the one who has committed a crime, but the one who clings to his crime and lives it over and over. We are all guilty of crime, the great crime of not living life to the full. But we are all potentially free. We can stop thinking of what we have failed to do and do whatever lies within our power. What these powers that are in us may be no one has truly dared to imagine. That they are infinite we will realize the day we admit to ourselves that imagination is everything. Imagination is the voice of daring. If there is anything Godlike about God it is that He has dared to imagine everything.

SHADOWY MONOMANIA

(From *Random Notes on D. H. Lawrence*)

NOTICE: *These notes were written in 1933 and '34; since then I have come across a book on Lawrence * which I consider the best to date. It is the work of a painter, not a writer. It gives a picture of Lawrence which is far from ideal, without in the least diminishing his stature. It is a warm, glowing document written with great effort and with no thought but that of telling the truth. I should like to recommend it to all who are interested in the Lawrence legend.*

HENRY MILLER

WHENEVER Lawrence's name comes up there is sure to arise a discussion as to the relative merits of *Sons and Lovers* and *Lady*

* A *Poet and Two Painters*, by Knud Merrild, published by George Routledge & Sons, Ltd., London, and reprinted by The Viking Press, New York. Both editions now exhausted.

232

Chatterley's Lover. These two works, the one representing the youthful Lawrence and the other representing the mature man, are contrasted as if they exemplified antagonistic elements in his nature. Those who prefer the former regard his later works as a decline in thought and creation—not a decline, merely, but a progressive deterioration, with *Lady Chatterley's Lover* touching the abyss. Very few of those who admire the latter work are inclined to see in it anything like an approach to artistic perfection, yet they persist in regarding it as one of his most important creations. Superficially there is a great gulf between the two works, but it is no more profound a division than that which characterizes the passage from youth to maturity. In the works of every creative individual there should be, and usually is, this divergence. Sometimes it is so strongly marked that between the early and the late works there is scarcely anything to bind them except the author's name.

At best we are able to detect in the artist's early works the seeds of the future man, and this not so much by the individuality of his expression as by the transparency of his influences. The origins of the man and the germs of future conflict lie clearly exposed in the works of youth. Henceforth we witness the struggle of the artist to free himself from the discordant elements of his being, to establish the superiority of certain values revealed to him during some crisis in his life, and to reject other values which had been of tremendous importance to him during the period of incubation. In the case of a great artist, such as Goethe, the whole conflict and development is summarized in one work, which covers a life-time. This work represents the man's life, and when it is completed he dies. The case of Proust is another example.

With Lawrence one feels dubious that he might have gone much beyond *Lady Chatterley's Lover*. The restricted life he led, his deliberate isolation from all the stimulating currents of art, his intensely personal vision, all this led to an inevitable withering at the roots.

Had he continued in the vein of *Sons and Lovers* he would undoubtedly have become a popular artist, the sort which the Anglo-Saxon world would have been proud to acclaim as its own. The high poetic feeling for Nature, which so many of the English poets share, and which permeates *Sons and Lovers*, represents in Lawrence the vast and compelling power of tradition: there runs through it that nostalgic feeling for death so noticeable in all the poets of Nature. Lawrence emerged from this adolescent union with Nature to die a bigger death. Under the spell of Idea he allowed a whole world of past to die in him; he killed the poet in himself in order to become the evangel of a new order. He sought to identify himself, and the world, with a greater cosmos. After *Sons and Lovers* he appears on the horizon of his unknown world as an archangel flourishing a glittering sword. His tongue becomes sharp, his words are bitter. He searches frantically for symbols of destruction, and admits of no solutions other than his own.

The world, I fear, may remember Lawrence only through his Lady Chatterley. And how is one to know Lawrence through this bitterly distorted, bitterly defiant expression of his soul? Not in any of his works does he reveal himself completely, and *Lady Chatterley's Lover* is one of his most extreme expressions. The phallic mystic! Phallic obviously enough, but where is the mysticism? It is there well enough for those who know him and understand him, but it is implicit in the work rather than expressed. The prophet who has expressed himself tyrannically by parable and symbol throughout all his works, the flaming archangel who rises to frenzy and ecstasy by his vision of the sacred aspect of life, this man, like the prophets of old who stalk through the Old Testament covered with excrement, finally despairs of making himself understood. Since there is no other way of making clear his message he does the crude and obvious thing of performing a miracle for the crowd: he gives them a genital banquet. *Lady Chatterley's Lover* is no more the substance of Lawrence's gospel than are the loaves and fishes which Christ distributed among the multitude: it is only the evidence of unseen powers.

The book is obscene and there is no justification for it. Because it requires none. And the miracles of Jesus are obscene. Because there is no justification for them either. Life is miraculous and obscene, and neither is there any justification for life. The crowd will accept neither life nor obscenity nor miracle; all that is sacred is taboo, nay, incomprehensible to the multitude. If *Lady Chatterley's Lover* represents another of Lawrence's "failures" it does so only because of its impurity, its compromise. And by that I mean that only wherein it is obscene is it magnificent; in its obscenity lies its great purity, its miraculous, its sacred quality. The rest, that padding, that cotton-wool in which all his visions were wrapped, is dead weight, the humus of decomposing bodies which he has not successfully sloughed off.

It is a pity that Lawrence ever wrote anything *about* obscenity, because in doing so he nullified his creation. Lawrence was a frightfully sensitive and a frightfully timid man. He sought to justify his violence, to explain it away. But violence is its own justification, a pure thing. And obscenity is one of the many forms of violence. It is the expression of the insufficiency of symbol, the explosion which occurs when the tension of antagonistic forces is no longer adequate to preserve the image. Of all the symbols which man has created to make his universe supportable, i.e., understandable, meaningful, the sexual symbols are the least secure; for in the riddle of sex man comes closest to tasting the full savour of death.

Sex is the Janus-faced symbol of creation-destruction. The great lie of life here comes to the surface; the contradiction refuses to be resolved.

When, consequently, in his effort to annihilate the fraud and sham of existence (all that which is embraced in the word "civilization"), Lawrence concentrates on the symbology of sex, it is with the cunning and malice of the female. It is an act of the deepest betrayal, a treachery toward that masculine world which he despairs of overthrowing. He understands too well the role of each. He struggles to go beyond that point at which they separated, to achieve some superhuman hermaphroditism which would unite the warring forces in him. But to achieve this mystical nexus demands a tension beyond any mortal man. Lawrence goes to pieces in this remote and frozen realm; he explodes with virulent obscenity, having arrived at some mysterious, utterly incomprehensible frontier of the mind whose outlines even are impossible to communicate.

In *Apocalypse* he writes: "What we want is to destroy our false inorganic connections, especially those related to money, and reestablish the living organic connections with the cosmos, the sun and earth, with mankind, and nation and family. Start with the sun and the rest will slowly, slowly happen."

Nothing vastly unfamiliar here, to those familiar with Lawrence's thinking. A certain triviality perhaps in his reference to the importance of money. But the important line, the really cryptic line, is the last: "start with the sun and the rest will slowly, slowly happen." From the very beginning of his development as thinker he has stressed the sun; it is the alpha and omega for him. In the *Fantasia of the Unconscious*, when paraphrasing Fraser's words (from *The Golden Bough*), he puts it thus: "it must have appeared to the ancient Aryan that the sun was periodically recruited from life." Frazer had written: "from the fire which resided in the sacred oak." And Lawrence concludes: "which is what the early Greek philosophers were always saying. And which seems to me the real truth, the clue to the cosmos."

Now this imperative need in him to restore the generative principle of life, which the sun symbolized for the older masculine Cultures, arose from his awareness and fear of the feminizing character of our civilization. The disintegration which he perceived everywhere he felt most keenly in the world of sex. He saw everything going grey, opaque—typical Laurencian adjectives. He did not want to accept the current idea of the sun being the source of life—our temporal planetary life—because he could not face the thought of a possible end to life. He not only will not concede that there are any dead planets, he will not even concede that the source of our earthly life is the sun. The idea is anathema to Lawrence— therefore he reverses the process. It is we, the living, who give life to the sun and stars, to the dead planets too. The origin of life, whence we come, whither we go—he admits that he knows nothing about these questions. There is no solution. He knows only this thing called Life, whose heart is mystery. If the intelligence of man denies this, then there is something wrong with the intellect—the intellect must be subordinated to the blood. It is the mind of man, he says, which has created all the snares and pitfalls. The mind would deny the very life instinct.

"If we come to think of it," says Lawrence, "light and dark mean whether we have our face or our back towards the sun. If we have our face to the sun, then we establish the circuit of cosmic or universal or material or infinite sympathy. These four adjectives—cosmic, universal, material, and infinite—are almost interchangeable, and apply, as we see, to that realm of the non-individual existence which we call the realm of the substantial death. It is the universe which has resulted from the death of individuals. And to this universe alone belongs the quality of infinity: to the universe of death. Living individuals have no infinity save in this relation to the total death-substance and death-being, the summed-up cosmos."

In coming now to a more detailed analysis of the ideas set forth in the *Fantasia of the Unconscious* I think it is important to recognize first of all that Lawrence regarded his cosmological views as the crude stammerings of an over-civilized being who had caught a few hints of a lost wisdom. He tries to draw a distinction between this subjective science of his, "established on data of living experience and sure intuition", and the objective science of modern thought "which concerns itself only with phenomena, and with phenomena as regarded in their cause-and-effect relationship." He has nothing to say against this science of ours, he adds. Perfect, as far as it goes. "But to regard it as exhausting the whole scope of human possibility in knowledge seems to me just puerile. Our science is a science of the dead world."

He goes on to say that this other science (in terms of life) was once universal, that it was esoteric, and invested in a large priesthood. He imagines that to have been so in a Glacial Period when men wandered back and forth from Atlantis to the Polynesian Continent, as men now sail from Europe to America. In that world, he says, men lived and taught and knew, and were in one complete correspondence over all the earth. "Then came the melting of the glaciers, and the world flood. The refugees from the drowned continents fled to the high places of America, Europe, Asia and the Pacific Isles. And some degenerated naturally into cave men, neolithic and paleolithic creatures, and some retained their marvellous innate beauty and life-perfection, as the South Sea Islanders, and some wandered savage in Africa, and some, like

Druids or Etruscans or Chaldeans or Amerindians or Chinese, refused to forget, but taught the old wisdom, only in its half-forgotten, symbolic forms. More or less forgotten, as knowledge: remembered as ritual, gesture, and myth-story."

Now this is all part of the scientific myth of to-day. At least, the picture is that which the men of science have bequeathed us. And Lawrence seems to recognize this, in part, when he says—"I am not a proper archaeologist nor an ethnologist. I am no 'scholar' of any sort. But I am very grateful to scholars for their sound work." *Grateful?* A strange way of putting it, indeed. As for the "sound work"—who is it that patronizingly admits this? Why the pompous little inheritor of the esoteric wisdom, who is neither a scientist nor a scholar of any sort. This is the treacherous foundation on which the whole superstructure is to rise.

It is important to bear this in mind constantly. "I have found hints, suggestions for what I say here in all kinds of scholarly books, from the Yoga and Plato and St. John the Evangel and the early Greek philosophers like Herakleitos down to Fraser and his *Golden Bough*, and even Freud and Frobenius. Even then I only remember hints—and I proceed by intuition. . . ." A delightfully childish attitude whereby he escapes all responsibility for error. He strove so desperately to save himself from attack—his ideas even more than himself. They were precious to him, his ideas, because they represented his universe. That was his universe: Idea. And that is why his language is so saturated with blood and feeling, with instinct and emotion. In himself he had little of it; he transfers it to his ideas, so that *they* at least may live. When he says that he was born a corpse, that we were all born corpses, he meant it. But he lulls himself into forgetfulness by his words.

Under the spell of his dark language we are almost convinced at times that we are in the presence of a Greek. Perhaps of all the peoples whose temples he ransacked the Greeks gave him most. Certainly it was they who gave him the notion of solid matter, of the substantial body, of the sublimity of the microcosm, of eternal recurrence, of the "thrice unknown darkness", of the one and all, of many, many things, so many things that he could not remember them all if he tried. But the Greeks lived out their drama of ideas. The fact that they borrowed them from older peoples is not to impugn their ideas in the least. It is the way in which they converted them to their own use which distinguishes them from all other peoples we have known. It is this travail of conversion, this agony of birth and death in which the Greek image of the universe was fixed, that gives us the feeling of their unique and splendorous existence. They did not simply pass into history. They made history.

The Greek in Lawrence is the faint (monomaniacal) shadow of something dimly remembered. It hovers over our modern world like a ghost. The modern world, which would turn again to the Orient for its inspiration, seems to ignore the fact that it was the poisonous wisdom of the East which sapped the courage of the Greeks. The emphasis on wisdom, as a relief from striving, which seems to be the last word of our present-day philosophers, the psychologists, is a return to that poisonous fount which destroyed the antique world. To have conquered the Centaur, to have liberated the soul from the lower regions, to mingle freely with the gods on earth, as men, one would imagine this the utmost that the race of man might aspire to. And so indeed it is. But there comes a time when man cannot support the idea of living as a god; he becomes self-conscious, he turns inward and dreams, he falls in love with his own image. Having completed his creation, having visualized his own representation, he dies in the mirror. The image fades out, and while the mirror itself is disintegrating there speaks the soothing voice of wisdom which would reconcile the loss of everything. In wisdom there is death. And in esoteric wisdom there is the quintessence of all the deaths which man has tasted. Mummy upon mummy, inlaid like pearls, in some vast edifice of death.

And now we come to the man: the "sex-crucified", the "sex-sodden", the "almost sexual weakling", the "spiritually precocious", etc. The man who wanted to make a God of himself, as Frieda said. The man who was definitely not a gentleman. The man who was an aristocrat—an aristocrat of the spirit, like Plato, like Jesus, like. . . .

Let us look at him for a moment in his Chaplinesque role. Let us look at him as a modern Don Quixote tilting against the windmills of white idealism. Let us look at him as the wanderer on the face of the earth. Let us look at him as a "productive neurotic".

He had twenty years of writing. And when one examines not the bulk alone but the quality of his work, when one considers the age in which he wrote—an age so hostile to artistic production, so paralyzing, so devastating!—when one considers these things quite impartially, it is only fair to say that he was a giant. Until almost the very end he was a poor and harried man. A sick man a good part of the time. Frail all his life. He was misunderstood, ostracized, rejected. He wandered over a good part of the globe. He darned his own socks, built his own fires, baked his own bread. He wrote novels, short stories, essays, poems, plays, books of travel and philosophy. He waged war wherever he went. He made enemies. He was loved too, but mostly he was hated. He dug among the Etruscan ruins in search of a civilization he loved. He translated one of the great novels of the age (Verga). He wrote some of the most trenchant criticism of American literature ever penned—the essays on Poe, Whitman and Melville, probably unsurpassed in all critical literature. He painted, and for the collection of his paint-ings he wrote an Introduction in which once again he said the most penetrating things, things about Cézanne particularly which are unsurpassed. He contracted tuberculosis for reasons which he himself has described. He died of the white sickness against which he had fought all his life, after explaining its symbolism. And on his death bed he wrote several volumes which contain more of life than can be found in the whole output of contemporary American literature. He burned so vividly and intensely that he left no ash. His critics and detractors are still picking the embers out of the fire.

It seems to me that in twenty years he showed enough activity to prove that he was alive. If, as he said, we are all born corpses, then it is also true that he was the most alive corpse in our time. The only value of an artist, he used to say, is whether he reveals life. Lawrence brought life and revealed life. Men will feed on him for generations to come, as they fed on him while he lived— "sucked the life out of him", to use his own words.

It seems to be forgotten, when it comes to looking at the man, that he was first and foremost an artist, a special kind of artist, one who consumed life, one who had to drain it to the full. He took nothing for granted: he experienced everything for himself. And having tested life for himself, having experienced for himself the truth of things, having forged for himself an iron conscience, he could say with all the vehemence of his positive spirit—"*I am not wrong. Who are you, who is anybody else, to tell me I am wrong? I am not wrong!*" When the tepid admiration of Richard Aldington halts before the violent extremism of Lawrence, when his mild, gentle spirit wishes to reprove the living man of genius, he says: "I fear that Lawrence will expire before the Bull" (i.e., The British Empire). Well, Mr. Aldington is wrong. D. H. Lawrence will outlive the British Empire. He will outlive all the present-day tottering empires. An empire lives only as long as it has living geniuses to give it flame and purpose. As for the British Bull, from all indications it is doing its best to snuff out its own life. No, the British Empire is not immortal. But the men who gave it life are immortal. Together, from whatever empires they arose, these spirits live on and help to bring about the only empire which can endure—the kingdom of the spirit.

So much for the heroic side of Lawrence. He had another side, as all men have, one that was pathetic and often ridiculous. This role Chaplin has immortalized in every film. It is the human role: man the homunculus waging an uneven battle against Fate. Here we see him as a sort of immortal bedbug, very tiny, very annoying, very smelly, managing by instinctive cunning to evade the squat, crushing thumb of the torporous giant Life. It is this side of him which the crowd relishes. They adore seeing him thumb his nose at the giant, or stick out his behind, or escape with his breeches coming down, or slip on a banana peel. The spokesmen of the crowd are the intellectuals who ponder over the imaginative life of the homunculus in order to detect the human traces in it—the human porcupine tracks which he left behind as he wriggled out of the giant's grasp. They come with their microscopic lenses and their testing and weighing apparatus, and they reconstruct a fine bedbug activity which they are arrogant enough to believe will make the mystery less mysterious. They analyze the lines so finely, and the spaces between the lines, that suddenly it seems possible for them to announce how it was that on a certain night in June or September the homunculus baptized David Herbert Lawrence failed to make proper love to his wife and so brought unto himself a train of misery and woe—and a few books to boot. They can even make the bed squeak, so marvellous are

243

their laboratory researches. They sweat and wrestle with these deeds and events in order to give a plausible—or shall I say "acceptable"?—reality to the man's life when all the while the man himself has been trying to establish another reality. While they write their biographies the author spills his heart's blood writing the autobiography of his soul.

Yes, Lawrence like other men of genius had his Chaplinesque moments—especially when he was surrounded by the women. Chaplin, as every one has probably observed, is most pathetic and ridiculous when posing as the lover. Woman is the dire test of reality. Woman is; man pretends. Lawrence the artist almost succeeded in becoming God. Lawrence the man gets plates smashed over his head by an irate spouse. (And he deserved it, too, from all accounts.) Lawrence the philosopher talks almost as well as Socrates, better sometimes, in my humble opinion. He can talk about "going beyond woman", can say the most magnificent things about "man's earnest purpose" . . . but in private life his wife leads him around by the apron-strings, as his mother did before her. Frieda's rages, as they are given us by eye-witnesses, are often more revelatory than Lawrence's magnificent speeches. "I'm just as important as you are!" she would blaze at him. And the more one reads about Frieda, the more one is inclined to agree with her. In fact, as a person, Frieda is much more important. There is a legendary aura about Frieda, an aura of splendid human opulence; she seems to dwarf all the figures with whom they came in contact. Particularly the incredible and horrendous female admirers. "You're not an aristocrat!" Frieda once flung at him, when she had been goaded beyond control. There were many things Frieda said which it hurt her to say, though they were true and just. But no one ought to pay attention to Frieda's words. Frieda Lawrence was a great mate, and perhaps the only woman Lawrence could have married and lived with successfully.

The aristocrat! If taking one's socks off and darning them in a train is any indication, then of course Lawrence was not an aristocrat. His language, too, was hardly that of the aristocrat. A bit coarse at times—perhaps *foul* would be a better word. And yet this coarse little collier's son with his Midlands accent and his uncontrollable temper could write the most magnificent prose, could describe most delicately and imaginatively how the Holy Ghost secreted itself in the seed of the dandelion beneath its umbrella of hairs. He wrote a great deal about the Holy Ghost, oddly enough, for a man who was not an aristocrat. He could write about the flame of life—and blow his nose in an old letter. So we are told. Indeed, we are told all sorts of terribly little intriguing things like this, all sorts of personal details that go to make up the daily humbuggery of a genius' life, by the admiring cows who flocked about him all his life.

It is my intention to give as many of these little items as possible, so that in addition to the heroic figure we shall have the every-day figure, the perpetual bedbug which the mob has to smell in order to know the thing lives or lived. It is necessary to present the "collective" side of him. For had he not been so human, Lawrence would not have gone up to the mountain top and died of the dread white disease.

One of the most poignant passages Lawrence wrote is given in *Kangaroo*, which is about the Australian adventure. The sense of desolation which is revealed in this extraordinary passage belongs as much to this side of the Pacific as the other. I give it here because in a moment I am coming again to the white man's disease. . . .

"To be alone, mindless and memoryless by the sea. To be alone

245

with a long, wide shore and land, heartless, soulless. As alone and as absent and as present as an aboriginal, dark on the sand in the sun. The strange falling-away of everything. The palms in the sea-wind were sere like old mops. The jetty straddled motionless from the shore. He had it all to himself. And there, with his hands in his pockets, he drifted into indifference. The far-off, far-off, far-off indifference. The world revolved and revolved and disappeared. Like a stone that has fallen into the sea, his old life, the old meaning, fell and rippled, and there was vacancy, with the sea and the shore in it. Far-off, far-off, as if he had landed on another planet, as a man might land after death. Leaving behind the body of care. Even the body of desire. Shed. All that had meant so much to him, shed. All the old world and self of care, the beautiful care as well as the weary care, shed like a dead body. The landscape?—he cared not a thing about the landscape. Love?—he was absolved from love, as if by a great pardon. Humanity?—there was none. Thought?—falling like a stone into the sea. The great, the glamorous past?—worn thin, frail, like a frail, translucent film of shell thrown up on the shore. The past all gone so frail and thin. What have I cared about, what have I cared for? There is nothing to care about. Absolved from it all. The world a new leaf. And on the new leaf, nothing. The white clarity of the fragile atmosphere. Without a mark, without a record. Why have I cared? I don't care. How strange it is, here, to be soulless and alone."

Was it love that killed him? In explaining this Lawrence pretends to give us the case of Edgar Allan Poe. You will notice that when Lawrence detests a man violently there is usually a strong affinity between that man and himself. Poe achieves honorable distinction in Lawrence's eyes as an unconscious prophet of doom. Speaking of Poe, he says: "Love can be terribly obscene. It is love that causes the neuroticism of the day. It is love that is the prime cause of tuberculosis. The nerves that vibrate most intensely in spiritual unisons are the sympathetic ganglia of the breast, of the throat, and the hind brain. Drive this vibration over-intensely, and you weaken the sympathetic tissues of the chest, the lungs, or of the throat, or of the lower brain, and the tubercles are given a ripe field. But Poe drove the vibrations beyond any human pitch of endurance."

Take that last line. Notice again that when Lawrence wishes to pay a man a great tribute, or when he wishes to annihilate him— it makes little difference which—he gives you a picture of himself. It seems to me that Edgar Allan Poe in no way deserved that last line. But Lawrence does. It is *he* who has driven the vibrations beyond all pitch of human endurance. The Luhan woman puts it baldly enough: "It seemed to me that the very thing he fought against in me, he capitulated to in her (Frieda): the surrender of the will. Why was he forever at her beck and call? If her judgment had been good for him, or if she at least carried him to places that were healthful for him to live in, it would not have been so bad. But the woman had no understanding of ill health and she invariably chose spots that put him down in bed and weakened his resistance to her . . . I need not mind if he called me destructive, for he has called her so in every line, in every book he has written, masking his accusations from her as best he could under many guises so she would let it pass. I wonder if she knew what she was doing, or if her instinct guided her to draw him, to her advantage and his despite, to the very worst climate and the most depressing surroundings?"

Here we have one of those instinctive feminine diagnoses which embroider the ever-growing biography of Lawrence. Trust the adoring female admirers to expose one another shamelessly. Mabel makes Brett out an idiot; Brett makes Frieda out a slut and a hussy; Frieda makes them all out to be a pack of intruders. The Carswell woman writes about him as if he were a saint; Brett writes about him as if he were a Sir Launcelot; the Luhan woman sees him as a composite of devil and saint. Her book, *Lorenzo in Taos*, pretends to give an authentic picture of what goes on behind the scenes, the private life of the genius, the mess he creates all about him, all that petty, trivial clap-trap of which he later weaves the fabric of his novels and poems. It tells us nothing at all about his genius, about what goes on in his soul; it gives only the raw materials of his life, the crude stuff of experience which his art refines and lends significance to. "The proper function of a critic," Lawrence once said, "is to save the tale from the artist who created it . . . Out of a pattern of lies art weaves the truth . . . Never trust the artist. Trust the tale."

"The scientific fact of sex is no more sex than a skeleton is a man."

"The mass of mankind should never be acquainted with the scientific biological facts of sex: never."

"Sex should come upon us as a terrible thing of suffering and privilege and mystery."

"The mystery, the terror, and the tremendous power of sex should never be explained away."

"The mystery must remain in its dark secrecy, and its dark, powerful dynamism."

"The reality of sex lies in the great dynamic convulsions of the soul."

These lines, torn from their context, will be found in the chapter called "The Birth of Sex" in the *Fantasia*. I quote them by way of showing Lawrence's approach to the subject of sex, that persistent and consistent attitude toward life which he reveals in all his writings: the emphasis on MYSTERY. Which is simply another way of acknowledging his deep religiousness.

"It is time to drop the word love, and more than time to drop the ideal of love. Every frenzied individual is told to find fulfillment in love . . . Whereas there is no fulfillment in love . . . The central fulfillment for a man is that he possess his own soul in strength, within him, deep and alone. The deep, rich aloneness, reached and perfected through love. And the passing beyond any further quest of love. . . . These are the two great ways of fulfillment. The first, the way of fulfillment through complete love, complete, passionate, deep love. And the second, the greater, the fulfillment through the accomplishment of religious purpose, the soul's earnest purpose."

"No man ever had a wife," says Lawrence, "unless he served a great predominant purpose. Otherwise he has a lover, a mistress . . . And if there be no further departure, no great way of belief on ahead, and if sex is the starting point and the goal as well: then sex becomes like the bottomless pit, insatiable . . . When sex is the starting and the returning point both, then the only issue is death." And this is the theme of almost all modern tragedy, he adds. "Our one, hackneyed, hackneyed theme."

In the novels one is almost baffled by the fierce antagonisms, the hatred of woman, which Lawrence displays. One is almost equally baffled by his search for a more perfect relationship with man, one based on love and yet not homosexual. The conflict, so the psychologists put it, had its origin in Lawrence's obsessive love for his mother. The Oedipus complex! *Sons and Lovers* is regarded as a work which depicts the tragic influence of the mother. In *Lady Chatterley's Lover* we have Bertha Coutts, who incarnates the "obscene love-will of the mother", which he refers to again and again in the *Fantasia*. "Always this infernal self-conscious Madonna starving our living guts and bullying us to death with her love."

A sexual failure, Murry calls him. A man so humiliated by his first experience with woman (Miriam in *Sons and Lovers*) that he can never exhaust his loathing and abomination of her. A man who has no business with sex at all, says Murry. "He is born to be a saint: then let him be one, and become a eunuch for the sake of the Kingdom of Heaven." But when, in *Aaron's Rod*, Lawrence reveals what it is that the saint craves Murry can't stick it either. As Murry explains it, "Lilly wants a homosexual relation with Tanny." From *Aaron's Rod*, he says, we learn that Lawrence will never be able to maintain that supremacy over the physical, of the masculine-creative over the female-sexual, which he asserted in the *Fantasia*. "What Lawrence is demanding in *Aaron's Rod* looks very like, but is different from, what Lawrence declares to be necessary in the *Fantasia*. To be united impersonally in creative and purposive activity on the basis of a true marriage fulfillment is one thing; to be homosexually united to a man of genius because he finds it impossible to achieve sexual fulfillment in marriage is quite another."

And so, using Lawrence's life as an explanation of his works, or vice versa, Murry reveals little by little the failure of the sexual creature, the male, the failure of the saint, the failure of the leader, the failure of the artist. Failure! Failure! Complete failure! The discovery of the failure of the artist seems coincident with the discovery of the psychological instrument of scientific approach. Every one, every thing, is failure, because everything is based on a study of disease. Psychology itself is a failure because it has its roots in that very disease which is eating man away. It may be convenient, satisfying, and convincing to regard the artist from the standpoint of failure and disease, but it leaves the problem of his appearance and his art untouched. It adds a new category of scientific terminology to the history of aesthetics.

Murry himself rather cravenly acknowledges this when he says: "Once more, it is easy to say that Lawrence is generalising an intensely individual life-history. And once more I reply that it is intensely individual only by its extremity; and, further, that this extremity is the cause of the fierce clarity of Lawrence's insight into the central issues. Lawrence was abnormal; his experience was abnormal. But if we think we can put him aside with the word, then our obtuseness shrieks to heaven. It is the abnormal men from whom we have to learn. They, and they alone, have something of import to teach us. Every man from whom humanity has learned how to make a real step forward into the future has been an abnormal man. He has been abnormal because he belongs to the future, because he was himself the soul of the future. Lawrence was the future; as much of it as we are likely to get in our time. Vital issues were tried out to a conclusion in him; the stress of suffering their resolution devoured and destroyed him. In so far as we understand the order of his significance, therefore, we understand also that it is impossible to *judge* him . . . A symbolic and prophetic man *cannot* make mistakes; all that he is and does is his destiny."

In the preface to his book Murry says: "This is the story of one of the greatest lovers the world has known: of a hero of love, of a man whose capacity for love was so great that he was afraid of it . . . It was not love of his mother only, but love of all men and all women and all things created: a devouring flame of universal love. This fierce and devouring flame of love would burn him up; it did burn him up. He was half burned away by it before the great fear took hold of him: a fear as mighty as the love which caused it. So he strove to kill his love; he fled away from it, he hid his face from it, he sought oblivion from it: in woman. The more avidly he sought oblivion from this consuming flame of love, the less he could find it, the less capable he became of finding it. And slowly and inevitably the love turned into hate. Hate, first and last, of himself who had feared his love and sought to kill it; hate, next, of woman, to whom he had fled for refuge from the fire that consumed him, and from whom he could not take the oblivion for which he hungered; hate, finally, of a world of men which had caused him to suffer as scarcely any man has suffered before."

I quote Murry at some length because this is the man to whom Lawrence turned in his anguish for faith and sympathy and love; this is the friend who rejected Lawrence and betrayed him, the man who had to wait for his friend to die in order to reveal his greatness, or his failure, to the world. And so, perhaps in remembrance of the love that Murry prated of, Lawrence, the great "sex-sodden" genius, when casting about for a title to that misunderstood book which now goes by the name of *Lady Chatterley's Lover*, thought for a long while of *Tenderness*. "In *Tenderness*," writes his biographer Catherine Carswell, "there was still a living test of a man's fidelity, while *love* was heavy with generations of betrayal." What Murry called love, she says, was that very thing which stank in Lawrence's nostrils as the festering of lilies.

In a letter to this same biographer, Lawrence, referring to the war, writes: "I have been reading St. Bernard's *Letters*, and I realise that the greatest thing the world has seen is Christianity, and one must be endlessly thankful for it, and weep that the world has learned the lesson so badly. But I count Christianity as one of the great historical factors, the has-been . . . I am not a Christian. Christianity is insufficient in me. . . . There is something beyond the past. The past is no justification. *Unless from us the future*

252

*takes place, we are death only.** The great Christian tenet must be surpassed, there must be something new: neither the war, nor the turning the other cheek. What we want is the fulfillment of our desires, down to the deepest and most spiritual desire. The body is immediate, the spirit is beyond: first the leaves and then the flower: but the plant is an integral whole: and therefore every desire, to the very deepest. And I shall find my deepest desire to be a wish for pure, unadulterated relationship with the universe, for truth in being. . . ."

It seems to me that this cuts clean through Murry's sickish twaddle about love and Jesus and sainthood and the spirit, the empty, ethereal scaffold on which he raises the spirit of his dead friend in order to give him the aesthetic guillotine. Murry has done precisely what Lawrence most hated and which he never would submit to: he has psychoanalyzed him according to a formula. He organized a chaos with logic, and for the sake of the persuasiveness of his brief he left out the most important Lawrence—the dreamer and creator. Because of his very physical weakness, and his struggle to combat it, certain things were revealed to Lawrence which were concealed from other men. To emphasize the weakness rather than the importance of the revelation is to be untrue to the creative dreams which are as much a part of the man as his human life. Truth demands that, in interpreting a man's life, the emphasis should be on the predominant characteristic of his nature, which in the case of Lawrence was the virility of his creative power. This certainly overshadowed any sexual or personal insufficiency. Murry's own admission that it is from the abnormal man we learn is one of those trite truisms which abound in his book and which he almost immediately proceeds to ignore. Instead of telling us what it is that we must learn from Lawrence he wastes his energies

* Italics mine.

in bewailing and lamenting the fact that Lawrence was abnormal. In other words, we learn from Murry that Lawrence was a genius because of his abnormality, and that to be abnormal is disastrous. In examining *Lady Chatterley's Lover*, for example, Murry finds it of no value whatsoever because Lawrence was merely trying to imagine a final triumph of his defeated masculinity. He rejects the creation because of its pathological basis. But if this tender book, as many believe it to be, provides a very adequate description of what sexual fulfillment can mean then the livingness of this creation, the perfection of its achievement, is what is valuable—not the fact that life itself failed to provide the author with any such fulfillment.

Lawrence's case, as Murry's admirable and treacherous book shows only too clearly, is precisely of the order which defies the cool, presumptuous, scientific method of analysis which the modern psychologist exploits. In fragmenting the man, in laying bare his conflicts, exploring his experiences, underscoring his shocks and his sufferings, it eats away the living man in order to put before us an articulated skeleton of seizable phenomena. The living dynamism, the unity which is the man, and which is composed of so much that eludes the instruments of scientific precision, escapes. In struggling to grasp the riddle of personality the inefficacy of the psychologic approach is still more patent when it is an artist who is the object of investigation. The fluid, protean nature of the man defies the rigid touch of science; the reality of his creation, the artist's whole *raison d'être*, is ignored—because the explanations which the psychologist furnishes us occupy a separate world from that vital, living world of the imagination which the artist has created. It seems almost like another of Mr. Murry's own truisms to say that genius is such by virtue of the fact that it constantly and forever eludes all formulation. The man of genius is he who makes his own laws, his own formulae; it is because they are uniquely his and that in obedience to them he alienates himself from the rest of men that he defies the categories of critics, scientists and philosophers.

Let us take another example of Murry's scientific dissection: the union of Anton and Ursula in *The Rainbow*, wherein Lawrence's "animality" is revealed. We are informed that it is a description of the disintegration which results from animality. Murry concludes that Lawrence's own terrific experience of self-immolation in the sexual experience left him unsatisfied because he was too weak to achieve satisfaction. But there may be quite another explanation of this violent union between Anton and Ursula. This devastating conflict might also be regarded, not as a mere sexual phenomenon, but as the creator's craving for a climax far bigger than the climaxes which life has to offer. It may well be a creative voraciousness beside which the average man's hunger is insignificant, because the creative individual is a magnified being. The creative being is obliged to absorb more because he must produce more. His voraciousness stands out as a symbolic portent for the others. More life! More hunger! More pain! More experience! And not merely quantitative, but qualitative experience—*intensity* of experience! This overwhelming urge for experience, this fierce, devouring hunger for life, it is true, usually costs the artist his life. He is divided between a desire to live out his deepest impulses and at the same time preserve himself from the destruction which inevitably ensues from such a course. The fear of ultimate physical extinction leads him to immortalize himself through his art. His experience of life then comes to be regarded by him as both a necessary aliment and as an evil, destructive thing. And since it is the sexual life which provides the greatest measure of experience and suffering, the symbolic, imaginative derivatives of that life

255

endow his art product with the most cruel and poignant emotional outlines. Just as he glorifies life, in order to slay it through his art, so he glorifies woman in order to execrate her, punish her, for the necessitous character of her role, which he recognizes only too clearly. It is because his creative instinct is so strong that he is obliged to deny, at least in his art, the tyranny of her power. Son of Woman he is, but it is as Father that he endows himself for his role in life. Born a mortal he craves immortality; born of woman he appoints himself begetter. Not of her are his children produced, but of Him who is all. He looks to her for his experience only in order to achieve final isolation. The sex act is not the consummation of the fulfillment—it is the point of departure. But it is just because his hunger is sharper, his need of experience more exigent, that his thirst for fulfillment, for an isolated union with the universe, emerges with such painful, discordant clarity.

The fulfillment which Lawrence depicts in *Lady Chatterley's Lover* is not the fulfillment of the artist. It is in *The Rainbow* that we witness this devastating, harrowing soul struggle. The struggle has a disintegrating character simply because it is an unequal struggle. That which the woman is terrified of, that urgent quest for something *beyond* her which makes a real union forever impossible is the sole preoccupation of the artist, because it is his problem, his conflict. No mortal woman will satisfy the demands of this demon. No mortal man either. That is why love, marriage, friendship, all prove to be insufficient, added tortures to his existence. But in his human moments the artist craves fulfillment through the woman—that is, as Lawrence says, *one way of fulfillment*. In *Lady Chatterley's Lover* it is the very human Lawrence, the eternal male, who reappears, as Murry says, after a lapse of eighteen years. Mellors and Annable are the same fundamental being, the human male, which Lawrence never wholly was, *could not be,* in fact. But if, after eighteen years of travail, of spiritual quest and soul struggle, the human Lawrence reemerged, with what wisdom and vision and sweetness! The antagonism is still there—male and female warring endlessly—but Mellors is a far riper individual than Annable. The eighteen years have been replete with the most varied experiences. In the person of Mellors, Lawrence has stripped away from the eternal male the ideal grave-clothes of the impossible lover and husband. *John Thomas and Lady Jane!* That was another title he had wished to give his book. . . . Penis and vagina. *Tenderness!* A true tenderness that would take the stench out of the word *love* because it would restore to the man and the woman the primacy of their roles. A union based on love, which is war, and thereby providing a perpetual renewal of the spirit. A faith built on the recognition of an innate antagonism, so that the man could go on to his beyond, to his business of creation in which the woman might participate. The clash of separate worlds resolved in the harmony of creation: such a fulfillment Lawrence envisaged and *realized,* through his art, as the possible destiny of the ordinary man and woman, the creatures of earth for whom the eternal conflict in sex has its importance also. As for his own creation and fulfillment, that he has given us in the reality of his art. He took the lives of ordinary men and women, and also of abnormal men and women, and by projecting into them the flame of his own unique personality he fused a creative reality restless, unseizable, enigmatic, but fecundating as his own life.

"The great thing," says Lawrence, "is to keep the sexes pure . . . We mean pure maleness in a man, pure femaleness in a woman. Woman is really polarized downwards, towards the centre of the earth . . . And man is polarized upwards, towards the sun and the

257

day's activity. Women and men are dynamically different, in every-thing. Even in the mind, where we seem to meet, we are utterly strangers . . . The *apparent* mutual understanding, in companion-ship between a man and a woman, is always an illusion, and always breaks down in the end. . . . The moment woman has got man's ideals and tricks drilled into her, the moment she's competent in the manly world—there's an end of it. . . . She becomes absolutely perverse, and her one end is to prostitute herself and her ideals to sex. Which is her business at the present moment. . . . You've got to know that you're a man, and being a man means you must go on alone, ahead of the woman, to break a way through the old world into the new . . . No man is a man unless to his woman he is a pioneer. You'll have to fight still harder to make her yield her goal to yours: her night goal to your day goal . . . Her goal is the deep, sensual individualism of secrecy and night-exclusiveness, hos-tile, with guarded doors. And you'll have to fight very hard to make a woman yield her goal to yours, to make her, in her own soul, *believe* in your goal beyond, in her goal as the way by which you go. She'll never believe until you have your soul filled with a profound and absolutely inalterable purpose that will yield to nothing, least of all to her. She'll never believe until, in your soul, you are cut off and gone ahead, into the dark. . . . Better the woman's goal, sex and death, than some *false* goal of man's. . . . The great goal of creative or constructive activity, or of heroic vic-tory in fight, must always be the goal of the day-time self. But the very possibility of such a goal arises out of the vivid dynamism of the conscious blood. A perfected sex circuit and a successful sex union. And there can be no successful sex union unless the greater hope of purposive, constructive activity fires the soul of the man all the time; or the hope of passionate, purposive, *destructive* ac-tivity: the two amount religiously to the same thing, within the

258

individual. Sex as an end in itself is a disaster: a vice. But an ideal purpose which has no roots in the deep sea of passionate sex is a greater disaster still. And now we have only these two things: sex as a fatal goal, which is the essential theme of modern tragedy; or ideal purpose as a deadly parasite. Sex passion as a goal in itself always leads to tragedy . . . But the automatic ideal-purpose is not even a tragedy, it is a slow humiliation and sterility."

I trust that the reader who is acquainted with Lawrence will forgive the excessive quotation, but even those who know the man's work are apt sometimes to forget what he said. And since Lawrence has come to be looked upon as the great "sex mystic" I have thought it well, if we are to study him from that angle, to bring forward again his own words, in his own language. The advantage of reading the *Fantasia* is merely that in it is summarized the wisdom which Lawrence derived from his experience of life. I do not regard it as a great book—quite the contrary—but it is at least an approach to the deeper, passionate content of the novels and poems. It does contain practically all of Lawrence's views, but diluted, filtered through the intellect. And his was not a great intellect.

It does seem significant that, with all the power that was in him, Lawrence strove to put woman back in her rightful place (a most un-modern view!), and that it is the women who are coming forward to champion him. Even the fatuous Luhan woman who, in giving us a portrait of Lawrence, has succeeded in giving us an even more vivid portrait of herself (a most abominable one) . . . even this spiritual fraud, I say, divined what Lawrence was aiming at. Everything conspired against him, she says. "The women who loved him seemed to be impelled to hold him back, even while they themselves most greatly needed his attainment." And when

259

she forgets herself and is annoyed by his masculine obstinacy, she says: "He was entombed in his recalcitrant body."

But they loved him, these women. They adored him and worshipped him. And they adored him and worshipped him not just because he inspired them with his great purposive faith, or because he went beyond them into his own dark futurity . . . no, they prostrated themselves before him because he revealed them to themselves in their nakedness. The masculine world, on the other hand, deeply and shamefully feminized, is more inclined to distrust and despise Lawrence's ideas. The masculine world, lulled to quiescence in the scorpion's nest, prefers the most fantastic cures to the simple, naked, horrible truth with which Lawrence confronts it.

Why is the incest motive so dominant in Lawrence's work—and not only in Lawrence but in so many men of genius, notably the moderns? Because it is the central theme in the artist's conflict with life, the root pattern of his struggle to emancipate himself, raise himself to fatherhood, i.e., to restore the great religious motive of life. "The woman," says Lawrence, "has not the courage to give up her hopeless insistence on love and her endless demand for love, demand of being loved. She has not the greatness of soul to relinquish her own self-assertion, and believe in the man who believes in himself and in his own soul's efforts—if there are any such men nowadays, which is very doubtful."

What Lawrence means to say, if I understand him rightly, is that man, in fulfilling his biologic function through sex, does not establish a sufficient value for woman. Though this is what she demands of him, through the rigorous laws of her being, in reality she as well as he requires the illusion of a greater purpose. The building of a masculine world—all that is implied by the word *Culture*—is a necessity *imposed on the man by the woman* in order to sustain an illusion. Deep down woman feels a large indifference toward man; she tolerates him in order that she may enjoy a larger life herself. At bottom he is almost unnecessary. If we read into the myth of evolution its deepest import then we can understand woman's role, her activity, her ceaseless war and depredation —and we can stand it! The eternal battle with woman sharpens our resistance, develops our strength, enlarges the scope of our cultural achievements: through her and for her we build our grandiose structures, our illusions, our myths, our legends, which become our religions, philosophies, and sciences.

But when this polarity breaks down, as it has to-day, when instead of a true blood polarity as the basis of sexual union we have "companions", "women who think like us," then beware! Lawrence's abuse, if you notice, goes out equally to man and woman. He is not a misogynist. Nor is he a misanthropist. "The rim of pallor between night and day"—the world of the monks— that is what he railed against and fought tooth and nail. The sickly, ideal love world of depolarized sex! The world based on a fusion of the sexes, instead of an antagonism. Right he was in saying—"not for a second do they (our mothers) allow us to escape from their ideal benevolence . . . Always the *will*, the will, the *love-will*, the ideal will, directed from the ideal mind. Always this stone, this scorpion of maternal nourishment."

The great Christian ideal of love, that spiritual perversion which has triumphed over the animal nature of man, it is this which has ushered in the bodily disintegration now so painfully visible. We have made woman our equal and now we are indoctrinated with her ideas; our whole idealistic corpus of thought is saturated with the female principle. The perversion of the great maternal instinct in woman has resulted in woman's expressing her deeper, inimical role of all-sufficient one. Man's inability to throw off the yoke of swaddling clothes and apron-string has brought about an open scorn and contempt on the part of woman, a genuine usurpation of his role in life. The great leaders of to-day, before making a decisive move, must first consult their wives or their mistresses. An artist, like Proust, must first wait until his mother dies before he can set about the great task of his life. Joyce drags us through the dreariest pages to attack an outworn institution like the Catholic Church, which is really his mother. The result, in the case of Proust, is his love for an invert; in the case of Joyce it is the glorification of the eternal whore in woman. In the case of Lawrence it is the search for a mythical man who is not a pervert but who understands the finesse and the amplitude of earthly love. *Incest motive!* The root malady, the pain, the torture, the horror from which springs their art.

To get a fresh grip on the man let us recapitulate briefly the evolution he describes through his life and work . . .

Let us take as the fundamental starting point that significant word which appears in the mouths of his own characters so often, and which is also used by his critics, even those who admire him intensely: FAILURE.

In the world of living men he regarded himself as a failure. The realization of this comes early in life, in the very moment of his flowering into manhood, when, involved with Miriam, his first love, he divines the fearful grip, the paralyzing influence of his mother's love. Miriam is not wholly to blame, he is aware of that. She is partly, and perhaps greatly, to blame in that she suffers from the same stubborn idealistic love-mode of the mother. She should have been able to liberate him, but she wasn't. The hatred he ought to have had for his mother he transferred to Miriam, and later to the whole white world doomed by its idealism, as he saw it.

"Dark, ruddy pillar," he writes (in *Virgin Youth*), "forgive me!

I am helplessly bound to the rock of virginity. Thy tower impinges on nothingness. Pardon me!" Here at the threshold of sexual life he regards himself as a prisoner of life. The man who twenty years later will address his own penis *and glorify it*. He realizes at the very start that he is handicapped in his effort to establish communion with the world of living men and women. His great problem is to find release, find a means of entry into the world.

Idealism! The one besetting sin of the human race! Let us not forget these words which form the grand motif of his quarrel with the world. Let us not forget that the root of the malady lay in his mother's strangling love-will, that obscene mother's love-will which had poisoned him from the start. Let us realize again that it is only with his mother's death that he acquires a sense of liberation, an ability to turn inward and discover in himself the true source of his power and significance. Let us remember that the great shock of his mother's death provides him with his first illumination: "Now I must go on with bringing out what I know is in me —let my powers have room to develop!"

Until his mother dies and leaves him free to battle with the world he can find no escape or refuge or liberation in sex. The affair with Miriam, instead of aiding him to find himself, only leaves him in despair: he revolts against himself and the world which produced him, the world of white idealism. The horror of this gives expression to the fundamental conflict in his being on which all his actions are henceforth to be pivoted. He becomes a divided being, because too greatly preoccupied with himself . . . because he is in love with himself. The evil of modern times lies precisely in this, that men cannot have any real, true relationship with their fellow-men. There is a sterility, an atrophy, of the affective self. Man's sensuous nature is blighted at the roots. There is no liberation, only revolt. No one can achieve wholeness. What passion is permitted us is only the passion of destructiveness.

In *Women in Love*, when the problem had begun to shape itself quite definitely, when he saw what it was that the world represented and what his place in it must be, he describes the world as "corrupt", adding: "At best, my only rightness lies in the fact that I know it, I detest what I am outwardly. I *loathe* myself as a human being." This is the despair of a man who craves a full life, a free life, who recognizes that he is chained to the rock perpetually, and that all his activity will resemble nothing more than the eating away of the chains for a liberation he himself will never enjoy. In his own self he incarnates the vultures which gnaw at his body. When later he describes the great carrion birds and the hyaenas, it is in reality a description of his own incorrigible, devouring self, the gnawing Absolute which claws at his vitals.

"I want the world to hate me, because I can't bear the thought that it might love me . . . One must be able to disentangle oneself from persons, from people! So you must hate people and humanity, and you want to escape . . ."

What is it he is trying to escape from? What is it that crops out in his first big attempt at liberation, through sex? It is given us in the response to Ursula's question—"*what is there beside?*" "Why," answers Birkin, "there is a final me which is stark and beyond responsibility: so there is a final you! And it is there I would want to meet you . . . not a mingling but an equilibrium, a pure balance of two single beings." Now these two pure single beings are wholly imaginary, wholly idealistic, wholly conceptual. They represent the male and female freed of their inhibiting taboos and ideals. They are human absolutes in sex, something now quite unimaginable. They are human beings who, through self-creation, are able to stand apart from the corruptive flux of disintegration. The self

264

beneath the ego represents for Lawrence the incorruptible self, the immortal self, the absolute! Because, in his belief, the petty, willful ego, the superficial self that responds to ideals, etc., is nothing but a cold surface of consciousness, consumed by the horror of not-being; the self which is crippled from birth and unable to have experience of any sort.

Once aware that his destiny is to symbolize for all time this great conflict which is going on in man, once aware that he is victimized by this conflict and must dedicate himself to expressing it, he embarks with savage earnestness, power and fluency in expressing every phase of the conflict. Now and then, weary of this futile, Promethean struggle, he expresses a longing to be human again, to participate in life's struggles. "I want to do something with living people, somewhere, somehow, while I live on the earth. I write, but I write alone. And I live alone. Without any connection with the rest of men." So Somers speaks in *Kangaroo* when Lawrence, fully aware of his destiny, allows himself to probe the subject of leadership. In *The Ladybird*, as Dionys, he says: "As a man who is by nature an aristocrat, it is my sacred duty to hold the lives of other men in my hands." But he is a special kind of aristocrat, the aristocrat of aristocrats: Dionysus, the Redeemer of Man.

In *Kangaroo* he toys with the idea of active participation in life, with the idea of political leadership. But he can have no faith in this external, remedial character of leadership—that is for the Caesars of this world. His idea of leadership is something far beyond this: it is *spiritual* leadership. Again the idealistic conflict expresses itself. He is not a practical man of affairs, a Caesar, nor does he wish to be a leader in the sense that Christ was. "A man should remain himself, not try to spread himself over humanity," he says. If he is going to lead (though he does not quite admit this to himself), it is as artist henceforth. He is going to lead, but indirectly, as the man who reveals the life mystery and by his revelation creates a new possibility, a strange element in life. (*The Plumed Serpent.*)

Paradoxical though it may seem, it is always thus: it is only the dead who can reveal life's mystery. The revelation occurs only when one surrenders to life. For the acceptance of life is the acceptance of death, of final utter dissolution and extinction. The idea of dying, of sacrificing one's life in order to save mankind, is the innate, dominating impulse. It is the man who has no life, who is so nearly dead that he has been gripped by the mystery of life, who can preach abandonment, surrender, sacrifice in death. That is why Lawrence is able to make the distinction between that creative form of death which liberates life and allows rebirth, and the other kind of death, which is a perpetuity in biologic immortality. He says in effect that our life, which is based on a denial of all spiritual values, is the revolting death which creates an immortality of corruption, that when one embraces the spiritual one dies creatively and death, consequently, is robbed of its sting.

But let us not forget that he enters life already paralyzed, unable to participate, and that he condemns life at every turn because it does not allow him, the spiritual cripple, to function freely. The same applies to all men to-day, only in a Lawrence there is an intense awareness of the situation. The struggle, then, for Lawrence is to free himself of the spiritual strangle-hold. His worship goes out for the dark, animal side of his being. When referring to the Aztecs' religion, the importance given by them to the earth, etc., he says: "My sermons would not aim to make the spirit seem real. There have been enough metaphors for the spirit already. It would speak more of the body and the earth. The two halves of the world, the one of which I have always championed against the other, I shall now, in evidence of my new wholeness, express as two factors of one unity." And so we have the re-enthronement of the dark god, Quetzalcoatl, the bird serpent: a synthesis of the conflicting human spirit which reasserts the divinity by stressing the animal nature of man. He has realized now that there is an impasse which can never be resolved except by going beyond, and to go beyond, for him, is to fuse the two opposites. This then amounts to a glorification of the supreme conflict in which he is rooted. Since there is no ultimate solution for the divided being that is man, the thing to do is to deify the conflict. That is to say, instead of resolving the conflict, instead of arriving at a *false* and satisfying conclusion, such as the men of science attempt by "explaining things away", Lawrence sticks fast in the chaos and mystery, in the very heart of antagonism. But the ability to do this, to perceive with magistral eye the full purport of life, is inevitably to stand apart from life, to detach oneself from the living current which would blind one to and drown one in the ultimate issues. Mired as he is in the unquenchable Absolute, Lawrence nevertheless does revive in us the life instincts—at the cost of his own life. By his very detachment he was able to create a world, and though it is not a real world, it serves as a magnet, a goal, a motivating and inspiring force. By reanimating the old symbols it gives new meaning to the fundamental problems of life which were in danger of stagnation.

That Lawrence realized the element of paradox in his way of life seems to me to be brought out forcefully in the description of Lincoln Cathedral and in the description of the carrion beasts. In *Salvator Mundi* he has already previsaged the criticisms which will be launched against him: "It is *himself* is corrupt—him a Saviour!" To be sure, it is the saviour who is corrupt, since in him is contained all the seeds of corruption, since it is he who is sacrificed to corruption and by his death purifies the world of corruption. Through the saviours we have life, because through them we cast out corruption, rid ourselves of the devastating sense of guilt, of sin, and of responsibility. By investing the heroic scapegoat with all the burdens which have weighed us down we emancipate ourselves from struggle. When we kill the scapegoat we kill the evil in ourselves and become free again to worship, to partake of life religiously, to see life in its sacred, mysterious, unifying aspect. By eliminating duality we restore that unity with the universe which is our perpetual dream and longing. By letting go the struggle between the animal and the divine in us we surrender ourselves to life and dissolution. Hitherto we had been arresting life by standing awesomely and worshipfully before the symbols of life. Our fear of living led us to prostrate ourselves before the empty symbol; instead of living life out we poured our livingness into the symbols. All this is the meaning of Culture, of history, of the eternal flux: the cyclical whirl about the static symbol which becomes transformed by our revolutions.

The artist, in smashing the old symbols, struggles desperately and vainly to remind us by his very existence that the symbol is in itself nothing. See, he says, it is I who have created it! But the world does not see. What it sees is that the artist is himself a symbol, and when it has slain him, it consumes the dead body and symbol, the work in which the spirit lies entombed. And the process recommences. . . .

And so Lawrence can say: "Only man tries not to flow . . ." And again—"We are transmitters of life, and when we fail to transmit life, life fails to flow through us."

His search for God, and his finding God (*The Plumed Serpent*), is this attempt to arrive at the source of life, the fountain itself. It matters little whether God be a plumed serpent or an idea. When in *The Rainbow* he pays tribute to the spiritual forces in man, he admits by his very imagery the great dynamic principle which religion symbolizes, even though it be the tyrannical power of the spirit which the cathedral embodies. He sees the absolutism which carries humanity along like a great tide, and he sees also that, even as humanity is being borne along by the tide, engulfed and overwhelmed, it is conscious of its fate and resisting. "These sly little faces peeped out of the grand tide of the cathedral like something that knew better. They knew quite well, these little imps that retorted on man's own illusion, that the cathedral was not absolute . . . Apart from the lift and spring of the great impulse towards the altar, these little faces had separate wills, separate motions, separate knowledge, which rippled back in defiance of the tide . . ."

This is the woman's view of the cathedral. Woman anchored in the reality of flesh, anchored to earth. The clinching and mating of stone arches in the dusky beyond of man's spiritual world is regarded by her as a deadening thing, a life destroyer. Through woman Lawrence presents the realistic powers of earth, the wisdom of the serpent, the destroyer of divine innocence and youth. Woman it is who by her deep rootedness in nature resists the idealistic urge to mortify the flesh. In the sly, impish faces that peer out of the grand tide of the cathedral she sees the *separate* will, the *separate* knowledge, the human, individual defiance of the tyranny wielded by the abstract and the absolute. She divines that the hidden secret of that great communal sacrifice which enabled the cathedrals to be reared lies in the significant work of the humble craftsman, he who was not the great architect or the great artist, obeying an impulse beyond him, but a tiny microcosm that imposed on the grand façade of the cathedral this decorative touch of personal, individual will. She saw that this humble figure expressed his religiousness in obscene fashion—by creating these gargoyles, these self-likenesses. The God who is personified in this grand cathedral with flaming windows and rushing arches, this God is something in us that is borne along on a human tide, and it is we, the grotesque, the despised, the ignoble, who must also be immortalized in the body of the cathedral. We erect it, and we adorn it. And when it suits us we can destroy it too. It is not absolute. We have fashioned it in durable stone as a testimony to the permanency of the spirit within us; but we are not going to be engulfed in the tide; we will peep out eternally, with sly, incorrigible, human faces, to mock the eternal spirit of man, to remind him of that which he wishes to ignore, albeit it is his glory.

Something of all this Lawrence hints at when in his poem on the Etruscan cypresses he recalls the living memory of the Etruscans, saying: "They are dead, the Etruscans, and all that is left is the shadowy monomania of some cypresses and tombs." *The shadowy monomania!* As if he wished to impress it deep in us, this eternal quest of the Absolute which has strewn life with monuments, with mournful trees, with regrets, with tombs. This comes out in its extremest when, as if to present this spirit which he himself so deeply represented, he transfers his hatred for the Absolute to the carrion beasts, the vulture and the hyaena.

"The carrion birds, aristocrats, sit up high and remote, on the sterile rocks of the old absolute, their obscene heads gripped hard and small, like knots of stone clenched upon themselves for ever!" One of the most revelatory passages in all Lawrence's writing, a self-portrait as convincing and terrifying as were the obscene figures in the cathedral to the woman.

"The vulture can neither see nor hear the living world, it is one supreme glance, the glance in search of carrion, its own absolute quenching, beyond which is nothing." Is this not Lawrence himself, the ultimate Lawrence? The stony self beyond the ego, inhuman, uncompromising, devouring and tenacious, annihilating woman, sex, friendship, loyalty, etc. The stony eye, petrified in that one supreme glance. Always smelling corruption, perched on that rock of the absolute: aristocrat of aristocrats, high up and remote, drawn back on its own nullity, because beyond it there is nothing. Like the hyaena again, which "can scarcely see and hear the living world." Deaf and blind to the human tide, to the roar and crimson flood of life: fixed eternally on the sterile rock of the self, the divine spirit of man in search of its own corruption.

How well Lawrence understood the complete and fulfilled man we understand from the portraits of his heroes, who are for him simply the self which he has denied and which haunts him like the accusing voice of conscience. They are the reverse Hamlets of his idealistic world.

Such a type is Aaron Sisson, whose friendship fails him. Aaron Sisson who refuses to yield himself up to the leadership of this blind fanatic which the real Lawrence was. This type of man is the *ideal* for Lawrence; he is the man Lawrence can never hope to be. And here, it seems to me, Lawrence deserves the highest recognition. Here, like Dostoievski whom he resembles in that he is a completely divided being, he has been able to objectify for us the two halves of himself, to oppose them one to another in the most diabolically sincere and truthful manner. In the person of Aaron Sisson, Lawrence puts back all those elements which Shakespeare withdrew from man in the character of Hamlet. Aaron Sisson is the man who achieves freedom of movement and freedom of thought by renouncing his petty, imperious ego. Unlike Lawrence, Aaron Sisson does not hold himself up as an ideal, does not try to alter people or the world. But, on the other hand, *he will not allow others to alter him!* Aaron Sisson proclaims in his own personality the majesty of his unique being. He neither accommodates himself to the world nor asks it to accommodate itself to him. Such a type is indubitably an ideal, for the world has never seen such a man. This is what Lawrence would like himself to be. And though, in the person of Lilly (his other, truer self) he seems to point to the possession of something beyond that which Aaron holds, in reality he is investing his antagonist with heroic qualities by virtue of his ability to resist the snares and enchantments of the ideal. Aaron is a loyal, steadfast, loving friend, the essence of humanness. Lilly is loyal only to his Holy Ghost, i.e., his conscience. For him friendship, in the ultimate sense, has no significance. What he wants of Aaron is fidelity. He wants him to obey, to trust in his leadership. It is the inhuman principle at work, the remote, detached love of all mankind which refuses to go out in human sympathy and warmth.

This steady drift away from the human does not end with the mere denial of the value of friendship. When Lawrence has finally retreated upon that "proud, isolate self", when he has disentangled himself from persons and people, rid his consciousness of the domination of humanity, he is able to turn beyond, to go out with a new sense of wholeness to his dark god, Quetzalcoatl. But his dark god inspires horror too. The woman, Kate, voices this feeling. And so, utterly, devastatingly sincere and consistent, he replies: "Why not? Horror is real. Why not a bit of horror, as you say, among all the rest? Get used to it that there must be a bit of fear and a bit of horror in your life." This is said as a sort of brave echo to his own timidity, for he is the man who, in his great love of man and of life, in his desperate desire to participate and not be set apart and aloof from others, has had finally to accept the full horror of life also. It was his deep tenderness which made him susceptible to the apathy and dullness, the morbidity, of the world about him.

He had had to recognize that what he feared he must learn to embrace, and he embraces it in the figure of Quetzalcoatl who personifies all the cruelty, horror and terror of life. Quetzalcoatl demands human sacrifices; he swims in the blood of the slain. And Lawrence, who had been so horrified, so maimed, by the cruel reality of the war—"this thing must not be . . . it was foul . . . as long as I am a man it shall not be, it shall not!"—this Lawrence finally comes to embrace the very incarnation of cruelty in his dark god. He sees that his fundamental human self is rooted in this cruelty, this eternal killing and sacrifice. The ideals which he had inherited had blinded him for a while to his real animal nature; they had tried to assert the supremacy of the one nature over against the other. Now, in the bird-serpent, he restores the validity of this cruel element in the human being. He not only restores and justifies it, he raises it to supreme importance by deifying it. It is again his idealistic nature at work, that driving quest of the Absolute, which never lets him be.

And here, like Freud, who opened up the realm of the Unconscious in order to liberate man's suppressed animal nature, Lawrence too plumbed his deepest being in order to find his own salvation. His dark god, and his whole dark world, are the dramatic and artistic expression of a suppressed libido. But, whereas the psychologists have sought in their theories to find a panacea for human ills, i.e., if not a remedy by the eradication of suffering, at least a remedy by the *explanation of their origins* (trusting to the belief that when we know the cause of a thing and can name it we shall be cured of our suffering), Lawrence refuses to name, refuses to explain, refuses the grace of salvation either through sublimation or abandonment of responsibility. Instead of avoiding the religious issue, Lawrence accepts it unqualifiedly. He seeks to re-establish the sacred character of life, to re-enthrone God, to make

God the only issue. All that is important to him, in surveying human endeavor, is—*how much of God is there in it?* He detests the psychologist's explanations because they would rid man of the God element. He beseeches man to abandon himself to his fate, to assert his power over fate by abandoning himself to it. "Out of the fight with the octopus of life, the dragon of degenerate or incomplete existence, one must win this soft bloom of living." This is the living duality in Lawrence, this is the instinct which enabled him to create his world. When he admires the life wisdom of the Egyptians, the Etruscans, or the Greeks, he is admiring the creative spirit in them which, while permitting them to accept the horror and the cruelty of life, also gave them the power to struggle, to combat their fate. Struggle is the creative element. ("Immortality is a question of character.") Immortality, he would say, is a by-product of the struggle, not the thing to be sought in itself. The fear of death, which brings about fear of life, is overcome by surrender to one's fate. But it is not a supine, fatalistic acquiescence; it is rather the complete fulfillment of and obedience to one's instincts, no matter where they lead. He has no fear of where they will lead, even if it be called destruction. The real fear, the real horror, he discovers, is in the frozen immortality of a life dedicated to ideals, a life that seeks to be protected by its ideals—the life of the tortoise whose blood is congealed, the life of the civilized man whose inner, sacred core is so hedged in, so protected by the crusts of dead beliefs, that he cannot *feel*, cannot *respond* to the currents of life. That is why, in *Women in Love*, he can say— "whatever single act is performed by any man now, in this condition, is an act of reduction, disintegration." He means by "act" the expression of a being asserting his will, his instincts. He means further that the deep, unconscious wish of the individual to-day is to die. *He must discover a means of dying.* By rediscovering his ani-

274

mal nature, by giving expression once again to his primal instincts, man will destroy the old being that was hidden away under the carapace of ideals. He must not go on in this hideous biologic immortality. He must learn to die in his corruption, in order to be reborn, to enjoy a new spirit and a new body and a new life!

MORE ABOUT ANAIS NIN

(Two letters)

1.

Letter to William A. Bradley, Literary Agent

> 4, Avenue Anatole France
> Clichy (Seine)
> August 2, 1933

DEAR MR. BRADLEY:

Since you are the one who has inspired the premeditated abortion of Anais Nin's Journal, some pages of which have just come to my attention, I am addressing myself to you directly in order to warn you that I shall use all my influence, and it is not inconsiderable, to belittle and ridicule your suggestions. Consider this an insolence, if you like. I have only one concern, and that is the preservation of what I consider a valuable document—more than that, a work of art.

I am not questioning your good intentions. It is your judgment, your taste, your vision that I condemn.

Let me remind you briefly that I am aware of your ideas as regards the Journal—first from Miss Nin's own lips, and secondly from your own. I listened to you in silence on the occasion of my last visit. I was baffled, and more than that, generous enough to concede that your judgment might have some weight. Now I am prepared to speak, to denounce you roundly.

There is one allowance to be made for you at present, and that is that you haven't been privileged to read the entire Journal. Neither have I, but I have read considerably more than you. And because of this advantage I feel I have the right to lay before you the monstrous nature of your error. In a little while you will have in your possession a great bloc of the Journal. Then, I should say, and only then, will you have the right to express your opinion. In the meantime I am asking Miss Nin to show you a criticism I made some time ago after reading a few volumes of the early section of the Journal. Regard it as prejudiced, if you wish, although the truth is I was prejudiced in advance unfavorably. The point is that in my rather extravagant appreciation I happened to unfold the heart and process of the Journal, something which I do not believe you have as yet grasped.

However, the important thing is that I instruct you, or remind you (which is a little less sententious, a little less insolent) of your proper role. Where you are dealing with nobodies it is fitting enough that you persuade the author to alter his manuscript. A little more or a little less of perfection does not matter, in the long run, where pure consumption is the sole desideratum. But when you have a genius to deal with it is an altogether different story. It may be, as in the case of Miss Nin, or myself for instance, a very imperfect genius. My impression of the genius, I must confess, is that he is usually imperfect. To be brief, it is for you to make up your mind whether the Journal is a thing of abiding value, a real contribution to the world's literature, or not. If in your opinion it is not, then I should imagine the kindest thing to do would be to drop it at once.

For me it is a foregone conclusion that the Journal is a work of the highest standing, that it is indeed altogether unique. Granting that my knowledge of the world's literature is not as extensive as your own, I nevertheless challenge you to cite me a worthy parallel to it. Myself I know of none. None by any man, and most certainly none by a woman. If it were due only to its uniqueness as a *female* contribution my unflinching endorsement of it would be entirely justified. But it does not owe its value or importance to this aspect in the least. It is a unique *human* contribution, doubly so because the female has been naturally more reticent, more reluctant to expose her soul.

I can think immediately of at least three eminent psychologists who would pounce with avidity on Miss Nin's work were they apprised of its existence. There would be little or no difficulty in securing the support of a medical publication, and subsequently by natural stages the attention and interest of more universal publishers. But that, it seems to me, is a poor way of going about it. As I tried to point out in my critical analysis of the early Journal, the great merit of her work is its universality of appeal. It is a tremendous cross-section of our life to-day. A tremendous revelation of the evolution of an artist. A most painfully naked exposal of a woman's soul.

278

By some definition which I am unable to accept you have apparently convinced yourself that Miss Nin is a personality but not an artist. And by a logic even worse than your faulty premise of a definition you ask her to obliterate what there is of art in her work in order to reveal her personality. I simply don't follow you at all. Perceiving in her case some far-fetched analogy to that of Isadora Duncan, you ask her to sit down and make a warm stew of her past in order to tickle a prurient public. You seem to think that Isadora Duncan (or her ghost) wrote an extremely interesting book, the proof being the receipts, the publicity, the hundred and one translations. Sheer nonsense, of course. It is only because your ego is involved that you fail to see what an atrocious thing it is, that it were much better for the memory of a great dancer that her memoirs had never been printed. No, if you can counsel nothing better than to emulate Isadora Duncan then Miss Nin had much better destroy her work.

What motivates your conduct is the public. True, you are the author's intermediary, his intercessor with the public. The public, however, can damned well take care of itself. As can the publisher. It is the author who requires the most of you, rightfully and justly. The test of an agent's worth is his ability to make the public swallow something it does not want. Any dolt can feed the public what it likes. Any pimp can pander to the perverted interests of the publishers. Everything begins and everything ends with the author —the public and the printer are simply accessories before God. I am sorry to be obliged to remind you of this, but it is no negligible point.

The author has need not of an agent only but of a friend, a confidant; some one who has unshakable faith in him, a faith based on taste and judgment. The history of any great work of art is the history of a friendship. Anything that is worth while is first fought against—that is axiomatic. To reduce the author to the mental stature of the public is obviously ridiculous. Yet that is what you are proposing to do.

You may say with some justice that it is not your business to devote your energies to championing unknown geniuses. "I am in business to earn a living." If that were true, if that were the whole truth, I would not waste the time writing you this long letter. I know that, like other business men, your greatest satisfaction lies outside the mere accumulation of money. You would like to be known as the man who discovered so-and-so or so-and-so. You tell yourself that, but do you always act up to it?

Let me revert to the Journal again. Let me tell you what I, an author, an impractical person, think ought to be done. I say after mature deliberation—*print the whole god-damned thing!* If there must be any alteration let it be in the nature of excision only, and that after great deliberation. You pick up one volume and find it fascinating. The next one you throw down in boredom or disgust. But you are one individual, not the public, not posterity. You are a man of strong prejudices, with tastes already formed and habits hard to uproot. Can you be certain that what you find uninteresting will not appeal to thousands, perhaps millions, of others? I don't say that the opposite holds true. More than likely, what you find interesting and what I find interesting, many many others will also find interesting. But have either of us an infallible test for measuring the interest of the world at large? I am thinking of the work as if it were actually launched. I am thinking of the Japanese reader, the Hindu reader, the Spanish reader, the Scandinavian reader. . . . I am thinking of the readers to come in the year 2000 A.D. and later, when the original manuscript, with the correct names, is brought to light, when some of those names will have become dear to millions of people whose existence you and I are unaware of, some of them not yet born. I am thinking of the whole unlived life yet before the author of this enormous document, the play of the dice, the love or the hatred, the popularity or the persecution of the public, the drama inextricably woven about her name, her deeds, her books. I am thinking that if her admittedly great personality is given the opportunity to blossom neither you nor I can predict how precious may be the words, the passages, the pages, the volumes that we are now ready to expunge.

But if her personality should never come to light her written testimony stands on its own legs, has a validity, has a right to be heard and read. If she were the very worst artist that ever lived, the author of some forty odd volumes recorded sedulously day by day with scarcely a break would possibly be regarded by those to come as, to say the least, a curious phenomenon of letters. En passant, with the exception of psychopathic cases, and I trust you do not regard Miss Nin as such, I know of no examples in the history of literature where such persistent and painstaking labor, such dire quest of truth, such rigorous self-analysis, such minutiae of observation, have ever led to nullity. The woman whose personality can communicate itself immediately is, as you know, hardly apt to be wasting her precious moments writing balderdash. Not unless she were at the same time an empty head, a beauty without brains, a vain and monstrous creature. I can testify that she is not, should you need any assurance on these points.

You who so keenly appreciated the opening volumes of her work have only to recollect that the fundamental note which she sounds —at an age when only an extraordinary intuition, a premonition, a foreboding, could explain it—is that of pain. The pain of isolation. The very keynote of the artist's eternal rack. Without any precocious knowledge, her education neglected rather, she gives in a simple and piercing narrative the complete frame-work of her whole future drama. She writes in the dark, but unfalteringly. She clings to her European authors, her European habits of mind, in the most formative years of her life, when any other child would have succumbed to the strong rhythm of American life. She holds herself silently superior to the whole American scene, a fact in itself which impresses me as quite magnificent. In her adolescence, which you quickly find rather tedious, she goes through a great struggle, the nature of which obviously eluded your grasp. She emerges into womanhood, passes into marriage, to carry on a still greater struggle. As a mature woman you have a product, to judge from her own testimony, as rich and as complicated, as interesting from the standpoint of art or personality, as any figure in the annals of literature. The tedious pages which you are so ready to relegate to the scrap-heap are as much a part of that full-fledged figure as the obviously interesting ones—perhaps more so, perhaps more important. Disabuse your mind of the idea that you are dealing with a work of art, intrinsically, or perhaps better, extrinsically; remember that it is a life, a human being, that you are dealing with, and that the document itself cannot be divided, first as literature and then as life. The two are wedded. "Who touches me touches a human being; who touches me touches a great book." The book and the woman are one. What you are calling art all the time is fraudulent. Art is always that for which there is no name, no definition. The "Pantagruel" was probably not considered art, in its day. The "Satyricon" of Petronius Arbiter was probably not art either, in its day. Consider the enormous defects of these two great works. How marvellous they are, how exciting! Thank God, they fell into the hands of no intercessor. Reflect, if you will, that Rabelais' motives were of the cheapest, when he began his great work. If not a plagiarist he was certainly a grand imitator, and a man to boot who knew on which side his bread was buttered. But

282

the complete work completed the man, ennobled the motive, drowned out all previous definitions of art.

I have a reason for making this seeming digression. I have seen in the span of some twenty volumes a geometric progression. I am almost afraid to envisage what the next twenty volumes may lead to. I hear you speak with an air of finality of the "setness" of the mind after a certain period. I must confess that I do not agree with you, not in *all* cases, at any rate. Not in the greatest, certainly, where the law works always contrary to your view. And what if I say that, bringing the whole work to an abrupt termination to-morrow, Miss Nin may proceed from this Gargantuan base to raise a towering and perplexing pyramid of art? Who can predict what she will do to-morrow? Who of us can say what the value of this formidable document really is? Or what its meaning?

If you can imagine the earnestness and sincerity, the vitality and inexhaustibility of such patriarchs as Titian and Michelangelo, or Goethe and Hardy, if you can imagine these sturdy and indomitable spirits more flexible, more liquid, you may then well imagine what is possible in this mysterious realm of art when a woman of genius dedicates her life to a high task.

It is highly plausible that no publisher to-day will care to risk a fortune in putting out Miss Nin's Journal. That, it seems to me, is of absolutely no concern. Sooner or later somebody will print it. Some love-sick fool may bankrupt himself in order to do it. There may be other ways of accomplishing it. Above all, it is not a question of how the public will receive it, or what the public will think of it. It is only a question of bringing it to light, of putting it in the hands of Fate. "Swann's Way", which was rejected on all sides, what would we not give to-day were there thirty more volumes like it. Every scrap about Joan of Arc, about Napoleon, especially about those celebrated authors whose very identity is in question, is sought after feverishly. Anais Nin gives a quotidian record of her life—in order to save posterity the labor of research. And what is there to justify this amazing minutiae of a woman's life? That, my dear man, nobody can answer. That belongs to the future.

Sincerely,

HENRY V. MILLER

2.

Letter to Anais Nin regarding one of her books

Clichy, 1933

DEAR ANAIS:

It was presumptuous of me to want to alter the language. If it is not English sometimes it is a language nevertheless, and the farther one goes along with it the more vital and necessary it seems. It is a violation of language which corresponds to the violation of thought and feeling. It could not have been written in an English which every capable writer knows how to employ. It required your own intimate imprint, and in the measure that one understands and appreciates you one understands and appreciates the strange language you have used. That is why I found it difficult, after I had passed a certain point, to suggest any radical changes in the text. If your thought is occasionally obscure it is only because what you are trying to put into words defies language; it would remain obscure even if an Anatole France had tried to formulate it.

Above all, it is the language of modernity, the language of nerves, repressions, larval thoughts and processes, the images not entirely divorced from their dream content; it is the language of the neurotic, the perverted, "marbled and veined with verdigris", as Gautier put it. It has in it all the elements of consumption which Chopin introduced into his music; it is diseased, as are the finest passages of Huysmans: a concentrated poison which only those may quaff who have been inoculated through too much living.

There are lines in it which are immortal—not lines only, but whole passages. There are passages which seem to defy all explanation, which hover on the borders of hallucination, madness, utter chaos. There are some so cruel and revolting as to seem inhuman: they are no longer thoughts or feelings but the raw essence of pain and malice. The whole thing is like a bloody emission, the orgasm of a monster, cluttered with snakes and jewels and bile and arsenic.

When I try to think to whom it is you are indebted for this style I am frustrated; I do not recall any one to whom you bear the slightest resemblance. You remind me only of yourself, of the latter books of the Diary in which you reveal your development. If you are indebted to men like Blake and Rimbaud you are unconscious of it; what you have taken from them you have put back in a form so unique, so fragile, and yet so durable, that the style bears no resemblance to that of your prototypes at all and can only be interpreted by reference to yourself. And if there are influences in literature of which you appear wholly unconscious, how many more are there in the realm of art—in painting and music—some of which are even unknown to you. Goya, yes . . . you have felt the savage mystery of him. But Rops, Felicien Rops, I am sure you have never heard of him. Debussy you know, and Debussy is there clearly in your beautiful impressionistic tapestries, in your overtones which leave your notes suspended above the body of your text like some phantasmal mirage. Richard Strauss too one feels in the mighty dissonances, in the superhuman effort to dissolve the very plexus of the medium. And like all these I mention you have worked with an almost Satanic glee. With a corrosive force you have broken down the veils of flesh and all the cushions that protect the nerves: you have played on the raw nerves, the very tenderest filaments of our sense organs. The effect is delirium, ecstasy which becomes insupportable. "You have borrowed from all palettes," to quote Gautier once again, with the result that one cannot transmute the music into words or the words into paint—one is drastically and irremediably exposed to the shock of a combined assault by all the instrumentalities of art. One is stunned, prostrated.

Leaving aside the external devices by which you accomplish your end, and examining the content itself. . . . What lies behind the confused welter of images, the ideas pyramided one on top of another to infinity? A woman stripped of all femininity, a woman with the raw, devastating power of her sex, a woman tearing from her symbols all the human masks which have made men behold in the monster the dangerous and unfathomable allure of his counterpart. Back of the glazed and shimmering Lesbianism stands the spectre of undivided sex, the original complete entity which had no need for the male to reproduce its kind; back of all the legends of friendship and love between man and man, woman and woman, or man and woman, lies this Narcissistic image of the single, all-sufficient self, the primal, generative force which fecundates itself.

"In the beginning was the Word and the Word became flesh." It is as though you were repeating this story of creation. The duality which you divine is the despair and the bankruptcy of logic and philosophy: it is the illusion which holds the human planetary system together, the great lie of creation which lends the piercing note of sorrow to all the great works of art. The lie which you expose sounds the death of art: it is fatal to trespass beyond a certain point. Since you are a woman, and since art is masculine, you as an artist rid yourself of the riddle by explaining it. In this inhuman struggle which your language reveals you are crucifying the world.

This is not language, this is the world being turned inside out; not mathematically in super-dimensional planes, not artistically in "violaceous" daring, but biologically, atomically, so that even the Creator can no more recognize his world.

The investigation which will follow the launching of your words will never end. Every line is pregnant with meaning, yet however much the meaning is explained the riddle will remain, because only you can explain it. And this riddle is your last triumph—you will never reveal it.

"I wait for a light as sulphurous as before the burial of Pompeii." That means for death, for the final catastrophe in which everything will be buried, because in the dissolution of death a flame is born whose secret is imparted only to those who are then and forever escaping the mould. The secret is incommunicable; it is that last knowledge to which we are driven by the most vital forces.

The opening, with your heart sticking in your throat, strangling you, with the legend of the quena and its haunting music, is prophetically accurate; it was prescribed by the very necessity of your choice. The heart is the great human organ, the sustainer of life, the most perfect and the most delicate organism of the body's complicated machinery. The blood purified of all poisons which the heart pumps through the system is the very juice of life, the invisible battleground where unknown conflicts are staged. In the blood are the messengers of the soul; the heart is the great seat of the soul. When the heart breaks, though the body live on, the soul dies; the individual is no longer a human being, but a galvanized corpse, a corpse that reaches extinction through petrefaction. When the heart is strangling one it means that the heart is usurping its natural function. It is a danger signal, but you disregarded it. You plucked out your heart, and while you were plucking it out you heard the music that is made of human bones, the sacrilegious music never heard by ordinary ears.

To find the proper setting for this music you reverted to the country of your heart, to the race from whose loins you sprang: the Incas. That is why, when you painted your Debussy vases (a superimposed culture) you gave us the unknown fragments of a lost world, a world whose vibrations still echo in our ears through oceans of blood. Your vases were made of volcanic ash, the residuum of other lost worlds; they were thickly encrusted, three-dimensional, and not baked, not burnt paint on clay, as with the antique vases which reveal a life without perspective.

"I waited for the leaden weight of destiny, the phantasmal wind of irreversibility, the tattered, low-hanging skies of fatalism." Pregnant words! You waited for the water to come out of the siphon and spread itself like a Norwegian lake. Yes, you had to wait for the deluge first, for the extinction of your own world, for the appearance of clear, cold waters in which icebergs float—and for the sound that comes over these waters when sun and moon stand still and all the human cries of suffering and despair have been silenced.

It is only in this polar night that your true self can emerge. From these Arctic waters there flows back again to the Equator the subterranean current which gives the earth its axis; as the eye of the sun opens wider and wider the wind grows hot, until finally it shrivels all vegetation. It is at the Pole that the meridians running their vertical course turn in circles round the sun. For six long months the sun stares ceaselessly, and in her stare there is the heavy knowledge of centuries: of peoples who stared at her lovingly, who prostrated themselves before her, who called her man and called her woman, who unfolded luxuriantly in the blaze of warmth, and were like seeds dropped into the ground, their histories a riotous repetition of changeless destinies. As long as the sun hung fixed and molten in the heavens there was the "phantasmal wind of irreversibility", and all things ran their course, people, cultures, times; but the "wild circling of craving" sped them on in vertical orbits ascending ever higher, ever farther. The sound of those days is heard still, when people get together in fever talk; it breaks whatever it touches because it has an eternal resonance. It is this voice traversing the centuries which renders nugatory all our hopes; it issues from the delta of all the great rivers that have fecundated the earth. The voice of creation whose song is death.

"The web of her dress moving always a moment before she moved, as if aware of her impulses, and stirring long after she was still, like waves ebbing back to the sea." Image of woman the spider throwing out her web of slenderest filament, web spun out of her own body according to immutable laws, web responsive to the least breath of wind, yet strong enough to support the weightiest victim.

"Her necklace thrown around the world's neck, unmeltable." The yoke which has never been shaken off; the yoke expressing itself in skyscrapers, in steel-stringed guitars, in cannon and prison bars: the yoke of substance indissoluble which goads man to a frenzy of activity, to war, to architecture and music, to laws, to prophecies: the yoke which holds him while he dances and foams at the mouth; the yoke which he feels after all the fetters are broken, the yoke which mocks his freedom, his learning, his metaphysical edifices, the yoke which keeps his nose to the grindstone and makes of his world an ironic thing, a defense, an excuse, a play-toy.

"The leaf fall of her words, the stained glass hues of her moods, the rust in her voice, the smoke in her mouth, her breath on my vision like human breath blinding a mirror." Image of nature, of fall coming on, the evening mist blurring the stained glass hues of the garden, the warm fireplace and the panting breath of love dulling the mirror. Outside her words are falling from the trees, noiselessly, slipping to earth on the wind, whirling with the smoke and mist, each dying leaf a remembrance; fall coming on to muffle the trend of pain, time intervening to cloud the mirror's image, the poignant drama closing in around you like the walls of a cathedral broken by stained glass conflicts. No possibility of looking out on the world; the luminous windows bleed with inner suffering and make the walls more rigid; the figures of saints and madonnas, of warriors and dervishes, convert the religious ecstasy into more fundamental phantasies—the legend of the grail, the miracle of the rose, the tribulations of the saints—all conspiring to remind you of the primordial pattern, the carpet of love woven in lust.

"The sibilance of her tongue. The muffled, close, half-talk of soft-fleshed women . . . all washing against the resonance of my memory." The sibilant tongue of woman is the serpent's tongue, the male organ speaking in them, tempting them; the language of women in love is like the hissing of serpents, their tongues curling and writhing with phallic fury, their mouths so close that their tongues intertwine; the sound of their love muffled, their talk broken, their fieriest efforts dissolving into softest flesh, their deepest yearning a painful memory of hard, cruel words, of flesh standing erect, lacerating, separating; the loveliest love between woman and woman is only the washing of tongues against the hard core of memory, bells without clappers producing a strange resonance. In the tomb of the vagina, written in sweet acid, is the record of one within another eternally in a far-reaching procession. The harlot's tomb in which the still-born open dead eyes one upon another.

"Back in Byzance, the idol dancing with legs parted." Image of Siva the Destroyer. Unforgettable image, obscene, predatory. Mona is always a woman with legs parted, with mouth half open, with eyes turning over. And in her hand she carries a hissing instrument, like the cistrum, which is the serpent's hiss, the phallic song of tongue-and-penis muffled in the web of her dress. With legs parted she is always the idol, always the unattainable—and the insatiable one. Her soft-yielding qualities had to be carved into man's brain with copper instruments because copper was the greatest metal of the antique world, the perdurable metal of the dawning civilizations.

"Her image I tattooed in their eyes." Cruel, cruel image, for the eye is the most sensitive sense organ of the body. If it is possible for the imagination to hold this image then it must suffer the most excruciating pain. Is this what Mona represents? An image ineradicable, a fixed image that is tattooed into the eyeballs?

"When your eyes are opened. . . ." Yes, that is the most terrifying thing that can happen, to one in love. Empty-handed . . . isolated . . . swimming in nothingness. Precisely, because all the connections are broken. Vision has nothing to do with sight. The world we see is the world we wish to see; there is no absolute, objective world which can be seized by truth, by a perfect sight. The eye is man's instrument of power; woman moves blindly, intuitively. Mona blindfolded, coveting her illusions, throwing out her lies, is the perfect symbol of the female principle.

In that long paragraph beginning—"Mona was not a demon"— you have said such tremendous things, such deeply significant and revelatory things, that you appear to me like a sorceress. How could you have divined all that in so short a time? Here is where I no longer believe you implicitly. What you showed me in your Diary was only a thin fragment of the truth. "She was copulating with the cosmic furies and demons." There is the pregnant line. Because to describe her copulation thus is to have put your finger on the very core of her being. "She had lost the power to fit body into body in human completeness." It could not have been said better. It explains the nymphomaniac in her, the aura of drugs, the sadism, the necrophilia, the infantilism, the regressions, the Stavrogin complex—everything, everything. In her sex usurps all the domains of life: things are thrown out of focus, relationships are twisted and perverted; sex, overflowing its proper channels, makes the image of the world distorted, magnified, swollen like a tumor; the orgasms which follow one another in quick succession are not dependent any longer on the one she embraces; she is copulating with an anonymous host; the idea has taken possession of her and the body becomes an insatiable machine whose repetitious movements dull the senses and leave one stupefied. This image, now fixed in my mind and which I was never able to put in words, I feel explains some of those early dreams in which the vagina became a billiard ball with teeth in it—in other words, a rotating machine, a hungry maw, a cruel, consuming mechanism that dehumanizes sex. And this machine, this tooth-like machine, produces no children. No "woman's joy of fecundation" here. No joy at all. Only insatiable desire—copulation on a cosmic scale.

And so, when you come to the next paragraph—"I had invaded the unique precincts of her being"—it is the logical termination of all that precedes. Whether it ever happened or not is immaterial: it was all experienced in the mind. . . . "She had a desire to flee . . ." What follows hereupon is the Sapphic song, the flight to the isle of Lesbos, the Mediterranean chant of love, the strong earth smells, the ardor that one woman rouses in another, and her longing to keep it apart, isolate, secret. All the softness of woman pleading, the decadent offering to another decadent her burnt offerings; the intrusion of the ploughman furrowing the earth, the ploughman trilling and cursing, dropping perspiration, all this is the both wished for and resented intrusion, the inevitable intrusion, the symbol of fecundation which is being frustrated, the symbol of man being cheated. . . . "Heavy, nerveless hours." Indeed! The nerves drained of their tonic lassitude. Not the sweet repose of copulation now, but the drugged, deathlike sleep of two whores who have embraced to exhaustion.

Signing off last night it occurred to me how false can be a work of art when the secret clues are withheld from us. The fusion of all these separate entities (paragraphs, lines, phrases, incidents, the jumbling of time and place) produces an artificial unity; what makes it baffling is that there are too many holes between your utterances. If one could read your Mona with an index in his hand, or opposite each page of script read the annotated document, or if you yourself would recast the thing and give us a psychological and metaphysical explanation of these incoherencies, then we would have something powerful to grapple with. Nobody will understand unless he is a master mind. This is the most intense and abstruse, the most abstracted sort of subjectivity possible.

If I am opening your eyes at all it is only that you may open mine still wider. The debris I am shovelling away uncovers only the topmost layers; there are eight or nine cities underneath still to be explored. None of these remarks are to be taken as detracting from your work; rather to inspire you, to point a way to the real handling of your theme—one way, at least.

All this is provoked by the recollection of your remark anent the conception, the genesis of the story. I am deliberately avoiding the knowledge you put into my hands because it was not mine; I want to continue to study it, unravel it, solely from the perspective I had originally created. But when I think of this dual thread of interpretation I realize how vast must be the complexity of the mind that created this Mona. To taste some of that labyrinthine delicacy is what I crave. . . .

"If Mona were now a memory. . . ." The revulsion expressed in this paragraph is overwhelming. Your head looking down from the ceiling on frog eyes and mouths of soiled leather. "Not even ugliness can stir a live hatred." Here again you approach my deepest feeling about her: that I had *invented* her qualities!

"Grayness is no ordinary grayness. . . ." Here I find some of your best writing, white and lucid—terrifying. If the real clue to the story is what you said, then see how this and the following paragraph express a double torture, a despair beyond despair: you go mad again in remembrance, a double despair, a double madness. "The breath of human beings is like the steam out of a laundry house." You carry over your previous Zolaesque revulsions and suddenly they expand and become the most poignant spiritual pangs.

"Laughter and tears. . . ." This is a remarkable passage, with that memorable closing—"like walking with a sword between your legs." To what does this last image correspond? It has many meanings. The first perhaps, that with each step you tread henceforth there is the danger of being cut in your most vital parts; there is also the sense of ridicule, since the military man who allows his sword to get between his legs is the inept man; it is a disgrace, it precedes a tumble, it is the stuff of film comedies. Then, bearing in mind your previous images—of danger being perpetually suspended above you (the Damocles sword), and of your head being lifted to the ceiling—now we have the world upside down and the sword threatens from below. No longer is it the throat which is in danger (cutting off all cerebral connections) but the womb itself. This is the mortal danger that the true woman fears. . . .

I haven't time to quote every line and phrase that strikes me so deeply. I pass over such beautiful things as the diamond-splintering rain on the windows, the rain dripping in the cells of the brain, etc. It will be difficult for me to disengage myself from these lines when I come to write again about Mona. You have obsessed me with your haunting lines. . . . I come now to the ships sinking with fire in their bowels, fires hissing in the cellars of every house. What does this portend? The spread of calamity everywhere, the discovery that nowhere is there peace or security. And then comes that line which has an irreplaceable quality: "the loved one's whitest flesh is what the broken glass will cut and the wheel crush." What a fierce, rending image that is! "Night is the collaborator of torturers." Mona's night, night of the great spider, in which are heard the long howls of death. "If a dog barks it is the man who loves wide gashes leaping in through the window." Think what a mélange this represents—how the images of fear and desire were intermingled and confused. When does the dog bark? Remember the dream of the man leaping in through the window? But not the same man. A man who loves wide gashes, a man who rapes with the corn-cob. Work it out and you will discover who the man is and what incites his greatest rage, his sadistic fury. You will discover too that you wanted the man to leap in through the window—the one man because it would solve your problems, the other man because it would save you from yourself, from the Mona complex. The wide gashes are the deep bruises you are willing to suffer at his hands; they are also something else. "Waiting for the heavy fall and the foam at the mouth." Waiting for the real dénouement. The foaming at the mouth is the futile helplessness, the rage insatiable which produces hysteria and epileptic fits.

Room with the scissor-arched ceiling. The completion of the drama. The key-word is "dispossessed". After the ruination, after the desertion by every one, comes the realization that you have been "dispossessed" of everything that belonged to you: that is why, standing before the blank walls, you hear more than is humanly bearable. And since you have the strength to go on living (the artist in you keeping you alive), you solder the flesh again. Terrible image—*solder!* Think how things are soldered together!

But the new life is a terrifying one. When all the illusions have been shattered there is left, as body, only the image of a whore, a madwoman, a criminal. You will move along only with the brain; an endless maggot feast of the past, inflaming your memory in order to nourish your cerebral life. A self-torture which nothing, no one, can assuage. That is why you picture yourself as a marionette; you are pulled by unseen strings, your movements are incomprehensible —unless they are explained by a hidden voice. The marionette show can render the most harrowing tragedy, a drama which human beings are incapable of enacting. . . . The thought of separating the circus twins, real flesh and blood beings, is an intolerable one: hence the pain endured by a wooden puppet being torn apart. The perpetual drama now, since you have gone mad, is the obsessive one of ridding yourself of your demon. . . . The woman with the Siamese cat eyes who smiles at herself in the mirror, or sees herself smiling when she is listening seriously, is the same old woman of the Diary who has always been listening to herself and smiling at the wrong time, who imagines herself slighted, unrecognized, unappreciated, who is always a step away from madness and looking for drama and suffering to justify her inexplicable misery.

All this description of pain is the description of the neurotic's, the introvert's, the invert's pain: the Hamlet soul which no European ever rids himself of. Excellent that you should have used "no separation between one and one's pain." Because it is this difference which demarcates the tragedies of the Greco-Roman world (with the possibility of catharsis for the audience as well as the writer) and the dramas of the modern world in which the audience goes away even more sick, more despairing, more ingrown. It is the malady of the soul for which there is no cure. It is the disease which has produced all our art, and the cure of the disease is the death of our art.

HENRY MILLER

THE MOST LOVELY INANIMATE
OBJECT IN EXISTENCE

(Fragment from The Air-conditioned Nightmare)

CORONADO seeking the Seven Cities of Cibola found them not. No white man has found on this continent what he came in search of. The dreams of the acquisitive whites are like endless journeys through petrified forests. On the River of Mercy they were borne to their graves. On the Mountain that was God they saw the City of the Dead. Through the waters of the Prismatic Lake they stared at the Endless Caverns. They saw Mountains of Superstition and mountains of shiny, jet-black glass. The Virgin River brought them to Zion where all was lovely and inanimate, most lovely, most inanimate. From the Garden of the Gods they moved in heavy armor to the Place of the Bird People and saw the City of the Sky. In the Fever River they saw the Sangre de Cristo. In the Echo River they heard the Desert of Hissing Sands. In the Dismal Swamp they came upon the passion flower, the fuzzy cholla, the snow-white blossoms of the yucca, the flaming orange of the trumpet-vine. Looking for the Fountain of Youth they came upon the Lake of the Holy Ghost wherein was reflected the Rainbow Forest. At Shiprock they were ship-wrecked; at Mackinac they were water-logged; at Schroon Lake they heard the loon and the wild antelope. The Gulf was lined with Cherokee roses, bougainvillea, hibiscus. They fell through Pluto's Chasm and awoke in Sleepy Hollow. They crossed the Great Divide (with Margaret Anglin) and came to soda canyons and borax fields. In the midst of the Thundering Waters, they stumbled on the Island of the Goat where Martha kept her Vineyard. Through the clear waters they saw jungles of kelp and phosphorescent marines. Near Avalon they saw the abalone and other shellfish lying on the ocean floor. Looking for the Black Hills they came upon the Bad Lands. Calling upon Manitou they found a Turquoise Spring and when they drank of its waters they were turned into obsidian. Searching for the Green Table they came upon the Cliff Palace where the red man kept his Medicine Hat. Passing through the Valley of the Shenandoah they came upon the Hanging Gardens and were swallowed up by the Mammoth Cave. . . .

Endless was the trek and endless the search. As in a mirage the bright nuggets of gold lay always beyond them. They waded through poisonous swamps, they tunneled through mountains, they reeled through scorching sands, they built natural and un-natural bridges, they erected cities overnight, they compressed steam, harnessed water-falls, invented artificial light, exterminated invisible microbes, discovered how to juggle commodities without touching or moving them, created laws and codes in such number that to find your way among them is more difficult than for a mariner to count the stars. To what end, to what end? Ask the Indian who sits and watches, who waits and prays for our destruction.

The end is a cold, dead mystery, like Mesa Verde. We sit on the top of an Enchanted Mesa, but we forget how we got there, and what is worse, we do not know how to climb down any more. We are on top of the Mountain that was God and it is extinct—"the most lovely inanimate object in existence."

HENRY MILLER was born in Manhattan in 1891, and attended elementary and high school in Brooklyn where his family moved when he was one. The rest of his education has been informal, acquired through wide reading and through travel. His first published book, *Tropic of Cancer*, appeared in Paris in 1934, although he had written many stories and two novels before that time. He lived in France for ten years, returning to the United States at the beginning of World War II after he had made an eight months' trip through Greece which resulted in *The Colossus of Maroussi*. In the early 1940's with the American artist, Abe Rattner, Miller made a cross-country tour of the United States which is recorded in *The Air-Conditioned Nightmare* and *Remember to Remember*. Mr. Miller settled in Big Sur, California, in 1945, but now spends much time travelling throughout Europe. In 1958 he was elected to membership in the National Institute of Arts and Letters, and in 1961 was awarded a special citation of the Prix International des Editeurs on the occasion of the coming publication of *Tropic of Cancer* in the United States and Italy.

BOOKS BY HENRY MILLER
published by NEW DIRECTIONS

THE AIR-CONDITIONED NIGHTMARE
The record of a year-long trip through the U.S., which is seen in mordant terms but with a vitality and freshness few writers could equal. Hardbound.

BIG SUR AND THE ORANGES OF HIERONYMUS BOSCH
Henry Miller here describes the earthly paradise he has found on the California coast and the devils, human and natural, which have threatened it. Hardbound.

THE BOOKS IN MY LIFE
A candid and self-revealing journey back into memory, sharing with the reader the thrills of new discovery that a lifetime of wide reading has brought to an original and questioning mind. Hardbound.

THE COLOSSUS OF MAROUSSI
A travel book about Greece. "It gives you a feeling of the country and the people that I have never gotten from any modern book." (Edmund Wilson.) Paperbound.

THE COSMOLOGICAL EYE
A miscellany of representative examples of Miller stories, sketches, prose poems, philosophical and critical essays, surrealist fantasies, and autobiographical notes. Included are several sections from *Black Spring*, together with the famous story "Max." Hardbound and paperbound.

THE HENRY MILLER READER
A cross-section designed to show the whole range of Miller's writing—stories, literary essays, "portraits" of people and places—interlarded with new autobiographical comments by Henry Miller. Edited, with an introduction, by Lawrence Durrell. Hardbound.

REMEMBER TO REMEMBER
Miller continues his examination of the American scene, in essays and stories, and finds men capable of resisting the dehumanizing pressures of civilization. Hardbound and paperbound.

SUNDAY AFTER THE WAR
Stories, essays, letters, long narratives, and other pieces, including three fragments from *The Rosy Crucifixion*, the story "Reunion in Brooklyn," an attack on Hollywood, and a study of the role of sex in the work of D. H. Lawrence. Hardbound and paperbound.

THE TIME OF THE ASSASSINS
A study of Rimbaud that is as much a study of Miller and has throughout the electric quality of miraculous empathy. Paperbound.

THE WISDOM OF THE HEART
A rich collection of Miller's stories and philosophical pieces, including his studies of D. H. Lawrence and Balzac. Paperbound.